Poetry
Others
Intersect
Coming to Canada

Novels
Unless
Larry's Party
The Stone Diaries
The Republic of Love
A Celibate Season (with Blanche Howard)
Swann
A Fairly Conventional Woman
Happenstance
The Box Garden
Small Ceremonies

Story Collections
Dressing Up for the Carnival
The Orange Fish
Various Miracles

Plays
Departures and Arrivals
Thirteen Hands
Fashion, Power, Guilt and the Charity of Families
(with Catherine Shields)
Anniversary (with David Williamson)

Criticism
Susanna Moodie: Voice and Vision

Anthology
Dropped Threads: What We Aren't Told (Edited with Marjorie Anderson)
Dropped Threads 2: More of What We Aren't Told
(Edited with Marjorie Anderson)

Biography
Jane Austen: A Penguin Lives Biography

CAROL SHIELDS

The Collected Stories

RANDOM HOUSE CANADA

www.randomhouse.ca

Epigraph is extracted from *The Stone Diaries* by Carol Shields. Copyright © 1993
by Carol Shields. Reprinted by permission of Random House Canada.

National Library of Canada Cataloguing in Publication

Shields, Carol, 1935–2003
The collected stories / by Carol Shields.

ISBN 0-679-31326-5

I. Title.

PS8587.H46A15 2004   C813'.54   C2004-900101-9

Jacket and text design: CS Richardson

Printed and bound in the United States of America

10   9   8   7   6   5   4   3   2   1

Contents

For Emma and Alden

Something has occurred to her—something transparently simple, something she's always known, it seems, but never articulated. Which is that the moment of death occurs while we are still alive. Life marches right up to the wall of that final darkness, one extreme state of being butting against the other. Not even a breath separates them. Not even a blink of the eye. A person can go on and on tuned in to the daily music of food and work and weather and speech right up to the last minute, so that not a single thing gets lost.

—From *The Stone Diaries*

Segue

SOMETHING IS ALWAYS SAYING TO ME: Be plain. Be clear. But then something else interferes and unjoints my good intentions.

Max and I were out yesterday morning, Sunday, a simple enough errand in our neighborhood. We "sallied forth" to buy a loaf of good seed bread and a potted plant, chrysanthemums in our case, with the smashed little faces that our daughter so admires, that bitter bronze color, matching the tablecloth she was sure to be laying right that moment out there in Oak Park. Eleven o'clock; my husband Max and I would be expected at half past twelve. We always arrive carrying a modest gift of some sort.

There, at the market, stimulated, probably, by the hint of frost in the air, I felt a longing to register the contained, isolated instant we had manufactured and entered, the purchase of the delicious hard-crusted bread, the decision over the potted plant—this was what I wanted to preserve. But an intrusive overview camera (completely imaginary, needless to say) bumped against me, so that instead of feeling the purity of the coins leaving my hand, I found myself watching the two of us, a man and a woman of similar height, both in their middle sixties, both slightly stooped—you'd hardly notice unless you were looking—and dressed in bright colors, making a performance of paying for their rounded and finite loaf of bread and then the burst of rusty chrysanthemums.

Wait a minute. Shouldn't there be a grandchild in this picture, a little boy or girl staying over with Nana and Poppa in downtown Chicago for the weekend? Well, no, our aging couple has not been so fortunate.

Our Sunday self-consciousness, the little mid-morning circle around Max and me, was bisected by light and dark. The day bloomed into mildness, October 7, one year and one month after the September 11 tragedy—event, spectacle, whatever you choose to call it. Max is a well-known Chicago novelist—he both loves and hates that regional designation—and he was, of course, spotted by other Sunday morning shoppers. *That's Max Sexton. Where? Over there. Really?* A little buzz travels with my husband, around him and above him, which, I believe, dishes out the gold dust that keeps him alive. To be noticed, to be recognized. With his white beard, white swifts of soft hair swept backward, his old-fashioned, too-large horn-rimmed spectacles, he is a familiar enough sight in our immediate neighborhood, and—allow me to say—in the national journals too, even to the point that he has been mentioned once or twice in the same breath with the Nobel Prize (as a dark horse, the darkest of horses). Not that we ever speak of this. It does not come up, we forbid it, the two of us. He has twice been nominated for the Pulitzer—we don't speak of that either.

There we were, yesterday morning, a fine Sunday.

Accompanying the novelist Max Sexton was his wife of forty years—me—whose name is Jane; I had my right arm crooked loosely through the great author's blue nylon jacket sleeve. Plain Jane. Well, not quite, God be thanked. My very good scarf gives me a certain look, not just its color, but the fact that it was knotted high up on the throat. Jane, the wife, the poet and editor, soon (tomorrow) to become past president of the American Sonnet Society—now known as Sonnet Revival—she with her hair in a smooth white pageboy and her reasonably trim body, *c'est moi*. Notice the earrings, handmade, Mexican. Wouldn't you just know! Oh God, yes. Yesterday, at the Andersonville market in Chicago's near-north side, Jane Sexton was sporting an excellent cashmere poncho-thingamajig, deep rose in color, and well-fitting black pants and expensive boots, which she always keeps nicely polished.

Let me say it: I am an aging woman of despairing good cheer—just look through the imaginary camera lens and watch me as I make the Sunday morning transaction over the bread, then the flowers, my straw tote from our recent holiday in Jamaica, my smile, my upturned sixty-seven-year-old voice, a voice so crying-out and clad with familiarity that, in fact, I can't hear it anymore myself, thank God; my ears are blocked. Lately everything to do with my essence has become transparent, neutral: Good morning, Jane Sexton smiles to one and all (such a friendly, down-to-earth woman). "What a perfect fall day." "What glorious blooms!" "Why, Mr. Henning, this bread is still warm! Can this be true?"

Max must surely hear the scattershot of my neighborhood greetings, so fond in their expression and so traditionally patterned, exactly what healthy, seasoned, amiable women learn to say in such chapters of their lives. He has, after so many years, a certain amount of faith in my voice, if nothing else, the voice that he's married to, but then he doesn't believe, I suspect, that the mystery of being is as deeply manifest in women as in men. The voice, as he perfectly well knows, is a social projection, an oral accomplishment, something I've created and maintained along with my feminine peers. I'm just being merry—that's how I imagine Max processing my ebullience—I'm being cordial in a way that may be slightly dishonest but that keeps life from bearing down with its solemn weight, keeps it nosing forward, and overrides the worst possible story the day might otherwise offer, his story, that is, which could quickly turn dreary and strangulated without my floating social descant riding overhead on strings of nylon. Oh, do shut up, Jane.

Yes, there we stood: the morning's excursion to the market, which we managed to stretch out an hour longer than it should have taken, then the taxi to our daughter's house in Oak Park, her austere three-story brick cube on East Avenue (built 1896) where she lives with her film agent husband, Ivan, with its wide front steps and shrubbery and cement cupids—where we were to have lunch, as usual on Sundays, something hot and savory in the dining room, followed by fresh fruit (on French fruit plates, each one different in design, and accompanied by knives with ceramic handles) and afterward coffee, and then the journey home. Ivan, without a word of complaint, will drive us back to our downtown apartment, silently ferrying his mother-in-law, his father-in-law (he is a man who cannot drive and talk at the same time), eastward through the light Sunday traffic, taking Chicago Avenue as usual. He will actually back his old Packard out of the Oak Park garage, slowly, down the narrow overgrown driveway with its scraping branches, wincing as he hears his beautifully restored car suffering instances of minute damage.

I have attempted in my life—at least in the last thirty years—to write one sonnet every fourteen days, and it is my especial (see *Fowler's* on the difference between *especial* and *special*) pleasure to spread the work out over the available working days. On Mondays, usually in the early morning after the house has been set right, I decide on the form—Italian (for

which I have a special fondness), Shakespearean, contemporary or what I, and some of my colleagues, call *essentialist.*
Surprisingly, this choice precedes the subject matter. "But how
do you decide what exactly to write *about?*" asked the *Chicago
Tribune* journalist, Meg Alford, in her early spring article.

As though I would tell her—and the world—about the tiny
spiral notebook in the upper-left-hand drawer of my desk
with its crowded list recorded randomly in ink or else pencil,
and even in one case lip-liner, of new and possible subjects:
the smell of taxis, the texture of bread, sleep, chewing gum,
Picasso, flints and arrowheads, the cello, the shape of coastal
islands and the children who are born on islands, cabbage,
shingle beaches, feet, Styrofoam, photographs of the new-
born as they appear in the newspaper (with sleek seal-baby
faces stroked in stone). Or a medieval wooden Christ image
that Max happened upon at the Art Institute, brooms and
brushes and dustpans and the concept of debris (how we half
treasure what we can't wait to throw away), a table set for
eight (and its companion sestet "Table Set for Seven"), the
beauty of coinage when neatly stacked on a counter, urban
alleys after dark, and—a mere jump away—the commingling
of hollyhocks and overhead wire, and then human faces and
their afterimage—an afterimage not being anything like an
aura, but possessing a different kind of density altogether.
I've worked on this particular afterimage/aura construct for
the last two weeks, finishing on Saturday afternoon (with a
slight alteration round about midnight, two closing words
pondered and then juxtaposed), and was more than usually
pleased with my efforts, that feeling every poet knows of
arrival home, the self returned to its self.

There is never a shortage of subjects, I explained to the
Chicago Trib reporter, hoping my teeth were not projecting an
idiotic over-gladness at the thought of such abundance

waiting to be expressed, matter and ideas swelling forward, eager to be sonnetized.

For the next two weeks my writing will approach the subject of my aging body; I have attempted this subject before, but always with indirection, as though I were peering at it from behind a shrub, so that it could be anyone's body. Now I must claim it, it seems, as mine. I see it close up: chin, breasts, stomach, hips and legs giving way to specific gravity, which will never relent, no matter what I do. The stars are speeding away from each other—we know that, so why are we surprised when the same thing happens to our various body parts, their willingness to spread and collapse and soften. My kneecaps, the skin that covers them, are as wrinkled as the fuzz of a poached peach, and sliding downward, always downward. But no one sees my knees anymore, so it doesn't matter.

Sonnet writing—and this is what I wanted the *Trib* reporter to understand—no longer confines itself to the professing and withdrawing of courtly love, although I insisted that a nod to such love is always hovering, or rather nudging. Is this notion true or just part of my fussy exegetic self? Courtly love? Who knows what shadow of that instinct survives? To be honest (not that I was honest with the slender, leather-skirted junior reporter and her tape recorder), it's only a suspicion borrowed from Max's belief that every novel, whatever its genre or subject, is about death. I certainly have never bought that one, not for a minute. A novel is about everything it touches upon, and so is a sonnet.

I reminded the reporter that sonnet means "little sound." "Oh," she said, and I could tell by the way her pen jumped in her hand that she was charmed by the idea; people almost always are.

Sonnets are taken so strenuously, so literally, when taught at school, or at least they used to be, and the definition—

fourteen lines of rhymed iambic pentameter—hardens and ends up gesturing toward an artifact, an object one might construct from a kit. But if you picture the sonnet, instead, as a little sound, a ping in the great wide silent world, you make visible a sudden fluidity to the form, a splash of noise, but a carefully measured splash that's saved from preciosity by the fact that it comes from within the body's own borders; one voice, one small note extended, and then bent; the bending is everything, the *volta,* the turn, and also important is where it occurs within the sonnet's "scanty plot of ground," to quote old Wordsworth. From there the "little sound" sparks and then forms itself out of the dramatic contrasts of private light and darkness.

Max's novels, on the other hand, come as a communal roar, especially the most recent one, *Flat Planet,* which was published with exquisitely poor timing, last year, 2001, on September 10.

Of course, no one had time to read the ensuing reviews of *Flat Planet,* no one cared about social novels and novelistic dioramas during that pinched, poisoned, vulnerable and shocking time, and it must be admitted that the contents of *Flat Planet,* with its wrangling families and chords of memory, sounded rancorously in the face of Ground Zero. *Flat Planet* became a note in the margin: NOTED CHICAGO WRITER PRESENTS NEUROTIC FATHER (who tries his damndest to persuade his adult kids to come home for Thanksgiving, when they'd rather be out in the world making money or enjoying alternative forms of sex or fine dining.) One critic did go so far as to say that Max Sexton *at least* had the stones to resist the excesses of postmodernism. Stones; Max loved that, I could tell. Max also loves—has always loved— Thanksgiving, the Thanksgiving of the old, weird America that lived in the woods or behind sets of green hills. He wanted so much for the book to sum up all that the word *thanksgiving* illuminates in America. But, really, what does the idea of thanks mean when a spectacularly fortunate country has been smacked in the chin? Has been flattened. Thanks to whom and for what?

Somewhere, someday, probably soon, a scholar will write a comparative thesis on pre- and post–World Trade Center literature. I can imagine her (or him), an intrepid young person in her early, awkward twenties (Columbia or else Yale), her hair flattened by neglect, her body unbalanced by bad posture and fad diets, perpetually in a state of flinching, just slightly overawed by her male supervisor (or the other way around), but determined (nevertheless) to identify the fulcrum that she knows, by instinct, separates the now-world, which has seen the end of Fortress America, and the notion of giving thanks from the "olden days"—separates real terrorism from the old excuse of vengeance, striking back when power is denied.

Max, with his shy, proud, leftish politics, would never reduce the ill-timing of September 11 to a career complaint, but I know he has felt the injustice of it. I understand exactly how he could have emended the book's galleys, given a few weeks' grace, even a few days', and, having done so, he would have found himself credited by the literary media with a handsome sense of prophecy and the companionable embrace of *now* that shades, so subtly, toward the current state of inquietude in America *at this moment*.

Instead, he and his book *Flat Planet* have been swept into a cave of unfashionable hush, dismissed and somehow made to feel a triviality. Since *Flat Planet* (those quarreling family members and their generational rivalries and heroic accumulations of wealth), Max has stayed as far as he can from talking to me about his New Manuscript.

Ever since we were married (1957), since the publication of his early *Lincoln Park Beatitudes,* Max has always had on hand a New Manuscript. That's part of what I married at the altar of Euclid Methodist Church in Oak Park. He had never made a secret of the fact that he intended to spend his life writing novels; it was certainly not a thing hidden from the new young wife—me—who had pledged herself to be Max Sexton's *muse,* even though we never thought of employing the word muse. He believed in my support, and I believed in his ability to have, always, in the rim of his consciousness, a New Manuscript, the future offering, the work with which he was currently engaged and to which I would always take a second place. What did I pledge in return? Nothing, really, except my presence. My abiding presence, the value of which I have recently come to question.

The new, new, New Manuscript lives at this moment in Max's orange vinyl briefcase (a souvenir bought in a public market in Paris, which he uses for luck), really a child's 1960ish backpack, a *cartable.* The manuscript might comprise three pages or three hundred at this point. I haven't asked. He takes it with him in the morning when he goes to his office, which is a small, comfortless room over a hardware outlet a mere two blocks away on Rush Street.

It is surprising to me that in a busy urban high-tech city we still need a place to buy screws and nuts, nails and hammers. We continue to require these old-fashioned items, as well as a place where they can be procured. You have to enter the revolving door of our very successful local hardware store, then walk by the rubber-smelling stock of garden tools and housewares, then up a set of stairs, to find Max's office door, a plain gray-painted metal door that opens with difficulty, scraping hard against the cheap tiled floor. There's a stubby window (glass bricks, gritted with dirt) high up on one wall. There's a shared bathroom down the hall; Max formerly had to ask one of the cashiers downstairs for a key, but now he has acquired one of his own.

For my husband, Max, spartanness serves as a set of crossed fingers; he mustn't give way to greed or a taste for luxury, or it will eat him up the way it ate Bellow and Steinbeck. Probably this explains why the two of us have never owned a car, certainly an eccentricity for our generation.

In the late afternoon, after a day at his word processor, he locks his office door with a sigh—or so I imagine—and totes his briefcase down the stairs, across the street and home, and then the two of us sit down in the living room for coffee.

I use freshly ground beans from the freezer, also beautiful Mexican handmade cups and saucers on a polished wooden tray; we deserve this after all our work, and after, in Max's case, hours of self-denial in his blank cell. What do we talk about?

He seems—I can only guess at this from the way his face relaxes, his tongue caught in silence—to enjoy an account of my day of sonnet-making, as long as I remember to keep my merry voice, but he offers nothing in return about the contents of his briefcase and how the New Manuscript is progressing.

Our Andersonville apartment in the late afternoon catches the full orange of the western sun. This is the old Swedish immigrant neighborhood, now—who knows why?—a refuge for gays and lesbians. Look at us. We are two oldish, coupled heterosexuals drinking coffee after a day of writing, of transposing our thoughts onto the ephemera of paper. One of us speaks of it, and one of us doesn't. I can't be sure of holding his interest when I tell him of my daily progress, but he is always eager to hear about—and amused by—the latest news of our Monday meetings of Sonnet Revival. Today was the day when, after all these years, I handed over the society's chair to another sonneteer, or sonnet-maker as we prefer to be called nowadays, a man named Victor Glantz. Max knows Victor and despises him, yet he inclined his head when Victor's name came up, eager for details, and anxious, I could see, to avoid any reference to his own working day.

His side trips to the Newbury, his "research," assure me the New Manuscript is going slowly—and that means badly. Research is a postponement, as I've heard Max say a dozen times. A novel is a whole world; there's so much to get right, but you don't get it right from reading encyclopedia articles. Sonnets, on the other hand, are an entirely different matter, those little sounds.

I work on my sonnets at a small keyhole desk in a corner of our blue-and-gray bedroom. I actually work with real paper, lined paper from a thick tablet, and a ballpoint pen, with a great many crossings-out and dozens of arrows and question marks and sometimes such marginal scribblings as "No!" or "saccharine" or "derivative," or else I present myself with that bold command: "Make fresher?" Freshness is the most demanding task one faces when dealing with a traditional meter, no matter how forgiving that meter is.

The first several pages are a mess, but I like to allow the mess to flow and flower. I make it move, sitting back in my chair, rotating my shoulders every half hour or so; I try to unknot my muscles, go, go, go—as long as it is forward. Forget you are a sixty-seven-year-old woman with a girlish white pageboy. Forget all that business about fourteen lines of rhymed iambic pentameter; think of Leonardo and his sage wisdom: "Art breathes from containment and suffocates from freedom." Or the problems that accrue from the "weight of too much liberty" (Wordsworth). Drown out the noise of rhyme and rhythm. Think only of the small dramatic argument that's being brought into being—a handball court, or a courtroom itself, hard, demanding thick stone walls—between perseverance and its asymmetrical smash of opposition. Think of that rectangle, perfect in its proportions, that plastic cutlery tray in your kitchen drawer, with its sharp divisions for forks, knives, spoons. Or think of the shape of a human life, which, like it or not, is limited. I believe that humans are meant to live about a hundred years—after that the cells stop wanting to divide and replicate themselves. Chickens, if left alone, will live for thirty years. I wrote a sonnet once about a chicken in great old age, screeching into its decayed wing feathers. Every species has a probable life span, and this observation offers me a verification of sorts for my fourteen-line creations.

From week to week, the subject of my ongoing sonnet suggests itself. It's as though there's a small thread clinging to my sweater's sleeve, always there, waiting to be picked off. I look up from my desk at the framed poster of Rilke's "Sonnet to Orpheus no. 14" that's fixed to the wall, and think: this is me. This is I—getting more grammatical, now—my surroundings being a fine-furred extension of myself. These moments of mental vacancy are mine too, and the smothering way, according to Max, I have of signing my letters with amities and my poems with the turn in point of view at about—more or less—the eighth line. Me, always me. My inescapable self with its slightly off-balanced packaging, benignly decentered by an altered view. When I announce my name, Jane Sexton, to new acquaintances, in circumstances formal or informal, my attempt at musical elusion is also part of me, riding up the "a" in Jane, as though a twinkly uncertainty waited, then plunging down into the plainness of Sexton, with its embedded salute to hard churchly labor—the sexton being only a sort of janitor, and wouldn't I rather have a name like Bishop or Deacon? No, I would not want to lose my bell-ringing, steeple-climbing, altar-dusting self, unconditioned for awe, broken-tongued on the subject of reverence.

My aging is me too, as well as the subject of my current sonnet. Only two years ago the idea of aging belonged to the whole world. It was background. I hadn't been touched by it then. Now I am. Because I'm tall and thin, I am conscious of my bones, especially my hips, which are so shallowly buried, and also conscious of their curvature and sharpness. Often I feel like a walking ossuary. Shouldn't the exercise of staring at my body involve a little veneration? Well, yes. My knuckles have grown elaborate and curious, white and blue knobs in a setting of stringy flesh. I've learned to curl my hands in my lap, one inside the other, so that no one can see the wonder of their structure, no one but me.

I am more and more solitary, and so is my poor Max. Are we then starting to take responsibility for our own dying bodies? It seems that each of us will have to do this on our own.

For a long time I have been perfectly happy to chair the twice-monthly meetings of the Sonnet Society, known since 1988 as the Sonnet Revival. Every second Monday, noon to one-thirty. The time is manageable—an hour and a half every other week, and our location in Clark House behind the SUD Building is an easy walk for me. The other members of the society find their parking on the street, which they do happily, since parking rarely presents a problem on Mondays.

Until recently we had the wide, broad-beamed Clark House room on the ground floor to ourselves, our massive oak conference table and the files where we keep our archives, but a year ago the Oulipian Society became aware of our privileged location, and applied for the use of our official meeting room on alternate Mondays, which seemed only fair to me and not a great inconvenience. Several of our members, though, felt our space had been compromised. Those upstarts!

I tried to reason with my colleagues, explaining that there should be no conflict if we planned our calendar carefully. But, in fact, the sharing of the room has caused occasional confusion, since many of our ranks are getting forgetful with age. I made the mistake once myself not too long ago. I can't imagine how I had mixed up the weeks except that Max and I had been away to Jamaica. In any case I arrived at the Oulipian Society meeting with my latest sonnet and bag lunch to find *them* in the midst of what they called their "combinatorial stratagems." On that particular Monday they were doing poems in which every line was to contain two words with double consonants. Their chair, Douglas Pome, asked me to stay for their "workshop" (as an "honored guest," he said) and I did, feeling a little awkward about being thought a forgetful type who mixes up the weeks, and not so much enjoying the session as thinking it would make a good story to tell Max over coffee, something new for a change— my ever-present itch of compunction.

The Oulipians were younger than our group and more raffish, especially Doug Pome, with his careful midlife beard and his joke of a name. (He does write a nice fleet line.) I noticed they had catered sandwiches instead of doing the brown-bag thing as we've done for years. Most of their poems had a kind of tumbling, jesting humor, which they richly enjoyed. Humor is something sonnet-makers do badly, if at all.

I've always had a soft spot for the Oulipians. I understand that, at first glance, they might seem to resemble the sonnet revivalists in that they set up constrictive forms for their literary production. But—whether they pursue their experiments and practice under the ever-anxious gaze of consciousness or whether they use anagram or linguistic transplant or number series—they suffer the disadvantage that they can never repeat their forays.

A sonnet, on the other hand, comes with its coat of varnish. As Flaubert says, the words are like hair; they shine with combing. We can do what we want with a sonnet. It is a container ever reusable, ever willing to be refurbished, retouched, regilded and reobjectified.

"Congratulations," I said to Victor Glantz today as I handed over the gavel and welcomed him to the head of the table, where I always sit. For the next three years he will take charge of the society meetings and newsletter, and after that he may earn himself another term. I presented him with an African violet, which I saw as symbolically useful, though I'm not sure the others understood the subtleties. (African violets must be watered from the bottom, not the top, and this, I believe, is analogous to the writing of sonnets in the twenty-first century.)

"I promise," he said formally, in his irritating way, "to carry on the mandate of our society and to bring the sonnet into greater and greater public usage." (I do cherish my association with Sonnet Revival, but I sometimes wish we had fewer loonies among us, and not quite so much enthusiastic mediocrity.)

Because the meeting broke up earlier than usual, and because time is more and more a problem for me, I took a different route home, doubling the distance between Clark House and our apartment building. After all these years I know our Andersonville area well, but the darkening skies, or else the glare of city lights, confused me for a moment. I felt my hands trembling in my pockets. One of the familiar old buildings had been razed; that was what was confusing me, something as simple as that.

Nevertheless I recognized later that I had, in fact, panicked. Fear spread rapidly through my body and went with a rush to my head, so that I thought I might faint. What was the matter with me? I had simply turned right when I should have turned left. There was a coffee shop on the corner. I had seen it many times, but had never entered. Now I went in, sat down at a small table by the window and ordered a cup of hot tea. Here I am, I said to myself two or three times, here I am, here I am, sipping at the edge of the plastic cup. I am five blocks from home, an aging woman who has lost her bearings. But now it's all right. In fifteen minutes I'll be home.

I didn't tell Max about getting lost, but I did tell him what Victor Glantz had said when taking over the meeting, his hopes that the sonnet would gain in public usage. Max laughed at that, laughed harder than I had expected. I gave him a small smile in return. He stopped laughing then and gulped his coffee, struggling to straighten his face. We have to be terribly careful after forty years together. We are both so easily injured.

On Mondays, even on Sonnet Revival days, I try to get one or two lines down. Today I did what I do every day, exactly the same. I start at the beginning, the first line, the first word, and then work my way through to the end, thinking: this is familiar, oh yes. This—if it is to mean anything—*must* be familiar; familiarity is the point, after all. Spring and counter-spring. April, May, June, July. Then August, then September, straight through the tunnel of the chilly calendar. I am not thinking, in this early stage, of octave-sestet divisions.

Everything I need is within reach—my notes, my dictionary and thesaurus, my Leonardo quote taped to my desk, and, in fact, except for the steady accompaniment of good light, what else am I likely to require as I move from space to space, other than this tough little pad of paper and the stub of my pen?

But there will come a moment, possibly today—I came close early this morning—when my faith in my miniature art collapses. I can count on that; everything will be going well, the words adding themselves up, gorging on themselves, and saluting the friendly gathering of half-rhymes (which is what I favor these days), then the slow sexual stroke of the iamb arrives, and then, for reasons undisclosed to me, I will be stopped in my working tracks, unable to complete more than six lines. For the first week, the sonnet lives underground, where delay and containment are my chief concerns. It is as though I am looking at it with one eye squeezed shut. And then—this can happen quickly—by the second Monday, I have, mostly, managed to set up my scaffolding for all of the fourteen lines, but it is a scaffolding with several bits unnailed, and nothing yet committed. There are pressures working on particular words, but mostly I try to silence what I think of as a foot pedal of a piano, which is ever ready to stomp and shout and take an easy ride home. I want space for strangeness to enter—not obscurities or avoidances, but idiosyncrasies of grammar or lexicon, so that the sound is harsh, even hurtful.

Half a dozen syllables in the third line are being withheld from me, so temptingly, a few feet out of sight, suspended on the other side of the desk lamp. Or else they are unwilling to freeze themselves in the particular posture I have prepared for them. I refuse, possessing as I do a kind of preternatural *sprezzatura,* and this presents another hurdle, to invert the structure of ordinary spoken English, attaching adjectives to the end of a line for the sake of rhyme. Here's an example from the literature of sonnets: "With strange new hopes and fears and fancies wild." "Wild" to rhyme with "smil'd" (Wilmon Brewer, a ferocious old sonnet-writer, whose book, awful, was published in 1937, *Sonnets and Sestinas*). If I were at the helm, Wilmot Brewer's line would have to go "With strange new hopes and fears and wild fancies," and where would you find a rhyme for fancies? In any case, I don't believe *fancies* is a word I've ever used in a sonnet.

And I want, also, that short introductory beat, the primary iamb, followed by the heavier second beat, and I won't have it any other way, though many sonnet-makers give in at this early point, as though they are inserting a trumpet into the verse and daring it to blow.

My brain stem is ready, the iambic grasp of knit/purl engaged, and is so close to matching the rhythm of my breath that I don't even think of it. Its motor hums in the joints of my shoulders and wrists, knit/purl, knit/purl, ten items arranged on each clean glass shelf, though I don't like to be overly prescriptive when it comes to meter.

Sometimes I look around whatever room I happen to be in as a way of steadying my thoughts. It is seven o'clock now. After our coffee ceremony I moved from the living room to the kitchen, with its fused aroma of afternoon coffee and tonight's roasting chicken and fresh pepper. My little notepad occupies the clean edge of the corner table, and I have just heard a woman on the radio say to her interviewer, about a local celebrity murderer, "There was something about that man that made the hair on my spine stand up."

After a minute I pick up a pencil and jot down the word *spine*. Then *spinal*. No, *spinal* is an anapest. I turn the radio off. Color in its array of tints moves forward in my mind, but not the words I need. *Spinal fluid*. Not quite.

It is my aging body I want to write about, this oiled goatskin I live inside of. The body that rises now, a little creakily, though I attempt to disguise this lack of limberness with an effort of will. I lean over from the waist as smartly as I can (as though a witness were standing next to me taking notes) and check the chicken in the oven and the pair of baking potatoes, darkening in their hides. Max is reading the newspaper. I hear him turning over the pages in the living room and think how he has deprived himself all day of this pleasure. He's always been strict about the avoidance of the newspaper earlier in the day, he is like a puritan in that way: first he must perform his daily task, getting down onto hard disk or paper his own five hundred words, which tomorrow he may or may not delete. In ten minutes we will sit down at the dinner table, just the two of us. Are we to share the future or no? I've never made a fuss of things—why would I begin now?

Oh, these duo dinners! They've grown so hard for us. We'll be talking about the Middle East tonight, the two of us. Or else the obscenity of CEO salaries in America. We already know each other's views on these subjects; we speak in order to keep the silence away. It's as though we reheat these issues in our very dear little copper saucepan—so battered and beloved—hoping by accident to stir in something new. But we are inoculated against surprise. We can no longer make each other laugh. We can't even startle one another. We are both abashed at this imposed duty at the end of every day, even though we've done it for years: each of us is obliged to eat a meal in the presence of a stranger, and yet each is determined to be a self, a singular self. Music helps; this is something we've both noticed in the last year, and I can hear Max now, rising and shuffling among CDs on the shelf where we keep them. What's it to be tonight? Ah, Mozart. Good!

After dinner, which includes a single glass of red wine, sipped slowly, grape-sized sips, I will phone our daughter in Oak Park to see how she got through her day, to try to gauge from her voice her level of vitality. I can hear myself being distractingly glib in order to blunt all that I resist. Is she bearing up? Will she manage another day of effort as she tries to see through her life's obscuring clutter? I have to know before I can tuck myself into our queen-size water bed, where I will read for an hour or more, while Max in another room watches a documentary on television. I am reading a short, bleak Irish novel and he is watching something to do with elephant tusks, needless slaughter and corruption in the international market.

Sleep arrives early, and my arm lifts, as though under hypnosis, to switch off the bedside lamp. My last thought before drifting off collapses into a kind of formula of information directed to the center of my cortex, where a question awaits. What am I now? What is my position in the universe, in the fen and bog of my arrangements?

The reply comes promptly, mocking my tone of high seriousness: if it weren't for my particular circumstances I would be happy.

Various Miracles

Various Miracles

SEVERAL OF THE MIRACLES THAT OCCURRED this year have gone unrecorded.

Example: On the morning of January 3, seven women stood in line at a lingerie sale in Palo Alto, California, and by chance each of these women bore the Christian name Emily.

Example: On February 16 four strangers (three men, one woman) sat quietly reading on the back seat of the number 10 bus in Cincinnati, Ohio; each of them was reading a paperback copy of *Smiley's People*.

On March 30 a lathe operator in a Moroccan mountain village dreamed that a lemon fell from a tree into his open mouth, causing him to choke and die. He opened his eyes, overjoyed at being still alive, and embraced his wife, who was snoring steadily by his side. She scarcely stirred, being reluctant to let go of a dream she was dreaming, which was that a lemon tree had taken root in her stomach, sending its pliant new shoots upward into her limbs. Leaves, blossoms and finally fruit fluttered in her every vein until she began to tremble in her sleep with happiness and intoxication. Her husband got up quietly and lit an oil lamp so that he could watch her face. It seemed to him he'd never really looked at her before, and he felt how utterly ignorant he was of the spring that nourished her life. Now she lay sleeping, dreaming, her face radiant. What he saw was a mask of happiness so intense it made him fear for his life.

On May 11, in the city of Exeter in the south of England, five girls (aged fifteen to seventeen) were running across a playing field at ten o'clock in the morning as part of their physical education program. They stopped short when they saw, lying on the broad gravel path, a dead parrot. He was grassy green in color with a yellow nape and head, and was later identified by the girl's science mistress as *Amazona ochrocephala*. The police were notified of the find, and it was later discovered that the parrot had escaped from the open window of a house owned by a Mr. and Mrs. Ramsay, who claimed, while weeping openly, that they had owned the parrot (Miguel by name) for twenty-two years. The parrot, in fact, was twenty-five years old, one of a pair of birds sold in an open market in Marseilles in the spring of 1958. Miguel's twin brother was sold to an Italian soprano who kept it for ten years, then gave it to her niece Francesca, a violinist who played first with the Netherlands Chamber Orchestra and later with the Chicago Symphony. On May 11 Francesca was wakened in her River Forest home by the sound of her parrot (Pete, or sometimes Pietro) coughing. She gave him a dish of condensed milk instead of his usual whole-oats-and-peanut mixture, and then phoned to say she would not be able to attend rehearsal that day. The coughing grew worse. She looked up the name of a vet in the Yellow Pages and was about to dial when the parrot fell over, dead in his cage. A moment earlier Francesca had heard him open his beak and pronounce what she believed were the words "*Ça ne fait rien.*"

On August 26 a man named Carl Hallsbury of Billings, Montana, was wakened by a loud noise. "My God, we're being burgled," his wife, Marjorie, said. They listened, but when there were no further noises, they drifted back to sleep. In the morning they found that their favorite little watercolor—a pale rural scene depicting trees and a winding road and the usual arched bridge—had fallen off the living-room wall. It appeared that it had bounced onto the cast-iron radiator and then ricocheted to a safe place in the middle of the living-room rug. When Carl investigated, he found that the hook had worked loose in the wall. He patched the plaster methodically, allowed it to dry, and then installed a new hook. While he worked he remembered how the picture had come into his possession. He had come across it hanging in an emptied-out house in the French city of St. Brieuc, where he and the others of his platoon had been quartered during the last months of the war. The picture appealed to him, its simple lines and the pale tentativeness of the colors. In particular, the stone bridge caught his attention since he had been trained as a civil engineer (Purdue, 1939). When the orders came to vacate the house late in 1944, he popped the little watercolor into his knapsack; it was a snug fit, and the snugness seemed to condone his theft. He was not a natural thief, but already he knew that life was mainly a matter of improvisation. Other returning soldiers brought home German helmets, strings of cartridge shells and flags of various sorts, but the little painting was Carl's only souvenir. And his wife, Marjorie, is the only one in the world who knows it to be stolen goods; she and Carl belong to a generation that believes there should be no secrets between married couples. Both of them, Marjorie as much as Carl, have a deep sentimental attachment to the picture, though they no longer believe it to be the work of a skilled artist.

It was, in fact, painted by a twelve-year-old boy named Pierre Renaud, who until 1943 had lived in the St. Brieuc house. It was said that as a child he had a gift for painting and drawing; in fact, he had a gift merely for imitation. His little painting of the bridge was copied from a postcard his father had sent him from Burgundy, where he'd gone to conduct some business. Pierre had been puzzled and ecstatic at receiving a card from his parent, a cold, resolute man with little time for his son. The recopying of the postcard in watercolors—later Pierre saw all this clearly—was an act of pathetic homage, almost a way of petitioning his father's love.

He grew up to become not an artist but a partner in the family leather-goods business. In the late summer he liked to go south in pursuit of sunshine and good wine, and one evening, August 26 it was, he and Jean-Louis, his companion of many years, found themselves on a small stone bridge not far from Tournus. "This is it," he announced excitedly, spreading his arms like a boy, and not feeling at all sure what he meant when he said the words, "This is it." Jean-Louis gave him a fond smile; everyone knew Pierre had a large capacity for nostalgia. "But I thought you said you'd never been here before," he said. "That's true," Pierre said. "You are right. But I feel, *here*"—he pointed to his heart—"that I've stood here before." Jean-Louis teased him by saying, "Perhaps it was in another life." Pierre shook his head, "No, no, no," and then, "Well, perhaps." After that the two of them stood on the bridge for some minutes regarding the water and thinking their separate thoughts.

On October 31 Camilla LaPorta, a Cuban-born writer, now a Canadian citizen, was taking the manuscript of her new novel to her Toronto publisher on Front Street. She was nervous; the publisher had been critical of her first draft, telling her it relied too heavily on the artifice of coincidence. Camilla had spent many months on revision, plucking apart the faulty tissue that joined one episode to another, and then, delicately, with the pains of a neurosurgeon, making new connections. The novel now rested on its own complex microcircuitry. Wherever fate, chance or happenstance had ruled, there was now logic, causality and science.

As she stood waiting for her bus on the corner of College and Spadina that fall day, a gust of wind tore the manuscript from her hands. In seconds the yellow typed sheets were tossed into a whirling dance across the busy intersection. Traffic became confused. A bus skittered on an angle. Passersby were surprisingly helpful, stopping and chasing the blowing papers. Several sheets were picked up from the gutter, where they lay on a heap of soaked yellow leaves. One sheet was found plastered against the windshield of a parked Pontiac half a block away; another adhered to the top of a lamppost; another was run over by a taxi and bore the black herringbone of tire prints. From all directions, ducking the wind, people came running up to Camilla, bringing her the scattered pages. "Oh this is crazy, this is crazy," she cried into the screaming wind.

When she got to the publisher's office, he took one look at her manuscript and said, "Good God Almighty, don't tell me, Camilla, that you of all people have become a post-modernist and no longer believe in the logic of page numbers."

Camilla explained about the blast of wind, and then the two of them began to put the pages in their proper order. Astonishingly, only one page was missing, but it was a page Camilla insisted was pivotal, a keystone page, the page that explained everything else. She would have to try to recon-struct it as best she could. "Hmmmmm," the publisher said—this was late in the afternoon of the same day and they sat in the office sipping tea—"I truly believe, Camilla, that your novel stands up without the missing page. Sometimes it's better to let things be strange and to represent nothing but themselves."

The missing page—it happened to be page 46—had blown around the corner of College Street and through the open doorway of a fresh fruit and vegetable stand, where a young woman in a red coat was buying a kilo of zucchini. She was very beautiful, though not in a conventional way, and she was also talented, an actress, who for some months had been out of work. To give herself courage and cheer herself up she had decided to make a batch of zucchini-oatmeal muffins, and she was just counting out the change on the counter when the sheet of yellow paper blew through the doorway and landed at her feet.

She was the kind of young woman who reads everything, South American novels, Russian folk tales, Persian poetry, the advertisements on the subway, the personal column in the *Globe and Mail,* even the instructions and precautions on public fire extinguishers. Print is her way of entering and escaping the world. It was only natural for her to bend over and pick up the yellow sheet and begin to read.

She read: *A woman in a red coat is standing in a grocery store buying a kilo of zucchini. She is beautiful, though not in a conventional way, and it happens that she is an actress who—*

Mrs. Turner Cutting the Grass

OH, MRS. TURNER IS A SIGHT cutting the grass on a hot afternoon in June! She climbs into an ancient pair of shorts and ties on her halter top and wedges her feet into crepe-soled sandals and covers her red-gray frizz with Gord's old golf cap—Gord is dead now, ten years ago, a seizure on a Saturday night while winding the mantel clock.

The grass flies up around Mrs. Turner's knees. Why doesn't she use a catcher, the Saschers next door wonder. Everyone knows that leaving the clippings like that is bad for the lawn. Each fallen blade of grass throws a minute shadow that impedes growth and repair. The Saschers themselves use their clippings to make compost, which they hope one day will be as ripe as the good manure that Sally Sascher's father used to spread on his fields down near Emerson Township.

Mrs. Turner's carelessness over the clippings plucks away at Sally, but her husband, Roy, is far more concerned about the Killex that Mrs. Turner dumps on her dandelions. It's true that in Winnipeg the dandelion roots go right to the middle of the earth, but Roy is patient and persistent in pulling them out, knowing exactly how to grasp the coarse leaves in his hand and how much pressure to apply. Mostly they come up like corks with their roots intact. And he and Sally are experimenting with new ways to cook dandelion greens, believing as they do that the components of nature are arranged for a specific purpose—if only that purpose can be divined.

In the early summer Mrs. Turner is out every morning by ten with her sprinkling can of chemical killer, and Roy, watching from his front porch, imagines how this poison will enter the ecosystem and move by quick capillary surges into his fenced vegetable plot, newly seeded now with green beans and lettuce. His children, his two little girls aged two and four—that they should be touched by such poison makes him morose and angry. But he and Sally so far have said nothing to Mrs. Turner about her abuse of the planet because they're hoping she'll go into an old-folks home soon or maybe die, and then all will proceed as it should.

High school girls on their way home in the afternoon see Mrs. Turner cutting her grass and are mildly, momentarily repelled by the lapped, striated flesh on her upper thighs. At her age. Doesn't she realize? Every last one of them is intimate with the vocabulary of skin care and knows that what has claimed Mrs. Turner's thighs is the enemy called cellulite, but they can't understand why she doesn't take the trouble to hide it. It makes them queasy; it makes them fear for the future.

The things Mrs. Turner doesn't know would fill the Saschers' new compost pit, would sink a ship, would set off a tidal wave, would make her want to kill herself. Back and forth, back and forth she goes with the electric lawn mower, the grass flying out sideways like whiskers. Oh, the things she doesn't know! She has never heard, for example, of the folk-rock recording star Neil Young, though the high school just around the corner from her house happens to be the very school Neil Young attended as a lad. His initials can actually be seen carved on one of the desks, and a few of the teachers say they remember him, a quiet fellow of neat appearance and always very polite in class. The desk with the initials N.Y. is kept in a corner of Mr. Pring's homeroom, and it's considered lucky—despite the fact that the renowned singer wasn't a great scholar—to touch the incised letters just before an exam. Since it's exam time now, the second week of June, the girls walking past Mrs. Turner's front yard (and shuddering over her display of cellulite) are carrying on their fingertips the spiritual scent, the essence, the fragrance, the aura of Neil Young, but Mrs. Turner is as ignorant of that fact as the girls are that she, Mrs. Turner, possesses a first name—which is Geraldine.

Not that she's ever been called Geraldine. Where she grew up in Boissevain, Manitoba, she was known always—the Lord knows why—as Girlie Fergus, the youngest of the three Fergus girls and the one who got herself in hot water. Her sister Em went to normal school and her sister Muriel went to Brandon to work at Eaton's, but Girlie got caught one night—she was nineteen—in a Boissevain hotel room with a local farmer, married, named Gus MacGregor. It was her father who got wind of where she might be and came banging on the door, shouting and weeping. "Girlie, Girlie, what have you done to me?"

Girlie had been working in the Boissevain Dairy since she'd left school at sixteen and had a bit of money saved up, and so, a week after the humiliation in the local hotel, she wrote a farewell note to the family, crept out of the house at midnight and caught the bus to Winnipeg. From there she got another bus down to Minneapolis, then to Chicago and finally New York City. The journey was endless and wretched, and on the way across Indiana and Ohio and Pennsylvania she saw hundreds and hundreds of towns whose unpaved streets and narrow blinded houses made her fear some conspiratorial, punishing power had carried her back to Boissevain. Her father's soppy-stern voice sang and sang in her ears as the wooden bus rattled its way eastward. It was summer, 1930.

New York was immense and wonderful, dirty, perilous and puzzling. She found herself longing for a sight of real earth, which she assumed must lie somewhere beneath the tough pavement. On the other hand, the brown flat-roofed factories with their little windows tilted skyward pumped her full of happiness, as did the dusty trees, when she finally discovered them, lining the long avenues. Every last person in the world seemed to be outside, walking around, filling the streets, and every corner breezed with noise and sunlight. She had to pinch herself to believe this was the same sunlight that filtered its way into the rooms of the house back in Boissevain, fading the curtains but nourishing her mother's ferns. She sent postcards to Em and Muriel that said, "Don't worry about me. I've got a job in the theater business."

It was true. For eight and a half months she was an usherette in the Lamar Movie Palace in Brooklyn. She loved her perky maroon uniform, the way it fit on her shoulders, the way the strips of crinkly gold braid outlined her figure. With a little flashlight in hand she was able to send streams of light across the furry darkness of the theater and onto the plum-colored aisle carpet. The voices from the screen talked on and on. She felt after a time that their resonant declarations and tender replies belonged to her.

She met a man named Kiki her first month in New York and moved in with him. His skin was as black as ebony. *As black as ebony*—that was the phrase that hung like a ribbon on the end of his name, and it's also the phrase she uses, infrequently, when she wants to call up his memory, though she's more than a little doubtful about what *ebony* is. It may be a kind of stone, she thinks, something round and polished that comes out of a deep mine.

Kiki was a good-hearted man, though she didn't like the beer he drank, and he stayed with her, willingly, for several months after she had to stop working because of the baby. It was the baby itself that frightened him off, the way it cried, probably. Leaving fifty dollars on the table, he slipped out one July afternoon when Girlie was shopping, and went back to Troy, New York, where he'd been raised.

Her first thought was to take the baby and get on a bus and go find him, but there wasn't enough money, and the thought of the baby crying all the way on the hot bus made her feel tired. She was worried about the rent and about the little red sores in the baby's ears—it was a boy, rather sweetly formed, with wonderful smooth feet and hands. On a murderously hot night, a night when the humidity was especially bad, she wrapped him in a clean piece of sheeting and carried him all the way to Brooklyn Heights, where the houses were large and solid and surrounded by grass. There was a house on a corner she particularly liked because it had a wide front porch (like those in Boissevain) with a curved railing—and parked on the porch, its brake on, was a beautiful wicker baby carriage. It was here that she placed her baby, giving one last look to his sleeping face, as round and calm as the moon. She walked home, taking her time, swinging her legs. If she had known the word *foundling*—which she didn't—she would have bounded along on its rhythmic back, so airy and wide did the world seem that night.

Most of these secrets she keeps locked away inside her mottled thighs or in the curled pinkness of her genital flesh. She has no idea what happened to Kiki, whether he ever went off to Alaska as he wanted to or whether he fell down a flight of stone steps in the silverware factory in Troy, New York, and died of head injuries before his thirtieth birthday. Or what happened to her son—whether he was bitten that night in the baby carriage by a rabid neighborhood cat or whether he was discovered the next morning and adopted by the large, loving family who lived in the house. As a rule, Girlie tries not to think about the things she can't even guess at. All she thinks is that she did the best she could under the circumstances.

In a year she saved enough money to take the train home to Boissevain. She took with her all her belongings, and also gifts for Em and Muriel, boxes of hose, bottles of apple-blossom cologne, phonograph records. For her mother she took an embroidered apron and for her father a pipe made of curious gnarled wood. "Girlie, my Girlie," her father said, embracing her at the Boissevain station. Then he said, "Don't ever leave us again," in a way that frightened her and made her resolve to leave as quickly as possible.

But she didn't go so far the second time around. She and Gordon Turner—he was, for all his life, a tongue-tied man, though he did manage a proper proposal—settled down in Winnipeg, first in St. Boniface, where the rents were cheap, and then Fort Rouge and finally the little house in River Heights just around the corner from the high school. It was her husband, Gord, who planted the grass that Mrs. Turner now shaves in the summertime. It was Gord who trimmed and shaped the caragana hedge and Gord who painted the little shutters with the cut-out hearts. He was a man who loved every inch of his house, the wide wooden steps, the oak door with its glass inset, the radiators and the baseboards and the snug sash windows. And he loved every inch of his wife, Girlie, too, saying to her once and only once that he knew about her past (meaning Gus MacGregor and the incident in the Boissevain Hotel), and that as far as he was concerned the slate had been wiped clean. Once he came home with a little package in his pocket; inside was a diamond ring, delicate and glittering. Once he took Girlie on a picnic all the way up to Steep Rock, and in the woods he took off her dress and underthings and kissed every part of her body.

After he died, Girlie began to travel. She was far from rich, as she liked to say, but with care she could manage one trip every spring.

She has never known such ease. She and Em and Muriel have been to Disneyland as well as Disneyworld. They've been to Europe, taking a sixteen-day trip through seven countries. The three of them have visited the south and seen the famous antebellum houses of Georgia, Alabama and Mississippi, after which they spent a week in the city of New Orleans. They went to Mexico one year and took pictures of Mayan ruins and queer shadowy gods cut squarely from stone. And three years ago they did what they swore they'd never have the nerve to do: they got on an airplane and went to Japan.

The package tour started in Tokyo, where Mrs. Turner ate, on her first night there, a chrysanthemum fried in hot oil. She saw a village where everyone earned a living by making dolls and another village where everyone made pottery. Members of the tour group, each holding up a green flag so their tour leader could keep track of them, climbed on a little train, zoomed off to Osaka, where they visited an electronics factory, and then went to a restaurant to eat uncooked fish. They visited more temples and shrines than Mrs. Turner could keep track of. Once they stayed the night in a Japanese hotel, where she and Em and Muriel bedded down on floor mats and little pillows stuffed with cracked wheat, and woke up, laughing, with backaches and shooting pains in their legs.

That was the same day they visited the Golden Pavilion in Kyoto. The three-storied temple was made of wood and had a roof like a set of wings and was painted a soft old flaky gold.

Everybody in the group took pictures—Em took a whole roll—
and bought postcards; everybody, that is, except a single tour
member, the one they all referred to as the Professor.

The Professor traveled without a camera, but jotted notes
almost continuously into a little pocket scribbler. He was
bald, had a trim body and wore Bermuda shorts, sandals and
black nylon socks. Those who asked him learned that he really
was a professor, a teacher of English poetry in a small college
in Massachusetts. He was also a poet who, at the time of the
Japanese trip, had published two small chapbooks based
mainly on the breakdown of his marriage. The poems, sadly,
had not caused much stir.

It grieved him to think of that paltry, guarded, nut-like
thing that was his artistic reputation. His domestic life had
been too cluttered; there had been too many professional
demands; the political situation in America had drained him
of energy—these were the thoughts that buzzed in his skull as
he scribbled and scribbled, like a man with a fever, in the
back seat of a tour bus traveling through Japan.

Here in this crowded, confused country he discovered
simplicity and order and something spiritual too, which he
recognized as being authentic. He felt as though a flower,
something like a lily, only smaller and tougher, had unfurled
in his hand and was nudging along his fountain pen. He
wrote and wrote, shaken by catharsis, but lulled into a new
sense of his powers.

Not surprisingly, a solid little book of poems came out of
his experience. It was published soon afterward by a well-
thought-of Boston publisher who, as soon as possible, sent
him around the United States to give poetry readings.

The Professor read his poems mostly in universities and col-
leges where his book was already listed on the Contemporary
Poetry course. He read in faculty clubs, student centers,

classrooms, gymnasiums and auditoriums, and usually, part-way through a reading, someone or other would call from the back of the room, "Give us your Golden Pavilion poem."

He would have preferred to read his Fuji meditation or the tone poem on the Inner Sea, but he was happy to oblige his audiences, though he felt "A Day at the Golden Pavilion" was a somewhat light piece, even what is sometimes known on the circuit as a "crowd pleaser." People (admittedly they were mostly undergraduates) laughed out loud when they heard it; he read it well too, in a moist, avuncular amateur actor's voice, reminding himself to pause frequently, to look upward and raise an ironic eyebrow.

The poem was not really about the Golden Pavilion at all, but about three midwestern lady tourists who, while viewing the temple and madly snapping photos, had talked incessantly and in loud, flat-bottomed voices about knitting patterns, indigestion, sore feet, breast lumps, the cost of plastic rain-coats and a previous trip they'd made together to Mexico. They had wondered, these three—noisily, repeatedly—who back home in Manitoba should receive a postcard, what they'd give for an honest cup of tea, if there was an easy way to remove stains from an electric coffee maker, and where they would go the following year—Hawaii? They were the three furies, the three witches, who for vulgarity and tastelessness formed a shattering counterpoint to the Professor's own state of tran-scendence. He had been affronted, angered, half-crazed.

One of the sisters, a little pug of a woman, particularly stirred his contempt, she of the pink pantsuit, the red toe-nails, the grapefruity buttocks, the overly bright souvenirs, the garish Mexican straw bag containing Dentyne chewing gum, aspirin, breath mints, sun goggles, envelopes of sac-charine, and photos of her dead husband standing in front of a squat, ugly house in Winnipeg. This defilement she had spread before the ancient and exquisitely proportioned Golden Pavilion of Kyoto, proving—and here the Professor's tone became grave—proving that sublime beauty can be brought to the very doorway of human eyes, ears and lips and remain unperceived.

When he comes to the end of "A Day at the Golden Pavilion" there is generally a thoughtful half second of silence, then laughter and applause. Students turn in their seats and exchange looks with their fellows. They have seen such unspeakable tourists themselves. There was old Auntie Marigold or Auntie Flossie. There was that tacky Mrs. Shannon with her rouge and her jewelry. They know—despite their youth they know—the irreconcilable distance between taste and banality. Or perhaps that's too harsh; perhaps it's only the difference between those who know about the world and those who don't.

It's true that Mrs. Turner remembers little about her travels. She's never had much of a head for history or dates; she never did learn, for instance, the difference between a Buddhist temple and a Shinto shrine. She gets on a tour bus and goes and goes, and that's all there is to it. She doesn't know if she's going north or south or east or west. What does it matter? She's having a grand time. And she's reassured, always, by the sameness of the world. She's never heard the word *commonality,* but is nevertheless fused with its sense. In Japan she was made as happy to see carrots and lettuce growing in the fields as she was to see sunlight, years earlier, pouring into the streets of New York City. Everywhere she's been she's seen people eating and sleeping and working and making things with their hands and urging things to grow. There have been cats and dogs, fences and bicycles and telephone poles, and objects to buy and take care of; it is amazing, she thinks, that she can understand so much of the world and that it comes to her as easily as bars of music floating out of a radio.

Her sisters have long forgotten about her wild days. Now the three of them love to sit on tour buses and chatter away about old friends and family members, their stern father and their mother who never once took their part against him. Muriel carries on about her children (a son in California and a daughter in Toronto), and she brings along snaps of her grandchildren to pass round. Em has retired from school teaching and is a volunteer in the Boissevain Local History Museum, to which she has donated several family mementos: her father's old carved pipe and her mother's wedding veil and, in a separate case, for all the world to see, a white cotton garment labeled "Girlie Fergus's Underdrawers, handmade, trimmed with lace, circa 1918." If Mrs. Turner knew the word *irony* she would relish this. Even without knowing the word *irony*, she relishes it.

The professor from Massachusetts has won an important international award for his book of poems; translation rights have been sold to a number of foreign publishers; and recently his picture appeared in the *New York Times,* along with a lengthy quotation from "A Day at the Golden Pavilion." How providential, some will think, that Mrs. Turner doesn't read the *New York Times* or attend poetry readings, for it might injure her deeply to know how she appears in certain people's eyes, but then there are so many things she doesn't know.

In the summer, as she cuts the grass, to and fro, to and fro, she waves to everyone she sees. She waves to the high school girls, who timidly wave back. She hollers hello to Sally and Roy Sascher and asks them how their garden is coming on. She cannot imagine that anyone would wish her harm. All she's done is live her life. The green grass flies up in the air, a buoyant cloud swirling about her head. Oh, what a sight is Mrs. Turner cutting her grass, and how, like an ornament, she shines.

Accidents

AT HOME MY WIFE IS MODEST. She dresses herself in the morning with amazing speed. There is a flashing of bath towel across the fast frame of her flesh, and then, *voilà*, she is standing there in her pressed suit, muttering to herself and rummaging in her bag for subway tokens. She never eats breakfast at home.

But the minute we hit the French coast—we stay in a vacation flat owned by my wife's brother-in-law—there she is, on the balcony with her bare breasts rising up to the sun. And she has breakfasted, and so have I, on three cups of coffee and a buttered croissant.

Her breasts have remained younger than the rest of her body. When I see her rub them with oil and point them toward the fierce sunlight, I think of the Zubaran painting in the museum at Montpellier which shows a young and rather daft-looking St. Agatha cheerfully holding out a platter on which her two severed breasts are arranged, ordinary and bloodless as jam pastries.

One morning something odd happened to my wife. She was sitting on the balcony working on her new translation of Valéry's early poems and she had a cup of coffee before her. I should explain that the dishes and cutlery and cooking things in the flat are supplied, and that this particular coffee cup was made of a sort of tinted glass in a pattern that can be found in any cheap chain store in France. Suddenly, or so she told me later, there was a cracking sound, and her cup lay in a thousand pieces in the saucer.

It had simply exploded. She wondered at first if she had been shot at with an air rifle. There was another apartment building opposite under construction, and at any time of the day workmen could be seen standing on the roof. But clearly it would have required an extraordinary marksman to pick off a cup of coffee like that from such a distance. And when she sifted through the slivers of glass, which she did with extreme care, she found no sign of a pellet.

The incident unnerved her. She put on her blouse when she went out on the balcony later in the day, but I noticed she kept a cup of coffee in the middle of the table as though daring a second explosion to occur.

I knew, though I'm not a scientist, that occasionally tempered glass fractures spontaneously. It's thought to come about by a combination of heat, light and pressure. It happens sometimes to the windshields of automobiles, though it is extremely rare and not entirely understood.

I told all this to my wife. "I still don't understand how it could have happened," she said. I explained again, knowing my explanation was vague and lacking in precision. I was anxious to reassure her. I reached down and put my arms around her, and that was how my accident occurred. She turned to look at me, and as she did so, the back of her earring tore the skin of my face.

It was surprising how long the tear was, about four inches in all, and it was deeper than just a scratch, although the blood oozed out slowly, as though with reluctance. We both realized I would require stitches.

The doctor in the Montpellier clinic spoke almost perfect

English, but with a peculiar tonelessness, rather like one of those old-fashioned adding machines clicking away. "You will require a general anesthetic," he told me. "You will be required to remain in the hospital overnight."

My wife was weeping. She kept saying, "If only I hadn't turned my head just at that moment."

The doctor explained that since the hospital was full, I would have to share a room. Always, he said, gesturing neatly with both hands, always at vacation time there were accidents. A special government committee, in fact, had been established to look into this phenomenon of *accidents de la vacances,* and someone had suggested that perhaps it might be the simplest solution if vacations were eliminated entirely.

I speak French fluently, having grown up in Montreal, but I have difficulty judging the tone of certain speakers. I don't know when someone—the doctor, for example—is speaking ironically or sincerely; this has always seemed to me to be a serious handicap.

While still under the anesthetic I was put into a room occupied by a young man who had been in a motorcycle accident. He had two broken legs and a shattered vertebra and was almost completely covered in white plaster. Only his face was uncovered, a young face with closed eyes and smooth skin. I put my hand on my own face, which was numb beneath the dressing, and wondered for the first time if I would be left with a scar.

My wife came to sit by my bed for a while. She was no longer crying. She had, in fact, been shopping and had bought a new pale yellow cardigan with white flowers around the neck, very fresh and springlike. I was touched to see that she had removed her earrings. On her ear lobes there was nothing but a faint dimple, the tiny holes made, she once told me, by her own mother when she was fourteen years old.

There seemed little to talk about, but she had bought a *Herald Tribune,* something she normally refuses to do. She scorns the *Herald Tribune,* its thinness and its effete news coverage. And it's her belief that when you are in another country you should make an attempt to speak and read the language of that country. The last time she allowed herself to buy a *Herald Tribune* was in 1968, the week of Trudeau's first election.

The young man with the broken legs was moaning in his sleep. "I hope he doesn't go on like this all night," she said. "You won't get any sleep at this rate."

"Don't worry about me," I said. "I'll be fine tomorrow."

"Do you think we should still plan to go over to Aigues Mortes?" she asked, naming the place we try to visit every summer. Aigues Mortes is, as many people have discovered, an extraordinary medieval port with a twelfth-century wall in near-perfect condition. It has become a habit with my wife and me to go there each year and walk around this wall briskly, a distance of a mile. After that we take a tour through the Tower of Constance with an ancient and eccentric guide, and then we finish off the afternoon with a glass of white wine in the town square.

"It wouldn't feel like a holiday if we didn't do our usual run to Aigues Mortes," my wife said in a rather loud cheerful voice, the sort of voice visitors often acquire when they come to cheer the sick.

The man with the broken legs began to moan loudly and, after a minute, to sob. My wife went over to him and asked if she could do anything for him. His eyes were still closed, and she leaned over and spoke into his ear.

"Am I dead?" he asked her in English. "Did you say I was dead?"

"Of course you aren't dead," she said, and smiled over her shoulder at me. "You're just coming out of the anesthetic and you're not dead at all."

"You said I was dead," he said to her in clear carrying British tones. "In French."

Then she understood. "No, we were talking about Aigues Mortes. It's the name of a little town near here."

He seemed to need a moment to think about this.

"It means *dead waters,*" my wife told him. "Though it's far from dead."

This seemed to satisfy him, and he drifted off to sleep again.

"Well," my wife said, "I'd better be off. You'll be wanting to get to sleep yourself."

"Yes," I said. "That damned anesthetic, it's really knocked me for a loop."

"Shall I leave you the *Herald Tribune?*" she asked. "Or are you too tired to read tonight?"

"You take it," I told her. "Unless there's any Canadian news in it."

That's another thing we don't like about the *Herald Tribune.* There's hardly ever any news from home, or if there is, it's condensed and buried on a back page.

She sat down again on the visitor's chair and drew her cardigan close around her. In the last year she's aged, and I'm grieved that I'm unable to help her fight against the puckering of her mouth and the withering away of the skin on her upper arms. She went through the paper page by page, scanning the headlines with a brisk professional eye. "Hmmm," she said to herself in her scornful voice.

"Nothing?" I asked.

"Well, here's something." She folded back the page and began to read. "Gilles Villeneuve is dead."

"Who?"

"Gilles Villeneuve. You know, the racing driver."

"Oh?"

"Let's see. It says 'Canadian racing driver, killed in practice run.' Et cetera. Always claimed racing was dangerous and so on, said a year ago that he'd die on the track." She stopped. "Do you want to hear all this?"

"No, that's enough." I felt the news about Gilles Villeneuve calmly, but I hope not callously. I've never really approved of violent sports, and it seems to me that people foolish enough to enter boxing rings or car races are asking for their own deaths.

"It's sad to die so young," my wife said, as if required to fill the silence I'd left.

The young man in the next bed began to sputter and cough, and once again my wife went over to see if she could do anything.

"You mustn't cry," she said to him. She reached in her bag for a clean tissue. "Here, let me wipe those tears away."

"I don't want to die." He was blubbering quite noisily, and I think we both felt this might weaken the shell of plaster that enclosed him.

My wife—I forgot to mention that she is still a very beautiful woman—placed her hand on his forehead to comfort him.

"There, there, it's just your legs. You've been sleeping, and you're only a little bit confused. Where do you come from?"

He murmured something.

"What did you say?"

"Sheffield. In England."

"Maybe I can telephone someone for you. Has the hospital sent a message to your people?"

It was an odd expression for her to use—*your people*. I don't think I've ever heard her use that particular phrase before.

"It's all right," he said. He had stopped crying, but my wife kept her hand on his forehead for another moment or two until he had dropped off to sleep.

I must have dropped off to sleep as well because when I opened my eyes she had gone. And after that it was morning and a nurse was opening the shutters and twittering something at me in French. The bed next to mine was empty, and she began to strip off the sheets.

"Where is he?" I asked her in my old, formal schoolboy French. "Where's my comrade with the broken legs?"

"*Il est mort,*" she said in the same twittering singsong.

"But he can't be dead. His legs were broken, that's all."

"The spinal cord was damaged. And there were other injuries. Inside."

A minute later the doctor came in and had a look under my dressing. "You perhaps will have a little scar," he said. "For a woman this is terrible, of course. But for a man . . ." He smiled and revealed pink gums. "For a man it is not so bad."

"I understand that he's died," I said, nodding at the stripped bed.

"Ah yes. Multiple injuries, there was no hope, from the moment he was brought in here yesterday."

"Just a young man," I said.

He was pressing the bandage back into place. "*Les accidents de vacances.* Every year the same. What can one do? One should stay home, sit in the garden, be tranquil."

When my wife comes for me in half an hour or so, I will have prepared what I'll say to her. I know, of course, that the first thing she'll ask me is: How is the young man from Sheffield? She will ask this before she inquires about whether I've had a good night or whether I'm suffering pain. I plan my words with precision.

This, luckily, is my métier, the precise handling of words.

Mine is a profession that is close to being unique; at least I know of no one else who does the same sort of work on a full-time basis.

I am an abridger. When I tell people, at a party for instance, that I am an abridger, their faces cloud with confusion and I always have to explain. What I do is take the written work of other people and compress it. For example, I am often hired by book clubs to condense or abridge the books they publish. I also abridge material that is broadcast over the radio.

It's a peculiar profession, I'm the first to admit, but it's one I fell into by accident and that I seem suited for. Abridging requires a kind of inverse creativity. One must have a sharp eye for turning points and a seismic sensitivity for the fragile, indeed invisible, tissue that links one event with another. I'm well-paid for my work, but I sometimes think that the degree of delicacy is not appreciated. There are even times when it's necessary to interfere with the truth of a particular piece and, for the sake of clarity and balance, exercise a small and inconspicuous act of creativity that is entirely my own. I've never thought of this as dishonesty and never felt that I had tampered with the integrity of a work.

My wife will be here soon. I'll watch her approach from the window of my hospital room. She still walks with a kind of boyish clip-clop, as though determined to possess the pavement with each step. This morning she'll be wearing her navy blazer; it's chilly, but it will probably warm up later in the day. She'll probably have her new yellow cardigan on underneath, but I won't be able to tell from here if she's wearing earrings. My guess is that she won't be. In her hand she'll have a small cloth bag, and I can imagine that this contains the picnic we'll be taking with us to Aigues Mortes.

"And how is *he?*" she's going to ask me in a few minutes from now. "How is our poor young friend with the broken legs?"

"He's been moved to a different place." I'll say this with a small shrug, and then I'll say, quickly, before she has a chance to respond, "Here, let me carry that bag. That's too heavy for you."

Of course, it's not heavy at all. We both know that. How could a bag containing a little bread and cheese and perhaps two apples be heavy?

It doesn't matter. She'll hand me the bag without a word, and off we'll be.

Sailors Lost at Sea

ONE AFTERNOON, OUT OF CURIOSITY or else boredom, Hélène wandered into an abandoned church. A moment later she found herself locked inside.

This was in France, in Brittany, and Hélène was a girl of fourteen who had been walking home from the village school to the house where she and her mother were temporarily living. Why she had stopped and touched the handle of the church door, she didn't know. She had been told, several times, that the little church was kept tightly locked, but today the door had opened easily at her touch. This was puzzling, though not daunting, and she had entered bravely, holding her head high. She had recently, since arriving in France, come to understand the profit that could be had from paying attention to good posture, how she could, by a minor adjustment of her shoulders or a lifting of her chin, turn herself into someone who had certain entitlements.

She and her mother were from Canada and, despite her Manitoba accent—which she knew seemed quaint, even comic to French ears, funnier even than Québécois—she was regarded with envy and awe by the girls in the village school in St. Quay. That she was from a place called Winnipeg, the girls found exotic. "Weenie-pegg," they said, with a giggling way of hanging on to the final *g*. Her mother said this was because St. Quay was an out-of-the-way sort of place.

This was true. It was a fact that only two girls in her level had ever been to Paris, which was just five hours away by train, and a surprising number of them had never been even as far as Rennes. Also impressive to these girls was the fact that Hélène's mother was a poet, a real poet, who had published three books. *Trois livres? Vraiment?* Their eyes had opened wide at this, and they weren't giggling any longer. ("That's one thing about the French," Hélène's mother told her. "They respect writers.") The girls at l'école Jeanne d'Arc were forever asking Hélène how her mother was getting on with her poetry. *"Ta mère, elle travaille bien?"* Their own mothers were the wives of fishermen or shopkeepers. Hélène had been presented to some of these mothers in the village streets: thick-ankled, round-faced women wearing old woolen coats and carrying groceries in bags made of plastic net.

Hélène and her mother had never intended to spend the whole of the year in St. Quay. They had planned to travel, to drift like migrants along the edges of the country. (*La France* has the shape of a hexagon, Hélène has been taught in the village school; this fact is repeated often, as though it carries mystical significance.) Instead of traveling, they had attached themselves like barnacles—this was how Hélène's mother put it—to this quiet spot on the channel coast, and Hélène had enrolled in the local school. There was a very good reason for this, her mother surprised her by saying. "The only way to get the feel of the country is to become a part of it." Of course, as Hélène now knew, and as her mother would soon discover, it was not possible at all for them to become part of the community. Everywhere they went, to the *boulangerie*, to the post office, everywhere, there was a rustle and a whisper that went before them, announcing, just behind the weak smiles of welcome, "Ah, les Canadiennes!" It made Hélène feel weak; she always was having to compose herself, to imagine how she must look from the outside.

In St. Quay there were a number of old churches, though the largest, a church dating from the thirteenth century, had been torn down ten years earlier. It had been replaced with a brown brick building that was square and ugly like a factory, and distressingly empty, distressing, that is, to the local priest, a Father Dominic. He was an old man with creased yellow skin and a stiff manner, but he was the only friend Hélène's mother had so far found in St. Quay.

"Alas," said Father Dominic, rubbing his long chin, "Brittany was once the most religious corner of France, and now it has become, overnight"—he made a zigzag in the air to signify lightning—"*secularized.*" He said this in his loud, lonely voice, speaking as though there could be no reversal.

"The church," he said, "has lost out to television and motorbikes and modernism in general, and it has all happened in a flash."

Well, this was not quite the truth, Hélène's mother explained later. The truth was that during the French Revolution Brittany had been filled with ranting anticlerical mobs who tore the statues out of church niches and removed stone chunks (heads chiefly or the fingers of upraised hands) from the roadside cavalries that dotted the Côte du Nord. *Quel dommage,* Hélène's mother said, in sly imitation of Father Dominic, her only friend.

The particular church where Hélène found herself imprisoned on a Thursday afternoon was one of these small, desecrated churches, statueless and plain, its heavy doors shorn clean of carving and its windows replaced by dull opalescent glass. The church was officially closed. She knew that; it had been closed for many years.

Father Dominic had explained to them that it was no longer served by a priest. Nowadays there was but a single Mass celebrated here each year—it was he who had the privilege of serving—and that was on a certain spring day set aside by tradition to honor sailors who had been lost at sea. On that particular Sunday in early April, the doors would be thrown open and people would enter carrying armloads of spring flowers; after that, a procession would wind over the rocks and down the beach itself.

When Hélène's mother heard Father Dominic talking about this festival, her eyes had softened with feeling, and she had nodded as though she too had had occasion to pay tribute to lost seamen—which, of course, coming from Winnipeg, she had not.

"That will be something to see," she said to Hélène, and wrote the name of the festival in her notebook. At that moment, seeing her mother writing down the details of the fete and imagining the blond sunniness of this festive day, Hélène truly understood that they would be staying here the entire year, that their drifting, which she had loved, all ten days of it, was not to be resumed.

The old church stood just outside the village on the rue des Chiens, the same street where they had found a house to rent. "We've installed ourselves in a cheap stone house on Dog Street." Hélène's mother had written this in a cheerful letter to a friend back home, as though having an inelegant address gave them an unconquerable ascendancy over the difficulties the little stone house presented. There it stood, surrounded by drenched shrubbery, a dragging lace of rain falling from the corners of the steep roof. The landlord, a scowling, silent widower with three teeth in his head, lived in the basement, and his presence cast a spell of restraint over them so that they tiptoed about the house, *his* house, in bedroom slippers and spoke to each other in hushed formal voices, more like a pair of elderly sisters than a mother and daughter. The bathroom stank despite the minty blue deodorizer Hélène had bought and attached to the wall, and the kitchen was damp and without cupboards. The two arm-chairs in the living room were covered with ancient, oily tap-estry cloth, badly frayed. In the morning her mother made coffee, carried it to one of these repellent chairs and sat down with her notebooks. There she spent her time, scarcely getting up and looking out at the sea all day. Hélène knew without asking that the poems were not coming easily.

By good fortune the Canadian government had seen fit to award her mother a sum of money so that she could come to France for a year in order to write poetry. She had long desired—and this was explained at great length in the appli-cation—to touch the soil where her ancestral roots lay. (But these roots, she now admitted to Hélène in one of their long whispered talks, were more deeply buried than she had thought. Her forebears had gone to Canada a long time ago, first to Quebec, then making their way to Manitoba.) And she was not entirely certain which region of France they had come from, though it was generally believed to have been either Brittany or Normandy. Now she was here, breathing French air, eating French bread, drinking bitter black coffee and tak-ing weekend walks on the wild wetted path that went along the coast, but what really was the use of this? What had she expected? For the so-called roots to rise up and embrace her?

It seemed to Hélène that her mother had childish notions about the magic of places. A field of oats was a field of oats. The blackberries they'd found along the coast path had the same beaded precision as those at home. Her mother had a way of making too much of things, always seeing secondary meanings, things that weren't really there, and her eyes watered embarrassingly when she spoke of these deeper meanings. It was infantile, the way she went on and on about the *fond* of human experience. What was the *fond* but carrying home the groceries, trying to keep warm in the drafty stone house, walking down the dark road in the morning to school, where the other girls waited for her, admiring her warm wool sweaters and asking her how her mother, the poet, was doing.

Recently Hélène's mother, as if to make up for the lack of poems, had latched with fevered intensity on to particles of local lore, prising them out of Michelin guides and storing them up in notebooks—not the same notebooks the poems went into, but pale green spiral-bound books with squared-off pages, notebooks (meant for young school children) that she bought in the village at the Maison de la Presse. In one of these notebooks, she had recorded:

There are two legends surrounding the founding of St. Quay, stories that contain similar elements but that occupy different sides of a coin. In the "good" story, a fourth-century Irish saint called St. Quay arrives in a stone boat to bring Christianity to the wild Breton coast. A bird flies ahead to tell the villagers of his imminent arrival, and the women (why just women?) joyfully run to the shore to greet him, bringing with them armloads of flowers and calling "St. Quay, St. Quay," guiding the boat to safety with their cries.

In the second version, the "bad" version, the same bird arrives to say that a stranger is approaching in a stone boat. The women (women again!) of the village are suspicious and hostile, and they run to the shore with rough stalks of gorse in their hands which they brandish ferociously, all the time crying, *"Quay, quay,"* which means in old Gaelic, "Away, away."

Her mother asked Hélène one day which version she preferred, but before Hélène could decide, she herself said, "I think the second version must be true." Then she qualified. "Not true, of course, not in a real sense, but containing the elements, the *fond* of truth."

"Why?" Hélène asked. She saw the shine on her mother's face and felt an obligation to keep it there. "Why not the first version?"

"It's a matter of perspective," her mother said. "It's just where I am now. In my life, I mean. I can believe certain things but not others."

Because of the way she said this, and the way she squeezed her eyes shut, Hélène knew her mother was thinking about Roger, the man in Winnipeg she was in love with. She had been in love before, several times. Love, or something like it, was always happening to her.

But now something had happened to Hélène: she was locked inside a church, chosen somehow, the way characters in stories are chosen. The thought gave her a wavelet of happiness. And a flash of guilty heat. She should not have entered the door; it should not have been unlocked, and she should not be standing here—but she was. And what could she do about it—nothing. The feeling of powerlessness made her calm and almost sleepy. She looked about in the darkness for a place to sit down. There was nothing—no pews, no chairs, only the stone floor.

She tried the door again. The handle was heavy and made of some dull metal that filled her hand. She set her school bag on the floor and tried turning the handle and pushing on the door at the same time, leaning her shoulder into the wood. Then she pulled the door toward her, rattled it sharply and pushed it out again.

"Open," she said out loud, and heard a partial echo float

to the roof. It contained, surprisingly, the half-bright tone of triumph.

"I'm fourteen years old and locked in a French church." These words slid out like a text she had been asked to read aloud. Calm sounds surrounded by their own well of calm; this was a fact. It was no more and no less than what had happened.

Perhaps there was another door. She began to look around. The windows, high up along the length of the church, let in soft arches of webbed light, but the light was fading fast. It was almost five o'clock and would be dark, she knew, in half an hour. Her mother would be waiting at home, the kitchen light on already, something started for supper.

High overhead was a dense, gray collision of dark beams and stone arches, and the arches were joined in such a way that curving shadows were formed, each of them like the quarter slice out of a circle. Hélène had made such curves with her pencil and compass under the direction of Sister Ste. Adolphe at the village school, and had been rewarded with a dainty-toothed smile and a low murmur, "*Très, très bon.*" Sister Ste. Adolphe gave her extra pencils, showed her every favor, favors that, instead of exciting envy among the girls, stirred their approval. Hélène was a foreigner and deserved privileges. It was just.

It occurred to Hélène that there must have been a reason for the church to be open. Perhaps there was a workman about, or perhaps Father Dominic himself had come to see that the church was safe and undisturbed during its long sleep between festivals.

"Hello," she called out. "*Bonjour.* Is there anyone here?" She stood still, pulling her coat more closely around her and waiting for an answer.

While she waited, she imagined two versions of her death. She would be discovered in the spring when the doors were flung open for the festival. The crowds, rushing in with arm-loads of flowers, would discover what was left of her, a small skeleton, odorless, as neat on the floor as a heap of stacked kindling, and the school bag nearby with its books and pencils and notebooks would provide the necessary identification.

Or some miracle of transcendence might occur. This was a church, after all, and close by was the sea. She might be lifted aloft and found with long strands of seaweed in her hair; her skin would be bleached and preserved so that it gleamed with the lustre of certain kinds of shells, and her lips, caked with salt, would be parted to suggest a simple attitude of prayerfulness. (She and her mother, in their ten days of wandering, had visited the grave of an imbecile, a poor wit-less man who had lived as a hermit in the fourteenth century. It was said, a short time after his death and burial, that a villager had noticed a golden lily growing from the hermit's grave, and when the body was exhumed it was discovered that the bulb of the plant was located in his throat, a testi-monial to his true worth and a rebuke to those who had ignored him in his life.)

It occurred to Hélène that her mother would blame herself and not France. Lately, she was always saying, "One thing about France, the coffee has real flavor." Or, "At least the French aren't sentimental about animals," or, "You can say one thing for France: things are expensive, but quality is high." It seemed her mother was compelled to justify this place where she had deliberately settled down to being lonely and uncomfortable and unhappy.

It had all been a mistake, and now her mother, though she didn't say it, longed for home and for Roger. "A man friend" is what she called Roger, saying this phrase with special emphasis as though it was an old joke with a low wattage of energy left in it. Roger loved her and wanted to marry her.

They had known each other for two years. His first wife had left him. "He's very bitter," Hélène's mother said, "and for someone like Roger, this can be a terrible blow, a great humiliation."

He was a chef at the Convention Center in downtown Winnipeg. When he was a young man, he had been taken into the kitchens of the Ritz Carleton in Montreal, where he had learned sauces and pastries and salads. He had learned to make sculptures out of butter or lard or ice or sugar, and even—for it was an arduous apprenticeship, he tells Hélène—how to fold linen table napkins in twenty classic folds. Would she like a demonstration? She had said yes, despising herself, and Roger had instantly obliged, but he could remember only thirteen of the twenty ways. Now, at the Convention Center, he seldom does any cooking himself, but supervises the kitchen from a little office where he spends his time answering the phone and keeping track of grocery orders.

On Saturday nights he used to come to the apartment in St. Vital where Hélène and her mother lived, and there in the tiny kitchen he made them veal in cream or croquettes or a dish of steamed fish, pickerel with white mushrooms and pieces of green onion.

"Tell me what you like best," he'd say to Hélène, "and next week I'll try it out on you."

Of course, he often stayed the night. He was astonishingly neat, never leaving so much as a toothbrush in the bathroom. On Sunday mornings he made them poached eggs on toast—ducks in their nests he called them. He had a trick with the eggs, lifting them from the simmering water with a spatula, then flipping them onto a clean, cotton tea towel, patting them dry, and then sliding them onto buttered triangles of toast—all this without breaking the yolks. He had learned to do this at the Ritz Carleton when he was a young man. "It would not have been acceptable," he said, "to serve an egg that was *wet*." He does it all very quickly and lightly, moving like a character in a speeded-up movie. The first time he did it for Hélène—she was only twelve at the time—she had clapped her hands, and now he's made it into a ceremony, one of several that have unsettled the household.

"Come here, little duckie," he says, flashing his spatula. "Turn yourself over like a good little duck for Hélène." Hélène, when he said this, found it hard to look at her mother, who laughed loudly at this showmanship, her mouth wide and crooked.

Later, after Roger had left, there were a few minutes of tender questioning between them. Hélène's mother, settling down on the plumped cushions, talked slowly, evenly, taking, it would seem, full measure of the delicate temperamental balance of girls in their early adolescence. About the disruption to the household, she was apologetic, saying, "This is only temporary." And, saying with her eyes, "This is not how I planned things." ("Shhh," she said to Roger when he became too merry, when he was about to tell another joke or another story about his apprenticeship.) "How do you like Roger?" her mother asked her. Then, instead of waiting for an answer, her mother began to talk about Roger's ex-wife, how vicious she had been, how she left him for another man.

"I hope I'm not barging in," Roger said, if he dropped by in the middle of the week. He was always bringing presents, not just food, but jewelry, once an alarm clock, once a coat for her mother and a silk blouse for herself. ("I don't know what girls like," he'd said abjectly on this occasion. "I can take it back.")

This is what made Hélène numb. She couldn't say a word in reply, and her silence ignited a savage shame. What was the matter? The matter was that they were waiting for her. They were waiting for her to make up her mind, just as the girls in the schoolyard with their *cartables* and their regulation blouses wait for her to arrive in the dark mornings and bring some improbable substance into the cement schoolyard. "Tell us about Weenie-pegg. Tell us about the snow."

It was growing very cold inside the church, but then even the churches they had visited in September had been cold. Hélène and her mother had carried cardigans. "You can never tell about the weather here," her mother had said, puzzled. This was a point scored against France, a plus for Manitoba, where you at least knew what to expect.

And soon it would be dark. Frail moons of light pressed like mouths on the floor, though the walls themselves were darkly invisible. Hélène reached out and rubbed her hand along the rough surface. This was—she began to figure—this was a fourteenth-century church; twenty centuries take away fourteen—that left six; that meant this church was six hundred years old, walls that were planted by the side of a road called rue des Chiens in a village called St. Quay, which was hidden away in the hexagon that was France. And her body would not be found until spring.

O Mother of God, she said to herself, and rubbed at her hair. O Mother of Jesus.

She tried the door again, putting her ear to the wood to see if she could sound out the inner hardware. There was only a thickish sound of metal butting against wood and the severed resistance of moving parts. She was going to perish. Perish. At fourteen. The thought struck her that her mother would never get over this. She would go back home and tell Roger she couldn't marry him. She would stop writing poems about landscapes that were "jawbone simple and picked clean by wind" and about the "glacé moon pinned like a brooch in the west." She would sink into the *fond,* and her mouth would sag open—this was not how she had planned things. And whose fault was it?

By now the church was entirely dark, but at the far end the altar gleamed dully. It seemed a wonder to Hélène that she could summon interest in this faint light. What was it? There was no gold or ornamentation, only a wooden railing that had been polished or worn by use, and the last pale light lay trapped there on the smooth surface like a pool of summer water.

O Mother of God, she breathed, thinking of Sister Ste. Adolphe, her tiny teeth.

She ran her hand along its edge. There was something at one end. Altar candles. The light didn't reach this far, but her hand felt them in the darkness, a branched candle holder, rising toward the center. She counted the tall candles with her fingers. Up they went like little stairs, one, two, three, four, five, six and then down again on the other side.

There might be matches, she thought, and fumbled at the base of the candle holder. Then she remembered she had some in her school bag. Her mother had asked her to stop at the *tobagie* for cigarettes and matches. (At home in St. Vital they had refused to sell cigarettes to minors, but here in France no one blinked an eye; a point for France.)

She felt her way back to where she had left the bag, rummaged for the matches, and then moved back along the wall to the candles. She managed to light them all, using only three matches, counting under her breath. The stillness of the flames seemed of her own creation, and a feeling of virtue struck her, a ridiculous steamroller. She thought how she would never again in her life be able to take virtue seriously.

Astonishing how much light twelve candles gave off. The stone church shrank in the light so that it seemed not a church at all, but a cheerful meeting room where any minute people might burst through the door and call out her name.

And, of course, that was what would happen, she realized. The lit-up church would attract someone's notice. It was a black night, and rain was falling hard on the roof, but nevertheless someone—and soon—would pass by and see the light from the church. An immediate investigation would be in order. Father Dominic would be summoned at once.

This might take several minutes; he would have to find his overshoes, his umbrella, not to mention the key to the church. Then there would be the mixed confusion of embracing and scolding. How could you? Why on earth? Thank God in all his mercy.

Until then, there was a width of time she would enter and inhabit. There was nothing else she could do; it was laughable. All she had to do was stand here warming her hands in the heat of the twelve candles—how beautiful they were really!— and wait for rescue to come.

Purple Blooms

THERE IS A BOOK I LIKE by the Mexican poet Mario Valeso, who, by coincidence, lives here in this city and who, in the evening, sometimes strolls down this very street. The book is entitled *Purple Blooms* and it is said to resolve certain perplexing memories of the poet's childhood. It is a work that is full of tact, yet it is tentative, off-balance, dark and truncated—and it is just this lack of finish that so moved me the first time I read it.

I gave a copy of the book to my friend Shana, who's been "going through a bad time," as she puts it. People who meet her are generally struck by her beauty. She's young, well-off and in excellent health, yet she claims that the disconnectedness of life torments her. Everything makes her sad. Lilacs make her sad. Chopin makes her sad. The thought of rain falling in a turbulent and empty ocean makes her sad. But nothing makes her sadder than the collection of toby jugs that her mother, the film actress, left her in her will.

More than a hundred of these sturdy little creatures fill the shelves of her sunny apartment. I myself find it unnerving the way they glisten and grin and puff out their pottery cheeks as though oblivious to the silly pouring lip that deforms the tops of their heads. Knick-knacks, Shana calls them, willfully denying their value, but she refuses nevertheless to part with them, though I've given her the name of an auctioneer who would guarantee a fair price.

It could be said that she encourages her sadness. It could be demonstrated. On her glass-topped coffee table she keeps a large vase of lilacs and an alabaster bust of Chopin and, since last Saturday, my gift of Mario Valeso's book *Purple Blooms*. The denseness, the compaction of the closed text and the assertive angle with which it rests on the table suggest to me that she has not yet opened its pages.

I have also given a copy to Edward. He is attractive, my Edward. I've spent a considerable number of hours staring at him, hoping his handsome features would grow less perfect, more of a match for my own. What does he see in me? (This is the question I ask myself—though I like to think I put it rhetorically.)

"Purple Blooms," Edward murmured as he slipped the gift wrap off the book, and then he said it again—*"Purple Blooms"*—in that warm, sliding, beet-veined voice of his. His father, as everyone knows, sang tenor with the Mellotones in the late forties, and some say that Edward has inherited something of the color of his voice. Edward, of course, vehemently denies any such inheritance. When he hears old records of "Down by the Riverside" or "I'm Blue Turning Gray Over You," he cannot imagine how he came to be the son of such a parent. The line of descent lacks distinction and reason, and Edward is a distinguished and reasoning man. He is also a man attentive to the least sexual breeze, and the minute he pronounced the words, *"Purple Blooms,"* I began worrying that he would find the poems not sensual enough for his liking.

"These poems are about the poet's past," I explained to Edward, rather disliking myself for the academic tone I was taking. "Valeso is attempting to make sense of certain curious family scenes that have lingered in his memory."

Edward, wary of dark sublimities, examined the dust jacket. "It won't bite you," I said, joking. He placed the book in his briefcase and promised he would "look at it" on the weekend or perhaps on his summer holidays.

"If you're not going to read it," I said, testing him, "I'll give it to someone else."

For a minute we were pitched straight into one of those little arched silences that lean inward on their own symmetry as though no exterior force existed. Edward took my hand sweetly, then rubbed his thumb across the inside of my wrist, but I noticed he did not promise me anything, and that made me uneasy.

As always, when I'm uneasy, I go out and buy my mother a present. Sometimes I bring her roasted cashews or fresh fruit, but today I take her a copy of *Purple Blooms*. "A book?" she shouts. She has not read a book since she was a young girl.

Fat and full of fury, she stands most days by an upstairs window and spies on the world. What possible need does she have for books, she asks me. Life is all around her.

To be more truthful, life is all behind her. At eighteen she was crowned North America's Turkey Queen at Ramona, California, and wore a dress that was made up entirely of turkey feathers. She has the dress still, though I've never laid eyes on it since she stores it in a fur vault in San Diego, once a year mailing off a twelve-dollar check for storage fees and saying, as she drops the envelope in the mailbox, "Well, so much for misspent youth."

How I plead with her! Go to a movie, I say. Invite the neighbors in. Take a course in French conversation or gourmet cooking or music appreciation. A year ago she stopped the newspapers. When the picture tube went on the TV, she decided it wasn't worth fixing. It seems nothing that's happening in the world has any connection with the eighteen-year-old girl carried so splendidly through the streets of Ramona with a crown of dusky turkey feathers in her hair.

"What do I want with a book about flowers," my mother growls. Her tone is rough, though she loves me dearly. I explain that the book is not about flowers (and at the same time imagine myself slyly trading on her innocent error at some future gathering of friends). "This poet," I tell her, "is attempting to recall certain early scenes that bloomed mysteriously and darkly like flowers, and that he now wants to come to terms with."

This is rather an earful for my mother. She pulls at her apron, looks frowningly at the ceiling, then out the window; this last I recognize as a signal that she wants me to leave, and I do.

Later that afternoon I find myself in the park. Almost everyone knows about the very fine little park at 16th and Ossington—a gem of a park with a wide gravel path and a sprightly round-headed magnolia and smooth painted benches by the side of a bowling green. A cool, quiet place to sit and read, but today it is filled with people.

I stop and ask some schoolchildren what the excitement is about, and a little boy in a striped sweater tells me that Mario Valeso is autographing copies of *Purple Blooms* over in the shady spot under the magnolia tree. There is a great deal of pushing and shoving and general rowdyism. Everyone, it seems, has brought along a copy of *Purple Blooms* for Mr. Valeso to sign. Shana is there with Edward, her arm slipped through his, and they both tell me they have "been greatly helped and strengthened" by reading the poems. "It's all a matter of making connections," Shana says in her breathless way, and Edward says, "It's discovering that we all share the same ancestors."

Then, to my surprise, I catch sight of my mother ahead of me in the crowd, and it pleases me to see that she has put on her best cardigan and her white shoes and that she is holding forth loudly to someone or other, saying, "Letting go of the past means embracing the present." Someone else is saying, "The seeds of childhood grow on mysterious parental soil," and an old man in a baseball cap is muttering, "We are the sum of our collective memories."

The crowd grows even larger, and again and again I find myself pushed to the end of the line. I realize it will be hours before my turn comes, and so I pull a book out of my knapsack to help while away the time. It is a new book of poetry, untitled and anonymous, which appears to be a celebration of the randomness and disorder of the world. We are solitary specks of foam, the poet says, who are tossed on a meaningless sea. Every wave is separate, and one minute in time bears no relationship to the moment that precedes or follows it.

I read on and on, and soon forget about the people crowding around me and reading over my shoulder. The bowling green fades into dimness, as do the benches and the magnolia tree and the gravel path, until all that's left is a page of print, a line of type, a word, a dot of ink, a shadow on the retina that is no bigger, I believe, than the smallest violet in the woods.

Flitting Behavior

SOME OF MEERSHANK'S WITTIEST WRITING was done during his wife's final illness.

"Mortality," he whispered each morning to give himself comfort, "puts acid in the wine." Other times he said, as he peered into the bathroom mirror, "Mortality puts strychnine in the candy floss. It puts bite in the byte." Then he groaned aloud—but only once—and got straight back to work.

His novel of this period, *Malaprop in Disneyfield,* was said to have been cranked out of the word processor between invalid trays and bedpans. In truth, he wept as he set down his outrageous puns and contretemps. The pages mounted, two hundred, three hundred. The bulk taunted him, and meanwhile his wife, Louise, lingered, her skin growing as transparent as human skin can be without disintegrating. A curious odor, bitter and yellow, stole over the sickroom. Meershank had heard of the odor that preceded death; now he breathed it daily.

It was for this odor, more than anything else, that he pitied her, she who'd busied herself all her life warding off evil smells with scented candles and aerosol room fresheners. Since a young woman she'd had the habit of sweetening her bureau drawers, and his too, with sprigs of dried lavender, and carrying always in her handbag and traveling case tiny stitched sachets of herbs. He had sometimes wondered where she found these anachronistic sachets; who in the modern industrial world produced such frivolities?—the Bulgarians maybe, or the Peruvians, frantic for hard currency.

Toward the end of Louise's illness he had a surprise visit from his editor, a vigorous, leggy woman of forty who drove up from Toronto to see how the new manuscript was coming along. She came stepping from her car one Monday afternoon in a white linen jumpsuit. Bending slightly, she kissed Meershank on both cheeks and cried out, "But this is extraordinary! That you can even think of work at a time like this."

Meershank pronounced for her his bite-in-the-byte aperçu, very nearly choking with shame.

He was fond of his editor—her name was Maybelle Spritz—but declined to invite her into his wife's bedroom, though the two women knew and liked each other. "She's not strong enough for visitors," he said, knowing it was the smell of the room he guarded her from, his poor Louise's last corner of pride. "Maybe later."

He and Maybelle sat drinking coffee on the veranda most of the afternoon. The weather all week had been splendid. Birds sang in the branches of Meershank's trees, and sunlight flooded the long triangle of Meershank's side lawn. Maybelle, reading slowly as always, turned over the manuscript pages. Her nails were long and vivid. She held a pencil straight up in her hand, and at least once every three minutes or so she let loose a bright snort of laughter, which Meershank welcomed like a man famished. He watched her braided loop of auburn hair and observed how the light burned on the tips of her heavy silver earrings. There was a bony hollow at the base of her neck that deepened, suddenly, each time another snort was gathering. Later, at five o'clock, checking his watch, he offered gin and tonic. For Louise upstairs he carried cream of celery soup, weak tea and an injection for her hip, which the visiting nurse had taught him to administer.

"Are you feeling lonely?" his wife asked him, turning on one side and readying herself for the needle. She imagined, rightly, that he missed her chatter, that her long days spent in drugged sleep were a deprivation. Every day she asked the same question, plunging him directly into blocky silence. Yes, he was lonely. No, he was not lonely. Which would please her more? He kept his hand on her discolored hip and mumbled the news—testing it—that Maybelle Spritz was thinking of coming for a visit.

She opened her eyes and managed a smile as he rearranged the pillows. He had a system: one pillow under each knee, one at the small of her back and two to support her shoulders. The air in the room was suffocating. He asked again, as he did every day, if he might open a window. No, she said, as she always did; it was too cold. She seemed convinced that spring had not arrived in its usual way, she who'd always been so reasonable.

Downstairs Maybelle stood in the kitchen drinking a second gin and tonic and heating up a noodle pudding she had brought along. She had occasionally been a dinner guest in Meershank's house, but had never before penetrated the kitchen. She set a little table on the veranda. There was a breeze, enough to keep the mosquitoes away for a bit. Knives and forks she discovered easily in the first drawer she opened. The thick white dinner plates she found stacked on a shelf over the sink. There were paper napkins of a most ordinary sort in a cupboard. As she moved about she marveled at the domesticity of the famous, how simple things appeared when regarded close up, like picking up an immense orange and finding it all thick hide on a tiny fruit. She wondered if Meershank would ask her to spend the night.

———

They had only once before shared a bed, and that had been during the awful week after Louise's illness has been diagnosed.

The expression *terminal,* when the doctor first pronounced it, had struck Meershank with a comic bounce, this after a lifetime of pursuing puns for a living. His scavenger self immediately pictured a ghostly airline terminal in which scurrying men and women trotted briskly to and fro in hospital gowns.

The word *terminal* had floated out of the young doctor's wide pink face; it was twice repeated, until Meershank collected himself and responded with a polite nod. Then he put back his head, counted the ceiling tiles—twelve times fourteen—and decided on the spot that his wife must not be told.

The specialist laced clean hands across flannel knees and pressed for honest disclosure; there were new ways of telling people that they were about to die; he himself had attended a recent symposium in Boston and would take personal responsibility . . .

No. Meershank held up his hand. This was nonsense. Why did people insist that honesty was the only way of coping with truth? He knew his wife. After thirty-five years of marriage he knew his wife. She must be brought home from the hospital and encouraged to believe that she would recover. Rest, medication, country air—they would work their healing magic. Louise could always, almost always, be persuaded to follow a reasonable course.

The following day, having signed the release papers and made the arrangements to have his wife moved, Meershank, until then a faithful husband, took his editor, Maybelle Spritz, to a downtown hotel and made plodding love to her, afterward begging pardon for his age, his grief and his fury at the fresh-faced specialist who, concluding their interview, had produced one of Meershank's books, *Walloping Westward,* and begged the favor of an inscription. Meershank coldly took out a pen and signed his name. He reminded himself that the Persians had routinely put to death the bearer of bad news.

Home again, with Louise installed in the big front bedroom, he resumed work. His word processor hummed like a hornet from nine to five, and the pages flew incriminatingly out of the printer. During the day his brain burned like a lightbulb screwed crookedly into a socket. At night he slept deeply. He wondered if he were acquiring a reputation for stoicism, that contemptible trait! Friends stopped by with gifts of food or flowers. The flowers he carried up to Louise's bedroom, where they soon drooped and died, and the food he threw in the garbage. Coffee cakes, almond braids, banana loaves—his appetite had vanished.

"Eat," Maybelle commanded, loading his plate.

He loved noodle pudding, and wondered how Maybelle knew. "It's in your second novel," she reminded him. "*Snow Soup and Won Ton Drift.* Remember? Wentzel goes into the café at Cannes and demands that—"

"I remember, I remember." Meershank held up a hand. (He was always holding up a hand nowadays, resisting information.) He had a second helping, ingesting starch and sweetness. This was hardly fitting behavior for a grieving husband. He felt Maybelle's eyes on him. "I shoulda brought more," she said, sounding for a minute like a girl from Cookston Corners, which she was. "I said to myself, he'll be starving himself."

For dessert she rummaged in the refrigerator and found two peaches. Louise would have peeled them and arranged the slices in a cut glass bowl. Meershank and Maybelle sat eating them out of their hands. He thought to himself: this is like the last day of the world.

"Ripe," Maybelle pronounced. There was a droplet of juice on her chin, which she brushed away with the back of her hand. Meershank observed that her eyes looked tired, but perhaps it was only the eye shadow she wore. What was the purpose of eye shadow, he wondered. He had never known and couldn't begin to imagine.

A character in his first book, *Swallowing Hole,* had asked this question aloud to another character, who happened to be his wife. What was her name? Phyllis? Yes, Phyllis of the phyllo pastry and philandering nights. "Why do you smudge your gorgeous green eyes with gook?" he, the cockolded husband, had asked. And what had the fair Phyllis replied? Something arch, something unpardonable. Something enclosing a phallic pun. He had forgotten, and for that he blessed the twisted god of age. His early books with their low-altitude gag lines embarrassed him, and he tried hard to forget he had once been the idiot who wrote them.

Maybelle, on the other hand, knew his oeuvre with depressing thoroughness and could quote chapter and verse. Well, that was the function of an editor, he supposed. A reasonable man would be grateful for such attention. She was a good girl. He wished she'd find a husband so he would feel less often that she'd taken the veil on his account. But at least she didn't expect him to converse with wit. Like all the others, she'd bought wholesale the myth of the sad jester.

It was a myth that he himself regarded with profound skepticism. He'd read the requisite scholarly articles, of course, and had even, hypocrite that he was, written one or two himself. Humor is a pocket pulled inside out; humor is an anguished face dumped upside down; humor is the refuge of the grunting cynic, the eros of the deprived lover, the break-fast of the starving clown. Some of these cheap theories he'd actually peddled aloud to the graduating class at Trent a year ago, and his remarks had been applauded lustily. (How much better to lust applaudingly, he'd cackled, sniggered, snorted inside his wicked head.)

He suspected that these theories were leapt upon for their simplicity, their symmetry, their neat-as-a-pin ironic shim-mer. They were touted by those so facile they were unable to see how rich with ragged comedy the world really was. But Meershank knew, he knew! Was it not divinely comic that only yesterday he'd received a telephone solicitation from the Jackson Point Cancer Fund? Wasn't it also comic that the specter of his wife's death should fill him with a wobbly lust for his broad-busted, perfume-wafting, forty-year-old editor? For that matter, wasn't it superbly comic that a man widely known as a professional misogynist had remained happily married to one woman for thirty-five years? (Life throws these kinky curves a little too often, Meershank had observed, and the only thing to do was open your fool mouth and guffaw.)

At nine he checked once again on his wife, who was sleeping quietly. If she woke later, a second injection was permitted. He carried a bottle of brandy out on to the veranda. One for the road?, he asked Maybelle with his eyebrows. Why not, she said with a lift of her shoulders. Her upper lip went stiff as a ledge in the moonlight, and he shuddered to think he was about to kiss her. The moon tonight was bloated and white, as fretful as a face. Everywhere there was the smell of mock orange blossoms, which had bloomed early this year and in absurd profusion. Crickets ticked in the grass, like fools, like drunkards. Meershank lifted his glass. The brandy burned his throat and made him retreat for an instant, but Maybelle became attenuated, lively, sharp of phrase, amusing. He laughed aloud for the first time in a week, wondering if the world would crack down the middle.

It did. Or seemed to. A loud overhead popping noise like the cracking of whips made him jump. Maybelle slammed down her glass and stared. All around them the sky flashed white, then pink, then filled with rat-a-tat-tat fountains and sparks and towering plumes.

"Jesus," Maybelle said. "Victoria Day. I almost forgot."

"I did forget," Meershank said. "I never once thought."

A rocket whined and popped, made ropy arcs across the sky, burst into petals, leaving first one, then a dozen blazing trails. It was suddenly daylight, fierce, then faded, then instantly replaced by a volley of cracking gunpowder and new showers of brilliance.

The explosions, star-shaped, convulsive, leaping out of the other, made Meershank think of the chains of malignant cells igniting in his wife's body.

He set down his brandy, excused himself and hurried upstairs.

Meershank, marrying Louise Lovell in 1949, had felt himself rubbing bellies for the first time with the exotic. He, a Chicago Jew, the son of a bond salesman, had fallen in love with a gentile, a Canadian, a fair-haired girl of twenty who had been gently reared in the Ottawa Valley by parents who lived quietly in a limestone house that was a hundred years old. It faced on the river. There was a rose garden criss-crossed by gravel paths and surrounded by a pale pink brick wall. Oh, how silently those two parents had moved about in their large square rooms, in winter wrapping themselves in shawls, sitting before pots of raspberry-leaf tea and making their good-natured remarks about the weather, the books they were forever in the middle of, the tiny thunder of politics that flickered from their newspaper, always one day old.

The mother of Louise possessed a calm brow of marble. The father had small blue eyes and hard cheeks. He was the author of a history of the Canadian Navy. It was, he told Meershank, the *official* history. Meershank was given a signed copy. And he was given, too, with very little noise or trouble, the hand of Louise in marriage. He had been stunned. Effortlessly, it seemed, he'd won from them their beloved only daughter, a girl of soft hips and bland hair done roundly in a pageboy.

"What exactly do you do?" they only once asked. He worked as a correspondent for a newspaper, he explained. (He did not use the word *journalist*.) And he hoped one day to write a book. ("Ah! A book! Splendid!")

The wedding was in the month of June and was held in the garden. Meershank's relatives did not trouble to travel all the way up from Chicago. The wedding breakfast was served out-of-doors, and the health of the young couple—Meershank at twenty-seven was already starting to bald—was toasted with a non-alcoholic fruit punch. The family was abstemious; the tradition went back several generations; alcohol, tobacco, caffeine—there wasn't a trace of these poisons in the blood-stream of Meershank's virgin bride. He looked at her smooth, pale arms—and eventually, when legally married, at her smooth, pale breasts—and felt he'd been singularly, and comically, blessed.

There is a character, Virgie Allgood, in Meershank's book *Sailing to Saskatchewan,* who might be said to resemble Louise. In the book, Virgie is an eater of whole grains and leafy vegetables. Martyrlike, she eschews french fries, doughnuts and liver dumplings, yet her body is host to disease after disease.

Fortified milk fails. Pure air fails. And just when the life is about to go out of her, the final chapter, a new doctor rides into town on a motorbike and saves her by prescribing a diet of martinis and cheesecakes.

There is something of Louise, too, in the mother in Meershank's tour de force, *Continuous Purring*. She is a woman who cannot understand the simplest joke. Riddles on cereal boxes have to be laboriously explained. Puns strike her as being untidy scraps to be swept up in a dustpan. She thinks a double entendre is a potent new drink. She is congenitally immune to metaphor (the root of all comedy, Meershank believes), and on the day her husband is appointed to the Peevish Chair of Midbrow Humor, she sends for the upholsterer.

When *Encounter* did its full-length profile on Meershank in 1981, it erred by stating that Louise Lovell Meershank had never read her husband's books. The truth is she not only had read them, but before the birth of the word processor she had typed them, collated the pages, corrected their virulent misspelling, redistributed semicolons and commas with the aplomb of a goddess, and tactfully weeded out at least half of Meershank's compulsive exclamation points. She corresponded with publishers, arranged for foreign rights, dealt with book clubs and with autograph seekers, and she always—less and less frequently, of course—trimmed her husband's fluffy wreath of hair with a pair of silver-handled scissors.

She read Meershank's manuscripts with a delicious (to Meershank) frown on her wide pale brow—more and more she'd grown to resemble her mother. She turned over the pages with a delicate hand as though they possessed the same scholarly sheen as her father's *Official History of the Canadian Navy*. She read them not once, but several times, catching a kind of overflow of observance that leaked like oil and vinegar from the edges of Meershank's copious, verbal, many-leafed salads.

Her responses never marched in time with his. She was slower, and could wave aside sentimentality, saying, "Why not?—it's part of the human personality." Occasionally, she said the unexpected thing, as when she described her husband's novella, *Fiend at the Water Fountain,* as being, "cool and straight up and down as a tulip."

What she actually told the journalist from *Encounter* was that she never *laughed* when reading her husband's books. For this Meershank has always respected her, valued her, adored her. She was his Canadian rose, his furry imbiber of scented tea, his smiling plum, his bread and jam, his little squirrel, his girlie-girl, his Dear Heart who promised in the garden by the river beside the limestone house in 1949 to stay at his side forever and ever. What a joke she has played on him in the end.

She has, Meershank said to Maybelle, taken a turn for the worse. He phoned the doctor, who said he would come at once. Then he handed Maybelle a piece of paper on which two telephone numbers were written. "Please," he said. "Phone the children."

Maybelle was unprepared for this. And she had never met the children. "What should I tell them?" she asked.

"Tell them," Meershank said, and paused. "Tell them it could be sooner than we thought."

One of the daughters, Sonya, lived in London, Ontario, where she was the new director of the program for women's studies. (For those who trouble to look, her mirror image can be found in Ira Chauvin, post-doc researcher in male studies, in Meershank's academic farce, *Ten Minutes to Tenure.*) Sonya did not say to Maybelle, "Who is this calling?" or "How long does she have?" She said, "I'll be there in three hours flat."

The other daughter, Angelica, ran a health-food restaurant and delicatessen with her husband, Rusty, in Montreal. They were just closing up for the night when Maybelle phoned. "I can get a plane at midnight," Angelica said in a high, sweet, shaky voice. "Tell her to wait for me."

After that Maybelle sat on a kitchen chair in the dark. She could have switched on the light, but she preferred to sit as she was and puzzle over what level of probability had landed her on the twenty-fourth of May as a visitor—she was not such a fool as to mistake a single embrace for anything other than a mutation of grief.

The tiles of the kitchen wall, after a moment, took on a greenish glow, and she began to float out of her body, a trick she had perfected during her long years of commuting between Cookston Corners and downtown Toronto. First she became Sonya, flying down an eastbound highway, her hands suddenly younger and supple-jointed on the slippery wheel. She took the long cloverleafs effortlessly, the tires of her tough little car zinging over ramps and bridges, and the sleepy nighttime radio voices holding her steady in the middle lane.

Then, blinking once and shutting out the piny air, she was transformed into Angelica, candid, fearful, sitting tense in an aisle seat at the rear of a plane—she had her mother's smooth cheeks, her father's square chin and her own slow sliding tears. On her lap she clutched a straw bag, and every five minutes she pushed back the sleeve of her blouse and checked her wristwatch, trying to freeze its hands with her will.

Next she was the doctor—springing onto the veranda, tapping at the screen door and taking the stairs two at a time. She drifted then into the amorphous body of Louise, where it was hot and damp and difficult to breathe, but where shadows reached out and curved around her head. Her hands lay surprisingly calm on the sheet—until one of them was lifted and held to Meershank's beating heart.

She felt his bewilderment and heard with his ears a long popping chain of firecrackers going off. A window in the bedroom had been opened—at last—and the scent of the mock orange blossoms reached him with a rushing blow. Everything was converging. All the warm fluids of life came sliding behind Maybelle's eyes, and she had to hold on to the sides of the kitchen chair to keep herself from disappearing.

In each of Meershank's fictions there is what the literary tribe calls a "set piece," a jewel, as it were, set in a spun-out text, or a chunk of narrative that is somehow more intense, more cohesive, more self-contained than the rest. Generally theatrical and vivid, it can be read and comprehended, even when severed from the wider story, or it can be "performed" by those writers—Meershank is not one—who like to gad about the country giving "readings."

In Meershank's recently published book, *Malaprop in Disneyfield,* the set piece has four characters sitting at dusk on a veranda discussing the final words of the recently deceased family matriarch. The sky they gaze into is a rainy mauve, and the mood is one of tenderness—but there is also a tone of urgency. Three of the four had been present when the last words were uttered, and some irrational prompting makes them want to share with the fourth what they heard—or what they *thought* they heard. Because each heard something different, and there is a descending order of coherence.

"The locked door of the room," is what one of them, a daughter, heard.

"The wok cringes in the womb," is the enigmatic phrase another swears she heard.

The bereaved husband, a blundering old fool in shirt sleeves, heard, incredibly, "The sock is out of tune."

All three witnesses turn to their listener, as lawyers to a judge. Not one of them is superstitious enough to place great importance on final words. Illness, they know, brings a rainbow of distortion, but they long, nevertheless, for interpretation.

The listening judge is an awkward but compassionate woman who would like nothing better than to bring these three fragments into unity. Inside her head she holds a pencil straight up. Her eyes are fixed on the purpling clouds.

Then it arrives. Through some unsecured back door in her imagination she comes up with "The mock orange is in bloom."

"Of course, of course," they chime, nodding and smiling at each other, and at that moment their grief shifts subtly, the first of many such shiftings they are about to undergo.

Pardon

ON FRIDAY AFTERNOON MILLY STOPPED at Ernie's Cards 'n' Things to buy a *mea culpa* card for her father-in-law, whom she had apparently insulted.

"Sorry," Ernie's wife said in her testy way. "We're all out."

Milly found this hard to believe. The card rack was full. You could buy a happiness-in-your-new-home card or a mind-your-own-beeswax card, even a spectacular three-dollar pop-up card announcing to the world that you were feeling under-appreciated. Surely there was such a thing as an I'm-sorry card.

"You can believe what you want," Ernie's wife said. "But we're sold right out. At the start of the week I had at least a dozen sorry cards in stock. We had a real nice selection, all the way from 'I boobed' to 'Forgive me, Dear Heart.' They went like hotcakes, the whole lot. That's more than I sell in an average year."

"How strange," Milly said. "What on earth's everyone being sorry about all of a sudden?"

Ernie's wife made a gesture of impatience. She wasn't there to stand around jawing with the customers, she snapped. There was the inventory to do and the ordering and so on.

Milly at once apologized for taking up her time; she had only been speaking rhetorically when she asked what every-one was being sorry about.

At this, Ernie's wife had the grace to blush and make amends. She'd been under strain, she said, what with people in and out of the shop all week grousing about her stock of sorry cards. There was one poor soul who came in weeping her eyes out. She'd had a set-to with her husband and told him he was getting so fat he was no longer attractive to her. It turned out he wasn't really getting fat at all. She was just in a miffy mood because she didn't like the new statue of Louis Riel in the park. She didn't object to Louis in the buff, not that—it was more a question of where her tax dollars were going.

Milly, who was an intimate friend of the sculptor, said, "I'm really sorry to hear this."

"And then," Ernie's wife went on, "a gentleman came in here saying he'd had an out-and-out row with his next-door neighbor who'd been a true-blue friend for twenty years."

"These things happen," Milly said. "Just this week my own father-in-law—"

"Seems the man and his neighbor got on to the subject of politics—in my opinion not a subject for friends to be discussing. The neighbor called my customer a stuffed-shirt fascist right to his face."

"That seems a little extreme," Milly said. "But why should he be the one to send a sorry card when his friend was the one who—?"

"Exactly!" Ernie's wife held up a finger, and her eyes filled with fire. "My thoughts exactly. But later that same day who should come in but a sweet old white-haired gent who said his next-door neighbor had called him a pinko bleeding heart and he—"

"Do you mean to tell me he was the very—"

"You're interrupting," Ernie's wife cried.

Milly said she was terribly sorry. She explained that she was feeling unstrung because now she would have to go all the way downtown to buy a card for her father-in-law.

"Well, if you're going downtown," Ernie's wife said, "would you mind returning a pair of pajamas for me? I bought them in the sales last week and, lo and behold, I got them home and found a flaw in the left sleeve."

Milly disliked going all the way downtown. She disliked waiting for the bus, and when she got on the bus she disliked the way a man sitting next to her let his umbrella drip on her ankle.

"I'm most awfully sorry," he said. "I didn't realize. I didn't even notice. In a hundred years I would never have let—"

Milly managed a smile and made a gesture with her hand that said: It's all right, I accept your apology. She was glad the umbrella hadn't dripped on the pajamas Ernie's wife had given her to return. Returning merchandise can be tricky, especially when it's wet and when the receipt's been mislaid. More often than not you meet with suspicion, scorn, arrogance, rebuff.

But today the gentleman in the complaint department was wearing a yellow rose in his lapel, and his eyes twinkled.

"We take full responsibility for flaws," he said. "Head office will be sending your friend a letter begging her pardon, and I personally apologize in the name of our branch and in the name of the manufacturer."

Milly, triumphant, took the bus home. The driver apologized, as well he should, for splashing her as she stood at the bus stop.

"It's not your fault, it's all this blessed rain," Milly said.

The bus driver shook his head. "A regular deluge. But I should have been more careful."

The instant the words left his mouth, the rain began to fall more heavily. The sky turned an ugly black, and soon rain was pelting down, loud and musical, slamming on the roof of the bus and streaming in thick sheets down its sides. The windshield wipers did their best to beat back the water, but clearly they hadn't been designed for a storm of this magnitude and, after a few minutes, the driver pulled over to the curb.

"I'm awfully sorry, folks," he announced, "but we're going to have to wait this one out."

Nobody really minded. It was rather pleasant, almost like a party, to be sitting snug inside a parked bus whose windows had turned to silver, swapping stories about storms of other years. Several passengers remembered the flood of 1958 and the famous spring downpour of 1972, but most of them agreed that today's storm was the most violent they had ever seen. They would be going home to flooded basements and worried spouses, yet they remained cheerful. Some of the younger people at the back of the bus struck up an impromptu singsong, and the older folks traded their newspapers back and forth. The headline on one paper said TRUDEAU APOLOGIZES TO REAGAN, and another said REAGAN APOLOGIZES TO SUMMIT. By the time the sun burst through, many of the passengers had exchanged names and phone numbers and announced to each other how cleansing a good storm can be, how it sweeps away unspoken hostilities and long-held grudges.

Milly, walking home from her bus stop, breathed in the shining air. Her feet were drenched, and she was forced to step over several fallen tree branches, but she noted with pleasure the blue clarity of the sky. It was going to be a splendid evening. A single cloud, a fluffy width of cumulus, floated high in the air over her house. It was shaped like a pair of wings, thought Milly, who was in a fanciful mood. No, not like wings, but like two outstretched hands, wonderfully white and beseeching, which seemed to beckon to her and say: Sorry about all this fuss and bother.

Seeing the great cloudy hands made Milly yearn to absolve all those who had troubled her in her life. She forgave her father for naming her Milly instead of Jo Ann, and her mother for passing on to her genes that made her oversensitive to small hurts and slights. She forgave her brother for reading her diary, and her sister for her pretty legs, and her cat for running in front of a truck and winding up pressed flat as a transfer on the road. She forgave everyone who had ever forgotten her birthday and everyone who looked over her shoulder at parties for someone more attractive to talk to. She forgave her boss for being waspish and her lover for lack of empathy and her husband for making uncalled-for remarks about stale breakfast cereal and burned toast.

All this dispensing of absolution emptied Milly out and made her light as air. She had a sensation of floating, of weightlessness, and it seemed to her that bells were chiming inside her head.

But it was only the telephone ringing—without a doubt her father-in-law phoning to ask forgiveness. She hurried inside so she could sing into his ear, yes, yes, yes, yes, yes.

Words

WHEN THE WORLD FIRST STARTED HEATING UP, an international conference was held in Rome to discuss ways of dealing with the situation.

Ian's small northern country—small in terms of population, that is, not in size—sent him to the meetings as a junior observer, and it was there he met Isobel, who was representing her country as full-fledged delegate. She wore a terrible green dress the first time he saw her, and rather clumsy shoes, but he could see that her neck was slender, her waist narrow and her legs long and brown. For so young a woman, she was astonishingly articulate; in fact, it was her voice more than anything else that he fell in love with—its hills and valleys and its pliant, easy-sided wit. It was a voice that could be distinguished in any gathering, being both sweet and husky and having an edging of contralto merriment that seemed to Ian as rare and fine as a border of gold leaf.

They played truant, missing half the study sessions, the two of them lingering instead over tall, cool drinks in the café they found on the Via Traflori. There, under a cheerful striped canopy, Isobel leaned across a little table and placed long, ribbony Spanish phrases into Ian's mouth, encouraging and praising him when he got them right. And he, in his somewhat stiff northern voice, gave back the English equivalents:

table, chair, glass, cold, hot, money, street, people, mouth. In the evenings, walking in the gardens in front of the institute where the conference was being held, they turned to each other and promised with their eyes, and in two languages as well, to love each other for ever.

The second International Conference was held ten years later. The situation had become grave. One could use the word *crisis* and not be embarrassed. Ian—by then married to Isobel, who was at home with the children—attended every session, and he listened attentively to the position papers of various physicists, engineers, geographers and linguists from all parts of the world. It was a solemn but distinguished assembly; many eminent men and women took their places at the lectern, including the spidery old Scottish demographer who years earlier had made the first correlation between substrata temperatures and highly verbalized societies. In every case, these speakers presented their concerns with admirable brevity, each word weighted and frugally chosen, and not one of them exceeded the two-minute time limitation. For by now no one really doubted that it was the extravagance and proliferation of language that had caused the temperature of the earth's crust to rise, and in places—California, Japan, London—to crack open and form long ragged lakes of fire. The evidence was everywhere and it was incontrovertible; thermal maps and measurements, sonar readings, caloric separations, a network of subterranean monitoring systems—all these had reinforced the integrity of the original Scottish theories.

But the delegates, sitting in the plenary session of the second International Conference, were still reluctant to take regulatory action. It was partly a case of heads-in-the-sand; it was—human nature being what it is—partly a matter of political advantage or commercial gain. There lingered, too, a somewhat surprising nostalgia for traditional liberties and for the old verbal order of the world. Discussion at the conference had gone around and around all week, pointless and wasteful, and it looked very much as though the final meeting would end in yet another welter of indecision and deferral. It was at that point that Ian, seated in the front row, rose and requested permission to speak.

He was granted a one-minute slot on the agenda. In fact, he spoke for several minutes, but his eloquence, his sincerity (and no doubt his strong, boyish appearance, his shaggy hair and his blue eyes) seemed to merit an exception. Certainly not one person sitting in that gathering had any wish to stop him.

It was unfortunate, tragic some thought, that a freak failure in the electronic system—only a plug accidentally pulled from its socket—prevented his exact words from being recorded, but those who were present remembered afterward how passionately he pleaded his love for the planet. (In truth—though who could know this?—he was thinking chiefly of his love for Isobel and his two children.)

We are living in a fool's dream, he told his fellow delegates, and the time has come for us to wake. Voluntary restraints were no longer adequate to preserve the little earth, which was the only home we know. Halfway measures like the old three-hour *temps tranquilles* were next to useless since they were never, or almost never, enforced. The evening curfew-lingua was ridiculously lenient. Abuses of every sort abounded, particularly the use of highly percussive words or words that were redolent with emotional potency, even though it had been established that these two classes of words were particularly damaging to bedrock and shales. Multilingualism continued to flourish. Wasteful antiphonic structures were actually on the increase in the more heavily populated regions, as was the use of elaborate ceremonial metaphor. It was as though, by refusing to make linguistic sacrifices, the human race had willed its own destruction.

When he finished speaking, the applause was prolonged and powerful. It perhaps held an element of shame, too; this young man had found the courage to say at last what should have been said long before. One after another the delegates rose to their feet, and soon their clapping fell into a steady rhythmic beat that had the effect of holding Ian hostage on the platform. The chairman whispered into his ear, begging him for a few additional words.

He assented. He could not say no. And, in a fever that was remarkably similar to the fever he had suffered as a child during a severe case of measles, or like the fever of love he had succumbed to ten years earlier in Rome, he announced to the audience, holding up a hand for attention, that he would be the first to take a vow of complete silence for the sake of the planet that had fathered him.

Almost at once he regretted his words, but hubris kept him from recanting for the first twenty-four hours and, after that, a kind of stubbornness took over. Isobel met him at the airport with the words, "You went too far." Later, after a miserable, silent attempt at lovemaking, she said, "I'll never forgive you." His children, clamoring to hear about his moment of heroism, poked at him, at his face and chest and arms, as though he were inert. He tried to tell them with his eyes that he was still their father, that he still loved them.

"Leave him alone," Isobel said sharply. "He might as well be a stranger now. He's no different than anyone else."

She became loud and shrewish. When his silent followers arrived at their door—and in time there were thousands of them, each with the same blank face and gold armband—she admitted them with bad grace. She grew garrulous. She rambled on and on, bitter and blaming, sometimes incoherent, sometimes obscene, sometimes reverting to a coarse, primitive schoolyard Spanish, sometimes shouting to herself or cursing into the mirror or chanting oaths—anything to furnish the emptiness of the house with words. She became disoriented. The solid plaster of the walls fell away from her, melting into a drift of vapor. There seemed to be no shadows, no sense of dimension, no delicate separation between one object and another. Privately, she pleaded with her husband for an act of apostasy. Later she taunted him. "Show me you're still human," she would say. "Give me just one word." The word *betrayal* came frequently out of her wide mobile mouth, and so did the scornful epithet *martyr.*

But time passes and people forget. She forgot, finally, what it was that had betrayed her. Next she forgot her husband's name. Sometimes she forgot that she had a husband at all, for how could anything be said to exist, she asked herself loudly, hoarsely—even a husband, even one's self—if it didn't also exist in the shape of a word.

He worried that she might be arrested, but for some reason—his position probably—she was always let off with a warning. In their own house she ignored him, passing him on the stairs without a look, or crossing in front of him as though he were a stuffed chair. Often she disappeared for hours, venturing out alone into the heat of the night, and he began to suspect she had taken a lover.

The thought preyed on him, though in fact he had long since forgotten the word for *wife* and also the word for *fidelity.* One night, when she left the house, he attempted to follow her, but clearly she was suspicious because she walked very quickly, looking back over her shoulder, making a series of unnecessary turns and choosing narrow old streets whose curbs were blackened by fire. Within minutes he lost sight of her; soon after that he was driven back by the heat.

The next night he tried again, and this time he saw her disappear into an ancient, dilapidated building, the sort of enclosure, he remembered, where children had once gone to learn to read and write. Unexpectedly, he felt a flash of pity; what a sad place for a tryst. He waited briefly, then entered the building and went up a flight of smoldering stairs that seemed on the point of collapse. There he found a dim corridor, thick with smoke, and a single room at one end.

Through the door he heard a waterfall of voices. There must have been a dozen people inside, all of them talking. The talk seemed to be about poetry. Someone—a woman—was giving a lecture. There were interruptions, a discussion, some laughter. He heard his wife's voice, her old gilt-edged contralto, asking a question, and the sound of it made him draw in his breath so sharply that something hard, like a cinder or a particle of gravel, formed in his throat.

It stayed stubbornly lodged there all night. He found it painful to breath, and even Isobel noticed how he thrashed about in bed, gasping wildly for air. In the morning she called a doctor, who could find nothing wrong, but she remained uneasy, and that evening she stayed home and made him cups of iced honey-and-lemon tea to ease his throat. He took her hand at one point and held it to his lips as though it might be possible to find the air he needed inside the crevices of her skin. By now the scraping in his throat had become terrible, a raw agonizing rasp like a dull knife sawing through limestone. She looked at his face, from which the healthy, blood-filled elasticity had gone and felt herself brushed by a current of air, or what might have been the memory of a name.

He began to choke violently, and she heard something grotesque come out of his mouth, a sound that was only half-human, but that rode on a curious rhythmic wave that for some reason stirred her deeply. She imagined it to be the word *Isobel*. "Isobel?" she asked, trying to remember its meaning. He said it a second time, and this time the syllables were more clearly formed.

The light of terror came into his eyes, or perhaps the beginning of a new fever; she managed to calm him by stroking his arm. Then she called the children inside the house, locked the doors and windows against the unbearable heat, and they began, slowly, patiently, hands linked, at the beginning where they had begun before—with table, chair, bed, cool, else, other, sleep, face, mouth, breath, tongue.

Poaching

ON OUR WAY TO CATCH the Portsmouth ferry, Dobey and I stayed overnight at a country hotel in the village of Kingsclere. The floors sloped, the walls tipped, the tap leaked rusty water and the bedclothes gave out an old, bitter odor.

At breakfast we were told by the innkeeper that King John had once stayed in this hotel and, moreover, had slept in the very room where we had spent the night.

"Wasn't he the Magna Carta king?" Dobey said, showing off. "That would make it early thirteenth century."

"Incredible," I said, worrying whether I should conceal my fried bread beneath the underdone bacon or the bacon beneath the bread. "Extraordinary."

The innkeeper had more to tell us. "And when His Royal Highness stopped here, he was bit by a bedbug. Of course, there's none of that nowadays." Here he chuckled a hearty chuckle and sucked in his red cheeks.

I crushed my napkin—Dobey would call it a serviette—on top of my bacon and fried bread and egg yolk and said to myself: next he'll be rattling on about a ghost.

"And I didn't like to tell you people last night when you arrived," the innkeeper continued, "but the room where the two of you was—it's haunted."

"King John?" I asked.

"One of the guards, it's thought. My wife's seen 'im many the time. And our Barbara. And I've heard 'im clomping about in his great boots in the dark of the night and making a right awful noise."

Dobey and I went back to our room to brush our teeth and close our haversacks, and then we lay flat on our backs for a minute on the musty bed and stared at the crooked beams.

"Are you thinking kingly thoughts?" I said after a while.

"I'm thinking about those poor bloody Aussies," said Dobey.

"Oh, them," I said. "They'll make out all right."

Only the day before we'd picked up the two Australians on the road. Not that they were by any stretch your average hitchhikers—two women, a mother, middle-aged, and a grown daughter, both smartly dressed. Their rented Morris Minor had started to smoke between Farrington and Kingsclere, and we gave them a lift into the village.

They'd looked us over carefully, especially the mother, before climbing into the back seat. We try to keep the back seat clean and free of luggage for our hitchhikers. The trick is to put them at their ease so they'll talk. Some we wring dry just by keeping quiet. For others we have to prime the pump. It's like stealing, Dobey says, only no one's thought to make a law against it.

Within minutes we knew all about the Australians. They were from Melbourne. The mother had recently been widowed, and her deceased husband, before the onset of Addison's disease, had worked as an investment analyst. Something coppery about the way she said "my late husband" suggested marital dullness, but Dobey and I never venture into interpretation. The daughter taught in a junior school. She was engaged to be married, a chap in the military. The wedding was six months away, and the two of them, mother and daughter, were shoring themselves up by spending eight weeks touring Britain, a last fling before buckling down to wedding arrangements. It was to be a church ceremony, followed by a lobster lunch in the ballroom of a large hotel.

The two of them made the wedding plans sound grudging and complex and tiresome, like putting on a war. The daughter emitted a sigh; nothing ever went right. And now they'd only been in England a week, had hardly made a dent, and already the hired car had let them down. It looked serious too, maybe the clutch.

Everything the mother said seemed electrically amplified by her bright, forthcoming Australia-lacquered voice. She had an optimistic nature, quickly putting the car out of mind and chirping away from the back seat about the relations in Exeter they planned to visit, elderly aunts, crippled uncles, a nephew who'd joined a rock band and traveled to America, was signed up by a movie studio but never was paid a penny—all this we learned in the ten minutes it took us to drive them into Kingsclere and drop them at the phone box. The daughter, a pretty girl with straight blond hair tied back in a ribbon, hardly said a word.

Nor did we. Dobey and I had made a pact at the start of the trip that we would conceal ourselves, our professions, our antecedents, where we lived, what we were to each other. We would dwindle, grow deliberately thin, almost invisible, and live like aerial plants off the packed fragments and fictions of the hitchhikers we picked up.

One day we traveled for two hours—this was between Conway and Manchester—with a lisping, blue-jeaned giant from Canada who'd come to England to write a doctoral thesis on the early language theories of Wittgenstein.

"We owe tho muth to Withgenstein," he sputtered, sweeping a friendly red paw through the air and including Dobey and me in the circle of Wittgenstein appreciators. He had run out of money. First he sold his camera; then his Yamaha recorder; then, illegally, the British Rail Pass his parents had given him when he finished his master's degree. That was why he was hitchhiking. He said, "I am going to Oxthford" as though he was saying, "I am a man in love."

He talked rapidly, not at all embarrassed by his lisp—Dobey and I liked him for that, though normally we refrain from forming personal judgments about our passengers. He spoke as though compelled to explain to us his exact reason for being where he was at that moment.

They all do. It is a depressing hypothesis, but probably, as Dobey says, true: people care only about themselves. They are frenzied and driven, but only by the machinery of their own adventuring. It has been several days now since anyone's asked us who we are and what we're doing driving around like this.

Usually Dobey drives, eyes on the road, listening with a supple, restless attention. I sit in the front passenger seat, my brain screwed up in a squint from looking sideways. At times I feel that giving lifts to strangers makes us into patronizing benefactors. But Dobey says this is foolish; these strangers buy their rides with their stories.

Dobey prefers to pick up strangers who are slightly distraught, saying they "unwind" more easily. Penury or a burned-out clutch—these work in our favor and save us from having to frame our careful questions. I am partial, though, to the calm, to those who stand by the roadside with their luggage in the dust, too composed or dignified to trouble the air with their thumbs. There was the remarkable Venezuelan woman who rode with us from Cardiff to Conway and spoke only intermittently and in sentences that seemed wrapped in their own cool vapors. Yes, she adored to travel alone. She liked the song of her own thoughts. She was made fat by the sight of mountains. The Welsh sky was blue like a cushion. She was eager to embrace rides from strangers. She liked to open wide windows so she could commune with the wind. She was a doctor, a specialist in bones, but alas, alas, she was not in love with her profession. She was in love with the English language because every word could be picked up and spun like a coin on the table top.

The shyest traveler can be kindled, Dobey maintains—often after just one or two strikes of the flint. That sullen Lancashire girl with the pink-striped hair and the colloid eyes—her dad was a coward, her mum shouted all the time, her boyfriend had broken her nose and got her pregnant. She was on her way, she told us, to a hostel in Bolton. Someone there would help her out. She had the address written on the inside of a cigarette packet. I looked aslant and could tell that Dobey wanted to offer her money, but part of our bargain was that we offer only rides.

Another thing we agreed on was that we would believe everything we were told. No matter how fantastic or eccentric or crazy the stories we heard, we'd pledged ourselves to respect their surfaces. Anyone who stepped into our back seat was trusted, even the bearded, evil-smelling curmudgeon we picked up in Sheffield who told us that the spirit of Ben Jonson had directed him to go to Westminster and stand at the abbey door preaching obedience to Mrs. Thatcher. We not only humored the old boy—who gave us shaggy, hand-rolled cigarettes to smoke—but we delivered him at midnight that same day.

Nevertheless, I'm becoming disillusioned. (It was my idea to head for Portsmouth and cross the channel.) I long, for instance, to let slip to one of our passengers that Dobey and I have slept in the bedchamber where King John was nipped by a bedbug. It's not attention I want and certainly not admiration. It's only that I'd like to float my own story on the air. I want to test its buoyancy, to see if it holds any substance, to see if it's true or the opposite of true.

And I ask myself about the stories we've been hearing lately: Have they grown thinner? The Australian mother and daughter, for example—what had they offered? Relations in Exeter. A wedding in Melbourne. Is that enough? Dobey says to be patient, that everything is fragmentary, that it's up to us to supply the missing links. Behind each of the people we pick up, Dobey believes, there's a deep cave, and in the cave is a trap door and a set of stone steps that we may descend if we wish. I say to Dobey that there may be nothing at the bottom of the stairs, but Dobey says, how will we know if we don't look.

Scenes

IN 1974 FRANCES WAS ASKED to give a lecture in Edmonton, and on the way there her plane was forced to make an emergency landing in a barley field. The man sitting next to her—they had not spoken—turned and asked if he might put his arms around her. She assented. They clung together, her size 12 dress and his wool suit. Later, he gave her his business card.

She kept the card for several weeks, poked in the edge of her bedroom mirror. It is a beautiful mirror, a graceful rectangle in a pine frame, and very, very old. Once it was attached to the back of a bureau belonging to Frances's grandmother. Leaves, vines, flowers and fruit are shallowly carved in the soft wood of the frame. The carving might be described as primitive—and this is exactly why Frances loves it, being drawn to those things that are incomplete or in some way flawed. Furthermore, the mirror is the first thing she remembers seeing, *really* seeing, as a child. Visiting her grandmother, she noticed the stiff waves of light and shadow on the frame, the way square pansies interlocked with rigid grapes, and she remembers creeping out of her grandmother's bed, where she had been put for an afternoon nap, and climbing on a chair so she could touch the worked surface with the flat of her hand.

Her grandmother died. It was discovered by the aunts and uncles that on the back of the mirror was stuck a piece of adhesive tape and on the tape was written: "For my vain little granddaughter Frances." Frances' mother was affronted, but put it down to hardening of the arteries. Frances, who was only seven, felt uniquely, mysteriously honored.

She did not attend the funeral; it was thought she was too young, and so instead she was taken one evening to the funeral home to bid goodbye to her grandmother's body. The room where the old lady lay was large, quiet and hung all around with swags of velvet. Frances's father lifted her up so she could see her grandmother, who was wearing a black dress with a white crepe jabot, her powdered face pulled tight, as though with a drawstring, into a sort of grimace. A lovely blanket with satin edging covered her trunky legs and torso. Laid out, calm and silent as a boat, she looked almost generous.

For some reason Frances was left alone with the casket for a few minutes, and she took this chance—she had to pull herself up on tiptoe—to reach out and touch her grandmother's lips with the middle finger of her right hand. It was like pressing in the side of a rubber ball. The lips did not turn to dust—which did not surprise Frances at all, but rather confirmed what she had known all along. Later, she would look at her finger and say to herself, "This finger has touched dead lips." Then she would feel herself grow rich with disgust. The touch, she knew, had not been an act of love at all, but only a kind of test.

With the same middle finger she later touched the gelatinous top of a goldfish swimming in a little glass bowl at school. She touched the raised mole on the back of her father's white neck. Shuddering, she touched horse turds in the back lane, and she touched her own urine springing onto the grass as she squatted behind the snowball bush by the fence. When she looked into her grandmother's mirror, now mounted on her own bedroom wall, she could hardly believe that she, Frances, had contravened so many natural laws.

The glass itself was beveled all the way around, and she can remember that she took pleasure in lining up her round face so that the beveled edge split it precisely in two. When she was fourteen she wrote in her diary, "Life is like looking into a beveled mirror." The next day she crossed it out and, peering into the mirror, stuck out her tongue and made a face. All her life she'd had this weakness for preciosity, but mainly she'd managed to keep it in check.

She is a lithe and toothy woman with strong, thick, dark brown hair, now starting to gray. She can be charming. "Frances can charm the bees out of the hive," said a friend of hers, a man she briefly thought she loved. Next year she'll be forty-five—terrible!—but at least she's kept her figure. A western sway to her voice is what people chiefly remember about her, just as they remember other people for their chins or noses. This voice sometimes makes her appear inquisitive, but, in fact, she generally hangs back and leaves it to others to begin a conversation.

Once a woman got into an elevator with her and said, "Will you forgive me if I speak my mind? This morning I came within an inch of taking my life. There was no real reason, only everything had got suddenly so dull. But I'm all right now. In fact, I'm going straight to a restaurant to treat myself to a plate of french fries. Just fries, not even a sandwich to go with them. I was never allowed to have french fries when I was a little girl, but the time comes when a person should do what she wants to do."

The subject of childhood interests Frances, especially its prohibitions, so illogical and various, and its random doors and windows that appear solidly shut, but can, in fact, be opened easily with a touch or a password or a minute of devout resolution. It helps to be sly, also to be quick. There was a time when she worried that fate had penciled her in as "debilitated by guilt," but mostly she takes guilt for what it is, a kind of lover who can be shrugged off or greeted at the gate. She looks at her two daughters and wonders if they'll look back resentfully, recalling only easy freedoms and an absence of terror—in other words, meagerness—and envy her for her own stern beginnings. It turned out to have been money in the bank, all the various shames and sweats of growing up. It was instructive; it kept things interesting; she still shivers, remembering how exquisitely sad she was as a child.

"It's only natural for children to be sad," says her husband, Theo, who, if he has a fault, is given to reductive statements. "Children are unhappy because they are inarticulate and hence lonely."

Frances can't remember being lonely, but telling this to Theo is like blowing into a hurricane. She was spoiled—a lovely word, she thinks—and adored by her parents, her plump, white-faced father and her skinny, sweet-tempered mother. Their love was immense and enveloping like a fall of snow. In the evenings, winter evenings, she sat between the two of them on a blue nubby sofa, listening to the varnished radio and taking sips from their cups of tea from time to time or sucking on a spoonful of sugar. The three of them sat enthralled through "Henry Aldrich" and "Fibber Magee and Molly," and when Frances laughed they looked at her and laughed too. Frances has no doubt that those spoonfuls of sugar and the roar of Fibber Magee's closet and her parents' soft looks were taken in and preserved so that she, years later, boiling an egg or making love or digging in the garden, is sometimes struck by a blow of sweetness that seems to come out of nowhere.

The little brown house where she grew up sat in the middle of a block crowded with other such houses. In front of each lay a tiny lawn and a flower bed edged with stones. Rows of civic trees failed to flourish, but did not die either. True, there was terror in the back lane, where the big boys played with sticks and jackknives, but the street was occupied mainly by quiet, hard-working families, and in the summertime hop-scotch could be played in the street, there was so little traffic.

Frances's father spent his days "at the office." Her mother stayed at home, wore bib aprons, made jam and pickles and baked custard, and every morning before school brushed and braided Frances's hair. Frances can remember, or thinks she can remember, that one morning her mother walked as far as the corner with her and said, "I don't know why, but I'm so full of happiness today I can hardly bear it." The sun came fretting through the branches of a scrubby elm at that minute and splashed across her mother's face, making her look like someone in a painting or like one of the mothers in her school reader.

Learning to read was like falling into a mystery deeper than the mystery of airwaves or the halo around the head of the baby Jesus. Deliberately she made herself stumble and falter over the words in her first books, trying to hold back the rush of revelation. She saw other children being matter-of-fact and methodical, puzzling over vowels and consonants and sounding out words as though they were dimes and nickels that had to be extracted from the slot of a bank. She felt suffused with light and often skipped or hopped or ran wildly to keep herself from flying apart.

Her delirium, her failure to ingest books calmly, made her suspect there was something wrong with her or else with the world, yet she deeply distrusted the school librarian, who insisted that a book could be a person's best friend. (Those subject to preciosity instantly spot others with the same affliction.) This librarian, Miss Mayes, visited all the classes. She was tall and soldierly with a high, light voice. "Boys and girls," she cried, bringing large red hands together, "a good book will never let you down." She went on; books could take you on magic journeys; books could teach you where the rain came from or how things used to be in the olden days. A person who truly loved books need never feel alone.

But, she continued, holding up a finger, there are people who do shameful things to books. They pull them from the shelves by their spines. They turn down the corners of pages; they leave them on screened porches where the rain and other elements can warp their covers; and they use curious and inappropriate objects as bookmarks.

From a petit point bag she drew a list of objects that had been wrongly, criminally inserted between fresh clean pages: a blue-jay feather, an oak leaf, a matchbook cover, a piece of colored chalk and, on one occasion—"on one occasion, boys and girls"—a *strip of bacon.*

A strip of bacon. In Frances's mind the strip of bacon was uncooked, cold and fatty with a pathetic streaking of lean. Its oil would press into the paper, a porky abomination, and its ends would flop out obscenely. The thought was thrilling: someone, someone who lived in the same school district, had had the audacity, the imagination, to mark the pages of a book with a strip of bacon. The existence of this person and his outrageous act penetrated the fever that had come over her since she'd learned to read, and she began to look around again and see what the world had to offer.

Next door lived Mr. and Mrs. Shaw, and upstairs, fast asleep, lived Louise Shaw, aged eighteen. She had been asleep for ten years. A boy across the street named Jackie McConnell told Frances that it was the sleeping sickness, that Louise Shaw had been bitten by the sleeping sickness bug, but Frances's mother said no, it was the coma. One day Mrs. Shaw, smelling of chlorine bleach and wearing a flower-strewn housedress, stopped Frances on the sidewalk, held the back of her hand to the side of Frances's face and said, "Louise was just your age when we lost her. She was forever running or skipping rope or throwing a ball up against the side of the garage. I used to say to her, don't make such a ruckus, you'll drive me crazy. I used to yell all the time at her, she was so full of beans and such a chatterbox." After that Frances felt herself under an obligation to Mrs. Shaw, and whenever she saw her she made her body speed up and whirl on the grass or do cartwheels.

A little later she learned to negotiate the back lane. There, between board fences, garbage cans, garage doors and stands of tough weeds, she became newly nimble and strong. She learned to swear—damn, hell and dirty bastard—and played piggy-move-up and spud and got herself roughly kissed a number of times, and then something else happened: one of the neighbors put up a basketball hoop. For a year, maybe two—Frances doesn't trust her memory when it comes to time—she was obsessed with doing free throws. She became known as the queen of free throws; she acquired status, even with the big boys, able to sink ten out of ten baskets, but never, to her sorrow, twenty out of twenty. She threw free throws in the morning before school, at lunchtime, and in the evening until it got dark. Nothing made her happier than when the ball dropped silently through the ring without touching it or banking on the board. At night she dreamed of these silky baskets, the rush of air and sinuous movement of the net, then the ball striking the pavement and returning to her hands. ("Sounds a bit Freudian to me," her husband, Theo, said when she tried to describe for him her time of free-throw madness, proving once again how far apart the two of them were in some things.) One morning she was up especially early. There was no one about. The milkman hadn't yet come, and there was dew shining on the tarry joints of the pavement. Holding the ball in her hands was like holding onto a face, it was so dearly familiar with its smell of leather and its seams and laces. That morning she threw twenty-seven perfect free throws before missing. Each time the ball went through the hoop she felt an additional oval of surprise grow round her body. She had springs inside her, in her arms and in the insteps of her feet. What stopped her finally was her mother calling her name, demanding to know what she was doing outside so early. "Nothing," Frances said, and knew for the first time the incalculable reward of self-possession.

There was a girl in her sewing class named Pat Leonard. She was older than the other girls, had a rough pitted face and a brain pocked with grotesqueries. "Imagine," she said to Frances, "sliding down a banister and suddenly it turns into a razor blade." When she trimmed the seams of the skirt she was making and accidentally cut through the fabric, she laughed out loud. To amuse the other girls she sewed the skin of her fingers together. She told a joke, a long story about a pickle factory that was really about eating excrement. In her purse was a packet of cigarettes. She had a boyfriend who went to the technical school, and several times she'd reached inside his pants and squeezed his thing until it went off like a squirt gun. She'd flunked math twice. She could hardly read. One day she wasn't there, and the sewing teacher said she'd been expelled. Frances felt as though she'd lost her best friend, even though she wouldn't have been seen dead walking down the hall with Pat Leonard. Melodramatic tears swam into her eyes, and then real tears that wouldn't stop until the teacher brought her a glass of water and offered to phone her mother.

Another time, she was walking home from a friend's in the early evening. She passed by a little house not far from her own. The windows were open and, floating on the summer air, came the sound of people speaking in a foreign language. There seemed to be a great number of them, and the conversation was very rapid and excited. They might have been quarreling or telling old stories; Frances had no idea which. It could have been French or Russian or Portuguese they spoke. The words ran together and made queer little dashes and runs and choking sounds. Frances imagined immense, wide-branching grammars and steep, stone streets rising out of other centuries. She felt as though she'd been struck by a bolt of good fortune, and all because the world was bigger than she'd been led to believe.

At university, where she studied languages, she earned pocket money by working in the library. She and a girl named Ursula were entrusted with the key, and it was their job to open the library on Saturday mornings. During the minute or two before anyone else came, the two of them galloped at top speed through the reference room, the periodical room, the reading room, up and down the rows of stacks, filling that stilled air with what could only be called primal screams. Why this should have given Frances such exquisite pleasure she couldn't have said, since she was in rebellion against nothing she knew of. By the time the first students arrived, she and Ursula would be standing behind the main desk, date stamp in hand, sweet as dimity.

One Saturday, the first person who came was a bushy-headed, serious-minded zoology student named Theodore, called Theo by his friends. He gave Frances a funny look, then in a cracked, raspy voice asked her to come with him later and have a cup of coffee. A year later he asked her to marry him. He had a mind unblown by self-regard and lived, it seemed to Frances, in a nursery world of goodness and badness with not much room to move in between.

It's been mainly a happy marriage. Between the two of them, they've invented hundreds of complex ways of enslaving each other, some of them amazingly tender. Like other married people, they've learned to read each other's minds. Once Theo said to Frances as they drove around and around, utterly lost in a vast treeless suburb, "In every one of these houses there's been a declaration of love," and this was exactly the thought Frances had been thinking.

To her surprise, to everyone's surprise, she turned out to have an aptitude for monogamy. Nevertheless, many of the scenes that have come into her life have involved men. Once she was walking down a very ordinary French street on a hot day. A man, bare-chested, drinking Perrier at a café table, sang out, "*Bonjour.*" Not "*Bonjour, madame*" or "*Bonjour, mademoiselle,*" just "*Bonjour.*" Cheeky. She was wearing white pants, a red blouse, a straw hat and sunglasses. "*Bonjour,*" she sang back and gave a sassy little kick, which became the start of a kind of dance. The man at the table clapped his hands over his head to keep time as she went dancing by.

Once she went to the British Museum to finish a piece of research. There was a bomb alert just as she entered, and everyone's shopping bags and briefcases were confiscated and searched. It happened that Frances had just bought a teddy bear for the child of a friend she was going to visit later in the day. The guard took it, shook it till its eyes rolled, and then carried it away to be X-rayed. Later he brought it to Frances, who was sitting at a table examining a beautiful old manuscript. As he handed her the bear, he kissed the air above its fuzzy head, and Frances felt her mouth go into the shape of a kiss too, a kiss she intended to be an expression of her innocence, only that. He winked. She winked back. He leaned over and whispered into her ear a suggestion that was hideously, comically, obscene. She pretended not to hear, and a few minutes later she left, hurrying down the street full of cheerful shame, her work unfinished.

These are just some of the scenes in Frances's life. She thinks of them as scenes because they're much too fragmentary to be stories and far too immediate to be memories. They seem to bloom out of nothing, out of the thin, uncolored air of defeats and pleasures. A curtain opens, a light appears, there are voices or music or sometimes a wide transparent stream of silence. Only rarely do they point to anything but themselves. They're difficult to talk about. They're useless, attached to nothing, can't be traded in or shaped into instruments to prise open the meaning of the universe.

There are people who think such scenes are ornaments suspended from lives that are otherwise busy and useful. Frances knows perfectly well that they are what a life is made of, one fitting against the next like English paving-stones.

Or sometimes she thinks of them as little keys on a chain, keys that open nothing, but simply exist for the beauty of their toothed edges and the way they chime in her pocket.

Other times she is reminded of the Easter eggs her mother used to bring out every year. These were real hens' eggs with a hole poked in the top and bottom and the contents blown out. The day before Easter, Frances and her mother always sat down at the kitchen table with paint brushes, a glass of water and a box of watercolors. They would decorate half a dozen eggs, maybe more, but only the best were saved from year to year. These were taken from a cupboard just before Easter, removed from their shoebox and carefully arranged, always on the same little pewter cake stand. The eggs had to be handled gently, especially the older ones.

Frances, when she was young, liked to pick up each one in turn and examine it minutely. She had a way of concentrating her thoughts and shutting everything else out, thinking only of this one little thing, this little egg that was round like the world, beautiful in color and satin to the touch, and that fit into the hollow of her hand as though it were made for that very purpose.

Fragility

WE ARE FLYING OVER THE ROCKIES on our way to Vancouver, and there sits Ivy with her paperback. I ask myself: Should I interrupt and draw her attention to the grandeur beneath us?

In a purely selfish sense, watching Ivy read is as interesting as peering down at those snowy mountains. She turns the pages of a book in the same way she handles every object, with a peculiar respectful gentleness, as though the air around it were more tender than ordinary air. I've watched her lift a cup of tea with this same abstracted grace, cradling a thick mug in a way that transforms it into something precious and fragile. It's a gift some people have.

I decide not to disturb her; utterly absorbed in what she's reading, she's seen the Rockies before.

In the seat ahead of us is a young man wearing a bright blue jacket—I remember that once I had a similar jacket in a similar hue. Unlike us, he's clearly flying over the Rockies for the first time. He's in a half-standing position at the window, snapping away with his camera, pausing only to change the film. From where I'm sitting I can see his intense, eager trigger hand, his steadying elbow, his dropped lower lip. In a week he'll be passing his slides around the office, holding them delicately at their edges up to the light. He might set up a projector and screen them one evening in his living room; he might invite a few friends over, and his wife—who will resemble the Ivy of fifteen years ago—will serve coffee and wedges of cheese cake; these are the Rockies, he'll say—magnificent, stirring, one of the wonders of the continent.

I tell myself that I would give a great deal to be in that young man's shoes, but this is only a half-truth, the kind of lie Ivy and I sometimes spin for our own amusement. We really don't want to go back in time. What we envy in the young is that fine nervous edge of perception, the ability to take in reality afresh. I suppose, as we grow older, that's what we forfeit, acquiring in its place a measure of healthy resignation.

Ivy puts down her book suddenly and reaches for my hand. A cool, light, lazy touch. She's smiling.

"Good book?"

"Hmmm," she says, and stretches.

Now, as a kind of duty, I point out the Rockies.

"Beautiful," she exclaims, leaning toward the window.

And it *is* beautiful. But unfortunately the plane is flying at a height that extracts all sense of dimension from the view. Instead of snow-capped splendor, we see a kind of Jackson Pollock dribbling of white on green. It's a vast abstract design, a linking of incised patterns, quite interesting in its way, but without any real suggestion of height or majesty.

"It looks a little like a Jackson Pollock," Ivy says in that rhythmic voice of hers.

"Did you really say that?"

"I think so." Her eyebrows go up, her mouth crimps at the edges. "At least, if I didn't, someone did."

I lift her hand—I can't help myself—and kiss her fingertips.

"And what's that for?" she asks, still smiling.

"An attack of poignancy."

"A serious new dietary disease, I suppose," Ivy says, and at that moment the steward arrives with our lunch trays.

Ivy and I have been to Vancouver fairly often on business trips or for holidays. This time it's different; in three months we'll be moving permanently to Vancouver, and now the two of us are engaged in that common-enough errand, a house-hunting expedition.

Common, I say, but not for us.

We know the statistics: that about half of all North Americans move every five years, that we're a rootless, restless, portable society. But for some reason, some failing on our part or perhaps simple good fortune, Ivy and I seem to have evaded the statistical pattern. The small stone-fronted, bow-windowed house we bought when Christopher was born is the house in which we continue to live after twenty years.

If there had been another baby, we would have considered a move, but we stayed in the same house in the middle of Toronto. It was close to both our offices and close too to the clinic Christopher needed. Curiously enough, most of our neighbors also stayed there year after year. In our neighborhood we know everyone. When the news of my transfer came, the first thing Ivy said was, "What about the Mattisons and the Levensons? What about Robin and Sara?"

"We can't very well take everyone on the street along with us."

"Oh Lordy," Ivy said, and bit her lip. "Of course not. It's only—"

"I know," I said.

"Maybe we can talk Robin and Sara into taking their holidays on the coast next year. Sara always said—"

"And we'll be back fairly often. At least twice a year."

"If only—"

"If only what?"

"Those stupid bulbs." (I love the way Ivy pronounces the word *stupid*: *stewpid*, giving it a patrician lift.)

"Bulbs?"

"Remember last fall, all those bulbs I put in?"

"Oh," I said, remembering.

She looked at me squarely: "You don't mind as much as I do, do you?"

"Of course I do. You know I do."

"Tell me the truth."

What could I say? I've always been impressed by the accuracy of Ivy's observations. "The truth is—"

"The truth is—?" she helped me along.

"I guess I'm ready."

"Ready for what?" Her eyes filled with tears. This was a difficult time for us. Christopher had died in January. He was a tough kid and lived a good five years longer than any of us ever thought he would. His death was not unexpected, but still, Ivy and I were feeling exceptionally fragile.

"Ready for what?" she asked again.

"For something," I admitted. "For anything, I guess."

The first house we look at seems perfect. The settled neighborhood is dense with trees and shrubbery and reminds us both of our part of Toronto. There are small repairs that need doing but nothing major. Best of all, from the dining room there can be seen a startling lop of blue water meeting blue sky.

I point this out to Ivy; a view was one of the things we had put on our list. There is also a fireplace, another must, and a capacious kitchen with greenhouse windows overlooking a garden.

"And look at the bulbs," I point out. "Tulips halfway up. Daffodils."

"Lilies," Ivy says.

"I think we've struck it lucky," I tell the real-estate woman who's showing us around, a Mrs. Marjorie Little. ("Call me Marge," she'd said to us with west-coast breeziness.)

Afterward, in the car, Ivy is so quiet I have to prompt her. "Well?"

Marge Little, sitting at the wheel, peers at me, then at Ivy.

"It's just," Ivy begins, "it's just so depressing."

Depressing? I can't believe she's saying this. A view, central location, a fireplace. Plus bulbs.

"Well," Ivy says slowly, "it's a divorce house. You must have noticed?"

I hadn't. "A divorce house? How do you know?"

"I looked in the closets. Her clothes were there but *his* weren't."

"Oh."

"And half the pictures had been taken off the wall. Surely you noticed that."

I shake my head.

"I know it sounds silly, but wouldn't you rather move into a house with some good"—she pauses—"some good vibrations?"

"Vibrations?"

"Did you notice the broken light in the bathroom? I'll bet someone threw something at it. In a rage."

"We could always fix the light. And the other things. And with our own furniture—"

Ivy is an accountant. Once I heard a young man in her firm describe her as a *crack* accountant. For a number of years now she's been a senior partner. When this same young man heard she was leaving because of my transfer, he couldn't help ragging her a little, saying he thought women didn't move around at the whim of their husbands anymore, and that, out of principle, she ought to refuse to go to Vancouver or else arrange some kind of compromise life—separate apartments, for instance, with weekend rendezvous in Winnipeg.

Ivy had howled at this. She's a positive, good-natured woman and, as it turned out, she had no trouble finding an opening in a good Vancouver firm at senior level. As I say, she's positive. Which is why her apprehension over good or bad vibrations is puzzling. Can it be she sees bad times ahead for the two of us? Or is it only that she wants solid footing after these long years with Christopher? Neither of us is quite glued back together again. Not that we ever will be.

"I can't help it," Ivy is saying. "It just doesn't feel like a lucky house. There's something about—"

Marge Little interrupts with a broad smile. "I've got all kinds of interesting houses to show you. Maybe you'll like the next one better."

"Does it have good vibes?" Ivy asks, laughing a little to show she's only half-serious.

"I don't know," Marge Little says. "They don't put that kind of info on the fact sheet."

The next house is perched on the side of the canyon. No, that's not quite true. It is, in fact, falling into the canyon. I notice, but don't mention, the fact that the outside foundation walls are cracked and patched. Inside, the house is alarmingly empty; the cool settled air seems proof that it's been vacant for some time.

Marge consults her fact sheet. Yes, the house has been on the market about six months. The price has been reduced twice. But—she glances at us—perhaps we noticed the foundation . . .

"Yes," I say. "Hopeless."

"Damn," Ivy says.

We look at two more houses; both have spectacular views and architectural distinction. But one is a bankruptcy sale and the other is a divorce house. By now I'm starting to pick up the scent: it's a compound of petty carelessness and strenuous neglect, as though the owners had decamped in a hurry, angry at the rooms themselves.

To cheer ourselves up, the three of us have lunch in a sunny Broadway restaurant. It seems extraordinary that we can sit here and see mountains that are miles away; the thought that we will soon be able to live within sight of these mountains fills us with optimism. We order a little wine and linger in the sunlight. Vancouver is going to be an adventure. We're going to be happy here. Marge Little, feeling expansive, tells us about her three children and about the problem she has keeping her weight down. "Marge Large they'll be calling me soon," she says. It's an old joke, we sense, and the telling of it makes us feel we're old friends. She got into the business, she says, because she loves houses. And she has an instinct for matching houses with people. "So don't be discouraged," she tells us. "We'll find the perfect place this afternoon."

We drive through narrow city streets to a house where a famous movie idol grew up. His mother still lives in the house, a spry, slightly senile lady in her eighties. The tiny house—we quickly see it is far too small for us—is crowded with photographs of the famous son. He beams at us from the hallway, from the dining room, from the bedroom bureau.

"Oh, he's a good boy. Comes home every two or three years," his mother tells us, her large teeth shining in a diminished face. "And once I went down there, all the way down to Hollywood, on an airplane. He paid my way, sent me a ticket. I saw his swimming pool. They all have swimming pools. He has a cook, a man who does all the meals, so I didn't have to lift a finger for a whole week. What an experience, like a queen. I have some pictures someplace I could show you—"

"That would be wonderful," Marge Little says, "but"—she glances at her watch—"I'm afraid we have another appointment."

"—I saw those pictures just the other day. Now where—? I think they're in this drawer somewhere. Here, I knew it. Take a look at this. Isn't that something? That's his swimming pool. Kidney-shaped. He's got another one now, even bigger."

"Beautiful," Ivy says.

"And here he is when he was little. See this? He'd be about nine there. We took a trip east. That's him and his dad standing by Niagara Falls. Here's another—"

"We really have to—"

"A good boy. I'll say that for him. Didn't give any trouble. Sometimes I see his movies on the TV and I can't believe the things he does, with women and so on. I have to pinch myself and say it's only pretend—"

"I think—"

"I'm going into this senior-citizen place. They've got a nice TV lounge, big screen, bigger than this little bitty one, color too. I always—"

"Sad," Ivy says, when we escape at last and get into the car.

"The house or the mother?" I ask her.

"Both."

"At least it's not a D.H." (This has become our shorthand expression for divorce house.)

"Wait'll you see the next place," Marge Little says, swinging into traffic. "The next place is fabulous."

Fabulous, yes. But far too big. After that, in a fit of desperation, we look at a condo. "I'm not quite ready for this," I have to admit.

"No garden," Ivy says in a numb voice. She looks weary, and we decide to call it a day.

The ad in the newspaper reads: WELL-LOVED FAMILY HOME. And Ivy and Marge Little and I are there, knocking on the door, at nine-thirty in the morning.

"Come in, come in," calls a young woman in faded jeans. She has a young child on one hip and another—they must be twins—by the hand. Sunlight pours in the front window and there is freshly baked bread cooling on the kitchen counter.

But the house is a disaster, a rabbit warren of narrow hallways and dark corners. The kitchen window is only feet away from a low brick building where bodywork is being done on imported sports cars. The stairs are uneven. The bedroom floors slope, and the paint is peeling off the bathroom ceiling.

"It just kills us to leave this place," the young woman says. She's following us through the rooms, pointing with unmistakable sorrow at the wall where they were planning to put up shelving, at the hardwood floors they were thinking of sanding. Out of the blue, they got news of a transfer.

Ironically, they're going to Toronto, and in a week's time they'll be there doing what we're doing, looking for a house they can love. "But we just know we'll never find a place like this," she tells us with a sad shake of her head. "Not in a million zillion years."

After that we lose track of the number of houses. The day bends and blurs; square footage, zoning regulations, mortgage schedules, double-car garages, cedar siding only two years old—was that the place near that little park? No, that was the one on that little crescent off Arbutus. Remember? The one without the basement.

Darkness is falling as Marge Little drives us back to our hotel. We are passing hundreds—it seems like thousands—of houses, and we see lamps being turned on, curtains being closed. Friendly smoke rises from substantial chimneys. Here and there, where the curtains are left open, we can see people sitting down to dinner. Passing one house, I see a woman in a window, leaning over with a match in her hand, lighting a pair of candles. Ivy sees it too, and I'm sure she's feeling as I am, a little resentful that everyone but us seems to have a roof overhead.

"Tomorrow for sure," Marge calls cheerily. (Tomorrow is our last day. Both of us have to be home on Monday.)

"I suppose we could always rent for a year." Ivy says this with low enthusiasm.

"Or," I say, "we could make another trip in a month or so. Maybe there'll be more on the market."

"Isn't it funny? The first house we saw, remember? In a way, it was the most promising place we've seen."

"The one with the view from the dining room? With the broken light in the bathroom?"

"It might not look bad with a new fixture. Or even a sky-light."

"Wasn't that a divorce house?" I ask Ivy.

"Yes," she shrugs, "but maybe that's just what we'll have to settle for."

"It *was* listed at a good price."

"I live in a divorce house," Marge Little says, pulling in front of our hotel. "It's been a divorce house for a whole year now."

"Oh, Marge," Ivy says. "I didn't mean—" she stops. "Forgive me."

"And it's not so bad. Sometimes it's darned cheerful."

"I just—" Ivy takes a breath. "I just wanted a lucky house. Maybe there's no such thing—"

"Are you interested in taking another look at the first house? I might be able to get you an appointment this

— 121 —

evening. That is, if you think you can stand one more appointment today."

"Absolutely," we say together.

This time we inspect the house inch by inch. Ivy makes a list of the necessary repairs, and I measure the window for curtains. We hadn't realized that there was a cedar closet off one of the bedrooms. The lights of the city are glowing through the dining-room window. A spotlight at the back of the house picks out the flowers just coming into bloom. There'll be room for our hi-fi across from the fireplace. The basement is dry and very clean. The wallpaper in the downstairs den is fairly attractive and in good condition. The stairway is well proportioned and the banister is a beauty. (I'm a sucker for banisters.) There's an alcove where the pine buffet will fit nicely. Trees on both sides of the house should give us greenery and privacy. The lawn, as far as we can tell, seems to be in good shape. There's a lazy Susan in the kitchen, also a built-in dishwasher, a later model than ours. Plenty of room for a small table and a couple of chairs. The woodwork in the living room has been left natural, a wonder since so many people, a few years back, were painting over their oak trim.

Ivy says something that makes us laugh. "Over here," she says, "over here is where we'll put the Christmas tree." She touches the edge of one of the casement windows, brushes it with the side of her hand and says, "It's hard to believe that people could live in such a beautiful house and be unhappy."

For a moment there's silence, and then Marge says, "We could put in an offer tonight. I don't think it's too late. What do you think?"

———

And now, suddenly, it's the next evening, and Ivy and I are flying back to Toronto. Here we are over the Rockies again, crossing them this time in darkness. Ivy sits with her head back, eyes closed, her shoulders so sharply her own; she's not quite asleep, but not quite awake either.

Our plane seems a fragile vessel, a piece of jewelry up here between the stars and the mountains. Flying through dark air like this makes me think that life itself is fragile. The miniature accidents of chromosomes can spread unstoppable circles of grief. A dozen words carelessly uttered can dismantle a marriage. A few gulps of oxygen are all that stand between us and death.

I wonder if Ivy is thinking, as I am, of the three months ahead, of how tumultuous they'll be. There are many things to think of when you move. For one, we'll have to put our own house up for sale. The thought startles me, though I've no idea why.

I try to imagine prospective buyers arriving for appointments, stepping through our front door with polite murmurs and a sharp eye for imperfections.

They'll work their way through the downstairs, the kitchen (renewed only four years ago), the living room (yes, a real fireplace, a good draft), the dining room (small, but you can seat ten in a pinch). Then they'll make their way upstairs (carpet a little worn, but with lots of wear left). The main bedroom is fair size (with good reading lamps built in, also bookshelves).

And then there's Christopher's bedroom.

Will the vibrations announce that here lived a child with little muscular control, almost no sight or hearing and no real consciousness as that word is normally perceived? He had, though—and perhaps the vibrations will acknowledge the fact—his own kind of valor and perhaps his own way of seeing the world. At least Ivy and I always rewallpapered his room every three years or so out of a conviction that he took some pleasure in the sight of ducks swimming on a yellow sea. Later, it was sailboats; then tigers and monkeys dodging jungle growth; then a wild op-art checkerboard; and then, the final incarnation, a marvelous green cave of leafiness with amazing flowers and impossible birds sitting in branches.

I can't help wondering if these prospective buyers, these people looking for God only knows what, if they'll enter this room and feel something of his fragile presence alive in a fragile world.

Well, we shall see. We shall soon see.

The Metaphor Is Dead—Pass It On

"THE METAPHOR IS DEAD," bellowed the gargantuan professor, his walrus mustache dancing and his thundery eyebrows knitting together rapaciously. "Those accustomed to lunching at the high table of literature will now be able to nosh at the trough on a streamlined sub minus the pickle. Banished is that imperial albatross, that dragooned double agent, that muddy mirror lit by the false flashing signal *like* and by that even more presumptuous little sugar lump *as*. The gates are open, and the prisoner, freed of his shackles, has departed without so much as a goodbye wave to those who would take a simple pomegranate and insist it be the universe.

"Furthermore," trumpeted the cagey professor, warming to his thesis and drumming on the lectern, "the dogged metaphor, that scurfy escort vehicle of crystalline simplicity, has been royally indicted as the true enemy of meaning, a virus introduced into a healthy bloodstream and maintained by the lordly shrewdness of convention. Oh, it was born innocently enough with Homer and his wine-dark sea (a timid offering, perhaps, but one that dropped a velvet curtain between what *was* and what *almost* was). Then came Beowulf, stirring the pot with his cunning kennings, and before you could count to sixteen, the insidious creature had wiggled through the window and taken over the house. Soon it became a private addiction, a pipe full of opium taken behind a screen—but the wavelet graduated to turbulent ocean, and the sinews of metaphor became, finally, the button and braces that held up the pants of poesy. The commonest object was yoked by adulterous communion with unlike object (bread and wine, as it were, touching the salty lips of unreason like a capricious child who insists on placing a token toe in every puddle).

"Initially a toy of the literati," the fiery professor cried, "the metaphor grew like a polyp on the clean chamber of poetry whose friendly narrative lines had previously lain as simply as knives and forks in a kitchen drawer and whose slender, unjointed nouns, colloquial as onions, became puffed up like affected dowagers, swaying, pelvis forward, into a Victorian parlor of cluttered predicates, where they took to sitting about on the embroidered cushions of metonymy and resting their metered feet on quirky mean-spirited oxymorons.

"Once established they acquired an air of entitlement, the swag and flounce and glitter of the image boxed within another image, one bleating clause mounting another, sometimes marinated in irony, other times drenched in the teacup of whimsy. Grown fat with simile and the lace of self-indulgence, the embryo sentence sprouted useless tentacles and became an incomprehensible polyhedron, a glassine envelope enclosing multiple darting allusions that gave off the perfume of apples slowly rotting in a hermit's cryptic cellar. There followed signs of severe hypochondria as these verbal clotheshorses stood contemplating one another and noting the inspired imbroglio lodged beneath each painted fingernail. The bell had clearly sounded. It was time to retreat.

"And now," the professor essayed, stabbing the listening air, "like light glancing off a bowling ball, the peeled, scrubbed and eviscerated simplicity of language is reborn. Out onto the rubbish heap goes the fisherman's net of foxy allusions. A lifeboat has been assigned to every passenger—and just in time too—and we are once again afloat on the simple raft of the declarative sentence (that lapsed Catholic of the accessible forms) and sent, shriven and humble, into orbit, unencumbered by the debris of dusty satellites, no longer pretending every object is *like* another; instead every object *is* (*is,* that frosty little pellet of assertion that sleeps in the folds of the newly minted, nip-wasted sentence, simple as a slug bolt and, like a single hand clapping, requiring neither nursemaid to lean upon nor the succor of moth-eaten mythology to prop it up). With watercolor purity, with soldierly persistence and workmanlike lack of pretence, the newly pruned utterance appears to roll onto the snowy page with not a single troubling cul-de-sac or detour into the inky besmudged midnight of imagery.

"But, alas," the ashen professor hollowly concluded, "these newly resurrected texts, for all their lean muscularity (the cleanly gnawed bones of *noun,* the powerful hamstrings of *verb*) carry still the faulty chromosome, the trace element, of metaphor—since language itself is but a metaphoric expression of human experience. It is the punishing silence around the word that must now be claimed for literature, the pure uncobbled stillness of the caesura whose unknowingness throws arrows of meaning (palpable as summer fruit approaching ripeness) at the hem of that stitched under-skirt of affirmation/negation, and plants a stout flag once and forever in the unweeded, unchoreographed vacant lot of being.

"And now, gentle people, the chair will field questions."

A Wood

(with Anne Giardini)

THE OTHER EVENING ROSS AND STANLEY arrived at the rehearsal hall in time to see Elke go through her violin concert to be performed at the end of the month. It has taken all these years for recognition to come, though she began composing when she was sixteen. How serene she looked in the middle of the bare stage. But she was wearing that damned peasant skirt; Ross had begged her not to dress like that. It made her look like a twelve-tone type. It made her look less than serious.

"Isn't she magnificent!" Stanley said, breathless. "The coloring! The expression! Like little gold threads pouring out."

"She'll never be ready," Ross said. "She should have been working all summer."

"You're hard on her. Don't be hard on her. She's human. She needed to get away."

"We're all hard on each other, all the Woods are hard on each other. Papa used to say, 'A Wood will only settle for standards of excellence. A Wood asks more of himself than he asks of others.'"

Stanley hadn't thought of poor Papa for some months, and now he joined in. "'A Wood knows that work is the least despised of human activities.'"

"Shhhh," Ross said. "She's starting her *Chanson des Fleurs.*"

"'A Wood values accomplishment above all,'" said Stanley, who, now that he had started, couldn't stop.

"Shhhh."

The first searching notes of the song were spirited from the instrument. Elke heard each note as a reproach. She hadn't yet seen her two brothers in the back row; the lights at the top of the stage were on, blinding her. The song was coarse and coppery, not as it sounded when she wrote it. Why did she write it? How could she expect substance to come out of nothing?

The violin dug uncompromisingly into the soft flesh of her neck and chin. Today the bow seemed malicious and sharp. These benign forms—she had let them take her over and become something else. The song, mercifully, ended, and so did her dark thoughts.

"Bravo! Encore!" Stanley's voice rang out. Was he here then? If only they'd shut off the lights. Why would they need them on so long before the actual concert? Today wasn't even a real rehearsal. How has Stanley tracked her down? If only it could be hoped that he hadn't brought Ross.

"Stanley?" Her wavery voice. It was a good thing she hadn't been trained as an actress. "Was that you, love?"

At the restaurant Elke was drinking red wine instead of white because Ross said it was more calming for her; she could scarcely afford to have one of her spells with the concert so near at hand. And only one glass, said Ross, then she must go home and get a good night's sleep.

Stanley watched her closely, thinking how regal she was. The long Wood nose. The Wood eyes. An almost-Wood chin, but less resolute than his or Ross's, which was perhaps a good thing.

"Well, of course I'm glad you came," she was saying to Stanley. "But who told you where the rehearsal hall was? Ross, I suppose."

"When you played the *Danse du Feu*, I had tears in my eyes," Stanley said. "Even now, two hours later, just thinking about it brings tears."

Ross said, "But you always cry at concerts."

"And at art galleries," said Elke. "I remember taking you to the Picasso retrospective at the Art Gallery when you were fifteen, and you got weepy and had to go to the men's room."

"Papa cried when he heard Callas," Ross said. "You could hear him sniffling all over the balcony."

Elke turned to Stanley and touched the top of his wrist. "Promise me you won't cry at the concert. I don't know what I'd do if I heard someone blowing into a handkerchief from the third row. I'd lose my place. I'd lose my sense of balance."

"I can't promise," Stanley said, his eyes filling with tears.

Elke found it hard to breathe. She was overwhelmed the way she had been with Papa before the accident. There was Ross, so brusque and demanding. And Stanley, too sweet, too sweet. The two were inseparable and, it seemed lately, inescapable. She would have to invent strategies to keep them out.

"Do you believe," she asked them, "do you believe that there is hidden meaning in what we dream?"

"Oh, yes," said Stanley at once.

Ross poured himself another glass of his chilled, ivory-colored wine.

"Well," Elke began, "I'll tell you my dream then, and you must interpret it for me." The only question in her mind was which dream to describe. She chose the one they might be most likely to understand.

"Papa gave me, in this dream, a set of heavy, leather-bound books. They were encyclopedias, very old and very valuable. They filled the long shelf above my desk. One day, as I sat looking through volume R to S, I noticed that the binding, under the leather, was made of old sheet music. I was certain that this was one of Schiffmann's lost symphonies, although I don't know why I was so sure of this. So, of course, I ripped apart every book and peeled away the pages of the symphony. And just as I became aware that I was mistaken, that the music was only a series of piano exercises, I also became aware that you and Papa had come into the room and were looking at me with expressions of enormous reproach."

"She made it up," Ross said later, when he and Stanley had turned out the light and were about to go to sleep. "She made up the whole dream."

From the other side of the room Stanley's voice was muffled. He liked to pull the blanket up so that it reached his lips. "How do you know it wasn't a real dream?"

"Woods don't dream, at least not dreams as vivid or as detailed as that. Besides, I talked to her psychiatrist after the last episode, and he told me she made up dreams all the time."

"I have dreams," said Stanley.

"She makes up dreams in order to reinforce her image of herself as a victim. In her made-up dreams there is always someone shouting at her or scolding her or pointing out her faults. In one of the dreams Papa was telling her she'd ruined her career because she'd cut her hair. It took all the creative force out of her."

"Like Sampson," Stanley said.

"There was another dream, more extreme, when Papa was accusing her of causing his accident. She invited him to supper, and then she phoned and told him not to come after all; she was too tired even to make him an omelet. That was how he happened to be wandering down Sherbrooke on his way to the delicatessen when the motorbike knocked him down. Of course, it was all invented. She prefers to think she's the guilty cause of disaster. You might say she's greedy for guilt. But she didn't fool the psychiatrist at all. Real dreams have a different texture, and he's convinced Elke never really dreamed these dreams."

"I have dreams," Stanley said.

Elke started awake so suddenly her left leg cramped beneath her. Gently she kneaded at the hard knot in her calf. The window was open, and the moon floated full and fat as though for her inspection. Last summer she'd been sent to study in Paris, and in the bank where she'd gone to change her grant checks there had been a sign: DEMANDEZ-VOUS DE LA LUNE. Of course she never did. Instead, she'd spent the tissuey franc notes and the long August afternoons in the café nearest her hotel.

She was seized, as always, in the middle of the night by regrets. She'd been so close to something original; it had flickered at the edge of her vision, in one of the darker corners of the café.

She must try to sleep. She would have to focus her energy and try to concentrate, if only for their sake. At least they found her worth their trouble. That was something.

"Too much, too much." She whispered these words out loud.

Then she slept, and her head again filled with dreams.

Despite being a Wood, Stanley had at least one vivid little dream every night. In the morning, as soon as he woke, he wrote a summary in a spiral-bound notebook. Sometimes he dreamed of food, chiefly artichokes, which he loved immoderately; sometimes he dreamed of music; and very frequently he dreamed of wandering down corridors with labyrinthine rooms going off to the left and right. He never dreamed about Papa. In fact, he seldom thought about him for weeks at a time, and he was naturally a little ashamed of this.

But he excused himself; he was busy. He woke early every day, drank a glass of hot tea and was in his workroom by eight-thirty. He had a great many orders—everyone seemed suddenly to want a handmade guitar. A student from a technical school helped him in the afternoons. They talked as they worked, which Stanley found charming. At 4:45, he locked the door and walked the mile and a half to the concert hall in order to catch the end of Elke's rehearsal. Usually, Ross was there when he arrived, sitting with a copy of the score on his lap and holding a little penlight so he could see in the dark.

One day after the rehearsal, a week before the performance, Stanley slipped Elke a note. "Dear Elke," it read. "The night before Papa's accident I forgot to remind him to take his heart pill. You remember how forgetful he was. I am certain that he had a heart attack on the way to the delicatessen and collapsed just as the motorbike came around the corner. Love, Stanley."

Elke was too tired to read yet another of Stanley's little notes. She accepted it with a small smile, then slipped it between the sheets of music on her stand. She never saw it again and assumed that it had fallen during the night and been swept up and thrown away—which was what she would have done with it herself.

In any case, the note wouldn't have comforted her. She worried less about the actual cause of Papa's death than everyone thought. It was what he'd meant to her that she fretted about, and his expectations. Her psychiatrist had assured her that the death would release her, but she knew she was going through with the concert for Papa's sake. For Papa, everything must be flawless.

Stanley told her her playing was perfect. It was impossible for her to improve. "Don't change a thing," he begged.

Ross told her he would select her clothes for the concert. He had examined her wardrobe. Only the red blouse would, perhaps, do. She needed a skirt, shoes, a scarf—everything. She was not to worry about it. He would look for the clothes and would buy her what she needed.

Elke found herself thanking him.

Ross was happy. Stanley had not seen him so happy since before Papa died. He smiled; he pranced; he showed Stanley the new clothes that he'd spread out on his bed. (Once this had been Papa's bed.)

There was a long black skirt made of some silky material, a pair of black shoes that consisted of thin little straps, and a printed scarf with red fleurs-de-lis on a black background.

That night, however, Stanley dreamed that the scarf became wound around Elke's neck during the performance and strangled her. He said to Ross in the morning, "I like everything but the scarf. Elke should wear the gold necklace instead of a scarf."

"It's too heavy for Elke," Ross said.

"It might bring her luck," said Stanley.

Many generations of Woods had worn the gold necklace. Three Woods had been married in it. A Wood had worn it to a funeral mass for Czar Nicholas. A Wood had shaken the hand of the great Schiffmann while wearing it. A Wood had hidden it behind a plaster wall in the city of Berlin. Another Wood had carried it out of Spain in 1936 sewn into the hem of a blanket.

"Gold can be vulgar," said Ross. "A scarf has more *esprit*."

"Papa would have insisted she wear the necklace," said Stanley. He was tired. He'd worked later than usual.

"All right," Ross said. "Tomorrow I'll go to the bank and get it out of the vault. But don't tell Elke. I want to surprise her."

On the day of the concert, Elke woke refreshed and alert after what seemed to her to have been a dream-free night. She lay for a few minutes in her bed and tried to remember when she'd last felt so almost happy. Her bedroom was filled with sunny shades of yellow and red—colors she'd chosen herself. The room was quiet. She could lie here as long as she wanted, and no one would come to tell her to get up.

She was at the hall by noon, before the technicians, before her brothers, before the audience and critics. Today the stage felt friendly; it welcomed the sound of her steps and her soft humming of the music she would play tonight. There was no terror in this.

"How do you feel?" Ross's voice sounded sharply at her feet. He was standing, suddenly, at the stairs leading from the front row to the stage. "Did you sleep well?"

"Woods always sleep well." Her rare teasing voice.

"But *did* you?" He paused, then walked up the stairs to where she was standing. His arms stretched toward her in a curious, beseeching gesture. "I've brought you the necklace. I got it from the bank yesterday, just before it closed for the weekend. I was so worried, I hid it underneath my pillow all night."

"Are you sure—?" Elke asked.

"Papa would have wanted you to wear it."

"Then I must, of course."

"Hurry," Ross said to Stanley. "We want to be there at least twenty minutes before the program begins."

"I should polish my shoes one more time," said Stanley. The two brothers stood by the door, dressed alike in their black suits and dark ties, the coarse Wood hair brushed back from their foreheads.

"Your shoes are fine as they are," Ross said, but he did not want to start a quarrel. He had quarreled with Papa the night he died, a circuitous quarrel about bonds and about the little Monet drawing—what should be done with it. It was just after the quarrel, in fact, that Papa had rushed out into the street and fallen in the path of the motorcyclist.

"I'll only be a minute," Stanley said. He found a soft cloth and rubbed at the toes of his black shoes. Then he pulled at his shirt cuffs and examined them. Elke must be proud of them tonight.

The air outside was spicy and cold, and the chilly white light of the moon coated the pavement and the tops of parked cars. Ross and Stanley fell into step, left-right, left-right. They were silent, guarding their thoughts and guarding at the same time, it seemed, Elke's good luck. Stanley wondered if she were anxious, if the little nerves were jumping under the skin of her playing arm, if she were finding it painful to breathe, if her vision were blurred or her thoughts scattered.

Walking along dark streets always made Stanley think of how piteously men and women struggle to make themselves known to one another, how lonely they can be.

At least he wasn't alone. He would never be alone. Thinking this, he stumbled slightly with happiness and bumped up against Ross. The two of them bounced lightly off each other as two eggs will do when boiled in a little pan.

Elke had persuaded Ross and Stanley to let her eat supper alone. She had eaten two peeled peaches and a bowl of corn flakes, and had drunk a small glass of Scotch. Now she was wandering the corridor beneath the stage.

There seemed an endless number of rooms: dressing rooms like her own, larger rooms filled with props and costumes, one tiny room with row after row of wigs, several rooms of mops and rags and buckets, then a little library whose shelves were weighted down with scripts and scores, next a delightful room full of instruments in need of repair, and still another room full of instruments beyond repair. This labyrinth of rooms had the surprising and inevitable logic of a dream.

She glanced at the watch given to her by Papa for her last birthday; the slim gold pointers had moved alarmingly fast. She had only a few minutes to get dressed. Before turning back to her room, where Ross's clothes lay spread out on a divan waiting for her, Elke opened one last door.

Costumes, costumes. These must be the costumes for the Saturday matinee performances of fairy tales given to bus-loads of children; Rapunzel's gown, Goldilocks's frilled pinafore, Sleeping Beauty's nightdress, Cinderella's slippers, Red Riding Hood's cape. The costumes were made to last for years of performances, and were lovely enough to enchant the most disenchanted of children. Rapunzel's gold-green gown, with its square neck and high empire waist, was by far the most beautiful and, as it happened, fit Elke perfectly.

The gold necklace, retrieved from a hiding place in her dressing room, sat solidly on her throat, framed by the square of satin and velvet. Elke caught up her violin and bow and walked lightly up to the wings.

"Four more minutes."

"Five. Shhhh."

"A worthy audience. A very fine audience. Wouldn't you say so, Ross? A fine audience?"

"Well, of course. A Wood always—"

"Ross?"

"What?"

"Papa."

"What about Papa?"

"Do you think he—? Do you ever believe that . . . after people die, that they—"

"Yes."

"Yes, what? You mean, you think—"

"Yes, I'm sure of it. Papa is here. With us. Tonight."

"I don't."

"What do you mean, you don't?"

"I don't think he's here."

"Of course he's here."

"I think he's gone. I'm sure of it. He's left us."

"He'll never leave us."

"Isn't that—?"

"Yes. Shhhh. She's coming."

Elke had just arrived in the wings when the lights were dimmed and the noise from the audience thinned to a softer sound. She stood, bent slightly forward, with one arm crooked around the violin and the bow held lightly in the opposite hand. Under the surprising folds of the costume, which she now realized smelled strongly of mothballs and dust, her body felt cool and determined.

It seemed suddenly as though Papa were near—in the chamber of the violin or wrapped around the rosined strings of her bow. But she knew this was only an illusion stirred by the hard lights and the rising excitement.

"He's gone," she told herself, looking down at the backs of her hands. "I'm sure of that, at least."

It was time to begin. It was past time to begin. A hand

pressed on her spine between her neck and her waist, between her shoulder blades, an encouraging, insistent pressure. "Go, go, they are waiting."

Elke bent her neck to show she was ready, then followed the angle of her head out onto the stage. A few minutes of surging noise—was someone shouting something to her?—then she laid her chin and her cheek on the violin, positioned her arm and bow. She closed her eyes and clearly saw the notes of her *Chanson des Fleurs* lined up before her. With a slight nod to the notes, to the audience, to herself, to whoever might be watching, she began to play.

Stanley was on his feet. "Bravo! Bravissimo!"

The two, bright, flag-shaped words were out of his mouth before he realized it and before Elke had played a single note. The shame, the shame. He felt the blood go out of his clapping hands and then their unbearable weight at his sides. The disgrace! For Elke, for Ross, for Papa, whose wide, pale, disappointed face came sliding before his eyes.

To himself, he said, "I'm going to faint."

But he didn't. All around him people were rising to their feet and applauding. For Elke, darling Elke. Even Ross, looking stunned, rose and opened his mouth and whispered, "Bravo."

She began. Her *Chanson* first, each note rounded like the bowl of a spoon. Stanley held his breath in the final bars, where the notes seemed to heap themselves one on top of the other. Then her *August Suite* and, after that, her *Fleuve Noir,* so slow, so stately that Stanley would have cried if he hadn't felt carried to a calm, rivery place beyond tears. Last, Elke played her silky little *Lament* in memory of Papa.

She bowed deeply. It was intermission already. The gold necklace burned at her throat, and the great golden-green dress swept the floor—where had she found such a dress? Stanley turned to ask Ross, who was staring straight ahead, "Where has she found such a dress?"

"We picked it out together," Ross was saying. "It seemed to set off the necklace."

It was over. She was back in the dressing room, exhausted, happy, her fingers aching for the resistance of the strings, her heart rocking. All those people; all those eyes scraping against the skin of her face.

She hesitated only a moment before opening the door to Ross's knock. One, two, three, she counted, then opened it.

Stanley followed Ross into the room, carrying—by the stems, heads downward—an enormous bouquet of flowers, an absurd bouquet of flowers. "Ecstasies! Ecstasies!" His eyes rolled, his arms swung, and the flowers fell to the floor, their sharp fragrance mingling with the odor of mothballs.

Ross blinked, then smiled, then bent down and picked up the strewn flowers. "For you," he said, presenting them and kissing Elke in the Wood way, first on one cheek, then on the other, finally on the forehead. "You are a true Wood," he said into her ear. He did not look into her eyes.

"The truest Wood," added Stanley, who liked the last word, and who was always permitted to have it.

Love so Fleeting, Love so Fine

WENDY IS BACK! the sign said. It caught his eye.

It was a handprinted sign and fairly crude—not that he was a man who objected to crudeness; crayon lettering on a piece of cardboard: WENDY IS BACK! it said.

The sign was in the window of an orthopedic shoe store on a dim back street in downtown Winnipeg. He passed it one morning on his way to the office, and the image of the sign, and all the questions it raised, stayed with him, printed as it were on the back wall of his eye.

Who is Wendy?

Where has she been?

Why is she back?

And why is her return the cause of joy?

Joy, there was no other word for it. The sign taped flat against the plate glass window was a joyful announcement, a public proclamation, reinforced, too, by its light, high floater of an exclamation point (that fond crayoned slash of exuberance) testifying to the fact that Wendy's return, whether from visiting her grandmother in Portage or from vacationing with a girlfriend in Hawaii, was an event worthy of celebration. The question was, why?

She would be about his own age, he reasoned—which was thirty. Nobody over thirty was named Wendy, at least nobody he'd ever met. But where had she been? Perhaps she'd been sick; flu was going the rounds, a persistent strain. (He himself had missed three days at work only the week before, and now his wife had come down with it.) Or an operation. Impossible.

It was more likely that she'd been sent away to Toronto or Montreal or St. Catharines for a job-upgrading course at some obscure community college specializing in the modern fitting of difficult feet. He mused, as he walked along, on what a narrow specialty it must be, the fitting of orthopedic footwear, but necessary, of course, and how, like chimney cleaning and piano tuning, it was a vocation whose appeal to youth might not be immediately apparent. Undoubtedly, she, Wendy, had come back from the east with a new sense of buoyancy, brimming with the latest theories and "tips," which she now felt eager to pass on to her customers.

It was easy to see that her popularity with customers was established. The store manager—a fatherly type—might even refer to it as "phenomenal." (Else, why this sign in his window? And why the Christmas bonus already set aside for her?) Customers doubtless experienced an upsurge of optimism at the sight of her wide blue eyes or at hearing her cheery early morning "Hello there!" Her particular humor would be difficult to pin down, being neither dry nor wry nor witty, but consisting, rather, of a wink for the elderly gents and broad teasing compliments for the ladies—"These shoes'll put you right back in the chorus line, Mrs. Beamish." They loved it; they lapped it up; how could they help but adore Wendy.

"Our little Wendy's back," he imagined these old ones cackling one to another as they came in for fittings, "and about time too."

From North Winnipeg they came, from East Kildonan and Fort Garry and Southwood and even Brandon so that their warped and crooked and cosmically disfavored feet could be taken into Wendy's smooth young hands, examined minutely and murmured over—but in that merry little voice of hers that made people think of the daughters they'd never had. Into her care they could safely put the shame of their ancient bunions, their blue-black swollen ankles, their blistered heels. Her strong, unerring touch never shrank when it came to straightening out crippled toes or testing with her healthy thumbs that peculiar soft givingness that indicates a fallen arch. By sheer banter, by a kind of chiding playfulness, she absolved her clients of the rasp of old calluses, the yellowness of soles, the damp dishonor attached to foot odor, foot foulness, foot obloquy, foot ignominy.

All this and more Wendy was able to neutralize—with forehead prettily creased—by means of her steady, unflinching manner. These feet are only human, she would be ready to say if asked. Tarsus and metatarsus; corn, callus and nail; her touch is tender and without judgment. Willingly she rises from her little padded stool and fetches the catalog sent from the supply house in Pittsburgh, and happily she points to Figure 42. "This little laced oxford doesn't look like much *off*," she concedes to Mrs. Beamish or whomever happens to be in her charge, "but it's really a very smart little shoe *on*."

He imagines that her working uniform is some kind of smock in a pastel shade, the nature of her work being, after all, primarily medical. A caring profession. A caring person. A person one cared about. Wendy! She was back!

And he loved her.

He admitted it to himself. Oh yes, it was like light spilling through a doorway, his love for her. Arriving at work and traveling in the elevator to the eleventh floor, he kept his eyes lowered, searching the feet of his fellow workers, noting here and there sturdy, polished, snub-nosed models with thickish heels. Had these people felt his Wendy's warm ministrations? He might, if he were bolder, announce loudly, "Wendy is back!" as if it were an oblation, and watch as smiles of recognition, then euphoria and a kind of relief, too, spread across their faces.

Later, alone, at the end of the workday, while his wife lay reading the newspaper in bed, he examined his own feet under a strong light. Would they soon require professional attention? Might they benefit from extra bracing or support, a foam lift at the heel, say, or—well, whatever Wendy would care to suggest now that she was up on the latest theories from the east. But what could he say to her that would not seem callow or self-serving or, worse, a plea for her attention. She might look at his two feet, stripped of their socks and laid bare and damp, and suspect he had come because of ulterior motives. Namely love. He is sure she is vigilant against those who would merely love her.

He is a man who has been in love many times. Before the transfer to the Winnipeg office, he spent two years in Vancouver, and once, standing in line at a bakery on 41st Avenue, he found himself behind two solemn young women who were ordering a farewell cake for a friend. "What would you like written on top?" the woman behind the counter asked them. They paused, looked uncertain, regarded each other, and then one of them said decisively, "So long, Louise."

Louise. Gold hair set off by a blue cotton square. Louise was leaving. Instinctively, he felt she didn't really want to go. All her friends were here. This was a beautiful city. She had a decent job, a pleasant apartment full of thick-leaved plants and bamboo furniture; she had a modest view of the mountains and a membership in a health club, but nevertheless she was leaving. SO LONG, LOUISE, the pink icing on her farewell cake spelled out.

Something had forced the move on her—a problem that might be professional or personal—and now she would have to deal—alone, for how could he help her?—with storing her furniture, canceling her subscriptions and giving away to friends the books and oddments she loved. Her medical insurance would have to be transferred, and there would be the last heartbreaking task of going down to the post office to arrange to have her mail forwarded. It seemed unpardonable to ask so much of a young woman who had barely had time to savor her independence and to study love's ingenious rarefaction. She would have to face the horror of apartment-hunting elsewhere; a whole new life to establish, in fact. If only he could put his arms around her, his poor Louise, whom he suddenly realized he cared deeply, deeply, deeply about.

His lost Louise. That is how he thinks of her, a woman standing in the airport—no, the bus station—in her dark cloth coat of good quality and with her two pieces of soft-sided luggage, in which lay folded a number of pale wool skirts and sweaters and her little zippered bag of cosmetics, toiletries, talcum powder and emery boards, which would be traveling, ineluctably, with her out to the edges of the city and over the mountain ranges and away from his yet-to-be declared love.

Still, he won't forget her, just as he has never forgotten his young and lovely Sherri, whom he first encountered thirty miles north of Kingston—where his first transfer took him. There he had seen, spray-painted in red on a broad exposed rock face, the message HANK LOVES SHERRI in letters that were at least three feet high.

He knows, of course, what the Hanks of the world are like: loud-mouthed and jealous, with the beginnings of a beer belly, the kind of lout who believes the act of love was invented to cancel out the attachment of the spirit, the sort of person who might dare to fling a muscled, possessive arm across

Sherri's shoulders while coming out of a coffee shop on Princess Street and later swear to her that she was different from the other girls he'd known. *His* Sherri, who, with her hyacinth cologne and bitten nails, was easily, fatally, impressed by male joviality and dark sprinklings of chest hairs. She would never stand a chance. For a while, a few months, she might be persuaded that Hank really did love her in his way, and that she, in return, loved him. But familiarity, intimacy—those enemies of love—would intervene, and one day she would wake up and find that something inside her had withered, that core of sweet vulnerability that was what *he* had loved in her from the first day when HANK LOVES SHERRI had stopped him cold on the highway.

And now it's Wendy who sets off wavelets of heat in his chest. WENDY IS BACK! He walks by the orthopedic footwear store again the next day—but this time more slowly. The loose leather wrappings on his feet scrape the pavement absurdly. His breath comes with pleasure and difficulty as though the air has been unbearably sweetened by her name—Wendy, Wendy, Wendy. Of course, he is tempted to peer closely through the dark plate glass, but finds it to be full of reflections—his own, mainly, his hungry face. He might go in—not today, but tomorrow—on the pretext of asking the time or begging change for the parking meter or telephone. He'll think of something. Love invents potent strategies, and people in love are resourceful as well as devious. Wendy, Wendy is back. But for how long?

The end of his love affairs always brings a mixed nightmare of poignancy and the skirmishings of pain. He feels stranded, beached, with salt in his ears. What is over, is over; he is realist enough to recognize that. But his loves, Sherri, Louise, Wendy—and the others—never desert him entirely. He has committed to memory the minor physics of veneration and, on dark nights, after his wife has fallen asleep and lies snoring quietly beside him, he likes to hang on to consciousness for an extra minute or two and listen to the sound of the wind rocking the treetops and brushing silkily against the window. It's then he finds himself attended by a false flicker on the retina—some would say vision—in which long, brightly colored ribbons dance and sway before him. Their suppleness, their undulations, cut deeply into his heart and widen for an instant the eye of the comprehended world. Often he can hear, as well, the muted sound of female voices and someone calling out to him by name.

Dolls, Dolls, Dolls, Dolls

DOLLS. ROBERTA HAS WRITTEN ME a long letter about dolls, or more specifically about a doll factory she visited when she and Tom were in Japan.

"Ha," my husband says, reading her letter and pulling a face, "another pilgrimage to the heart's interior." He can hardly bring himself to read Roberta's letters anymore, though they come addressed to the two of us; there is a breathlessness about them that makes him squirm, a seeking, suffering openness that I suspect he finds grotesque in a woman of Roberta's age. Forty-eight, an uneasy age. And Roberta has never been what the world calls an easy woman. She is one of my oldest friends, and the heart of her problem, as I see it, is that she is incredulous, still, that the color and imagination of our childhood should have come to rest in nothing at all but these lengthy monochrome business trips with her husband, a man called Tom O'Brien; but that is neither here nor there.

In this letter from Japan, she describes a curious mystical experience that caused her not exactly panic and not precisely pleasure, but that connected her for an instant with an area of original sensation, a rare enough event at our age. She also unwittingly stepped into one of my previously undeclared beliefs. Which is that dolls, dolls of all kinds—

those strung-together parcels of wood or plastic or cloth or whatever—possess a measure of energy beyond their simple substance, something half-willed and half-alive.

Roberta writes that Tokyo was packed with tourists; the weather was hot and humid, and she decided to join a touring party on a day's outing in the countryside—Tom was tied up in meetings, as per usual.

They were taken by air-conditioned bus to a village where ninety percent—the guide vigorously repeated this statistic—where ninety percent of all the dolls in Japan were made. "It's a major industry here," Roberta writes, and some of the dolls still were manufactured almost entirely by hand in a kind of cottage-industry system. One house in the village, for example, made nothing but arms and legs, another the bodies; another dressed the naked doll bodies in stiff kimonos of real silk and attached such objects as fans and birds to the tiny lacquered female fingers.

Roberta's party was brought to a small house in the middle of the village where the heads of geisha dolls were made. Just the heads and nothing else. After leaving their shoes in a small darkened foyer, they were led into a surprisingly wide, matted workroom that was cooled by slow-moving overhead fans. The air was musty from the mingled straw and dust, but the light from a row of latticed windows was softly opalescent, a distinctly mild, non-industry quality of light, clean-focused and just touched with the egg yellow of sunlight.

Here in the workroom nine or ten Japanese women knelt in a circle on the floor. They nodded quickly and repeatedly in the direction of the tourists, and smiled in a half-shy, half-neighborly manner; they never stopped working for a second.

The head-making operation was explained by the guide, who was a short and peppy Japanese with soft cheeks and a sharp "arfing" way of speaking English. First, he informed them, the very finest sawdust of a rare Japanese tree was taken and mixed with an equal solution of the purest rice paste. (Roberta writes that he rose up on his toes when he reached the words *finest* and *purest* as though paying tribute to the god of superlatives.) This dough-like material then was pressed into wooden molds of great antiquity (another toe-rising here) and allowed to dry very slowly over a period of days. Then it was removed and painted; ten separate and exquisitely thin coats of enamel were applied, so that the resulting form, with only an elegant nose breaking the white egg surface, arrived at the weight and feel and coolness of porcelain.

The tourists—hulking, Western, flat-footed in their bare feet—watched as the tiny white doll heads were passed around the circle of workers. The first woman, working with tweezers and glue, applied the eyes, pressing them into place with a small wooden stick. A second woman painted in the fine red shape of a mouth and handed on the head to a woman who applied to the center of the mouth a set of chaste and tiny teeth. Other women touched the eyes with shadow, the cheeks with bloom, the bones with highlight, so that the flattened oval took on the relief and contours of sculptured form. "Lovely," Roberta writes in her letter, "a miracle of delicacy."

And finally, the hair. Before the war, the guide told them, real hair had been used, human hair. Nowadays a very fine quality of blue-black nylon was employed. The doll's skull was cunningly separated into two sections so that the hair could be firmly, permanently rooted from the inside. Then the head was sealed again, and the hair arranging began. The two women who performed this final step used real combs and brushes, pulling the hair smoothly over their hands so that every strand was in alignment, and then they shaped it, tenderly, deftly, with quick little strokes, into the intricate knots and coils of traditional geisha hair dressing.

Finally, at the end of this circular production line, the guide held up a finished head and briefly propagandized in his sharp, gingery, lordly little voice about the amount of time that went into making a head, the degree of skill, the years of apprenticeship. Notice the perfection of the finished product, he instructed. Observe the delicacy, mark the detailing. And then, because Roberta was standing closest to him, he placed the head in her hands for a final inspection.

And that was the moment Roberta was really writing me about. The finished head in her hands, with its staring eyes and its painted veil of composure and its feminine, almost erotic crown of hair, had more than the weight of artifact about it. Instinctively, Roberta's hands had cupped the head into a laced cradle, protective and cherishing. There was something *alive* about the head.

An instant later she knew she had overreacted. "Tom always says I make too much of nothing," she apologizes. The head hadn't moved in her hands; there had been no sensation of pulse or breath, no shimmer of aura, no electrical charge, nothing. Her eyes went to the women who had created this little head. They smiled, bowed, whispered, miming a busy humility, but their cool, waiting eyes informed her that they knew exactly what she was feeling.

What she *had* felt was a stirring apprehension of possibility. It was more than mere animism; the life, or whatever it was that had been brought into being by those industriously toiling women, seemed to Roberta to be deliberate and to fulfill some unstated law of necessity.

She ends her letter more or less the way she ends all her letters these days: with a statement that is really a question. "I don't suppose," she says, "that you'll understand any of this."

———

Dolls, dolls, dolls, dolls. Once—I forget why—I wrote those words on a piece of paper, and instantly they swam into incomprehension, becoming meaningless ruffles of ink, squiggles from a comic strip. Was it a Christmas wish list I was making? I doubt it. As a child I would have been shocked had I received more than one doll in a single year; the idea was unworthy, it was *unnatural.* I could not even imagine it.

Every year from the time I was born until the year I was ten I was given a doll. It was one of the certainties of life, a portion of a large, enclosing certainty in which all the jumble of childhood lay. It now seems a long way back to those particular inalterable surfaces: the vast and incomprehensible war; Miss Newbury, with her ivory-colored teeth, who was principal of Lord Durham Public School; Euclid Avenue, where we lived in a brown house with a glassed-in front porch; the seasons with their splendors and terrors curving endlessly around the middle eye of the world that I shared with my sister and my mother and father.

Almost Christmas: there they would be, my mother and father at the kitchen table on a Saturday morning in early December, drinking drip coffee and making lists. There would come a succession of dark, chilly pre-Christmas afternoons in which the air would grow rich with frost and longing, and on one of those afternoons our mother would take the bus downtown to buy the Christmas dolls for my sister and me.

She loved buying the Christmas dolls, the annual rite of choosing. It's the faces, she used to say, that matter, those dear molded faces. She would be swept away by a pitch of sweetness in the pouting lips, liveliness and color in the lashed eyes, or a line of tenderness in the tinted cheeks—"The minute I laid eyes on that face," she would say, helplessly

— 152 —

shaking her head in a way she had, "I just went and fell head over heels."

We never, of course, went with her on these shopping trips, but I can see how it must have been: Mother, in her claret-wine coat with the black squirrel collar, bending over, peering into glass cases in the red-carpeted toy department and searching in the hundreds of stiff smiling faces for a flicker of response, an indication of some kind that this doll, this particular doll, was destined for us. Then the pondering over price and value—she always spent more than she intended—having just one last look around, and finally, yes, she would make up her mind.

She also must have bought on these late afternoon shopping excursions Monopoly sets and dominoes and sewing cards, but these things would have been carried home in a different spirit, for it seems inconceivable for the dolls, our Christmas dolls to be boxed and jammed into shopping bags with ordinary toys; they must have been carefully wrapped—she would have insisted on double layers of tissue paper—and she would have held them in her arms, crackling in their wrappings, all the way home, persuaded already, as we would later be persuaded, in the reality of their small beating hearts. What kind of mother was this with her easy belief, her adherence to seasonal ritual? (She also canned peaches the last week in August, fifty quarts, each peach half-turned with a fork so that the curve, round as a baby's cheek, gleamed lustrous through the blue glass. Why did she do that—go to all that trouble? I have no idea, not even the seed of an idea.)

The people in our neighborhood on Euclid Avenue, the real and continuing people, the Browns, the McArthurs, the Sheas, the Callahans, lived as we did, in houses, but at the end of our block was a large yellow brick building, always referred to by us as The Apartments. The Apartments, frilled at the back with iron fire escapes, and the front of the building solid with its waxed brown foyer, its brass mailboxes and nameplates, its important but temporary air. (These people only rent, our father had told us.) The children who lived in the apartments were always a little alien; it was hard for us to believe in the real existence of children who lacked backyards of their own, children who had no fruit cellars filled with pickles and peaches. Furthermore, these families always seemed to be moving on after a year or so, so that we never got to know them well. But on at least one occasion I remember we were invited there to a birthday party given by a little round-faced girl, an only child named Nanette.

It was a party flowing with new pleasures. Frilled nutcups at each place. A square bakery cake with shells chasing each other around the edges. But the prizes for the games we played—pin the tail on the donkey, musical chairs—were manipulated so that every child received one—was that fair?— and these prizes were too expensive, overwhelming completely the boxed handkerchiefs and hair ribbons we'd brought along as gifts. But most shocking of all was the present that Nanette received from her beaming parents.

We sat in the apartment under the light of a bridge lamp, a circle of little girls on the living-room rug, watching while the enormous box was untied. Inside was a doll.

What kind of doll it was I don't recall except that her bronzed hair gleamed with a richness that was more than visual; what I do remember was the affection with which she was lifted from her wrappings of paper and pressed to Nanette's smocked bodice, how she was tipped reverently backward so that her eyes clicked shut, how she was rocked to and fro, murmured over, greeted, kissed, christened. It was as though Nanette had no idea of the inappropriateness of this gift. A doll could only begin her life at Christmas. Was it the rigidities of my family that dictated this belief, or some obscure and unconscious approximation to the facts of gestation? A birthday doll, it seemed to me then, constituted a violation of the order of things, and it went without saying that the worth of all dolls was diminished as a result.

Still, there sat Nanette, rocking back and forth in her spun rayon dress, stroking the doll's stiff wartime curls and never dreaming that she had been swindled. Poor Nanette, there could be no heartbeat in that doll's misplaced body; it was not possible. I felt a twist of pity, probably my first, a novel emotion, a bony hand yanking at my heart, an emotion oddly akin—I see it clearly enough now—to envy.

In the suburbs of Paris is one of the finest archeological museums in Europe—my husband had talked, ever since I'd known him, about going there. The French, a frugal people, like to make use of their ancient structures, and this particular museum is housed inside a thirteenth-century castle. The castle, if you block out the hundreds of surrounding villas and acacia-lined streets, looks much as it always must have looked, a bulky structure of golden stone with blank, primitive, upswept walls and three round, brutish towers whose massiveness might be a metaphor for that rough age that equated masonry with power.

The interior of this crude stone shell has been transformed by the Ministry of Culture into a purring, beige-toned shrine to modernism, hived with climate-controlled rooms and corridors, costly showcases and thousands of artifacts, subtly lit, lovingly identified. The pièce de résistance is the ancient banqueting hall where today can be seen a wax reconstruction of pre-Frankish family life. Here in this room, a number of small, dark, hairy manikins squat naked around a cleverly simulated fire. The juxtaposition of time—ancient, medieval and modern—affected us powerfully; my husband

and young daughter and I stared for some time at this strange tableau, trying to reconcile these ragged eaters of roots with the sleek, meaty, well-clothed Parisians we'd seen earlier that day shopping on the rue Victor Hugo.

We spent most of an afternoon in the museum, looking at elegantly mounted pottery fragments and tiny vessels clumsily formed from cloudy glass. There was something restorative about seeing French art at this untutored level, something innocent and humanizing in the simple requirement for domestic craft. The Louvre had exhausted us to the glitter of high style and finish, and at the castle we felt as though the French had allowed a glimpse of their coarser, more likable selves.

"Look at that," my husband said, pointing to a case that held a number of tiny clay figures, thousands of years old. We looked. Some of them were missing arms, and a few were missing their heads, but the bodily form was unmistakable.

"They're icons," my husband said, translating the display card: "From the pre-Christian era."

"Icons?" our daughter asked, puzzled. She was seven that summer.

"Like little gods. People in those days worshipped gods made of clay or stone."

"How do you know?" she asked him.

"Because it says so," he told her. "*Icône.* That's the French word for icon. It's really the same as our word."

"Maybe they're dolls," she said.

"No. It says right here. Look. In those days people were all pagans, and they worshipped idols. Little statues like these. They sort of held them in their hands or carried them with them when they went hunting or when they went to war."

"They could be dolls," she said slowly.

He began to explain again. "All the early cultures—"

She was looking at the figures, her open hand resting lightly on the glass case. "They look like dolls." For a minute I thought he was going to go on protesting. His lips moved, took the necessary shape. He lifted his hand to point once again at the case. I felt sick with sudden inexplicable anger.

Then he turned to our daughter, shrugged, smiled, put his hands in his pockets. He looked young, twenty-five, or even younger. "Who knows," he said to her. "You might be right. Who knows."

My sister lives three hundred miles away in Ohio, and these days I see her only two or three times a year, usually for family gatherings on long weekends. These visits tend to be noisy and clamorous. Between us we have two husbands and six children, and then there is the flurry of cooking and cleaning up after enormous holiday meals. There is never enough time to do what she and I love to do most, which is to sit at the kitchen table—hers or mine, they are inter-changeable—with mugs of tea before us and to reconstruct, frame by frame, the scenes of our childhood.

My memory is sharper than hers, so that in these discus-sions, though I'm two years younger, I tend to lead while she follows. (Sometimes I long for a share of her forgetfulness, her leisured shrugging acceptance of past events. My own recollections, not all happy, are relentlessly present, kept stashed away like ingots, testifying to a peculiar imprisoning muscularity of recall.) The last time she came—early October—we talked about the dolls we had been given every Christmas. Our husbands and children listened, jealously it seemed to me, at the sidelines, the husbands bemused by this ordering of trivia, the children open-mouthed, disbelieving.

I asked my sister if she remembered how our dolls were presented to us, exactly the way real children are presented, the baby dolls asleep in stenciled cradles or wrapped in receiving blankets; and the schoolgirl dolls propped up by the Christmas tree, posed just so, smiling brilliantly and fingering the lower branches with their shapely curved hands. We always loved them on sight.

"Remember Nancy Lynn?" my sister said. She was taking the lead this time. Nancy Lynn had been one of mine, one of the early dolls, a large, cheerful baby doll with a body of cloth and arms and legs of painted plaster. Her swirled brown hair was painted on, and at one point in her long life she took a hard knock on the head, carrying forever after a square chip of white at the scalp. To spare her shame, we kept her lacy bonnet tied on day and night. (Our children, listening, howled at this delicacy.)

One wartime Christmas we were given our twin dolls, Shirley and Helen. The twins were small and hollow and made of genuine rubber, difficult to come by in those years of shortages, and they actually could be fed water from a little bottle. They were also capable of wetting themselves through tiny holes punched in their rubber buttocks; the vulnerability of this bodily process enormously enlarged our love for them. There was also Barbara the Magic Skin Doll, wonderfully pliable at first, though later her flesh peeled away in strips. There was a Raggedy Ann, not to our minds a real doll, but a cloth-stuffed hybrid of good disposition. There was Brenda, named for her red hair, and Betty, with jointed knees and a brave little tartan skirt. There was Susan—her full name was Brown-Eyed Susan—my last doll, only I didn't know it then.

My sister and I committed the usual sins, leaving our dolls in their pajamas for days on end, and then, with a rush of shame and love, scooping them up and trying to make amends by telescoping weeks and even years into a Saturday afternoon. Our fiercely loved dolls were left out in the rain. We always lost their shoes after the first month; their toes broke off almost invariably. We sometimes picked them up by the arm or even the hair, but we never disowned them or gave them away or changed their names, and we never buried them in ghoulish backyard funerals as the children in our English stories seemed to do. We never completely forgot that we loved them.

Our mother loved them too. What was it that stirred her frantic devotion? Some failure of ours? Some insufficiency in our household? She spent hours making elaborate wardrobes for them; both my sister and I can remember the time she made Brenda a velvet cape trimmed with scraps of fur from her old squirrel collar. Sometimes she helped us give them names: Patsy, Gloria, Merry Lu, Olivia.

"And the drawer," my sister said. "Remember the drawer?"

"What drawer?" I asked.

"You remember the drawer. In our dresser. That little drawer on the left-hand side, the second one down."

"What about it?" I asked slowly.

"Well, don't you remember? Sure you do. That's where our dolls used to sleep. Remember how Mother lined it with a doll blanket?"

"No," I said.

"She thumbtacked it all around, so it was completely lined. That's where Shirley and Helen used to sleep."

"Are you sure?"

"Absolutely."

I remind her of the little maple doll cribs we had.

"That was later," she said.

I find it hard to believe that I've forgotten about this, especially this. A drawer lined with a blanket; that was exactly the kind of thing I remembered.

But my sister still has the old dresser in the attic of her house. And she told me that the blanket is still tacked in place; she hasn't been able to bring herself to remove it. "When you come at Christmas," she said, "I'll show it to you."

"What color is it?" I asked.

"Pink. Pink with white flowers. Of course, it's filthy now and falling apart."

I shook my head. A pink blanket with white flowers. I have no memory of such a blanket.

Perhaps at Christmas, when I actually look at the drawer, it all will come flooding back. The sight of it may unlock what I surely have stored away somewhere in my head, part of the collection of images that has always seemed so accessible and true. The fleecy pink drawer, the dark night, Shirley and Helen side by side, good night, good night as we shut them away. Don't let the bedbugs bite. Oh, oh.

It happened that in the city where I grew up a little girl was murdered. She was ten years old, my age.

It was a terrible murder. The killer entered her bedroom window while she was sleeping. He stabbed her through the heart; he cut off her head and her arms and her legs. Some of these pieces were never found.

It would have been impossible not to know about this murder; the name of the dead girl was known to everyone, and even today I have only to think the syllables of her name and the whole undertow of terror doubles back on me. This killer was a madman, a maniac who left notes in lipstick on city walls, begging the police to come and find him. He couldn't help himself. He was desperate. He threatened to strike again.

Roberta Callahan and JoAnn Brown and I, all of us ten years old, organized ourselves into a detective club and determined to catch the killer. We never played with dolls anymore. The Christmas before, for the first time, there had been no doll under the tree; instead, I had been given a wristwatch. My mother had sighed, first my sister, now me.

Dolls, which had once formed the center of my imagination, now seemed part of an exceedingly soft and sissified past, something I used to do before I got big. I had wedged Nancy Lynn and Brown-Eyed Susan and Brenda and Shirley and all the others onto a shelf at the back of my closet, and now my room was filled with pictures of horses and baseball stickers and collections of bird nests. Rough things, rugged things, tough things. For Roberta Callahan and JoAnn Brown and I desired, above all else, to be tough. I don't remember how it started, this longing for toughness. Perhaps it was our approaching but undreamed of puberty. Or the ebbing of parental supervision and certain possibilities of freedom that went with it.

Roberta was a dreamy girl who loved animals better than human beings; she had seen *Bambi* seven times and was always drawing pictures of spotted fawns. JoAnn Brown was short and wiry and wore glasses, and could stand any amount of pain; the winter before she had been hospitalized with double pneumonia. *Double pneumonia.* "But I had the will to live," she told us solemnly. The three of us were invited to play commandos with the boys on the block, and once the commando leader, Terry Shea, told another boy, in my hearing, that for a girl I was tough as nails. *Tough as nails.* It did not seem wildly improbable to JoAnn and Roberta and me that we should be the capturers of the crazed killer. Nancy Drew stalked criminals. Why not us?

In JoAnn Brown's house there was a spare room, and in the spare room there was a closet. That closet became the secret headquarters for the detective club. We had a desk, which was a cardboard carton turned upside down, and there, sitting on the floor with Mr. Brown's flashlight and stacks of saltines, we studied all the newspaper clippings we could find. We discussed and theorized. Where did the killer hide out? When and where would he strike again? Always behind our plotting and planning lay certain thoughts of honor and reward, the astonishment of our parents when they discovered that we had been the ones who led the police to the killer's hideout, that we had supplied the missing clue; how amazed they would be, they who all summer supposed that their daughters were merely playing, believing that we were children, girls, that we were powerless.

We emerged from these dark closet meetings dazed with heat and determination, and then we would take to the streets. All that summer we followed suspicious-looking men. Short men. Swarthy men. Men with facial scars or crossed eyes. One day we sighted a small dark man, a dwarf, in fact, carrying over his shoulder a large cloth sack. A body? Perhaps the body of a child? We followed him for an hour, and when he disappeared into an electrical-supply shop, JoAnn made careful note of the address and the time of entry.

Back in the closet we discussed what we should do. Should we send a letter to the police? Or should we make our way back to the shop and keep watch?

Roberta said she would be too frightened to go back.

"Well, I'll go, then," I spoke bravely.

Bravely, yes, I spoke with thrilling courage. But the truth was this: I was for all of that summer desperately ill with fear. The instant I was put to bed at night, my second-floor bedroom became a cave of pure sweating terror. Atoms of fear conjoined in a solid wall of darkness, pinning me down as I lay paralyzed in the middle of my bed; even to touch the edges of the mattress would be to invite unspeakable violence. The window, softly curtained with dotted swiss, became the focus of my desperate hour-by-hour attention. If I shut my eyes, even for an instant, he, the killer, the maniac, would seize that moment to enter and stab me through the heart. I could hear the sound of the knife entering my chest, a wet, injurious, cataclysmic plunge.

It was the same every night; leaves playing on the window pane, adumbration, darkness, the swift transition from neighborhood heroine, the girl known to be tough as nails, the girl who was on the trail of a murderer, to this, this shallow-breathing, rigidly sleepless coward.

Every night my mother, cheerful, baffled, innocent as she said good night, would remark, "Beats me how you can sleep in a room with the window closed." Proving how removed she was from my state of suffering, how little she perceived my nightly ordeal.

I so easily could have told her that I was afraid. She would have understood; she would have rocked me in her arms, bought me a night light at Woolworth's, explained how groundless my fears really were; she would have poured assurance and comfort on me and, ironically, I knew her comfort would have brought release.

But it was comfort I couldn't afford. At the risk of my life I had to go on as I was, to confess fear to anyone at all would have been to surrender the tough new self that had begun to grow inside me, the self I had created and now couldn't do without.

Then, almost accidentally, I was rescued. It was not my mother who rescued me, but my old doll Nancy Lynn. I had a glimpse of her one morning in my closet, a plaster arm poking out at me. I pulled her down. She still wore the lacy bonnet on her chipped head, gray with dirt, the ribbons shredded. She had no clothes, only her soft, soiled, mattressy body and the flattened joints where the arms and legs were attached. After all these years her eyes still opened and shut, and her eyelids were a bright youthful pink in contrast to the darkened skin tone of her face.

That night she slept with me under the sheet, and malevolence drained like magic from the darkened room; the night pressed friendly and familiar through the dotted swiss curtains; the Callahan's fox terrier yapped at the streaky moon. I opened the window and could hear a breeze loosened in the elms. In bed, Nancy Lynn's cold plaster toe poked reassuringly at my side. Her cloth body, with its soiled cottony fragrance, lay against my bare arm. The powerful pink eyelids were inexpressibly at rest. All night, while I slept, she kept me alive.

For as long as I needed her—I don't remember whether it was weeks or months before the killer was caught—she guarded me at night. The detective club became over a period of time a Gene Autry Fan Club, then a Perry Como Record Club, and there must have been a day when Nancy Lynn went back to her closet. And probably, though I don't like to think of it, a day when she and the others fell victim to a particularly heavy spree of spring cleaning.

There seems no sense to it. Even on the night I first put her on the pillow beside me, I knew she was lifeless, knew there was no heart fluttering in her soft chest and no bravery in her hollow head. None of it was real, none of it.

Only her power to protect me. Human love, I saw, could not always be relied upon. There would be times when I would have to settle for a kind of parallel love, an extension of my hidden self, hidden even from me. It would have to do, it would be a great deal better than nothing, I saw. It was something to be thankful for.

Invitations

ON MONDAY SHE LOOKED IN HER MAILBOX, although she had no reason to expect a letter so soon. But there it was, a small, square card. She held it in her two hands, testing its weight.

It was an invitation to an exhibition of drawings at a private gallery. The name of the artist was only faintly familiar to her, and she couldn't decide if she'd ever seen his work or not. She tried to imagine what kind of drawings she was being invited to view—would they be primitive or abstract or what was sometimes called "magic realism"? She summoned these categories to mind and then decided it didn't matter. What mattered was that she had been invited.

The invitation pleased her, though she wasn't such a fool as to think she'd been specifically singled out because of her aesthetic sensitivity or because of her knowledge of modern graphics or even because of the pleasure of her company. The address on the card had been typed; her name, in fact, was misspelled, the last two letters transposed. Somewhere, no doubt, she'd turned up on a mailing list—that was all.

She would wear a certain printed velvet skirt she had and with it a black turtleneck sweater. No one would expect her to buy a drawing or even to comment on the exhibition. It was necessary only to accept a glass of wine and a cube of orange cheese and stand for a minute or two in front of each drawing, nodding comprehendingly and perhaps murmuring something properly neutral into the air such as "nicely detailed" or "wonderful sense of space." There was a good chance no one would even speak to her, but it would be better than spending Saturday evening in her new apartment, sitting in an armchair with a book and feeling loneliness drink her drop by drop.

The previous tenant had left behind a single item, which was a paperback copy of Jane Austen's *Mansfield Park,* a book that, oddly enough, she had always intended to read. She couldn't help feeling that there had been something deliberate—and something imperative too—about this abandoned book, as though it had been specifically intended for her, and that she was being enjoined to take it seriously. But how much better it would be to be going *out;* how much easier it would be to say, should anyone ask, that on Saturday evening she would be attending an opening of an interesting new exhibition.

On Tuesday she was again taken by surprise, for in her mailbox there was another invitation, this time for a cocktail party given by a distant friend of a friend, someone she'd never met but whose name she dimly remembered having heard. It was a disappointment that the party was being held on the same night as the gallery opening and that, furthermore, it was at the same hour. For a minute she entertained the possibility of attending both functions, galloping breathlessly from one to the other. But no, it was not feasible; the two parties were at opposite ends of the city. It was a great pity, she felt, since invitations are few and far between when one moves to a new address. She would have to make a choice.

Of course she would choose the cocktail party. The gallery opening, now that she stopped to think about it, was no more than a commercial venture, an enticement to buyers and patrons. It would be fraudulent of her to attend when she'd no intention of buying a picture, and besides, she was drawn to cocktail parties. She was attracted, in fact, to parties of all kinds, adding them as an opportunity to possess, for a few hours at least, a life that was denser, more concentrated and more vigorous than the usual spun-out wastes of time that had to be scratched endlessly for substance. She could still wear her certain velvet skirt, but with a pretty red satin blouse she'd recently acquired.

On Wednesday, strangely, she received a third invitation— and it, too, was for Saturday evening. This time the invitation was handwritten, a rather charming note that she read through quickly three times. She was being invited to a small buffet supper. There would be only a dozen or so guests, it was explained. The author of a new biography would be there, and so would the subject of the biography, who was, by chance, also a biographer. A particular balding computer scientist would be in attendance along with his wife, who was celebrated for her anti-nuclear stance and for her involvement in Navajo rugs. There would be a professor of history and also a professor of histology, as well as a person renowned for his love of Black Forest cakes and cheese pastries. There would be a famous character actor whose face was familiar, if not his name, and also the hairdresser who'd invented the Gidget cut and raised razor cuts to their present *haute* status.

Of course she could not say no. How much more congenial to go to a supper party than to peer at violent works of art and mutter, "Interesting, interesting," and how much more rewarding than standing about with a drink and a salty canapé and trying to make conversation with a room full of strangers. Her green silk dress would be suitable, if not precisely perfect, and she could gamble safely enough on the fact that no one would have seen it before.

Thursday's mail brought still another invitation, also unfortunately for Saturday evening. She smiled, remembering how her mother used to say, "It never rains but it pours." The invitation, which was for a formal dinner party, was printed on fine paper, and there was a handwritten note at the bottom. "We do hope you can make it," the note said. "Of course, we know you by reputation, and we've been looking forward to meeting you for years."

It had been some time since she'd attended a formal dinner party, and she was flattered to be sent an invitation with a handwritten note at the bottom. It pleased her to imagine a large, vaulted dining room and parade of courses elegantly served, each with a different wine. The gleam of light through cut glass would sparkle on polished linen and on the faces of the luminaries gathered around the table. Her green silk, with perhaps the double strand of pearls, would be festive enough, but at the same time subdued and formal.

She wasn't entirely surprised to look into her mailbox on Friday and see that she'd been sent yet another invitation. The paper was a heavy, creamy stock and came enclosed in a thick double envelope. There was to be a reception—a *gala* it was called—at the top of a large downtown hotel on Saturday evening. The guest of honor, she read, was to be herself.

She felt a lurch of happiness. Such an honor! But a moment later her euphoria gave way to panic, and when she sat down to collect herself, she discovered she was trembling not with excitement but with fear.

On Saturday she surveyed the five invitations, which were arranged in a circle on her coffee table. These missives, so richly welcoming, persuading and honoring, had pleased her at first, then puzzled her. And now she felt for the first time directly threatened. Something or someone was conspiring to consume a portion of her life, of herself, in fact—entering her apartment and taking possession of her Saturday evening just as a thief might enter and carry off her stereo equipment or her lovely double rope of pearls or a deep slice of her dorsal flesh.

She decided to stay home, instead, with a cup of coffee and her adventitiously acquired copy of *Mansfield Park*. Already it was dark, and she switched on the small reading lamp by her chair. The shade of the lamp was made of a pale, ivory-yellow material, and the light that shone through it had the warm quality of very old gold.

It happened that people passing her window on their way to various parties and public gatherings that night were moved to see her, a woman sitting calmly in an arc of lamp-light, turning over—one by one—the soft pages of a thick book. Clearly she was lost in what she was reading, for she never once glanced up. Her look of solitary containment and the oblique angle with which the light struck the left side of her face made her seem piercingly lovely. One of her hands, curved like a comma, lay on her lap; the other, slowly, thoughtfully, turned over the pages.

Those who passed by and saw her were seized by a twist of pain, which was really a kind of nostalgia for their childhood and for a simplified time when they, too, had been bonded to the books they read and to certain golden rooms they remembered as being complete and as perfect as stage settings. They felt resentment, too, at the cold rain and the buffeting wind and the price of taxis and the hostility of their hosts. They felt embarrassed by their own small, proffered utterances and by the expanded social rubric they had come to inhabit.

As they moved to and fro in large, brightly lit rooms, so high up in glittering towers that they felt they were clinging to the sides of cliffs, their feet began to ache and exhaustion overcame them. Soon it was past midnight, no longer the same day, but the next and the next. New widths of time clamored to be filled, though something it seemed, some image of possibility, begged to be remembered.

Outside, the wind blew and blew. The sky slipped sideways, turning first yellow, then a mournful, treasonous purple, as though time itself was drowning in a waterfall of shame.

Taking the Train

GWENETH MCGOWAN, THE DISRAELI SCHOLAR, was awarded the Saul Appeldorf Medal at a gala reception. She carried it home and put it in a dresser drawer under a pile of underwear. Her morale was high. Recognition in the academic world seemed assured, her rent was paid up for six months and, in addition, she had a number of good friends, some deserving of her friendship, and some not.

"Dear Gweneth," came a letter from Calgary, Alberta, where one of the deserving friends lived. "So! Now you're famous! Well, well. Why not treat yourself to a visit—come and see me."

Within a week Gweneth was on a plane. Northie McCord, her friend and former roommate at school, met her at the airport with a bouquet of daisies. "Ah, daisies," Gweneth said, without amazement. Memory was the first bag they reached into on their infrequent meetings, and Northie's offering of daisies was meant to dislodge and recover images of her wedding day, when bride and bridesmaids, Gweneth included, had worn crowns of daisies on their heads. They also had worn peace buttons pinned to their smooth silk bodices.

"Just who the hell did we think we were?" Northie asked Gweneth later that day when the two of them were settled on canvas chairs in Northie's untidy backyard. "Who exactly did we think we were performing for?"

She passed Gweneth what was left of a joint. "I don't know about you, but I think I was trying to say I hadn't capitulated just because I was marrying a chemical engineer. What I should have said was that I was damn well ready to capitulate."

"We were tired," said Gweneth, who had no recollection of being tired, but wasn't ready yet to talk about Northie's husband, who had been mauled to death by a grizzly in a provincial park the year before. (According to a news report in an eastern paper, the attack had been "provoked" by the ham sandwich he carried in the pocket of his jacket; such an innocent act, Gweneth had thought at the time, to carry a ham sandwich.)

"A remarkable sky," she said to Northie, and the two of them fell into a loop of silence that only very old friends can enter easily.

There had been a period of several years when they'd been out of touch. In those years Gweneth was working on a Ph.D. and, for the most part, was without money. Being without money made her wayward, and waywardness permitted her a series of small abdications: letters, phone calls, reunions—they all went by the board. Sometimes, too, she lacked courage. "I don't have anything to show!" she confessed to an early lover, not sure whether she meant silverware or children or that hard lacquer she thought of as happiness. Later, she came to see happiness as something chancy and unreliable, a flash of light beating at the edge of a human eye or a thin piece of glass to be carried secretly inside her head.

Northie McCord's fifteen-year-old daughter, also named Gweneth but called Gwen for short, was excited by Gweneth's visit and insisted on making supper for the three of them. On a card table on the back porch she set out cold sliced beef, potato salad from a carton and glasses of iced tea.

Along with the cold beef there was a ceramic pot of fiery mustard. "Superb," Gweneth pronounced, as her mouth filled with splendid heat. "Whenever did you get such wonderful stuff?"

Northie and her daughter exchanged sly smiles. "It's our own," Northie said. "Didn't you notice those mustard plants in the yard?"

Gweneth helped herself to more beef and mustard. "God forgive me, I thought it was weeds." She felt for a moment that rare sensation of stepping outside her body and entering a narrative that belonged not to any one of them, but that was shared equally.

After supper, Gwen washed the dishes and Northie led Gweneth over to the cedar fence, where there was a double row of mustard plants. There are two types, Northie explained, black and white, and the best mustard in the world is made by combining the two.

"I didn't know what to do with myself last winter," Northie said, "but I remembered how you read right through Carthusian-to-Crockroft when you were seventeen. What was it—volume four of the encyclopedia?"

"Volume five. If I remember, I was troubled by my virginity and looked up *coitus* one day, and then just buried myself in all those lovely *C*'s. That's how I discovered John Clare, and that led me to the nineteenth century, and that led to Disraeli."

"I settled down with volume fifteen," Northie said. "Maybe because Gwen was fifteen. Maximinus-to-Naples, that's what volume fifteen is called. Maximinus, in case you're wondering, was one of the Roman emperors. About February I got to *mustard*. According to the encyclopedia, mustard grows plentifully in Montana, and so I thought, well, why not in Alberta? I had a devil of a time getting the right seedlings. You can cook the greens, too, if you rinse them twice, but I thought I'd better not inflict that on you."

She bent down to pick a leaf for Gweneth, and when she stood up her eyes were filled with tears. "It's a diversion," she said. "It's something to show people when they drop in."

"You are," Gweneth said loudly, hugging her, "the most successful mustard farmer I've ever met."

The girl, Gwen, flushed from the heat of the kitchen, carried two cups of coffee into the yard. "For McCord and McGowan," she said, and dropped a mock curtsy.

"We sound like sweater manufacturers."

"Or quality chocolates."

The two women moved the lawn chairs into a last remaining patch of sun and sat talking about the past, about what they had been like as girls of sixteen and seventeen. They'd done this before, but it seemed to Gweneth that they'd never done it so thoroughly—it was as though they were obliged, for the sake of the future, to rescue every moment. She remembered what one of her lovers had said: "What is the point of nostalgia if not to wring memory dry?"

The evening grew chilly. A breeze came up, and Gweneth swore she could smell mustard in the air. Gwen brought them more coffee, a cardigan for her mother and a lacy wool shawl for Gweneth. "She's playing handmaiden tonight," Northie said, when the girl had gone back into the house to her Bruce Springsteen records. "She's got very maternal since Mac was killed. She thinks this is what I need, to sit and talk with an old friend."

Gweneth asked, "And is it what you need?"

"Yes," Northie said. "But I don't need to talk about *it.* You don't want that, and I can't quite manage it."

"It isn't a question of my wanting it or not wanting it. If you want to talk, well, that's—"

"That's what you came for?"

"I was going to say that, but it's not true, of course. I don't think comfort is what you and I are able to do for each other. It wasn't in our syllabus, as the saying goes."

"The night before Mac left for that hiking trip we sat out here. Just like tonight. Except, the most extraordinary thing happened. There was a display of northern lights—have you ever seen the northern lights?"

Gweneth said no, glad she could say no.

"It's rather rare just here. Normally, you have to be away from the city because the general illumination interferes. But something was just right with the atmosphere that night, and it was a dazzling show. I hadn't imagined it would be so precisely outlined as it's shown in pictures—those folded curtains dragging down from the heavens. Mac said—I remember his exact words—he said all we needed was a celestial choir. Straight out of MGM, corny as hell. You know I'm not one for omens and portents, but it's given me something to hang on to. Along with Maximinus and mustard. And Gwen, of course."

"You're lucky to have a child. That's something I'm sorry I missed." Gweneth said this even though it wasn't true. (The lie bothered her not at all since she knew it did people good to be fulsomely envied.) She had never wished for a child. Once she said to a man she was living with, "The saddest thing in the world is a woman who thinks with her womb." "No," he said, "the saddest thing in the world is an artist whose work speaks to no one." This man, an abstract painter by profession, was always watering down her observations, and eventually it drove her straight into the arms of a Guggenheim Fellowship.

When her thesis was published, she liked to pat its brown covers and say, "Hi there, baby." When she was interviewed, shaking, on the BBC—the Third Programme yet—she found herself talking about her research like a mother, and indulging in a mother's fond praising, defensive and fault-finding by turn. And once she sat in the Reading Room of the British Museum and examined a tiny nineteenth-century book of essays written by an obscure country clergyman. The binding had long since deteriorated, and the pages had been tied together by someone—who?—when?—with a piece of ribbon. Slowly, respectfully, she'd tried to undo the knot, but the ribbon was so stiff with age that it crumbled on the table into a kind of white powder. She had examined the severed pages with more tenderness and sense of privilege than she'd ever felt toward anything in her life, and it occurred to her that perhaps this is what mothers feel for the secret lives of their children. Surely—she glanced at Northie—such moments keep people from flying into pieces.

"I didn't know you ever wanted children," Northie said after a while. "I mean, you never said."

They sat in silence a little longer until they began to shiver with cold.

When they came into the house, they found Gwen sitting on the living-room floor, listening to a Bruce Springsteen record, a long moaning song. She held up the record sleeve, which said: "New York City Serenade."

"It's coming," she told the two of them as they stood in the doorway. "The best part is coming." She shut her eyes and held up a finger, just as the song changed abruptly from gravel-weighted melody to anguished wail and the repeated phrase, "'She won't take the train, she won't take the train.'" Listening, her face went luminous with sorrow, and her lips mouthed the tragic words. "'No, she won't take the train, no, she won't take the train.'"

Who won't take the train? Gweneth wanted to demand roughly. Why not? And did it matter? The mystery was that a phrase so rich with denial could enthrall a young girl.

Gweneth felt an impulse to rescue her with logic, with exuberance, but stopped just in time. An image came into her mind, an old, traditional image of women who, after a meal, will take a tablecloth, shake it free of crumbs and put it away, each taking a corner, folding it once, then twice, then again. They never hesitate, these women, moving in and out, in and out, as skilled and graceful as dancers. And now, Gweneth thought: here we are, the three of us, holding on to this wailing rag-tag of music for all we're worth, and to something else that we can't put a name to, but don't dare drop.

Home

IT WAS SUMMER, THE MIDDLE OF JULY, the middle of the twentieth century, and in the city of Toronto one hundred people were boarding an airplane.

"Right this way," the lipsticked stewardess cried. "Can I get you a pillow? A blanket?"

It was a fine evening, and they climbed aboard with a lightsome step, even those who were no longer young. The plane was on its way to London, England, and since this was before the era of jet aircraft, a transatlantic flight meant twelve hours in the air. Ed Dover, a man in his mid-fifties who worked for the post office, had cashed in his war bonds so that he and his wife, Barbara, could go back to England for a twenty-one-day visit. It was for Barbara's sake they were going; the doctor had advised it. For two years she had suffered from depression, forever talking about England and the village near Braintree where she had grown up and where her parents still lived. At home in Toronto she sat all day in dark corners of the house, helplessly weeping; there was dust everywhere, and the little back garden where rhubarb and raspberries had thrived was overtaken by weeds.

Ed had tried to cheer her first with optimism, then with presents—a television set, a Singer sewing machine, boxes of candy. But she talked only about the long, pale Essex twilight, or a remembered bakeshop in the High Street, or sardines on toast around the fire, or the spiky multicolored lupines that bloomed by the back door. If only she could get lupines to grow in Toronto, things might be better.

Ed and Barbara now sat side by side over a wing, watching the propellers warm up. She looked out the window and dozed. It seemed to her that the sky they traveled through was sliding around the earth with them, given thrust by the fading of the sun's color. She thought of the doorway of her parents' house, the green painted gate and the stone gateposts that her father polished on Saturday mornings.

Then, at the same moment, and for no reason, the thought of this English house fused perfectly with the image of her own house, hers and Ed's, off Keele Street in Toronto, how snug it was in winter with the new fitted carpet and the work Ed had done in the kitchen, and she wondered suddenly why she'd been so unhappy there. She felt something like a vein reopening in her body, a flood of balance restored, and when the stewardess came around with the supper tray, Barbara smiled up at her and said, "Why, that looks fit for a king."

Ed plunged into his dinner with a good appetite. There was duckling with orange sauce and, though he wasn't one for fancy food, he always was willing to try something new. He took one bite and then another. It had a sweet, burned taste, not unpleasant, which for some reason reminded him of the sharpness and strangeness of sexual desire, the way it came uninvited at queer moments—when he was standing in the bathroom shaving his cheeks, or when he hurried across Eglinton Avenue in the morning to catch his bus. It rose bewilderingly like a spray of fireworks, a fountain that was always brighter than he remembered, going on from minute to minute, throwing sparks into the air and out onto the coolness of grass. He remembered, too, something almost forgotten: the smell of Barbara's skin when she stepped out of the bath and, remembering, felt the last two years collapse softly into a clock tick, their long anguish becoming something he soon would be looking back upon. His limbs seemed light as a boy's. The war bonds, their value badly nibbled away by inflation, had been well exchanged for this moment of bodily lightness. Let it come, let it come, he said to himself, meaning the rest of his life.

Across from Ed and Barbara, a retired farmer from Rivers, Manitoba, sat chewing his braised duckling. He poked his wife's knee and said, "For God's sake, for God's sake," referring, in his withered tenor voice, to the exotic meal and also to the surpassing pleasure of floating in the sky at nine o'clock on a fine summer evening with first Quebec, then the wide ocean skimming beneath him.

His wife was not a woman who appreciated being poked in the knees, but she was too busy thinking about God and Jesus and loving mercy and the color of the northern sky, which was salmon shading into violet, to take offense. She sent the old man, her husband for forty years, a girlish, newminted smile, then brought her knuckles together and marveled at the sliding terraces of grained skin covering the backs of her hands. Sweet Jesus our Savior—the words went off inside her ferny head like popcorn.

Not far from her sat a journalist, a mole-faced man with a rounded back, who specialized in writing profiles of the famous. He went around the world phoning them, writing to them, setting up appointments with them, meeting them in hotels or in their private quarters to spy out their inadequacies, their tragedies, their blurted fears, so that he could then treat them—and himself—to lavish bouts of pity. It was hard work, for the personalities of the famous vanish into their works, but always, after one of his interviews, he was able to persuade himself that it was better, when all was said and done, to be a nobody. In Canada he had interviewed the premier of a large eastern province, a man who had a gray front tooth, a nervous tremor high up on one cheek and a son-in-law who was about to go to jail for a narcotics offense. Now the journalist was going home to his flat in Notting Hill Gate; in twenty-four hours he would be fingering his collection of tiny glass animals and thinking that, despite his relative anonymity, his relative loneliness, his relatively small income and the relatively scanty degree of recognition that had come his way—despite this, his prized core of neutrality was safe from invaders. And what did that mean? He asked himself this with the same winning interrogation he practiced on the famous. It meant happiness, or something akin to happiness.

Next to him sat a high school English teacher, a woman of forty-odd years, padded with soft fat and dressed in a stiff shantung travel suit. Once in England, she intended to take a train to the Lake District and make her way to Dove Cottage, where she would sign her name in the visitors' book as countless other high school teachers had done. When she returned to Toronto, a city in which she had never felt at home though she'd been born there, and when she went back to her classroom in September to face unmannerly adolescents who would never understand what *The Prelude* was about, it would be a comfort for her to think of her name inscribed in a large book on a heavy oak table—as she imagined it—in the house where William Wordsworth had actually lived. The world, she suddenly saw, was accessible; oceans and continents and centuries could be spryly overleapt. From infancy she'd been drawn toward those things that were transparent—glass, air, rain, even the swimmy underwaterness of poetry. The atmosphere on the plane, its clear chiming ozone, seemed her true element, rarified, tender, discovered. Thinking this, she put back her head and heard the pleasurable crinkle of her new perm, a crinkle that promised her safe passage—or anything else she desired or could imagine.

They were all happy, Ed and Barbara Dover, the lip smacking farmer and his prayerful wife, the English journalist, and the Toronto teacher—but they were far from being the only ones. By some extraordinary coincidence (or cosmic dispensation or whatever), each person on the London-bound flight that night was, for a moment, filled with the steam of perfect happiness. Whether it was the oxygen-enriched air of the fusiform cabin, or the duckling with orange sauce, or the soufflé-soft buttocks of the stewardess sashaying to and fro with her coffeepot, or the unchartable currents of air bouncing against the sides of the vessel, or some random thought dredged out of the darkness of the aircraft and fueled by the proximity of strangers—whatever it was, each of the one hundred passengers—one after another, from rows one to twenty-five, like little lights going on—experienced an intense, simultaneous sensation of joy. They were for that moment swimmers riding a single wave, tossed upward by infection or clairvoyance or a slant of perception uniquely heightened by an accident of altitude.

Even the pilot, a Captain Walter Woodlock, a man plagued by the most painful and chronic variety of stomach ulcers, closed his eyes for the briefest of moments over Greenland and drifted straight into a fragment of dream. It couldn't have lasted more than thirty seconds, but in that short time he felt himself falling into a shrug of relaxation he'd almost forgotten. Afloat in his airy dimension, he became a large wet rose nodding in a garden, a gleaming fish smiling on a platter, a thick slice of Arctic moon reaching down and tenderly touching the small uplifted salty waves. He felt he could go on drifting forever in this false loop of time, so big and so blue was the world at that moment.

It must have been that the intensity and heat of this gathered happiness produced a sort of gas or ether or alchemic reaction—it's difficult to be precise—but for a moment, perhaps two, the walls of the aircraft, the entire fuselage and wings and tail section became translucent. The layers of steel, the rivets and bracing and ribwork turned first purple, then a pearly pink, and finally metamorphosed to the incandescence of pure light.

This luminous transformation, needless to say, went unnoticed by those in the aircraft, so busy was each of them with his or her private vision of transcendence.

But there was, it turned out, one witness: a twelve-year-old boy who happened to be standing on a stony Greenland beach that midsummer night. His name was Piers, and he was the son of a Danish Lutheran clergyman who had come to the tiny Greenland village for a two-year appointment. The boy's mother had remained behind in Copenhagen, having fallen in love with a manufacturer of pharmaceuticals, and none of this had been adequately explained to the boy— which may have been why he was standing, lonely and desperately confused, on the barren beach so late at night.

It was not very dark, of course. In Greenland, in the middle of the summer, the sky keeps some of its color until eleven o'clock, and even after that there are traces of brightness, much like the light that adheres to small impurities suspended in wine. The boy heard the noise of the motors first, looked up frowningly and saw the plane, shiningly present with its chambered belly and elegant glassy wings and the propellers spinning their milky webs. He was too dazzled to wave, which was what he normally did when a plane passed overhead. What could it be? he asked himself.

He knew almost nothing of science fiction, a genre scorned by his father, and the church in which he had been reared strictly eschewed angelic hosts or other forms of bodily revelation. A trick of the atmosphere? He had already seen the aurora borealis and knew this was different. The word *phenomenon* had not yet entered his vocabulary, but when it did, a few years later, dropping like a ripe piece of fruit into his consciousness, he found that it could usefully contain something of the spectacle of that night.

Such moments of intoxication, of course, quickly become guilty secrets—this is especially true of children—so it is not surprising that he never told anyone about what he had seen.

Like his father, he grew up to become a man of God, though like others of his generation he wore the label with irony. He went first to Leiden to study, and there lost his belief in the Trinity. After that he received a fellowship to the Union Theological Seminary in New York, where his disbelief grew, as did his reputation for being a promising young theologian. Before long he was invited to join the faculty; he became, in a few short years, the author of a textbook and a sought-after lecturer, and in his late thirties he fell in love with a nervous, intelligent woman who was a scholar of medieval history.

One night, when wrapped in each other's arms, she told him how women in the Middle Ages had pulled their silk gowns through a golden ring to test the fineness of the cloth. It seemed to him that this was the way in which he tested his belief in God, except that instead of determining the fineness of faith, he charted its reluctance, its lumpiness, its ultimate absurdity. Nevertheless, against all odds, there were days when he was able to pull what little he possessed through the ring; it came out with a ripply whoosh of surprise, making him feel faint and bringing instantly to mind the image of the transparent airplane suspended in the sky of his child-hood. All his life seemed to him to have been a centrifugal voyage around that remembered vision—the only sign of mystery he had ever received.

One day, his limbs around his beloved and his brain burning with pleasure, he told her what he had once been privileged to see. She pulled away from him then—she was a woman with cool eyes and a listening mouth—and suggested he see a psychiatrist.

Thereafter, he saw less and less of her, and finally, a year later, a friend told him she had married someone else. The same friend suggested he should take a holiday.

It was summertime, the city was sweltering, and it had been some time since he had been able to pull anything at all through his gold ring. He considered returning to Greenland for a visit, but the flight schedule was unbelievably complicated and the cost prohibitive; only wealthy bird watchers working on their life lists could afford to go there now. He found himself one afternoon in a travel agent's office next to a pretty girl who was booking a flight to Acapulco.

"Fabulous place," she said. Glorious sun. Great beaches. And grass by the bushel.

Always before, when the frivolous, leisured world beckoned, he had solemnly refused. But now he bought himself a ticket, and by the next morning he was on his way.

At the airport in Acapulco, a raw duplicity hangs in the blossom-sweat air—or so thinks Josephe, a young woman who works as a baggage checker behind the customs desk. All day long fresh streams of tourists arrive. From her station she can see them stepping off their aircraft and pressing forward through the wide glass doors, carrying with them the conspiratorial heft of vacationers-on-the-move. Their soft-sided luggage, their tennis rackets, their New York pallor and anxious brows expose in Josephe a buried vein of sadness, and one day she notices something frightening: 109 passengers step off the New York plane, and each of them—without exception—is wearing blue jeans.

She's used to the sight of blue jeans, but such statistical unanimity is unnerving, as though a comic army has grotesquely intruded. Even the last passenger to disembark and step onto the tarmac, a man who walks with the hesitant gait of someone in love with his own thoughts, is wearing the ubiquitous blue jeans.

She wishes there had been a single exception—a woman in a bright flowered dress or a man archaic enough to believe that resort apparel meant white duck trousers. She feels oddly assaulted by such totality, but the feeling quickly gives way to a head-shaking thrill of disbelief, then amusement, then satisfaction and, finally, awe.

She tries hard to get a good look at the last passenger's face, the one who sealed the effect of unreality, but the other passengers crowd around her desk, momentarily threatened by her small discoveries and queries, her transitory power.

In no time it's over; the tourists, duly processed, hurry out into the sun. They feel lighter than air, they claim, freer than birds, drifting off into their various inventions of paradise as though oblivious to the million invisible filaments of connection, trivial or profound, that bind them one to the other and to the small planet they call home.

The Journal

WHEN HAROLD AND SALLY TRAVEL, Sally keeps a journal, and in this journal Harold becomes *H.* She will write down such things as "H. exclaimed how the cathedral (Reims) is melting away on the outside and eroding into abstract lumps—while the interior is all fluidity and smoothness and grace, a seemingly endless series of rising and arching."

Has Harold actually *exclaimed* any such thing? The phrase *seemingly endless* sounds out of character, a little spongy, in fact, but then people sometimes take on a different persona when they travel. The bundled luggage, the weight of the camera around the neck, the sheer cost of air fare make travelers eager to mill expansive commentary from minor observation. Sally, in her journal, employs a steady, marching syntax, but allows herself occasional forays into fancy.

Both Harold and Sally are forty years old, the parents of two young children, boys. Harold possesses a mild, knobby face—his father was Swedish, his mother Welsh—and the natural dignity of one who says less than he feels. After he and his wife, Sally, leave the cathedral, they walk back to the Hotel du Nord, where they are staying, down one of those narrow, busy streets that the French like to describe as *bien animé,* and everywhere, despite a thick mist of rain, people are busy coming and going. Since it is close to five o'clock, they're beginning to gather in small cafés and bars and *salons du thé* in order to treat themselves to glasses of wine or beer or perhaps small cups of bitter espresso. A *quotidian quaff* is the tickling phrase that pops into Harold's head, and it seems to him there is not one person in all of Reims, in all of France for that matter, who is not now happily seated in some warm public corner and raising pleasing liquids to his lips. He experiences a nudge of grief because he does not happen to live in a country where people gather publicly at this hour to sip drinks and share anecdotes and debate ideas. He and Sally live on the fringe of Oshawa, Ontario, where, at the end of the working day, people simply return to their homes and begin to prepare their evening meal as though lacking the imagination to think of more joyous activities. But here, at a little table in France, the two of them have already gone native—"H. and I have gone native . . ."— and sit sipping cups of tea and eating little pancakes sprinkled with sugar. Harold feels inexpressibly at peace—which makes him all the more resentful that he can't live the rest of his life in this manner, but he decides against mentioning his ambivalent feelings to Sally for fear she'll write them down in her journal. ("H. laments the sterility of North American life which insists on the isolation of the family rather than daily ceremony of . . .")

The Hotel du Nord is much like other provincial hotels in its price bracket, possessing as it does a certain dimness of light bulbs, rosy wallpaper printed with medallions, endless creaking corridors lined with numbered doors and, especially, a proprietor's young brown-eyed son who sits in the foyer at a little table doing his homework, his *devoir* as he calls it. It's a lesson on the configuration of the Alps that occupies this young boy and keeps his smooth dark head bent low. The angle of the boy's bent neck sharpens Harold's sorrow, which has been building since he and Sally left the cathedral. ("H. was deeply moved by the sight of . . .")

Their room is small, the bed high and narrow and the padded satin coverlet not quite clean. Between coarse white sheets they attempt to make love, and almost, but not quite, succeed. Neither blames the other. Sally curses the remnant of jet lag, and Harold suspects the heaviness of the bedcovers; at home they've grown used to the lightness of a single electric blanket. But the tall shutters at the Hotel du Nord keep the little room wonderfully, profoundly, dark, and the next morning Harold remarks that there's probably a market in Canada for moveable shutters instead of the merely decorative Colonial type. ("H. has become an enthusiastic advocate of . . .")

It seems that the hotel, despite its great number of rooms, is almost empty. At least, there is only one other guest having breakfast with Sally and Harold the next morning, a young man sitting at the table next to theirs, drinking his coffee noisily and nibbling a bun. Out of pity—for the young, for the solitary—they engage him in conversation. He's an Australian, hungry for cricket scores, scornful of New Zealanders, and illiterate in French—altogether a dull young man; there's no other word for it. ("What a waste, H. says, to come so far and be so dull!!")

Rain, rain, rain. To cheer themselves up, Sally and Harold drive their rented Peugeot to Dijon and treat themselves to a grand lunch at an ancient *auberge*. ("Awnings, white tablecloths, the whole ball of wax.") Sally starts with a lovely and strange salad of warm bacon, chicken livers, tomatoes, lettuce and parsley. Then something called *Truite Caprice*. When she chews, an earnest net of wrinkles flies into her face, and Harold finds this so endearing that he reaches for her hand. ("H. had the alternate menu—herring—which may be the cause of his malaise!")

Sunshine, at last, after days of rain, and Sally and Harold arrive at the tall gates of a château called Rochepot, which their *Guide Michelin* has not awarded the decency of a single star. Why not? they wonder aloud.

Because it is largely a restoration, their tour guide says. She's middle-aged, with a broad fused bosom, and wears an apron over her green wool suit. Stars, she says, are reserved for those things that are authentic. Nevertheless, the château is spectacular with its patterned roofs and pretty interior garden—and Sally and Harold, after the rain, after yet another night of sexual failure, are anxious to appreciate. The circular château bedchambers are filled with curious hangings, the wide flagged kitchen is a museum of polished vessels and amusing contrivances, but what captures Harold's imagination is a little plaque on the garden wall. It shows a picture of a giraffe, and with it goes a brief legend. It seems that the King of Egypt gave the giraffe to the King of France in the year 1827, and that this creature was led, wearing a cloak to keep it from the chill, through the village of Rochepot, where it was regarded by all and sundry as a great spectacle. Harold loves the nineteenth century, which he sees as an exuberant epoch that produced and embraced the person he would like to have been: gentleman, generalist, amateur naturalist, calm but skeptical observer of kingships, comets and constellations, of flora and fauna and humanistic philosophy, and at times he can scarcely understand how he's come to be a supervisor in the public school system on the continent of North America. ("H. despairs because . . .")

In Le Grand Hotel in Beaune, in a second-floor room that faces onto the rue Principal and that is directly accessible all night long to the river of loud traffic destined for the south, Sally and Harold achieve one of those rare moments of sexual extravagance that arrives as a gift perhaps two or three times in one's life. Whether it was an enabling exhaustion—exhaustion can be cumulative, as all travelers know—or whether it was the bottle of soft, pale red dinner wine—softer than rain, softer even than the sound of the word *rain*—or whether they felt themselves previously and uniquely abandoned in the strange, many-veined hexagon of France, where their children and their children's babysitter and their aged parents and even the Canadian embassy in Paris could not possibly track them down—whatever the reason, they've been led, extraordinarily, into the heaven of ecstasy and then into the cool, air-filled condition of deep rest. Harold sleeps, his eyelids unmoving, and Sally, entering a succession of linked dreams, transcends herself, becoming S., that brave pilgrim on a path of her own devising. The ubiquitous satin coverlet presses and the shutters preserve darkness—though they do next to nothing to keep out the sound of traffic—and the long night leans in on them, blessing the impulse that coaxed them away from Oshawa and from the North American shore into this alien wine-provisioned wilderness where they are minutely and ecstatically joined and where they exchange, as seldom before in their forty-year lives, those perfect notices of affection and trust and rhapsody. ("H. and I slept well and in the morning . . .")

Salt

HALFWAY THROUGH HIS CANADIAN lecture tour, Thornbury found himself at an all-male dinner where the conversation had begun to flag. It seemed to him that much human effort went into separating men from women, and he often wondered why and to what effectiveness. Here, at the—what was it called? The Manitoba Club—there was still a quaint prohibition against women, yet there was something distinctively feminine about the pink-shaded wall lamps and the bowls of wet roses on every table. Women, Thornbury could not help thinking, might have kept the evening livelier; women would not have permitted the sudden falling off of discussion that brings official functions to a self-conscious halt.

This happened between the salad and the dessert course, the final stretch of a small club dinner organized in Thornbury's honor. Politics had been discussed, national and local, and flattering—though vague—references had been made to Thornbury's afternoon lecture. He supposed that, somewhere within his bloated body, his star of celebrity still twinkled, and for that reason he felt an obligation to keep the evening lively. Part of his arrogance, his wife, Flora, charged, was his belief that he had to assist others over the difficult sill of language. This was not so, he maintained, but he rightly felt that, were it not for his visit, the six men seated at the table would be at home enjoying the company of their wives and children.

Gathered around him were a judge, two lawyers, a deputy provincial minister, the publisher of a small literary quarterly, and a man who had been introduced earlier as a theologian. Thornbury turned to the theologian, who was sitting on his left, and said, "There's something I've been wondering about lately. It's a biblical question, and perhaps you would be able to provide me with an answer."

At this the theologian looked mildly disoriented, and a bridge of bone over his eyes pushed forward. "Well I'm afraid my Bible's a bit rusty—"

"It's just this," Thornbury said. "Why was it that Lot's wife was turned into a pillar of salt?"

"Disobedience, wasn't it?" The theologian was vague, engagingly so, probing his salad with a busy fork. "She disobeyed God by turning and looking back at the burning city."

"Yes," Thornbury said, "of course. But my question is, why salt? Why not limestone, for instance? Or marble?"

"Salt is soluble," someone pronounced, not very helpfully. One of the lawyers. "Highly perishable, a pillar of salt. Wouldn't last long in this part of the world, not in the springtime, anyway."

"But in that part of the world where the rainfall—"

"Didn't Lot's wife have a name?" It was the judge who was speaking, a mild, contemplative man, ridiculously young to be a judge, in Gordon Thornbury's opinion. Earlier, he had predicted that the judge would be the one most likely, as the evening sank beneath the tipping horizon of drink, to address him as *Gord*. (On the Australian tour it had been *Gordo*; in America, once, *Gord-boy*.)

"No woman would stand for it nowadays," the theologian said. "Being labeled Lot's wife, that is. Not my wife, at any rate."

Thornbury felt the conversation drifting off again. This

seemed a pattern he had observed elsewhere in North America, the impulse to broaden rather than focus, and he imagined it must have to do with a perceived obligation to democratize even the smallest social discussion. There was something compelling about New World discursiveness, particularly in this flat, pleasant prairie city where the trickle-down despair of the century—like the elm beetle—seemed not to have reached; this width of fresh faces, this courtesy, this absurd willingness to offer up an evening from their connubial lives! But he steered back, nevertheless, to his original question. "Why salt?" he said again.

The two lawyers scowled as though pretending to think, and the theologian looked bewildered—in fact, at that moment, though Thornbury could not have known it, a gas pain shot across the man's heart, causing him to abruptly set down his wineglass. A little wine leapt from the glass onto the table-cloth, a pink stain from which eyes were quickly withdrawn.

The local publisher, springy as an athlete, jumped in with, "I expect it's an example of synecdoche, a term my wife's recently introduced me to. She would be able to explain it better than I, but it means that the word *salt*, as used in this case, could imply a broader category—mineral, for instance. Just as," he looked around the table, "just as the apple in the story of Adam and Eve stands for all manner of fruit."

"Hmmmm," said Thornbury, who saw the logic of this but was reluctant to surrender the image of salt—he was a man with a gift for selling his private visions to others, and it piqued him, more than it should, to be diverted.

A number of points were raised. Wasn't salt considered a luxury? Not in the Mediterranean, where salt was plentiful. Wasn't salt a preservative? Perhaps Lot's wife was just being salted away temporarily until she pulled up her socks. (Gruff laughter here, and Thornbury felt for an instant a chill maleness breezing off the fairway.) *Was* there, when it came down to it, such a thing as an actual pillar of salt? The deputy minister cleared his throat at last and said that, yes, indeed there was, and that such pillars occurred naturally in underground caves. It happened that he had been a mining engineer before entering public life, and he and his wife could vouch for such curious structures.

"The injustice of it," sighed the youthful judge, not inappropriately. "Which of us, even Gord here—or our wives—*wouldn't* have looked back when specifically told not to? I'm not sure I'd call that disobedience." He shot the theologian a look. "I'd call it a justifiable compulsion."

"Almost an invitation."

"The gauntlet thrown."

"Absolutely."

"I picture a sort of Ionian column," said the publisher in his speculative way. "With the wind howling around it."

This remark produced a sudden flush of intimacy. "Well," one of the lawyers said, clearly the cleverer one, "what I picture is the female form preserved in the pillar. Like one of those temple goddesses who support the cornices of classical buildings. Last summer my wife and I—"

Thornbury thought of his own wife, Flora, as he had last seen her in London. She was striding away from him at Heathrow, chip-chipping on her high, very slender shoes. He had kissed her lips, something he seldom did in public; she'd been cross with him that day, unexpectedly argumentative and, with some logic, accused him of seizing upon travel as a retreat from difficulty. There was nothing saline about Flora's lips. More like summer fruit, though some would say past ripeness. He recalled the day he first met her. Her hair was a crown of auburn; they had taken a taxi across London, and she had been wearing a rather short skirt which exposed a pair of sharp, carved knees, reminding him, more than any-thing else, of the small shrewd heads of foxes. His hands had wanted to reach out and cover them.

A week ago, at Heathrow, he'd gone through the barrier and turned for a final look at her, wondering almost abstractly whether she would turn at the same moment. She hadn't. She'd walked briskly to the automatic doors and dis-appeared. He'd felt himself stiffen with loneliness. Montreal lay ahead—woods, deep lakes—then Toronto, Winnipeg, Calgary, Vancouver, a stretched follow-the-dot ganglia of effort and rich meals. It was then he thought of Lot's wife, wondering if it had been tears that turned her to salt, her wish to stay rooted in one spot. He was about to risk this thought aloud when he saw that dessert was being served.

Dessert was maple mousse, one of the club specialties, almost always trotted out for foreign guests (or overseas visi-tors, as the somewhat old-fashioned chef would have put it). In Quebec, Thornbury had been served *jambon au sirop d'érable,* in Toronto a bizarre maple liqueur, and he imagined that, esophagus to gut, he soon would be lined with a bed of sweetness. His health, his celebrity, were toasted with brandy.

"I'm sure you gentlemen will be wanting an early night," he said, acting out of the guilt that attaches to guests of honor and imagining the faithful, waiting wives.

It is a trick of perception, he believes, that makes him see these absent wives as faithful. He has absorbed, in the barely glimpsed cities—Melbourne, Perth, Tulsa, Austin, Denver, San Francisco—an impression of marital order, an ongoing pageant celebrating the richness of that phantom, fidelity. A mirage, of course. Sweet and druggy, fleeting as music that leaks from car windows, he breathes it in as a necessary potion. "My wife and I" is a phrase he leaps upon. "My wife said to me—" "My wife read your recent article—" These wives, with their unassailable good faith, have won his love. It's they he thinks about before falling asleep in his first-class hotel rooms, though his dreams are about Flora and the helpless worries that gabble behind him like starved geese. He and Flora had once talked about emigrating. Rhodesia was mentioned, he recalls. Well, that would have been a mistake, anyway.

Good night. A pleasure. An honor. Enchanting. Good night. Within minutes, with almost painful haste, the guests scatter, going out through the heavy club doors into a moist spring night. Only the theologian lingers for a moment. His voice is breathy and excited. He intends to pursue the question of Lot's wife, he tells Thornbury. Why salt, indeed? An interesting question. No doubt one of the biblical commentaries he has at home will have something to say on the subject. He promises to drop Thornbury a line if he discovers anything.

Thornbury looks at the man's round face, its open, large-eared symmetry and nascent jowls, and clearly sees how he must have looked as an infant, imagining first a fair wisp of hair and then the beginnings of a knitted bonnet with matching satin ribbon bow fixing it to his head. He also divines in him an anxious groping toward recognition—someone in the same boat, as *he* might put it—and even a flimsy uprooted reaching for love. What can he say under the circumstances? Speaking from the heart, Flora always says, turns him to pulp.

He pictures the now inevitable postcard winging its way across the Atlantic, its tough little Canadian stamp and post-mark, its cramped, pedantic printing, the horror of a cheery set of exclamation points, hail-fellow-searcher-after-truth. Dear God.

Flora, elegant and angular, will stoop and pick it up, peer at it and say, slippingly, "What's all *this* about salt?" She cannot imagine his life, what it's composed of and how he conspires to preserve it.

Others

FOR THEIR HONEYMOON, Robert and Lila went to France. Neither of them had been to Europe before, but Lila's mother had given them a surprisingly generous check, and they said to each other: Why not?

They started out in Normandy, and their first night there, as they sat puzzling over the menu, a man approached them. He was an English civil servant on holiday. "Excuse me," he said, "I overheard you and your wife speaking English, and I wonder if I might ask an enormous favor of you."

The favor was to cash a personal check—the hotel in the village was being sticky for some reason. Robert agreed to cash it—it was only for fifty pounds—but with some concern. The world, after all, was full of con artists with trustworthy faces, and one couldn't be too careful.

The check went through, however, with no trouble, and the Englishman now sends Robert and Lila Christmas greetings every year. He signs them with a joint signature—Nigel and Jane—and adds a few words about the weather, the state of their health (both his and Jane's) and then thanks them yet again for coming to their rescue in Normandy. This has been going on now for twenty-five years.

————

Lila's grandfather was William White Westfield, the prosperous Toronto lawyer, who, in the twenties, wrote a series of temperance novels that were printed by a church-owned press and distributed free to libraries across Ontario.

When Robert married Lila, her mother's wedding gift was a set of these books—this, of course, was in addition to the honeymoon check. "Even if you never read them, Robert," she said, "I know you'll be amused by the titles."

He was. *Journey to Sobriety, The Good Wife's Victory, A Farewell to Inner Cravings* and, his favorite, *Tom Taylor, Battles and Bottles.* Robert and Lila displayed the books in a little bookcase that Robert made out of bricks and plain pine boards. It gave their apartment a look of solidarity, a glow. They lived, when they were first married, in an old duplex just north of High Park that had three rooms, all painted in deep postwar colors—a purple kitchen, a Wedgwood blue bedroom, and a Williamsburg green living room. That winter they sanded the living-room floor by hand. Later, this became their low-water mark: "Remember when we were so broke we couldn't afford to rent a floor sander?" It took them a whole month, square foot by square foot, to sand their way through the sticky old varnish. Robert, who was preparing for exams, remembers how he would study for an hour—memorizing the names of the cranial nerves or whatever—and then sand for an hour.

When they finished at last with the sanding and with the five coats of wax, and when Robert had passed his examinations, they bought a bottle of cheap wine, and sat in the middle of the shining floor drinking it. Lila lifted her glass toward the shelf of temperance books and said, "Cheers."

"Cheers" was what Nigel and Jane had written on their first Christmas card. Just a simple "Cheers, and again our hearty thanks."

The next winter they wrote, or rather Nigel wrote, "A damp winter, but we've settled into our new house and find it comfortable."

By coincidence, Robert and Lila had moved as well—to a new apartment that had an elevator and was closer to the hospital where Robert was interning. Thinking of Nigel and Jane and their many other friends, Lila arranged to have the mail forwarded to the new address. She missed the old duplex, especially the purple kitchen with its high curving cornices. She suspected Robert of having a cyst of ambition, hard as a nut. She was right. This made her feel lonely and gave her a primal sense of deprivation, but she heard in her head a voice saying that the deprivation was deserved.

It was only at night, when she and Robert lay in each other's arms, that everything slipped back into its proper place. Her skin became mysteriously feathered, like an owl's or some other fast-flying night bird. "Open, open," she begged the dark air of their little bedroom, and often it did.

It was different for Robert, who felt himself settling into marriage like a traveler without provisions. Sleeping with Lila in the first year of their marriage, he often thought: How can I use this moment? What can it teach me?

But finally he let himself be persuaded that he had come under the power of love, and that he was helpless.

Robert and Lila had a baby that was stillborn. It must not be thought of as a tragedy, friends told them; it was nature's way of weeding out the imperfect. They left soon afterward for three weeks in England because they were persuaded that a change of scene would do them good. The flight was very long, but smooth. Fresh Canadian blueberries were served on the plane, and all the passengers piled off, smiling at each other with blue teeth. "We should get in touch with Nigel and Jane," said Lila with her blue mouth.

But when they tried to find them in the telephone book, they discovered they weren't listed. There was nothing to be done. The Christmas cards had carried no return address, only a London postmark, and so Robert and Lila were forced to admit defeat. Both of them were more disappointed than they said.

The year before, Nigel had written: "Our garden gives us great pleasure." Lila had felt envious and wished she had a garden to give her pleasure.

Both Lila and Robert liked to stay in bed on Sunday morning and make love, but occasionally, four or five times a year, they went to church. There was pleasure to be had in passing through a set of wide oak doors into the calm carpeted Protestant sanctuary, and they enjoyed singing the familiar old hymns, Robert for their simple melodies and Lila for their shapely words, which seemed to meet in the final verse like a circle completed. "Reclothe me in my rightful mind," was a phrase she loved, but was puzzled by. What was her rightful mind? All autumn she'd wondered.

At Christmas, the card from England came zipping through the mail slot with the message, "An exceptional winter. Our pond has frozen over completely, and Jane has taken up ice skating, North American style."

Robert read the message over several times. Each inky letter was crisply formed and the *T*s were crossed with merry little banners. "How can they have a pond if they live in London?" he asked. He was thinking about Jane, imagining her whirling and dashing to and fro in a sky blue skating costume and showing a pronounced roundness of thigh.

"Do you have any recollection at all of what Nigel looked like?" Lila asked Robert once, but Robert couldn't remember anything about him except that he had looked respectable and solid, and not much older than himself. Neither of them could remember Jane at all.

Lila took a job teaching in a French school, but quit six weeks later when she discovered she was pregnant. Twin boys were born. They were exquisite, lively and responsive, following with their quick little eyes the faces of their parents, the turning blades of a butterfly mobile and bright lights of all kinds. Robert and Lila carried them into the big chilly Protestant church one rainy Sunday and had them officially christened. The little house they rented filled up overnight with the smell of talcum powder and oats cooking; Robert became an improbable night visitor who smelled dark and cold in his overcoat. From across the ocean come the message: "Summer found us back in Normandy, reliving old memories."

"Where does the time go?" Robert said one morning in a voice that was less a lament than a cry of accomplishment. It seemed to him a good thing for time to pass quickly. He wondered sometimes, when he went off in the mornings, especially in the winter, if work wasn't just a way of coping with time. He also wondered, without jealousy or malice, what kind of salary Nigel pulled down.

They were surprised at how quickly routines and habits accrued. Patterns, rhythms, ways of doing things—they evolved without a need for conscious decision. The labor of the household split itself, not equitably, perhaps, but neatly. Robert ruled over the garage and the cement-linked kingdom of the basement, keeping an ear permanently cocked for the murmuring of machinery and for its occasional small failures.

For Lila there was the house, the children, the bills and the correspondence. The task of writing Christmas cards fell mainly to her. One year she sat down at Grandfather Westfield's roll-top desk and wrote 175 cards. So many friends, so many acquaintances! Still, she paused, lifted her head and melodramatically said to herself, "I am a lonely woman." She wished once again that she knew Nigel and Jane's address so she could send them a snap of the boys and ask them if they had any children—she suspected they didn't, in which case she would like to write them a few words of comfort, perhaps counsel patience.

Nigel had written that year about the coal strike, about a fortnight he and Jane had spent in Scotland, about the flooding of a river near their house.

Eight people were seated around a table. There were candles, Lila had made a salmon mousse and surrounded it with cucumber slices and, after that, there was a leg of lamb, wild rice and fresh asparagus. Robert walked around the table and poured wine. The conversation had taken a curious turn, with each couple recounting the story of their honeymoon. Some of the stories were touched-up sexual burlesques—the red wine brought a slice of the ribald to the table—and some were confused, unedited accounts of misunderstandings or revelations.

Robert and Lila described their month in France, and Robert, making a fine story of it, told the others about the check they had cashed for an English stranger who now sends them Christmas cards.

"And I've saved every single one of them," Lila said.

This surprised Robert, who was proud to be married to a woman who was not a collector of trivia. Lila sent him a wide, apologetic smile across the roasted lamb and a shrug that said: Isn't it absurd, the things we do.

"You took a real chance," someone at the table remarked. "You could have lost the whole bundle."

Robert nodded, agreeing. He thought again as he had thought before, how generous, open and trusting he and Lila must have been in those days. It was an image he cherished, the two of them, lost in their innocence and in each other.

Lila went to visit her mother one day, and they had a quarrel. The argument was over something of no importance, a photograph Lila had misplaced. They both apologized afterward, but Lila cried on her way out to the parking lot, and a man stopped her and said, "Pardon me. You seem to be in distress. May I help you?"

He had a kind, anonymous face. Lila told him she was upset because she had quarreled with someone. The man understood her to mean she had quarreled with a lover, and that was what Lila intended him to understand.

He walked her to her car, held her arm for a moment and said a few kind words. Things would look different in the morning. Things had a way of blowing over. Misunderstandings were inevitable, but sometimes they yielded a deeper sense of the other person.

Lila drove home in that state of benign suspension which can occur when a complete stranger surprises one by an act of intimacy. She felt not only rescued, but deserving of rescue.

Often, she thought how it would be possible to tell Nigel things she could never tell Robert. He would never drum his fingers on the table or interrupt or correct her. He would be patient, attentive and filled with a tender regard for women.

She seldom thought about him concretely, but an impression of him beat at the back of her head, a pocket watch ticking against a silky lining. "Jane has made a splendid recovery," he wrote rather mysteriously at Christmas.

"A wonderful year," Lila wrote to friends at Christmas. "The children are growing so fast."

When she wrote such things, she wondered what happened to all the other parts of her life that could not be satisfyingly annotated. She tried at first to rescue them with a series of graceful, old-fashioned observations, but she soon became tired and discouraged and suspected herself of telling lies.

Robert and Lila acquired a cat, which ran up a tree in a nearby park and refused to come down. "He'll come down when he's good and hungry," Lila assured her children, but several days passed and still the cat refused to descend. At length, Robert dipped a broomstick into a tin of tuna fish and, standing on a ladder, managed to coax the cat down by waving this fragrant wand before his stubborn nose.

A photographer for a Toronto newspaper happened to be standing not ten feet away, and he snapped a picture of Robert in the act of rescue. The picture and story were picked up by a wire service as a human-interest piece a few days later—this was during a quiet spell between elections and hijackings—and appeared on the inside pages of newspapers across the continent. Robert was amazed. He was, he realized, mildly famous, perhaps as famous as he would ever be again. It was not the kind of fame he had imagined for himself and, in fact, he was a little ashamed of the whole episode. Friends phoned from distant cities and congratulated him on his act of heroism. "Yes," Lila said with expansive good humor, "I am indeed married to the illustrious cat rescuer."

Robert couldn't help wondering if the picture had been published in the English dailies, and if Jane had seen it. It might have made her laugh. Jane, Jane. He imagined she was a woman who laughed easily. "Jane and I are both in excellent spirits," a recent Christmas greeting had reported.

Whenever Lila went into a café or restaurant, she slipped the little packets of sugar into her purse, even though she and Robert no longer used sugar. They had grown health conscious. Robert swam laps twice a week at the sports club he joined, and he was making an effort to cut down on martinis. All this dieting and exercise had stripped away his flesh so that when they made love Lila felt his hip bones grinding on hers. She believed she should feel healthier than she did, what with all the expensive, fresh vegetables she carried home and cooked in the special little steamer Robert had brought back from San Francisco.

She wondered if Jane had to watch her figure as carefully as she herself did. She wondered if Jane were attractive. Sometimes, she saw women on the street, women who had a look of Englishness about them, someone wearing a simple linen dress or with straight graying hair. If these women wore perfume, it was something grassy. They were determinedly cheerful; they put a smiling face on everything, keeping life joyful, keeping it puffing along, keeping away from its dark edges. They swallowed their disappointments as though to do so was part of a primordial bargain.

"Jane and I are seriously considering a walking tour of the Hebrides next year," Nigel had written.

Robert applied for a year off in order to do some research on the immune system, but almost from the start things went badly. The data he required accumulated slowly and yielded little that was specific. He learned too late that someone else, someone younger and with a larger grant, was on the same track at Stanford. He insisted on being given computer time in order to correlate his findings, and then discovered he was painfully, helplessly inept at using a computer. He began drifting to his club in the early afternoons to swim laps, or sometimes he drank in the bar and told Lila that he swam laps. His disappointment, his difficulty, his lies, his drunkenness, his life sliding away from him down a long blind chute, made him decide that the time had come to buy a house.

The house was expensive, ten rooms of glass and dark-stained wood cunningly perched on the side of a ravine, but it saved his life, or so he said at the time. He and Lila and the boys moved in at the end of November. As always, when they moved, Lila made careful, tactful, heroic efforts to have their mail forwarded. She looked forward to the barrage of Christmas greetings. Nigel and Jane's card came from the Hebrides that year, just a short note saying, "We made it at last. The birds are magnificent."

Lila had the use of her mother's summer cottage in Muskoka, and she and Robert and the children liked to spend four or five weeks there every summer. There was a particular nightgown she wore at the lake. It was altogether different from her city nightgowns, which were long, sliplike things in shiny materials and in colors such as ivory or melon or plum. The cottage nightgown was white cotton printed with quite large red poppies. There was a ruffle at the neck and another at the feet. On a bigger woman, it would have been comic; it was large, loose, a balloon of a garment.

Robert couldn't imagine where it had come from. It was difficult to think of someone as elegant as Lila actually going out to buy such a thing. She kept it in an old drawer at the cottage, and one summer they arrived and found that a family of mice had built a nest in its flower-strewn folds. The children ran screaming.

"Throw it away," Robert told her.

But she had washed it in the lake with strong detergent and dried it in the sun. "As good as new," she said, after she mended one small hole.

For a week the children called it her mouse gown and refused to touch it.

But Robert loved her in it. How he loved her! The wet, lakey smell was in her hair all summer long, and on her skin. She was his shining girl again, easy and ardent and restored to innocence.

Summer was one thing, but for most of the year Lila and Robert lived in a country too cold for park benches or al fresco dining or cuddling on yachts or unzipping the spirit. They suffered a climate more suitable for sobering insights, for guilt, for the entrenchment of broad streams of angst and darkness.

England, too, was a cold country, yet Nigel wrote: "We've had a cheerless autumn and no summer to speak of, but as long as Jane and I have our books and a good fire, we can't complain."

Just as heavy drinkers gather at parties to condemn others for overindulgence, so Lila lovingly gathered stories of wrecked marriages and nervous breakdowns—as though an accumulation of statistics might guard her sanity and her marriage, as if the sheer weight of disaster would prevent the daily erosion of what she had once called her happiness. She wailed, loudly and frequently, about the numbers of her friends who popped Valium or let their marriages slide into boredom. "I'll go crazy if I hear about one more divorce." She said this mournfully, but with a sly edge of triumph. Her friends' children were taking drugs or running away from home. She could weep, she told Robert, when she looked around and saw the wreckage of human lives.

But she didn't weep. She was, if anything, reaffirmed by disaster. "I ran into Bess Carrier downtown," she told Robert, "and she looked about sixty, completely washed out, devastated. You wouldn't have known her. It was heartbreaking. I get so depressed sometimes. There must be something we can do for her."

Robert knew it would come to nothing, Lila's plans to take Bess Carrier out for lunch or send her flowers or invite her around for a drink. Lila's charity seldom got past the point of corpse-counting these days; it seemed to take most of her time.

No one escaped her outraged pity—except perhaps Nigel and Jane. They were safe, across the ocean, locked into their seasonal rhythms, consumed by their various passions. They were taking Portuguese lessons, they had written. And growing orchids.

Lila loved parties, and she and Robert went to a great many. But when they drove home past lighted houses and streets full of parked cars, she was tormented by the parties she had missed, assuming, as a matter of course, that these briefly glimpsed gatherings glittered with a brighter and kinder light. She imagined rooms fragrant with woodsmoke and fine food—and talk that was both grave and charming. Who could guess what her imagination had cost her over the years?

The same plunging sense of loss struck her each year when she opened the Christmas greeting from Nigel and Jane. Elsewhere, these cards said to her, people were able to live lives of deep trust. How had it happened—that others were able to inhabit their lives with such grace and composure?

"He probably sends out thousands of these things,"

Robert once said to Lila, who was deeply offended. "He must be a bit off his rocker. He must be a real nut."

It was the month of July. Robert bundled the boys into the station wagon, and they drove across the country, camping, climbing in the mountains, cooking eggs and coffee over an open fire, breathing fresh air. Lila went to Rome on a tour with a group from the art gallery. While she was gone, her mother died of heart failure on the platform of the College Street subway station. The moment she collapsed, her straw hat flying into the air, was the same moment when Lila stood in the nave of St. Peter's, looked up into its magisterial vaulting and felt that she had asked too much of life. Like Nigel and Jane, she must try to find a simpler way of being: playing word games at the kitchen table, being attentive to changes in the weather, taking an interest in local history, or perhaps collecting seashells on a beach, taking each one into her hand and minutely examining its color and pattern.

A snowy day. Lila was at home. There was a fire, a pot of Earl Grey and Beethoven being monumentally unpleasant on the record player. She turned the music off and was rewarded by a blow of silence. In the whole of the long afternoon there was not one interruption, not even a phone call. At seven, Robert arrived home and the peace was broken by this peaceful man.

A snowy day. Robert was up at seven. Granola in a bowl given to him by his wife. She was lost in a dream. He would like to have surprised her by saying something startling, but he was convinced, prematurely as it turned out, that certain rhythms of speech had left him forever. He knew this just as he knew that he was unlikely ever again to kiss the inner elbow of a woman and behave foolishly.

A snowy day. Nigel wrote: "We are wrapped in a glorious blizzard, an extraordinary North Pole of a day. Jane and I send good wishes. May you have peace, joy and blessings of every kind."

Loss of faith came at inappropriate times, settling on the brain like a coat of deadly lacquer. Lila thought of her dead baby. Robert thought of his abandoned research. But, luckily, seasonal tasks kept the demons down—the porch to open and clean, the storm windows to see to, the leaves. Robert and Lila always gave a party for the staff in the fall. After the fall party, there were the Christmas things to be done. The children were doing well in school. Soon it would be summer.

Occasionally, in a crowd, in an airport or a restaurant or in the street, Robert would see a woman's face so prepared in its openness for the appeal of passion, tenderness or love, so composed and ready, that he was moved to drop everything and take her in his arms. A thousand times he had been able to resist. Once he had not.

She was a woman not much younger than Lila and not as pretty. His feeling for her was intense and complicated. He was corrupted by the wish to make her happy, and the fact that it took little to make her happy touched him in the same way his children's simple wants had once aroused his extravagant generosity. He had no idea why he loved her. She rode a bicycle and pulled her hair back with a ribbon. Her hair ribbons, her candor, her books and records, and especially her strong rounded arms, put him in mind of Jane. When she closed a book she was reading, she marked her place with a little silk cord and folded her hands, one inside the other, in exactly the same way he imagined Jane would do.

———

Lila was stepping into a taxi on her way to see her lawyer. Nothing she could do, not even the bold, off-hand way she swung her handbag on her shoulder, could hide the touching awkwardness and clumsy surprise of a woman who had been betrayed by someone she loves.

The taxi driver drove through the late-afternoon traffic. "Would you object if I smoke?" he asked Lila, who was embarrassed by his courtesy. She wondered if he had a wife. His shoulder-length hair was clean and more than commonly fine, and on the fingers of his left hand there were three rings, so large and intricate and so brilliantly colored that she was moved to comment on them.

"I go with a girl who did a jewelry course in New Brunswick," he said. "She keeps making me rings. I don't know what I'm going to do if she keeps making me rings."

"Are you going to marry her?" Lila asked. Now that she was taking the first step to dissolve her marriage, she felt she had the right to ask all manner of outrageous questions.

"Marriage?" He paid grave attention to her question. "I don't know about marriage. Marriage is a pretty long haul."

"Yes, it is," Lila said. She rolled down the window and looked at the heavy, late-afternoon sky, which seemed now to form a part of her consciousness. Why wouldn't someone help her? She slumped, turned her face sideways and bit on the bitter vinyl of the upholstery. "Nigel, Nigel," her heart pleaded.

Robert missed his house, he missed his sons and often he missed Lila. Guilt might explain the trembling unease he felt when he stamped the snow off his shoes and rang the bell of what had been his front door. Inside he would find the smell of fresh coffee, that most forgiving of smells, and the spicy chalk smell of adolescent boys. And what else?—the teasing drift of Lila's perfume, a scent that reminded him of grass.

He arrived at nine every Saturday morning, insisting, he said rather quaintly, on doing the household chores. More often than not these chores consisted of tapping on the furnace gauge or putting a listening ear under the hood of Lila's car or filling out some forms for the fire insurance. He did all these things with a good—some would say guilty—heart. He even offered to do the Christmas cards and advise their many, many friends that he and Lila were now separated.

Most of the friends replied with short notes of condolence. Several of them said, "We know what you're going through." Some said, "Perhaps you'll find a way to work things out." One of them, Bess Carrier, wrote, "We've suspected for some time that things weren't right."

Nigel wrote: "We hope this Christmas finds you both joyous and eager for the new year. Time goes so quickly, but Jane and I often think of the two of you, so happy and young in Normandy, and how you found the goodness to come to our aid."

Lila missed Robert, but she didn't miss him all the time. At first, she spent endless hours shopping; all around her, in the department stores, in the boutiques, people were grabbing for the things they wanted. What did she want, she asked herself, sitting before a small fire in the evening and fingering the corduroy of the slipcover. She didn't know.

She rearranged the house, put a chair at an angle, had the piano moved so that the sun struck its polished top. She carried her Grandfather Westfield's temperance novels out of the basement and arranged them on a pretty little table, using a piece of quartz for a bookend. The stone scratched the finish, but she rubbed it with a bit of butter as her mother used to do, and forgot about it. Some days she woke up feeling as light as a girl, and as blameless. The lightness stayed with her all day, and she served her sons plates of soup and sandwiches for dinner. When summer came, she bought herself a pair of white cotton pants and a number of boyish T-shirts. One of them had a message across the front that said "Birds are people too."

She had a great many friends, most of them women, and sometimes it seemed to her that she spent all day talking to these women friends. She wondered now and then how Jane filled her days, if she knitted or visited the sick or what. She wished they could meet. She would tell Jane everything. She would trust her absolutely.

Certain kinds of magazines are filled with articles on how to catch a man and how, having caught him, to keep him happy, keep him faithful, keep him amorous. But Lila and her friends talked mainly about how few men were worth catching and how fewer still were worth keeping. Yet, when Robert asked if he might come back, she agreed.

She would have expected a woman in her situation to feel victorious, but she felt only a crush of exhaustion that had the weight and sound of continuous rain. Robert suggested they get away for a vacation, somewhere hot: Spain or Portugal. (Nigel and Jane had gone to Portugal, where they had spent many hours walking on the beaches.)

Lila said: "Maybe next year." She was too tired to think about packing a suitcase, but next year she was bound to have more energy.

Robert gave Lila an opal ring. Lila gave Robert a set of scuba equipment. Robert gave Lila a book of French poems that he'd found at a garage sale. Lila gave Robert a soft scarf of English wool and put it around his neck and patted it in place, saying, "Merry Christmas."

"Merry Christmas," Robert said back, and to himself he said: There's no place in the world I would rather be at this minute.

The card from England was late, but the buff envelope was reassuringly familiar and so was the picture—a scenic view of Salisbury Plain under a wafery layer of snow. Inside, Nigel had written: "Jane has been in a coma for some months now, but it is a comfort to me that she is not in pain and that she perhaps hears a little of what goes on about her."

Lila read the words several times before they swam into comprehension. Then she phoned Robert at his office. Hearing the news, he slumped forward, put a fist to his forehead and closed his eyes, thinking: *Jane, Jane.*

"How can he bear this?" Lila said several times. *Nigel.*

Later, they sat together in a corner of the quiet living room. A clock ticked on the wall. This room, like the other rooms in the house, was filled with airy furniture and thick rugs. Fragile curtains framed a window that looked out onto a wooded ravine, and beyond the ravine could be seen the tops of apartment buildings. From the triple-paned windows of these apartments one could glimpse a pale sky scratched with weather whorls, and a broad lake that joined, eventually, a wide gray river whose water emptied into the Atlantic Ocean. As oceans go, this was a mild and knowable ocean, with friendly coasts rising smoothly out of the waves and leading directly to white roads, forests and the jointed streets of foreign towns and villages. Both Robert and Lila, each enclosed in a separate vision, could imagine houses filled with lighted rooms, and these rooms—like the one they were sitting in—were softened by the presence of furniture, curtains, carpets, men and women and children, and by that curious human contrivance that binds them together.

They know after all this time about love—that it's dim and unreliable and little more than a reflection on the wall. It is also capricious, idiotic, sentimental, imperfect and inconstant, and most often seems to be the exclusive preserve of others. Sitting in a room that was slowly growing dark, they found themselves wishing they could measure its pure anchoring force or account for its random visitations. Of course they could not—which was why, after a time, they began to talk about other things: the weather, would it snow, would the wind continue its bitter course, would the creek freeze over, would there be another power cut, what would happen during the night.

The Orange Fish

The Orange Fish

LIKE OTHERS OF MY GENERATION I am devoted to food, money and sex, but I have an ulcer and have been unhappily married to Lois-Ann, a lawyer, for twelve years. As you might guess, we are both fearful of aging. Recently Lois-Ann showed me an article she had clipped from the newspaper, a profile of a well-known television actress who was described as being "deep in her thirties."

"That's what we are," Lois-Ann said sadly, "deep in our thirties." She looked at me from behind a lens of tears.

Despite our incompatibility, the two of us understand each other, and I knew more or less what it was she was thinking: that some years ago, when she was twenty-five, she made up her mind to go to Vancouver Island and raise dahlias, but on the very day she bought her air ticket, she got a letter in the mail saying she'd been accepted at law school. "None of us writes our own script," she said to me once, and of course she's right. I still toy—I confess this to you freely—with my old fantasy of running a dude ranch, with the thought of well-rubbed saddles and harnesses and the whole sweet leathery tip of possibility, even though I know the dude market's been depressed for a decade, dead, in fact.

Not long ago, on a Saturday morning, Lois-Ann and I had

one of our long talks about values, about goals. The mood as we sat over breakfast was sternly analytical.

"Maybe we've become trapped in the cult of consumerism and youth worship," I suggested.

"Trapped by our *zeitgeist*," said Lois-Ann, who has a way of capping a point, especially my point.

A long silence followed, twenty seconds, thirty seconds. I glanced up from an emptied coffee cup, remembered that my fortieth birthday was only weeks away, and felt a flare of panic in my upper colon. The pain was hideous and familiar. I took a deep breath as I'd been told to do. Breathe in, then out. Repeat. The trick is to visualize the pain, its substance and color, and then transfer it to a point outside the body. I concentrated on a small spot above our breakfast table, a random patch on the white wall. Often this does the trick, but this morning the blank space, the smooth drywall expanse of it, seemed distinctly accusing.

At one time Lois-Ann and I had talked about wallpapering the kitchen or at least putting up an electric clock shaped like a sunflower. We also considered a ceramic bas-relief of cauliflowers and carrots, and after that a little heart-shaped mirror bordered with rattan, and, more recently, a primitive map of the world with a practical acrylic surface. We have never been able to agree, never been able to arrive at a decision.

I felt Lois-Ann watching me, her eyes as neat and neutral as birds' eggs. "What we need," I said, gesturing at the void, "is a picture."

"Or possibly a print," said Lois-Ann, and immediately went to get her coat.

Three hours later we were the owners of a cheerful lithograph titled *The Orange Fish*. It was unframed, but enclosed in a sandwich of twinkling glass, its corners secured by a set of neat metal clips. The mat surrounding the picture was a generous three inches in width—we liked that—and the background was a shimmer of green; within this space the orange fish was suspended.

I wish somehow you might see this fish. He is boldly drawn, and just as boldly colored. He occupies approximately eighty percent of the surface and has about him a wet, dense look of health. To me, at least, he appears to have stopped moving, to be resting against the wall of green water. A stream of bubbles, each one separate and tear-shaped, floats above him, binding him to his element. Of course, he is seen in side profile, as fish always are, and this classic posture underlines the tranquillity of the whole. He possesses, too, a Buddha-like sense of being in the *right* place, the only place. His center, that is, where you might imagine his heart to be, is sweetly orange in color, and this color diminishes slightly as it flows toward the semi-transparency of fins and the round, ridged, non-appraising mouth. But it was his eye I most appreciated, the kind of wide, ungreedy eye I would like to be able to turn onto the world.

We made up our minds quickly; he would fit nicely over the breakfast table. Lois-Ann mentioned that the orange tones would pick up the colors of the seat covers. We were in a state of rare agreement. And the price was right.

Forgive me if I seem condescending, but you should know that, strictly speaking, a lithograph is not an original work of art, but rather a print from an original plate; the number of prints is limited to ten or twenty or fifty or more, and this number is always indicated on the piece itself. A tiny inked set of numbers in the corner, just beneath the artist's signature, will tell you, for example, that our particular fish is number eight out of an existing ten copies, and I think it pleased me from the start to think of those other copies, the nine brother fish scattered elsewhere, suspended in identical seas of green water, each pointed soberly in the same leftward direction. I found myself in a fanciful mood, humming, installing a hook on the kitchen wall, and hanging our new acquisition. We stepped backward to admire it, and later Lois-Ann made a Spanish omelet with fresh fennel, which we ate beneath the austere eye of our beautiful fish.

As you well know, there are certain necessary tasks that coarsen the quality of everyday life, and while Lois-Ann and I went about ours, we felt calmed by the heft of our solemn, gleaming fish. My health improved from the first day, and before long Lois-Ann and I were on better terms, often sharing workaday anecdotes or pointing out curious items to each other in the newspaper. I rediscovered the girlish angularity of her arms and shoulders as she wriggled in and out of her little nylon nightgowns, smoothing down the skirts with a sly, sweet glance in my direction. For the first time in years she left the lamp burning on the bedside table and, as in our early days, she covered me with kisses, a long nibbling trail up and down the ridge of my vertebrae. In the morning, drinking our coffee at the breakfast table, we looked up, regarded our orange fish, smiled at each other, but were ritualistically careful to say nothing.

We didn't ask ourselves, for instance, what kind of fish this was, whether it was a carp or a flounder or a monstrously out-of-scale goldfish. Its biological classification, its authenticity, seemed splendidly irrelevant. Details, just details; we swept them aside. What mattered was the prismatic disjection of green light that surrounded it. What mattered was that it existed. That it had no age, no history. It simply *was*. You can understand that to speculate, to analyze overmuch, interferes with that narrow gap between symbol and reality, and it was precisely in the folds of that little gap that Lois-Ann and I found our temporary refuge.

Soon an envelope arrived in the mail, an official notice. We were advised that the ten owners of *The Orange Fish* met on the third Thursday evening of each month. The announcement was photocopied, but on decent paper with an appropriate logo. Eight-thirty was the regular time, and there was a good-natured reminder at the bottom of the page about the importance of getting things going punctually.

Nevertheless, we were late. At the last minute Lois-Ann discovered a run in her pantyhose and had to change. I had difficulty getting the car started, and, of course, traffic was heavy. Furthermore, the meeting was in a part of the city that was unfamiliar to us. Lois-Ann, although a clever lawyer, has a poor sense of spatial orientation and told me to turn left when I should have turned right. And then there was the usual problem with parking, for which she seemed to hold me responsible. We arrived at 8:45, rather agitated and out of breath from climbing the stairs.

Seeing that roomful of faces, I at first experienced a shriek in the region of my upper colon. Lois-Ann had a similar shock of alarm, what she afterward described to me as a jolt to her imagination, as though an axle in her left brain had suddenly seized.

Someone was speaking as we entered the room. I recognized the monotone of the born chairman. "It is always a pleasure," the voice intoned, "to come together, to express our concerns and compare experiences."

At that moment the only experience I cared about was the sinuous river of kisses down my shoulders and backbone, but I managed to sit straight on my folding chair and to look alert and responsible. Lois-Ann, in lawyerlike fashion, inspected the agenda, running a little gold pencil down the list of items, her tongue tight between her teeth.

The voice rumbled on. Minutes from the previous meeting were read and approved. There was no old business. Nor any new business. "Well, then," the chairman said, "who would like to speak first?"

Someone at the front of the room rose and gave his name, a name that conveyed the double-pillared boom of money and power. I craned my neck, but could see only a bush of fine white hair. The voice was feeble yet dignified, a persisting quaver from a soft old silvery throat, and I realized after a minute or two that we were listening to a testimonial. A mystical experience was described. Something, too, about the "search for definitions" and about "wandering in the wilderness" and about the historic symbol of the fish in the Western Tradition, a secret sign, an icon expressing providence. "My life has been altered," the voice concluded, "and given direction."

The next speaker was young, not more than twenty, I would say. Lois-Ann and I took in the flare of dyed hair, curiously angled and distinctively punk in style. You can imagine our surprise: here of all places to find a spiked bracelet, black nails, cheeks outlined in blue paint, and a forehead tattooed with the world's most familiar expletive. *The Orange Fish* had been a graduation gift from his parents. The framing alone cost two hundred dollars. He had stared at it for weeks, or possibly months, trying to understand what it meant; then revelation rushed in. "Fishness" was a viable alternative. The orange fins and sneering mouth said no to "all that garbage that gets shoveled on your head by society. So keep swimming and don't take any junk," he wound up, then sat down to loud applause.

A woman in a neatly tailored mauve suit spoke for a quarter of an hour about her investment difficulties. She'd tried stocks. She'd tried the bond market. She'd tried treasury bills and mutual funds. In every instance she found herself buying at the peak and selling just as the market bottomed out. Until she found out about investing in art. Until she found *The Orange Fish.* She was sure, now, that she was on an upward curve. That success was just ahead. Recently she had started to be happy, she said.

A man rose to his feet. He was in his mid-fifties, we guessed, with good teeth and an aura of culture lightly worn. "Let me begin at the beginning," he said. He had been through a period of professional burnout, arriving every day at his office exhausted. "Try to find some way to brighten up the place," he told his secretary, handing her a blank check. *The Orange Fish* appeared the next day. Its effect had been instantaneous: on himself, his staff, and also on his clients. It was as though a bright banner had been raised. Orange, after all, was the color of celebration, and it is the act of celebration that has been crowded out of contemporary life.

The next speaker was cheered the moment he stood. He had, we discovered, traveled all the way from Japan, from the city of Kobe—making our little journey across the city seem trivial. As you can imagine, his accent was somewhat harsh and halting, but I believe we understood something of what he said. In the small house where he lives, he has hung *The Orange Fish* in the traditional tokonoma alcove, just above the black lacquered slab of wood on which rests a bowl of white flowers. The contrast between the sharp orange of the fish's scales and the unearthly whiteness of the flowers' petals reminds him daily of the contradictions that abound in the industrialized world. At this no one clapped louder than myself.

A fish is devoid of irony, someone else contributed in a brisk, cozy voice, and is therefore a reminder of our lost innocence, of the era that predated double meanings and trial balloons. But, at the same time, a fish is more and also less than its bodily weight.

A slim, dark-haired woman, hardly more than a girl, spoke for several minutes about the universality of fish. How three-quarters of the earth's surface is covered with water, and in this water leap fish by the millions. There are people in this world, she said, who have never seen a sheep or a cow, but there is no one who is not acquainted with the organic shape of the fish.

"We begin our life in water," came a hoarse and boozy squawk from the back row, "and we yearn all our days to return to our natural element. In water we are free to move without effort, to be most truly ourselves."

"The interior life of the fish is unknowable," said the next speaker, who was Lois-Ann. "She swims continuously, and is as mute, as voiceless as a dahlia. She speaks at the level of gesture, in circling patterns revived and repeated. The purpose of her eye is to decode and rearrange the wordless world."

"The orange fish," said a voice which turned out to be my own, "will never grow old."

I sat down. Later, my hand was most warmly shaken. During the refreshment hour I was greeted with feeling and asked to sign the membership book. Lois-Ann put her arms around me, publicly, her face shining, and I knew that when we got home she would offer me a cup of cocoa. She would leave the bedside lamp burning and bejewel me with a stream of kisses. You can understand my feeling. Enchantment. Ecstasy. But waking up in the morning we would not be the same people.

I believe we all felt it, standing in that brightly lit room with our coffee cups and cookies: the woman in the tailored mauve suit, the fiftyish man with the good teeth, even the young boy with his crown of purple hair. We were, each of us, speeding along a trajectory, away from each other, and away from that one fixed point in time, the orange fish.

But how helplessly distorted our perspective turned out to be. What none of us could have known that night was that *we* were the ones who were left behind, sheltered and reprieved by a rare congeniality and by the pleasure that each of us feels when our deepest concerns have been given form.

That very evening, in another part of the city, ten thousand posters of the orange fish were rolling off a press. These posters—which would sell first for $10, then $8.49, and later $1.95—would decorate the rumpled bedrooms of teenagers and the public washrooms of filling stations and beer halls. Within a year a postage stamp would be issued, engraved with the image of the orange fish, but a fish whose eye, miniaturized, would hold a look of mild bewilderment. And sooner than any of us would believe possible, the orange fish would be slapped across the front of a Sears flyer, given a set of demeaning eyebrows, and cruelly bisected with an invitation to stock up early on back-to-school supplies.

There can be no turning back at this point, as you surely know. Winking off lapel buttons and earrings, stamped onto sweatshirts and neckties, doodled on notepads and in the margin of love letters, the orange fish, without a backward glance, will begin to die.

Chemistry

IF YOU WERE TO WRITE ME a letter out of the blue, type-written, handwritten, whatever, and remind me that you were once in the same advanced recorder class with me at the YMCA on the south side of Montreal and that you were the girl given to head colds and black knitted tights and whose *Sprightly Music for the Recorder* had shed its binding, then I would, feigning a little diffidence, try to shore up a coarsened image of the winter of 1972. Or was it 1973? Unforgivable to forget, but at a certain distance the memory buckles; those are the words I'd use.

But you will remind me of the stifling pink heat of the room. The cusped radiators under the windows. How Madame Bessant was always there early, dipping her shoulders in a kind of greeting, arranging sheets of music and making those little throat-clearing chirps of hers, getting things organized—for us, everything for us, for no one else.

The light that leaked out of those winter evenings filled the skirted laps of Lonnie Henry and Cecile Landreau, and you, of course, as well as the hollows of your bent elbows and the seam of your upper lip brought down so intently on the little wooden mouthpiece and the bony intimacy of your instep circling in air. You kept time with that circling foot of yours, and also with the measured delay and snap of your chin. We sat in a circle—you will prod me into this remembrance. Our chairs drawn tight together. Those clumsy old-fashioned wooden folding chairs? Dusty slats pinned loosely with metal dowels? A cubist arrangement of stern angles and purposeful curves. Geometry and flesh. Eight of us, counting Madame Bessant.

At seven-thirty sharp we begin, mugs of coffee set to one side. The routines of those weekly lessons are so powerfully set after a few weeks that only the most exigent of emergencies can breach them. We play as one person, your flutey B minor is mine, my slim tonal accomplishment yours. Madame Bessant's blunt womanly elbows rise out sideways like a pair of duck wings and signal for attention. Her fretfulness gives way to authority. *Alors,* she announces, and we begin. Alpine reaches are what we try for. God marching in his ziggurat heaven. Oxygen mists that shiver the scalp. Music so cool and muffled it seems smoothed into place by a thumb. Between pieces we kid around, noodle for clarity, for what Madame Bessant calls roundness of tone, *rondure, rondure.* Music and hunger, accident and intention meet here as truly as they did in the ancient courts of Asia Minor. "*Pas mal,*" nods our dear Madame, taking in breath, not wanting to handicap us with praise; this is a world we're making, after all, not just a jumble of noise.

We don't know what to do with all the amorous steam in the room. We're frightened of it, but committed to making more. We start off each lesson with our elementary Mozart bits and pieces from the early weeks, then the more lugubrious Haydn, then Bach, all texture and caution—our small repertoire slowly expanding—and always we end the evening with an intricate new exercise, something tricky to bridge the week, so many flagged, stepped notes crowded together that the page in front of us is black. We hesitate. Falter.

Apologize by means of our nervy young laughter. "It will come," encourages Madame Bessant with the unlicensed patience of her métier. We read her true meaning: the pledge that in seven days we'll be back here again, reassembled, another Wednesday night arrived at, our unbroken circle. Foul-mouthed Lonnie H. with her starved-looking fingers ascends a steep scale, and you respond, solidly, distinctively, your head arcing back and forth, back and forth, a neat two-inch slice. The contraction of your throat forms a lovely knot of deliberation. (I loved you more than the others, but, like a monk, allowed myself no distinctions.) On and on, the timid fingerings repeat and repeat, picking up the tempo or slowing it down, putting a sonorous umbrella over our heads, itself made of rain, a translucent roof, temporary, provisional—we never thought otherwise, we never thought at all. Madame Bessant regards her watch. How quickly the time. . . .

In Montreal, in January, on a Wednesday evening. The linoleum-floored basement room is our salon, our conservatory. This is a space carved out of the nutty wood of foreverness. Windows, door, music stands and chairs, all of them battered, all of them worn slick and giving up a craved-for weight of classicism. The walls exude a secretive decaying scent, of human skin, of footwear, of dirty pink paint flaking from the pipes. Half the overhead lights are burned out, but it would shame us to complain. To notice. Madame Bessant—who tolerates the creaky chairs, the grudging spotted ceiling globes, our sprawling bodies, our patched jeans, our cigarette smoke, our outdoor boots leaking slush all over the floor, our long, uncombed hair—insists that the door be kept shut during class, this despite the closeness of the overheated air, choking on its own interior odors of jointed ductwork and mice and dirt.

Her baton is a slim metal rod, like a knitting needle—perhaps it *is* a knitting needle—and with this she energetically beats and stirs and prods. At the start of the lessons there seems such an amplitude of time that we can afford to be careless, to chat away between pieces and make jokes about our blunders, always our own blunders, no one else's; our charity is perfect. The room, which by now seems a compaction of the whole gray, silent frozen city, fills up with the reticulation of musical notes, curved lines, spontaneous response, actions and drawn breath. You have one of your head colds, and between pieces stop and shake cough drops, musically, out of a little blue tin.

Something else happens. It affects us all, even Mr. Mooney with his criminal lips and eyes, even Lonnie H., who boils and struts with dangerous female smells. We don't just play the music, we *find* it. What opens before us on our music stands, what we carry in with us on our snow-sodden parkas and fuzzed-up hair, we know for the first time, hearing the notes just as they came, unclothed out of another century when they were nothing but small ink splashes, as tentative and quick on their trim black shelves as the finger Madame Bessant raises to her lips—her signal that we are to begin again, at the beginning, again and again.

She is about forty. Old, in our eyes. Not a beauty, not at all, except when she smiles, which is hardly ever. Her face is a somatic oval with a look of having been handled, molded; a high, oily, worried forehead, but unlined. A pair of eye glasses, plastic framed, and an ardor for clear appraisal that tells you she wore those same glasses, or similar ones, through a long comfortless girlhood, through a muzzy, joyless adolescence, forever breathing on their lenses and attempting to polish them beyond their optical powers, rubbing them on the hems of dragging skirts or the tails of unbecoming blouses.

She has short, straight hair, almost black, and wears silvery ear clips, always the same pair, little curly snails of blackened silver, and loose cheap sweaters that sit rawly at the neck. Her neck, surprisingly, is a stem of sumptuous flesh, pink with health, as are her wrists and the backs of her busy, rhythmically rotating hands. On one wrist is a man's gold watch that she checks every few minutes, for she must be home by ten o'clock, as she frequently reminds us, to relieve the babysitter, a mere girl of fourteen. There are three children at home, all boys—that much we know. Her husband, *a* husband, is not in the picture. Not mentioned, not ever. We sense domestic peril, or even tragedy, the kind of tragedy that bears down without mercy.

Divorce, you think. (This is after class, across the street, drinking beer at Le Piston.) Or widowed. Too young to be a widow, Lonnie H. categorically says. Deserted, maybe. Who says that? One of us—Rhonda? Deserted for a younger, more beautiful woman? This seems possible and fulfills an image of drama and pain we are prepared to embrace; we begin to believe it; soon we believe it unconditionally.

We never talk politics after class, not in this privileged love-drugged circle—we've had enough of politics, more than enough. Our talk is first about Madame Bessant, our tender concern for her circumstances, her children, her babysitter just fourteen years old, her absent husband, her fretful attention to the hour, her sense of having always to hurry away, her coat not quite buttoned or her gloves pulled on. We also discuss endlessly, without a touch of darkness, the various ways each of us has found to circumvent our powerlessness. How to get cheap concert tickets, for instance. How to get on pogey. Ways to ride the Métro free. How to break a lease, how to badger a landlady into repairing the water heater. Where to go for half-priced baked goods. Cecile Landreau is the one who tells us the name of the baked goods outlet. She has a large, clean, ice-maiden face and comes from a little town out west, in Alberta, a town with a rollicking comical name. She gets a laugh every time she mentions it, and she mentions it often. A lively and obstinate girl—you remember—and highly adaptive. She moved to Montreal just one year before, and already she knows where to get things cheap: discount shoes, winter coats direct from the manufacturer, art supplies marked down. She never pays full price. ("You think I'm nuts?") Her alto recorder, a soft pine-colored Yamaha, she bought in a pawn shop for ten dollars and keeps in a pocketed leather case that she made herself in a leathercraft course, also offered at the Y.

The poverty we insinuate is part real and part desire. We see ourselves as accidental survivors crowded to the shores of a cynical economy. By evasion, by mockery, by a mutual nibbling away at substance, we manage to achieve a dry state of asceticism that feeds on itself. We live on air and water or nothing at all; you would think from the misty way we talk we had never heard of parents or cars or real estate or marital entanglements. The jobs we allude to are seasonal and casual, faintly amusing, mildly degrading. So are our living arrangements and our live-in companions. For the sake of each other, out of our own brimming imaginations, we impoverish ourselves, but this is not a burdensome poverty; we exalt in it, and with our empty pockets and eager charity, we're prepared to settle down after our recorder lesson at a corner table in Le Piston and nurse a single beer until midnight.

But Mr. Mooney is something else. Hungry for membership in our ranks, he insists loudly on buying everyone a second round, and a third. Robert is his first name, Robert Mooney. He speaks illiterate French and appalling English.

Reaching into his back pocket for his wallet, a thick hand gripping thick leather, he's cramped by shadows, blurred of feature, older than the rest of us, older by far, maybe even in his fifties, one of those small, compact, sweet-eyed, supple-voiced men you used to see floating around certain quarters of Montreal, ducking behind tabloids or grabbing short ryes or making endless quick phone calls from public booths.

Here in Le Piston, after our recorder lesson, he drops a handful of coins on the table and some bills, each one a transparent, childish offer of himself. My round, he says, without a shred of logic. He has stubby blackened fingers and alien appetites, also built-up shoes to give himself height, brutal hair oil, gold slashes in his back teeth. We drink his beer down fast, without pleasure, ashamed. He watches us, beaming.

All he wants is a portion of our love, and this we refuse. Our reasons are discreditable. His generosity. His age. His burnished leather coat, the way it fits snugly across his round rump. His hair oil and puttied jowls. Stubble, pores, a short thick neck, history. The way the beer foam nudges up against his dark lip. Any minute he's likely to roister or weep or tell a joke about a Jew and a Chinaman or order a plate of *frites*. The joke, if he tells it, we'll absorb without blinking; the *frites* we'll consume down to the last crystal of salt. Dispassionate acts performed out of our need to absolve him. To absolve ourselves.

Robert Mooney is a spoiler, a pernicious interloper who doesn't even show up until the third Wednesday, when we've already done two short Mozart pieces and are starting in on Haydn, but there he is in the doorway, his arms crossed over his boxer's chest. A shuffling awkward silence, then mumbled introductions, and bad grace all around, except for Madame Bessant, who doesn't even notice. Doesn't even *notice.* Our seven stretches to eight. An extra chair is found, clatteringly unfolded and squashed between yours and Pierre's. (Pierre of the cowboy boots and gold earring, as though you need reminding.) Into this chair Mr. Mooney collapses, huffing hard and scrambling with his thick fingers to find his place in the book Madame Bessant kindly lends him until he has an opportunity to buy one of his own.

Layers of incongruity radiate around him: the unsecured history that begs redemption, rough questions stored in silence. How has this man, for instance, this Robert Mooney, acquired a taste for medieval instruments in the first place? And by what manner has he risen to the advanced level? And through what mathematical improbability has he come into contact with Mozart and with the gentle Madame Bessant and the YMCA Winter Enrichment Program and with us, our glare of nonrecognition? When he chomps on his mouthpiece with his moist monkey mouth, we think of cigars or worse. With dwindling inattention he caresses his instrument, which is old and beautifully formed. He fingers the openings clumsily, yet is able to march straight through the first exercise with a rhythm so vigorous and unhesitating you'd think he'd been preparing it for months. He has nothing of your delicacy, of course, nor Pierre's, even, and he can't begin to sight-read the way Rhonda can—remember Rhonda? Of course you remember Rhonda, who could forget her? Mr. Mooney rides roughshod over poor Rhonda, scrambles right past her with his loud marching notes blown sharply forward as if he were playing a solo. "*Bon,*" Madame Bessant says to him after he bursts through to the end of his second lesson. She addresses him in exactly the same tone she uses for us, employing the same little fruited nodes of attention. "Clearly you know how to phrase," she tells him, and her face cracks with a rare smile.

The corners of our mouths tuck in; withholding, despising. But what is intolerable in our eyes is our own intolerance, so shabby and sour beside Madame Bessant's spontaneously bestowed praise. We can't bear it another minute; we surrender in a cloudburst of sentiment. And so, by a feat of inversion, Robert Mooney wins our love and enters our circle, enters it raggedly but forever. His contradictions, his ruptured history, match our own—if the truth were known. Seated at the damp table at Le Piston, he opens his wallet yet again and buys rounds of beer, and at the end of the evening, on a slicked white street, with the moon shrunk down to a chip, we embrace him.

We embrace each other, all of us, a rough huddle of wool outerwear and arms, our cold faces brushing together, our swiftly applied poultice of human flesh.

It was Rhonda of all people, timorous Rhonda, who initiated the ceremonial embrace after our first lesson and trip to Le Piston. Right there on the sidewalk, acting out of who knows what wild impulse, she simply threw open her arms and invited us in. We were shy the first time, not used to being so suddenly enfolded, not knowing where it would lead. We were also young and surprised to be let loose in the world so soon, trailing with us our differently colored branches of experience, terrified at presuming or pushing up too close. If it had been anyone other than Rhonda offering herself, we might have held back, but who could refuse her outspread arms and the particularity of her smooth camel coat? (Do you agree? Tell me yes or no.) The gravest possible pleasure was offered and seized, this hugging, this not-quite kiss.

Already, after three weeks, it's a rite, our end-of-evening embrace, rather solemn but with a suggestion of benediction, each of us taken in turn by the others and held for an instant, a moonlit choreographed spectacle. At this moment our ardor grows dangerous and threatens to overflow. This extemporaneous kind of street-love paralyzes the unsteady. (The youth of the eighties would snort to see it.) One step further and we'd be actors in a shabby old play, too loaded with passion to allow revision. For that reason we keep our embrace short and chaste, but the whole evening, the whole week, in fact, bends toward this dark public commerce of arms and bodies and the freezing murmur that accompanies it. Until next week. Next Wednesday. (A passport, a guarantee of safe conduct.) *A la prochaine.*

One night in early March, Rhonda appears in class with red eyes. The redness matches the long weepy birthmark that starts beneath her left ear and spills like rubbery fluid down the side of her neck.

You glance up at her and notice, then open your big woven bag for a Kleenex. "It's the wind," you say, to spare her. "There's nothing worse than a March wind." We're well into Bach by this time and, of all of us, Rhonda handles Bach with the greatest ease. This you remember, how she played with the unsupported facility that comes from years of private lessons, not that she ever mentions this, not a word of it, and not that we inquire. We've learned, even Mr. Mooney has learned, to fall back and allow Rhonda to lead us through the more difficult passages. But tonight her energy is frighteningly reduced. She falters and slides and, finally, halfway through the new piece, puts down her recorder, just places it quietly on the floor beneath her chair and runs, hobbling unevenly, out of the room.

Madame Bessant is bewildered—her eyes open wide behind her specs—but she directs us to carry on, and we do, limping along to an undistinguished conclusion. Then Lonnie H. goes off in search of Rhonda.

Lonnie H. is a riddle, a paradox. Her hair is as densely, dully orange as the plastic shopping bag in which she carries her portfolio of music and the beaded leather flip-flops she wears during class. That walk of hers—she walks with the savage assurance of the young and combative, but on Wednesday night, at least, she tries to keep her working-class spite in check; you can see her sucking in her breath and biting down on those orange lips.

Later, when we're doing our final exercise, the two of them, Rhonda and Lonnie H., reappear. A consultation has been held in the corridor or in the washroom. Rhonda is smiling fixedly. Lonnie H. is looking wise and sad. "An affair of the heart," she whispers to us later as we put on our coats and prepare to cross the street to Le Piston. An affair of the heart—the phrase enters my body like an injection of sucrose, its improbable sweetness. It's not what we've come to expect of the riddlesome Lonnie. But she says it knowingly—an affair of the heart—and the words soften her tarty tangle-haired look of anarchy, make her almost serene.

Some time later, weeks later or perhaps that very night, I see Pierre with his warpish charm reach under the table at Le Piston and take Rhonda's hand in his. He strokes her fingers as though he possesses the fire of invention. He has a set of neglected teeth, a stammer, and there is something amiss with his scalp, a large roundness resembling, under the strands of his lank Jesus hair, a wreath of pink plastic. His chin is short and witty, his long elastic body ambiguous. The left ear, from which a gold hoop dangles, is permanently inflamed.

It is Pierre who tells us one evening the truth about Madame Bessant's husband. The story has reached him through a private and intricately convoluted family pipeline: the ex-husband of a cousin of Pierre's sister-in-law (or something of this order) once lived in the same apartment block as Monsieur and Madame Bessant, on the same floor, in fact, and remembered that the nights were often disturbed by the noise of crying babies and the sound of Monsieur Bessant, who was a piano teacher, playing Chopin, often the same nocturne again and again, always the same. When the piano playing stopped abruptly one day, the neighbors assumed that someone had complained. There was also a rumor, because he was no longer seen coming or going, that Monsieur Bessant was sick. This rumor was verified one morning, suddenly and terribly, by the news of his death. He had, it seemed, collapsed in a downtown Métro station on a steamy summer day, just toppled off the platform into the path of an approaching train. And one more detail. Pierre swallows as he says it. The head was completely separated from the body.

What are we to do with this story? We sit for some time in silence. It is a story too filled with lesions and hearsay, yet it is also, coming from the artless, stammering Pierre, curiously intact. All its elements fit; its sequence is wholly convincing—Monsieur Bessant, swaying dizzily one minute and cut to ribbons the next, people screaming, the body collected and identified, the family informed, heat rising in waves and deforming the future. Everything altered, changed forever.

"Of course, it might have been a heart attack," Pierre says, wanting now to cancel the whole account and go back to the other, simpler story of an unfeeling husband who abandons his wife for a younger woman.

"Or a stroke," Cecile Landreau suggests. "A stroke is not all that unusual, even for a quite young man. I could tell you stories."

Robert Mooney keeps his eyes on the chilly neck of his beer bottle. And he keeps his mouth clapped shut. All the while the rest of us offer theories for Monsieur Bessant's sudden collapse—heat stroke, low blood sugar—Robert keeps a hard silence. "A helluva shock" is all he says, and then mumbles, "for her."

A stranger entering Le Piston and overhearing us might think we were engaged in careless gossip. And, seeing Pierre reach for Rhonda's hand under the table, might suspect carnal pressure. Or infer something flirtatious about Cecile Landreau, toying with her charm bracelet in a way that solicits our protection. And calculating greed (or worse, condescension) in our blithe acceptance of Robert Mooney's rounds of beer. Lonnie H. in a knitted muffler, pungent with her own bodily scent, could easily be misunderstood and her cynical, slanging raptures misread. A stranger could never guess at the kind of necessity, innocent of the sensual, the manipulative, that binds us together, that has begun as early as that first lesson, when we entered the room and saw Madame Bessant tensely handing out purple mimeographed sheets and offsetting the chaos of our arrival. We were ashamed in those first few minutes, ashamed to have come. We felt compromised, awkward, wanting badly to explain ourselves, why we were there. We came to learn, we might have said had anyone asked, to advance, to go forward, something of that order. Nothing crystallizes good impulses so much as the wish to improve one's self. This is one of the things that doesn't change.

After that first night, we relaxed. The tang of the schoolroom played to our affections, and so did the heat of our closely drawn chairs, knees almost touching so that the folds of your skirt aligned with my thigh, though from all appearances you failed to notice. The fretfulness with which Madame Bessant regarded her watch put us on our honor, declared meanness and mischief out of bounds, demanded that we make the allotted time count—and so we brought our best selves and nothing else. Our youth, our awkwardness, our musical naiveté yoked good will to virtue, as sacredness attaches itself invisibly to certain rare moments.

I exaggerate, I romanticize—I can hear you say this, your smiling reproach. I have already, you claim, given poor Pierre an earring and a stammer, accorded Lonnie H. an orange plastic bag and a sluttish mouth, branded Rhonda with the humiliation of a port-wine birthmark when a small white scar was all she had or perhaps only its psychic equivalent, high up on her cheek, brushed now and then unconsciously with the back of her hand. But there's too much density in the basement room to stop for details.

Especially now, with our time so short, five more weeks, four more weeks. Some nights we linger at Le Piston until well after midnight, often missing the last train home, preferring to walk rather than cut our time short. Three more weeks. Our final class is the fourteenth of May, and we sense already the numbered particles of loss we will shortly be assigned. When we say good night—the air is milder, spring now—we're reminded of our rapidly narrowed perspective. We hang on tighter to each other, since all we know of consequence tells us that we may not be this lavishly favored again.

Lately we've been working hard, preparing for our concert. This is what Madame Bessant calls it—a concert. A little program to end the term. Her suggestion, the first time she utters it—"We will end the season with a concert"—dumbfounds us. An absurdity, an embarrassment. We are being asked to give a recital, to perform. Like trained seals or small children. Called upon to demonstrate our progress. Cecile Landreau's eyebrows go up in protest; her chin puckers the way it does when she launches into one of her picaresque western anecdotes. But no one says a word—how can we? Enigmatic, inconsolable Madame Bessant has offered up the notion of a concert. She has no idea of what we know, that the tragic narrative of her life has been laid bare. She speaks calmly, expectantly; she is innocence itself, never guessing how charged we are by our guilty knowledge, how responsible. The hazards of the grown-up life are settled on her face. We know everything about the Chopin nocturne, repeated and repeated, and about the stumbling collapse on the hot tracks, the severed head and bloodied torso. When she speaks of a concert, we can only nod and agree. Of course there must be a concert.

It is decided, then. We will do nine short pieces. Nothing too onerous, though, the program must be kept light, entertaining.

And who is to be entertained? Madame Bessant patiently explains: we are to invite our friends, our families, and these *invitées* will form an audience for our concert. A *soirée,* she calls it now. Extra chairs have already been requisitioned, also a buffet table, and she herself—she brings her fingers and thumbs together to make a little diamond—she herself will provide refreshments.

This we won't hear of. Lonnie H. immediately volunteers a chocolate cake. Robert Mooney says to leave the wine to him, he knows a dealer. You insist on taking responsibility for a cheese and cold cuts tray. Cecile and Rhonda will bring coffee, paper plates, plastic forks and knives. And Pierre and I, what do we bring?—potato chips, pretzels, nuts? Someone writes all this down, a list. Our final celebratory evening is to be orderly, apt, joyous, memorable.

Everyone knows the fourteenth of May in Montreal is a joke. It can be anything. You can have a blizzard or a heat wave. But that year, our year, it is a warm rainy night. A border of purple collects along the tops of the warehouses across the street from the Y, and pools of oily violet shimmer on the rough pavement, tinted by the early night sky. Only Madame Bessant arrives with an umbrella; only Madame Bessant *owns* an umbrella. Spinning it vigorously, glancing around, setting it in a corner to dry. *Voilà,* she says, addressing it matter-of-factly, speaking also to the ceiling and partially opened windows.

We are all prompt except for Robert Mooney, who arrives a few minutes late with a carton of wine and with his wife on his arm—hooked there, hanging on tight. We see a thick girdled matron with square dentures and a shrub of bronze curls, dense as Brillo pads. Gravely, taking his time, he introduces her to us—"May I present Mrs. Mooney"—preserving the tender secret of her first name, and gently he leads her toward one of the folding chairs, arranging her cardigan around her shoulders as if she were an invalid. She settles in, handbag stowed on the floor, guarded on each side by powerful ankles. She has the hard compact head of a baby lion and a shy smile packed with teeth.

Only Robert Mooney has risked us to indifferent eyes. The rest of us bring no one. Madame Bessant's mouth goes into a worried circle, and she casts an eye across the room, where a quantity of food is already laid out on a trestle table. A cheerful paper tablecloth, bright red in color, has been spread. Also a surprise platter of baby shrimp and ham. Wedges of lemon straddle the shrimp. A hedge of parsley presses against the ham. About our absent guests, we're full of excuses, surprisingly similar—friends who canceled at the last minute, out-of-town emergencies, illness. Madame Bessant shrugs minutely, sighs and looks at her watch. She is wearing a pink dress with large white dots. When eight o'clock comes she clears her throat and says, "I suppose we might as well go through our program anyway. It will be good practice for us, and perhaps Madame Mooney will bear with us."

Oh, we play beautifully, ingeniously, with a strict sense of ceremony, never more alert to our intersecting phrases and spelled out consonance. Lonnie H. plays with her eyes sealed shut, as though dreaming her way through a tranced lifetime, backward and also forward, extending outward, collapsing inward. Your foot does its circling journey, around and around, keeping order. Next to you is Robert Mooney, whose face, as he puffs away, has grown rosy and tender, a little shy, embarrassed by his virtue, surprised by it too. Rhonda's forehead creases into that touching squint of hers. (You can be seduced by such intense looks of concentration; it's that rare.) Cecile's wrist darts forward, turning over the sheets, never missing a note, and Pierre's fingers move like water around his tricks of practiced tension and artful release.

And Mrs. Mooney, our audience of one, listens and nods, nods and listens, and then, after a few minutes, when we're well launched, leans down and pulls some darning from the brocade bag on the floor. A darkish tangle, a lapful of softness. She works away at it throughout our nine pieces. These must be Robert Mooney's socks she's mending, these long dark curls of wool wrapped around her left hand, so intimately stabbed by her darting needle. Her mouth is busy, wetting the thread, biting it off, full of knowledge. Between each of our pieces she looks up, surprised, opens her teeth and says in a good-natured, good-sport voice, "Perfectly lovely." At the end, after the conclusion has been signaled with an extra measure of silence, she stows the socks in the bag, pokes the needle resolutely away, smiles widely with her stretched mouth and begins to applaud.

Is there any sound so strange and brave and ungainly as a single person clapping in a room? All of us, even Madame Bessant, instinctively shrink from the rhythmic unevenness of it, and from the crucial difficulty of knowing when it will stop. If it ever does stop. The brocade bag slides off Mrs. Mooney's lap to the floor, but still she goes on applauding. The furious upward growth of her hair shimmers, and so do the silver veins on the back of her hands. On and on she claps, powerless, it seems, to stop. We half rise, hover in midair, then resume our seats. At last Robert Mooney gets up, crosses the room to his wife and kisses her loudly on the lips. A smackeroo—the word comes to me on little jointed legs, an artifact from another era, out of a comic book. It breaks the spell. Mrs. Mooney looks up at her husband, her hard lion's head wrapped in surprise. "Lovely," she pronounces. "Absolutely lovely."

After that the evening winds down quickly. Rhonda gives a tearful rambling speech, reading from some notes she's got cupped in her hand, and presents Madame Bessant with a pair of earrings shaped, if I remember, like treble clefs. We have each put fifty cents or maybe a dollar toward these earrings, which Madame Bessant immediately puts on, dropping her old silver snails into her coin purse, closing it with a snap, her life beginning a sharp new chapter.

Of course there is too much food. We eat what we can, though hardly anyone touches the shrimp, and then divide between us the quantities of leftovers, a spoiling surfeit that subtly discolors what's left of the evening.

Robert and his wife take their leave. "Gotta get my beauty sleep," he says loudly. He shakes our hands, that little muscular fist, and wishes us luck. What does he mean by luck? Luck with what? He says he's worried about getting a parking ticket. He says his wife gets tired, that her back acts up. "So long, gang," he says, backing out of the room and tripping slightly on a music stand, his whole dark face screwed up into what looks like an obscene wink of farewell.

Madame Bessant, however, doesn't notice. She turns to us, smiling, her odd abbreviated little teeth opening to deliver a surprise. She has arranged for a different babysitter tonight. For once there's no need for her to rush home. She's free to join us for an hour at Le Piston. She smiles shyly; she knows, it seems, about our after-class excursions, though how we can't imagine.

But tonight Le Piston is closed temporarily for renovations. We find the door locked. Brown wrapping paper has been taped across the windows. In fact, when it opens some weeks later it has been transformed into a produce market, and today it's a second-hand bookshop specializing in mysteries.

Someone mentions another bar a few blocks away, but Madame Bessant sighs at the suggestion; the sigh comes spilling out of an inexpressible, segmented exhaustion that none of us understands. She sighs a second time, shifts her shopping bag loaded with leftover food. The treble clefs seem to drag on her ear lobes. Perhaps, she says, she should go straight home after all. Something may have gone wrong. You can never know with children. Emergencies present themselves. She says good night to each of us in turn. There is some confusion, as though she has just this minute realized how many of us there are and what we are called. Then she walks briskly away from us in the direction of the Métro station.

The moment comes when we should exchange addresses and phone numbers or make plans to form a little practice group to meet on a monthly basis, perhaps, maybe in the undeclared territory of our own homes, perhaps for the rest of our lives.

But it doesn't happen. The light does us in, the too-soft spring light. There's too much ease in it, it's too much like ordinary daylight. A drift of orange sun reaches us through a break in the buildings and lightly mocks our idea of finding another bar. It forbids absolutely a final embrace, and something nearer shame than embarrassment makes us anxious to end the evening quickly and go off in our separate directions.

Not forever, of course; we never would have believed that. Our lives at that time were a tissue of suspense with surprise around every corner. We would surely meet again, bump into each other in a restaurant or maybe even in another evening class. A thousand spontaneous meetings could be imagined.

It may happen yet. The past has a way of putting its tentacles around the present. You might—you, my darling, with your black tights and cough drops—you might feel an urge to write me a little note, a few words for the sake of nostalgia and nothing more. I picture the envelope waiting in my mailbox, the astonishment after all these years, the wonder that you tracked me down. Your letter would set into motion a chain of events—since the links between us all are finely sprung and continuous—and the very next day I might run into Pierre on St. Catherine's. What a shout of joy we'd give out, the two of us, after our initial amazement. That very evening a young woman, or perhaps not so very young, might rush up to me in the lobby of a concert hall: Lonnie H., quieter now, but instantly recognizable, that bush of orange hair untouched by gray. The next day I imagine the telephone ringing: Cecile or Rhonda—why not?

We would burrow our way back quickly to those winter nights, saying it's been too long, it's been too bad, saying how the postures of love don't really change. We could take possession of each other once again, conjure our old undisturbed, unquestioning chemistry. The wonder is that it hasn't already happened. You would think we made a pact never to meet again. You would think we put an end to it, just like that—saying goodbye to each other, and meaning it.

Hazel

AFTER A MAN HAS MISTREATED A WOMAN he feels a need to do something nice, which she must accept.

In line with this way of thinking, Hazel has accepted from her husband, Brian, sprays of flowers, trips to Hawaii, extravagant compliments on her rather ordinary cooking, bracelets of dull-colored silver and copper, a dressing gown in green tartan wool, a second dressing gown with marabou trim around the hem and sleeves, dinners in expensive revolving restaurants and, once, a tender kiss, tenderly delivered, on the instep of her right foot.

But there will be no more such compensatory gifts, for Brian died last December of heart failure.

The heart failure, as Hazel, even after all these years, continues to think of it. In her family, the family of her girlhood, that is, a time of gulped confusion in a place called Porcupine Falls, all familiar diseases were preceded by the horrific article: *the* measles, *the* polio, *the* rheumatism, *the* cancer, and—to come down to her husband, Brian, and his final thrashing with life—*the* heart failure.

He was only fifty-five. He combed his uncolored hair smooth and wore clothes made of gabardinelike materials, a silky exterior covering a complex core. It took him ten days to die after the initial attack, and during the time he lay there, all his minor wounds healed. He was a careless man who bumped into things: shrubbery, table legs, lighted cigarettes, simple curbstones. Even the making of love seemed to him a labor and a recovery, attended by scratches, bites, effort, exhaustion and, once or twice, a mild but humiliating infection. Nevertheless, women found him attractive. He had an unhurried, good-humored persistence about him and could be kind when he chose to be.

The night he died, Hazel came home from the hospital and sat propped up in bed till four in the morning, reading a trashy, fast-moving New York novel about wives who lived in spacious duplexes overlooking Central Park, too alienated to carry on properly with their lives. They made salads with rare kinds of lettuce and sent their apparel to the dry cleaners, but they were bitter and helpless. Frequently they used the expression *fucked up* to describe their malaise. Their mothers or their fathers had fucked them up, or jealous sisters or bad-hearted nuns, but mainly they had been fucked up by men who no longer cared about them. These women were immobilized by the lack of love and kept alive only by a reflexive bounce between new ways of arranging salad greens and fantasies of suicide. Hazel wondered as she read how long it took for the remembered past to sink from view. A few miserable tears crept into her eyes, her first tears since Brian's initial attack, that shrill telephone call, that unearthly hour. Impetuously she wrote on the book's flyleaf the melodramatic words "I am alone and suffering unbearably." Not her best handwriting, not her usual floating morning-glory tendrils. Her fingers cramped at this hour. The cheap ballpoint pen held back its ink, and the result was a barely legible scrawl that she nevertheless underlined twice.

By mid-January she had taken a job demonstrating kitchenware in department stores. The ad in the newspaper promised on-the-job training, opportunities for advancement and contact with the public. Hazel submitted to a short, vague, surprisingly painless interview, and was rewarded the following morning by a telephone call telling her she was to start immediately. She suspected she was the sole applicant, but nevertheless went numb with shock. Shock and also pleasure. She hugged the elbows of her dressing gown and smoothed the sleeves flat. She was fifty years old and without skills, a woman who had managed to avoid most of the arguments and issues of the world. Asked a direct question, her voice wavered. She understood nothing of the national debt or the situation in Nicaragua, nothing. At ten-thirty most mornings she was still in her dressing gown and had the sense to know this was shameful. She possessed a softened, tired body and rubbed-looking eyes. Her posture was only moderately good. She often touched her mouth with the back of her hand. Yet someone, some person with a downtown commercial address and an official letterhead and a firm telephone manner had seen fit to offer her a job.

Only Hazel, however, thought the job a good idea.

Brian's mother, a woman in her eighties living in a suburban retirement center called Silver Oaks, said, "Really, there is no need, Hazel. There's plenty of money if you live reasonably. You have your condo paid for, your car, a good fur coat that'll last for years. Then there's the insurance and Brian's pension, and when you're sixty-five—now don't laugh, sixty-five will come, it's not that far off—you'll have your social security. You have a first-rate lawyer to look after your investments. There's no need."

Hazel's closest friend, Maxine Forestadt, a woman of her own age, a demon bridge player, a divorcée, a woman with a pinkish powdery face loosened by too many evenings of soft drinks and potato chips and too much cigarette smoke flowing up toward her eyes, said, "Look. You're not the type, Hazel. Period. I know the type and you're not it. Believe me. All right, so you feel this urge to assert yourself, to try to prove something. I know, I went through it myself, wanting to show the world I wasn't just this dipsy pushover and hanger-on. But this isn't for you, Haze, this eight-to-five purgatory, standing on your feet, and especially *your* feet, your arches; your arches act up just shopping. I know what you're trying to do, but in the long run, what's the point?"

Hazel's older daughter, Marilyn, a pathologist, and possibly a lesbian, living in a women's co-op in the east end of the city, phoned and, drawing on the sort of recollection that Hazel had already sutured, said, "Dad would not have approved. I know it, you know it. I mean, Christ, flogging pots and pans, it's so public. People crowding around. Idle curiosity and greed, a free show, just hanging in for a teaspoon of bloody quiche lorraine or whatever's going. Freebies. People off the street, bums, anybody. Christ. Another thing, you'll have to get a whole new wardrobe for a job like that. Eye shadow so thick it's like someone's given you a punch. Just ask yourself what Dad would have said. I know what he would have said, he would have said thumbs down, nix on it."

Hazel's other daughter, Rosie, living in British Columbia, married to a journalist, wrote: "Dear Mom, I absolutely respect what you're doing and admire your courage. But Robin and I can't help wondering if you've given this decision enough thought. You remember how after the funeral, back at your place with Grandma and Auntie Maxine and Marilyn, we had that long talk about the need to lie fallow for a bit and not to rush headlong into things and make major decisions, just to let the grieving process take its natural course. Now here it is, a mere six weeks later, and you've got yourself involved with these cookware people. I just hope you haven't signed anything. Robin says he never heard of Kitchen Kult, and it certainly isn't listed on the boards. We're just anxious about you, that's all. And this business of working on commission is exploitative to say the least. Ask Marilyn. You've still got your shorthand and typing and, with a refresher course, you probably could find something; maybe Office Overload would give you a sense of your own independence and some spending money besides. We just don't want to see you hurt, that's all."

At first, Hazel's working day went more or less like this: at seven-thirty her alarm went off; the first five minutes were the worst; such a steamroller of sorrow passed over her that she was left as flat and lifeless as the queen-size mattress that supported her. Her squashed limbs felt emptied of blood, her breath came out thin and cool and quiet as ether. What was she to do? How was she to live her life? She mouthed these questions to the silky blanket binding, rubbing her lips frantically back and forth across the stitching. Then she got up, showered, did her hair, made coffee and toast, took a vitamin pill, brushed her teeth, made up her face (going easy on the eye shadow), and put on her coat. By eight-thirty she was in her car and checking her city map.

Reading maps, the tiny print, the confusion, caused her headaches. And she had trouble with orientation, turning the map first this way, then that, never willing to believe that north must lie at the top. North's natural place should be toward the bottom, past the Armoury and stockyards, where a large, cold lake bathed the city edges. Once on a car trip to the Indian River country early in their married life, Brian had joked about her lack of map sense. He spoke happily of this failing, proudly, giving her arm a squeeze, and then had thumped the cushioned steering wheel. Hazel, thinking about the plushy thump, wished she hadn't. To recall something once was to remember it forever; this was something she had only recently discovered, and she felt that the discovery might be turned to use.

The Kitchen Kult demonstrations took her on a revolving cycle of twelve stores, some of them in corners of the city where she'd seldom ventured. The Italian district. The Portuguese area. Chinatown. A young Kitchen Kult salesman named Peter Lemmon broke her in, *familiarizing* her, as he put it, with the Kitchen Kult product. He taught her the spiel, the patter, the importance of keeping eye contact with customers at all times, how to draw on the mood and size of the crowd and play, if possible, to its ethnic character, how to make Kitchen Kult products seem like large, beautiful toys, easily mastered and guaranteed to win the love and admiration of friends and family.

"That's what people out there really want," Peter Lemmon told Hazel, who was surprised to hear this view put forward so undisguisedly. "Lots of love and truckloads of admiration. Keep that in mind. People can't get enough."

He had an aggressive pointed chin and ferocious red sideburns, and when he talked he held his lips together so that the words came out with a soft zither-like slur. Hazel noticed his teeth were discolored and badly crowded, and she guessed that this accounted for his guarded way of talking. Either that or a nervous disposition. Early on, to put him at his ease, she told him of her small-town upbringing in Porcupine Falls, how her elderly parents had never quite recovered from the surprise of having a child. How at eighteen she came to Toronto to study stenography. That she was now a widow with two daughters, one of whom she suspected of being unhappily married and one who was undergoing a gender crisis. She told Peter Lemmon that this was her first real job, that at the age of fifty she was out working for the first time. She talked too much, babbled in fact—why? She didn't know. Later she was sorry.

In return he confided, opening his mouth a little wider, that he was planning to have extensive dental work in the future if he could scrape the money together. More than nine thousand dollars had been quoted. A quality job cost quality cash, that was the long and short of it, so why not take the plunge. He hoped to go right to the top with Kitchen Kult. Not just sales, but the real top, and that meant management. It was a company, he told her, with a forward-looking sales policy and sound product.

It disconcerted Hazel at first to hear Peter Lemmon speak of the Kitchen Kult product without its grammatical article, and she was jolted into the remembrance of how she had had to learn to suppress the article that attached to bodily ailments. When demonstrating product, Peter counseled, keep it well in view, repeating product's name frequently and withholding product's retail price until the actual demo and tasting has been concluded.

After two weeks, Hazel was on her own, although Peter Lemmon continued to meet her at the appointed "sales venue" each morning, bringing with him in a company van the equipment to be demonstrated and helping her "set up" for the day. She slipped into her white smock, the same one every day, a smooth permapress blend with grommets down the front and Kitchen Kult in red script across the pocket, and stowed her pumps in a plastic bag, putting on the white crepe-soled shoes Peter Lemmon had recommended. "Your feet, Hazel, are your capital." He also produced, of his own volition, a tall collapsible stool on which she could perch in such a way that she appeared from across the counter to be standing unsupported.

She started each morning with a demonstration of the Jiffy-Sure-Slicer, Kitchen Kult's top seller, accounting for some sixty percent of total sales. For an hour or more, talking to herself, or rather to the empty air, she shaved hillocks of carrots, beets, parsnips and rutabagas into baroque curls or else she transformed them into little star-shaped discs or elegant matchsticks. The use of cheap root vegetables kept the demo costs down, Peter Lemmon said, and presented a less threatening challenge to the average shopper, Mrs. Peas and Carrots, Mrs. Corn Niblets.

As Hazel warmed up, one or two shoppers drifted toward her, keeping her company—she learned she could count on these one or two, who were elderly women for the most part, puffy of face and bulgy of eye. Widows, Hazel decided. The draggy-hemmed coats and beige tote bags gave them away. Like herself, though perhaps a few years older, these women had taken their toast and coffee early and had been driven out into the cold in search of diversion. "Just set the dial, ladies and gentlemen," Hazel told the discomfited two or three voyeurs, "and press gently on the Jiffy lever. Never requires sharpening, never rusts."

By mid-morning she generally had fifteen people gathered about her, by noon as many as forty. No one interrupted her, and why should they? She was free entertainment. They listened, they exchanged looks, they paid attention, they formed a miniature, temporary colony of good will and consumer seriousness, waiting to be instructed, initiated into Hazel's rituals and promises.

At the beginning of her third week, going solo for the first time, she looked up to see Maxine, in her long beaver coat, gawking. "Now this is just what you need, madam," Hazel sang out, not missing a beat, an uncontrollable smile on her face. "In no time you'll be making more nutritious, appealing salads for your family and friends and for those bridge club get-togethers."

Maxine had been offended. She complained afterward to Hazel that she found it embarrassing being picked out in a crowd like that. It was insulting, especially to mention the bridge club as if she did nothing all day long but shuffle cards. "It's a bit thick, Hazel, especially when you used to enjoy a good rubber yourself. And you know I only play cards as a form of social relaxation. You used to enjoy it, and don't try to tell me otherwise because I won't buy it. We miss you, we really do. I know perfectly well it's not easy for you facing Francine. She was always a bit of a you-know-what, and Brian was, God knows, susceptible, though I have to say you've put a dignified face on the whole thing. I don't think I could have done it; I don't have your knack for looking the other way, never have had, which is why I'm where I'm at, I suppose. But who are you really cheating, dropping out of the bridge club like this? I think, just between the two of us, that Francine's a bit hurt, she thinks you hold her responsible for Brian's attack, even though we all know that when our time's up, it's up. And besides, it takes two."

In the afternoon, after a quick pickup lunch (leftover grated raw vegetables usually or a hard-boiled egg), Hazel demonstrated Kitchen Kult's all-purpose non-stick fry pan. The same crowds that admired her julienne carrots seemed ready to be mesmerized by the absolute roundness of her crepes and omelets, their uniform gold edges and the ease with which they came pulling away at a touch of her spatula. During the early months, January, February, Hazel learned just how easily people could be hypnotized, how easily, in fact, they could be put to sleep. Their mouths sagged. They grew dull-eyed and immobile. Their hands went hard into their pockets. They hugged their purses tight.

Then one afternoon a small fortuitous accident occurred: a

crepe, zealously flipped, landed on the floor. Because of the accident, Hazel discovered how a rupture in routine could be turned to her advantage. "Whoops-a-daisy," she said that first day, stooping to recover the crepe. People laughed out loud. It was as though Hazel's mild exclamation had a forgotten period fragrance to it. "I guess I don't know my own strength," she said, shaking her curls and earning a second ripple of laughter.

After that she began, at least once or twice a day, to misdirect a crepe. Or overcook an omelet. Or bring herself to a state of comic tears over her plate of chopped onions. "Not my day," she would croon. Or "good grief" or "sacred rattlesnakes" or a shrugging, cheerful "who ever promised perfection on the first try?" Some of the phrases that came out of her mouth reminded her of the way people talked in Porcupine Falls back in a time she could not possibly have remembered. Gentle, unalarming expletives calling up wells of good nature and neighborliness. She wouldn't have guessed she had this quality of rubbery humor inside her.

After a while she felt she could get away with anything as long as she kept up her line of chatter. That was the secret, she saw—never to stop talking. That was why these crowds gave her their attention: she could perform miracles (with occasional calculated human lapses) and keep right on talking at the same time. Words, a river of words. She had never before talked at such length, as though she were driving a wedge of air ahead of her. It was easy, *easy*. She dealt out repetitions, little punchy pushes of emphasis, and an ever growing inventory of affectionate declarations directed toward her vegetable friends. "What a devil!" she said, holding aloft a head of bulky cauliflower. "You darling radish, you!" She felt foolish at times, but often exuberant, like a semi-retired, slightly eccentric actress. And she felt, oddly, that she was exactly as strong and clever as she need be.

But the work was exhausting. She admitted it. Every day the crowds had to be wooed afresh. By five-thirty she was too tired to do anything more than drive home, make a sandwich, read the paper, rinse out her Kitchen Kult smock and hang it over the shower rail, then get into bed with a thick paperback. Propped up in bed reading, her book like a wimple at her chin, she seemed to have flames on her feet and on the tips of her fingers, as though she'd burned her way through a long blur of a day and now would burn the night behind her too. January, February, the first three weeks of March. So this was what work was: a two-way bargain people made with the world, a way to reduce time to rubble.

The books she read worked braids of panic into her consciousness. She'd drifted toward historical fiction, away from Central Park and into the Regency courts of England. But were the queens and courtesans any happier than the frustrated New York wives? Were they less lonely, less adrift? So far she had found no evidence of it. They wanted the same things, more or less: abiding affection, attention paid to their moods and passing thoughts, their backs rubbed and, now and then, the tender grateful application of hands and lips. She remembered Brian's back turned toward her in sleep, well covered with flesh in his middle years. He had never been one for pajamas, and she had often been moved to reach out and stroke the smooth mound of flesh. She had not found his extra weight disagreeable, far from it.

In Brian's place there remained now only the rectangular softness of his allergy-free pillow. Its smooth casing, faintly puckered at the corners, had the feel of mysterious absence.

"But why does it always have to be one of my *friends*!" she had cried out at him once at the end of a long quarrel. "Don't you see how humiliating it is for me?"

He had seemed genuinely taken aback, and she saw in a

flash it was only laziness on his part, not express cruelty. She recalled his solemn promises, his wet eyes, new beginnings. She fondly recalled, too, the resonant pulmonary sounds of his night breathing, the steep climb to the top of each inhalation and the tottery stillness before the descent. How he used to lull her to sleep with this nightly music! Compensations. But she had not asked for enough, hadn't known what to ask for, what was owed her.

It was because of the books she read, their dense complications and sharp surprises, that she had applied for a job in the first place. She had a sense of her own life turning over page by page, first a girl, then a young woman, then married with two young daughters, then a member of a bridge club and a quilting club, and now, too soon for symmetry, a widow. All of it fell into small childish paragraphs, the print over-large and blocky like a school reader. She had tried to imagine various new endings or turnings for herself—she might take a trip around the world or sign up for a course in ceramics—but could think of nothing big enough to fill the vacant time left to her—except perhaps an actual job. This was what other people did, tucking in around the edges those little routines—laundry, meals, errands—that had made up her whole existence.

"You're wearing yourself out," Brian's mother said when Hazel arrived for an Easter Sunday visit, bringing with her a double-layered box of chocolate almond bark and a bouquet of tulips. "Tearing all over town every day, on your feet, no proper lunch arrangements. You'd think they'd give you a good hour off and maybe a lunch voucher, give you a chance to catch your breath. It's hard on the back, standing. I always feel my tension in my back. These are delicious, Hazel, not that I'll eat half of them, not with my appetite, but it'll be something to pass round to the other ladies. Everyone shares here, that's one thing. And the flowers, tulips! One or the other would have more than sufficed, Hazel, you've been extravagant. I suppose now that you're actually earning, it makes a difference. You feel differently, I suppose, when it's your own money. Brian's father always saw that I had everything I needed, wanted for nothing, but I wouldn't have minded a little money of my own, though I never said so, not in so many words."

One morning Peter Lemmon surprised Hazel, and frightened her too, by saying, "Mr. Cortland wants to see you. The big boss himself. Tomorrow at ten-thirty. Downtown office. Headquarters. I'll cover the venue for you."

Mr. Cortland was the age of Hazel's son-in-law, Robin. She couldn't have said why, but she had expected someone theatrical and rude, not this handsome curly-haired man unwinding himself from behind a desk that was not really a desk but a gate-legged table, shaking her hand respectfully and leading her toward a soft brown easy chair. There was genuine solemnity to his jutting chin and a thick brush of hair across his quizzing brow. He offered her a cup of coffee. "Or perhaps you would prefer tea," he said, very politely, with a shock of inspiration.

She looked up from her shoes, her good polished pumps, not her nurse shoes, and saw a pink conch shell on Mr. Cortland's desk. It occurred to her it must be one of the things that made him happy. Other people were made happy by music or flowers or bowls of ice cream—enchanted, familiar things. Some people collected china, and when they found a long-sought piece, *that* made them happy. What made *her* happy was the obliteration of time, burning it away so cleanly she hardly noticed it. Not that she said so to Mr. Cortland. She said, in fact, very little, though some dragging filament of intuition urged her to accept tea rather than coffee, to forgo milk, to shake her head sadly over the proffered sugar.

"We are more delighted than I can say with your sales performance," Mr. Cortland said. "We are a small but growing firm and, as you know"—Hazel did not know, how could she?—"we are a family concern. My maternal grandfather studied commerce at McGill and started this business as a kind of hobby. Our aim, the family's aim, is a reliable product, but not a hard sell. I can't stress this enough to our sales people. We are anxious to avoid a crude hectoring approach or tactics that are in any way manipulative, and we are in the process of developing a quality sales force that matches the quality of our product line. This may surprise you, but it is difficult to find people like yourself who possess, if I may say so, your gentleness of manner. People like yourself transmit a sense of trust to the consumer. We've heard very fine things about you, and we have decided, Hazel—I do hope I may call you Hazel—to put you on regular salary, in addition, of course, to an adjusted commission. And I would like also to present you with this small brooch, a glazed ceramic K for Kitchen Kult, which we give each quarter to our top sales person."

"Do you realize what this means?" Peter Lemmon asked later that afternoon over a celebratory drink at Mr. Duck's Happy Hour. "Salary means you're on the team, you're a Kitchen Kult player. Salary equals professional, Hazel. You've arrived, and I don't think you even realize it."

Hazel thought she saw flickering across Peter's guarded, eager face, like a blade of sunlight through a thick curtain, the suggestion that some privilege had been carelessly allocated. She pinned the brooch on the lapel of her good spring coat with an air of bafflement. Beyond the simple smoothness of her paycheck, she perceived dark squadrons of planners and decision makers who had brought this teasing irony forward. She was being rewarded—a bewildering turn of events—for her timidity, her self-effacement, for what Maxine called her knack for looking the other way. She was a shy, ineffectual, untrained, neutral-looking woman, and for this she was being kicked upstairs, or at least this was how Peter translated her move from commission to salary. He scratched his neck, took a long drink of his beer, and said it a third time, with a touch of belligerence, it seemed to Hazel: "a kick upstairs." He insisted on paying for the drinks, even though Hazel pressed a ten-dollar bill into his hand. He shook it off.

"This place is bargain city," he assured her, opening the orange cave of his mouth, then closing it quickly. He came here often after work, he said, taking advantage of the two-for-one happy hour policy. Not that he was tight with his money, just the opposite, but he was setting aside a few dollars a week for his dental work in the summer. The work was mostly cosmetic, caps and spacers, and therefore not covered by Kitchen Kult's insurance scheme. The way he saw it, though, was as an investment in the future. If you were going to go to the top, you had to be able to open your mouth and project. "Like this brooch, Hazel, it's a way of projecting. Wearing the company logo means you're one of the family and that you don't mind shouting it out."

That night, when she whitened her shoes, she felt a sort of love for them. And she loved, too, suddenly, her other small tasks, rinsing out her smock, setting her alarm, settling into bed with her book, resting her head against Brian's little fiber-filled pillow with its stitched remnant of erotic privilege and reading herself out of her own life, leaving behind her cut-out shape, so bulky, rounded and unimaginably mute, a woman who swallowed her tongue, got it jammed down her throat and couldn't make a sound.

Marilyn gave a shout of derision on seeing the company brooch pinned to her mother's raincoat. "The old butter-up trick. A stroke here, a stroke there, just enough to keep you going and keep you grateful. But at least they had the decency to get you off straight commission, for that I have to give them some credit."

"Dear Mother," Rosie wrote from British Columbia. "Many thanks for the waterless veg cooker, which is surprisingly well made and really very attractive too, and Robin feels that it fulfills a real need, nutritionally speaking, and also aesthetically."

"You're looking better," Maxine said. "You look as though you've dropped a few pounds, have you? All those grated carrots. But do you ever get a minute to yourself? Eight hours on the job plus commuting. I don't suppose they even pay for your gas, which adds up, and your parking. You want to think about a holiday; people can't be buying pots and pans 365 days a year. JoAnn and Francine and I are thinking seriously of getting a cottage in Nova Scotia for two weeks. Let me know if you're interested, just tell those Kitchen Kult moguls you owe yourself a little peace and quiet by the seaside, ha! Though you do look more relaxed than the last time I saw you—you looked wrung out, completely."

In early May, Hazel had an accident. She and Peter were setting up one morning, arranging a new demonstration, employing the usual cabbage, beets and onions, but adding a few spears of spring asparagus and a scatter of chopped chives. In the interest of economy she'd decided to split the asparagus lengthwise, bringing her knife first through the tender tapered head and down the woody stem. Peter was talking away about a new suit he was thinking of buying, asking Hazel's advice—should he go all out for a fine summer wool or compromise on wool and viscose? The knife slipped and entered the web of flesh between Hazel's thumb and forefinger. It sliced farther into the flesh than she would have believed possible, so quickly, so lightly that she could only gaze at the spreading blood and grieve about the way it stained and spoiled her perfect circle of cucumber slices.

She required twelve stitches and, at Peter's urging, took the rest of the day off. Mr. Cortland's secretary telephoned and told her to take the whole week off if necessary. There were insurance forms to sign, but those could wait. The important thing was—but Hazel couldn't remember what the important thing was; she had been given some painkillers at the hospital and was having difficulty staying awake. She slept the afternoon away, dreaming of green fields and a yellow sun, and would have slept all evening too if she hadn't been wakened around eight o'clock by the faint buzz of her doorbell. She pulled on a dressing gown, a new one in flowered seersucker, and went to the door. It was Peter Lemmon with a clutch of flowers in his hand. "Why Peter," she said, and could think of nothing else.

The pain had left her hand and moved to the thin skin of her scalp. Its remoteness as much as its taut bright shine left her confused. She managed to take Peter's light jacket—though he protested, saying he had only come for a moment—and steered him toward a comfortable chair by the window. She listened as the cushions subsided under him, and hurried to put the flowers, already a little limp, into water, and to offer a drink—but what did she have on hand? No beer, no gin, and she knew better than to suggest sherry. Then the thought came: What about a glass of red wine?

He accepted twitchily. He said, "You don't have to twist my arm."

"You'll have to uncork it," Hazel said, gesturing at her bandaged hand. She felt she could see straight into his brain, where there was nothing but rags and old plastic. But where had *this* come from, this sly, unpardonable superiority of hers?

He lurched forward, nearly falling. "Always happy to do the

honors." He seemed afraid of her, of her apartment with its settled furniture, lamps and end tables and china cabinet, regarding these things first with a strict, dry, inquiring look. After a few minutes, he resettled in the soft chair with exaggerated respect.

"To your career," Peter said, raising his glass, appearing not to notice how the word *career* entered Hazel's consciousness, waking her up from her haze of painkillers and making her want to laugh.

"To the glory of Kitchen Kult," she said, suddenly reckless. She watched him, or part of herself watched him, as he twirled the glass and sniffed its contents. She braced herself for what would surely come.

"An excellent vin—" he started to say, but was interrupted by the doorbell.

It was only Marilyn, dropping in as she sometimes did after her self-defense course. "Already I can break a collarbone," she told Peter after a flustered introduction, "and next week we're going to learn how to go for the groin."

She looked surprisingly pretty with her pensive, wet, youthful eyes and dusty lashes. She accepted some wine and listened intently to the story of Hazel's accident, then said, "Now listen, Mother, don't sign a release with Kitchen Kult until I have Edna look at it. You remember Edna, she's the lawyer. She's sharp as a knife; she's the one who did our lease for us, and it's airtight. You could develop blood poisoning or an infection, you can't tell at this point. You can't trust these corporate entities when it comes to—"

"Kitchen Kult," Peter said, twirling his glass in a manner Hazel found silly, "is more like a family."

"Balls."

"We've decided," Maxine told Hazel a few weeks later, "against the cottage in Nova Scotia. It's too risky, and the weather's only so-so, according to Francine. And the cost of air fare and then renting a car, we just figured it's too expensive. My rent's going up starting in July and, well, I took a look at my bank balance and said, Maxine kid, you've got to tighten the old belt. As a matter of fact, I thought—now this may surprise you—I'm thinking of looking for a job."

Hazel set up an interview for Maxine through Personnel, and in a week's time Maxine did her first demonstration. Hazel helped break her in. As a result of a dimly perceived office shuffle, she had been promoted to Assistant Area Manager, freeing Peter Lemmon for what was described as "Creative Sales Outreach." The promotion worried her slightly, and she wondered if she was being compensated for the nerve damage in her hand, which was beginning to look more or less permanent. "Thank God you didn't sign the release," was all Marilyn said.

"Congrats," Rosie wired from British Columbia after hearing about the promotion. Hazel had not received a telegram for some years. She was surprised that this austere printed sheet went by the name of telegram. Where was the rough gray paper and the little pasted together words? She wondered who had composed the message, Robin or Rosie, and whose idea it had been to abbreviate the single word, and if thrift were involved. *Congrats.* What a hard little hurting pellet to find in the middle of a smooth sheet of paper.

"Gorgeous," Brian's mother said of Hazel's opal-toned silk suit with its scarf of muted pink, pearl and lemon. Her lips moved appreciatively. "Ah, gorgeous."

"A helluva improvement over a bloody smock," Maxine sniffed, looking sideways.

"Most elegant!" said Mr. Cortland, who had called Hazel into his office to discuss her future with Kitchen Kult. "The sort of image we hope and try to project. Elegance and understatement." He presented her with a small box in which rested, on a square of textured cotton, a pair of enameled earrings with the flying letter K for Kitchen Kult.

"Beautiful," said Hazel, who never wore earrings. The clip-on sort hurt her, and she had never got around to piercing her ears. "For my sake," Brian had begged her when he was twenty-five and she was twenty and about to become his wife, "don't ever do it. I can't bear to lose a single bit of you."

Remembering this, the tone of Brian's voice, its rushing, foolish sincerity, Hazel felt her eyes tingle. "My handbag," she said, groping blindly.

Mr. Cortland misunderstood. He leaped up, touched by his own generosity, a Kleenex in hand. "We simply wanted to show our appreciation," he said, or rather sang.

Hazel sniffed, more loudly than she intended, and Mr. Cortland pretended not to hear. "We especially appreciate your filling in for Peter Lemmon during his leave of absence."

At this Hazel nodded. Poor Peter. She must phone tonight. He was finding the aftermath of his dental surgery painful and prolonged, and she had been looking, every chance she had, for a suitable convalescent card, something not too effusive and not too mocking—Peter took his teeth far too seriously. Perhaps she would just send one of her blurry impressionistic hasty notes, or better yet, a jaunty postcard saying she hoped he'd be back soon.

Mr. Cortland fingered the pink conch shell on his desk. He picked it up between his two hands and rocked it gently to and fro, then said, "Mr. Lemmon will not be returning. We have already sent him a letter of termination and, of course, a generous severance settlement. It was decided that his particular kind of personality, though admirable, was not quite in line with the Kitchen Kult approach, and we feel that you yourself have already demonstrated your ability to take over his work and perhaps even extend the scope of it."

"I don't believe you're doing this," Marilyn shouted over the phone to Hazel. "And Peter doesn't believe it either."

"How do you know what Peter thinks?"

"I saw him this afternoon. I saw him yesterday afternoon. I see him rather often, if you want to know the truth."

Hazel offered the Kitchen Kult earrings to Maxine, who snorted and said, "Come off it, Hazel."

Rosie in Vancouver sent a short note saying, "Marilyn phoned about your new position, which is really marvelous, though Robin and I are wondering if you aren't getting in deeper than you really want to at this time."

Brian's mother said nothing. A series of small strokes had taken her speech away and also her ability to leave her bed. Nothing Hazel brought her aroused her interest, not chocolates, not flowers, not even the fashion magazines she used to love.

Hazel phoned and made an appointment to see Mr. Cortland. She invented a pretext, one or two ideas she and Maxine had worked out to tighten up the demonstrations. Mr. Cortland listened to her and nodded approvingly. Then she sprang. She had been thinking about Peter Lemmon, she said, how much the sales force missed him, missed his resourcefulness and his attention to details. He had a certain imaginative flair, a peculiar usefulness. Some people had a way of giving energy to others, it was uncanny, it was a rare gift. She didn't mention Peter's dental work; she had some sense.

Mr. Cortland sent her a shrewd look, a look she would not have believed he had in his repertoire. "Well, Hazel," he said at last, "in business we deal in hard bargains. Maybe you and I can come to some sort of bargain."

"Bargain?"

"That insurance form, the release. The one you haven't got round to signing yet. How would it be if you signed it right now on the promise that I find some slot or other for Peter Lemmon by the end of the week? You are quite right about his positive attributes, quite astute of you, really, to point them out. I can't promise anything in sales though. The absolute bottom end of management might be the best we can do."

Hazel considered. She stared at the conch shell for a full ten seconds. The office lighting coated it with a pink, even light, making it look like a piece of unglazed pottery. She liked the idea of bargains. She felt she understood them. "I'll sign," she said. She had her pen in her hand, poised.

On Sunday, a Sunday at the height of summer in early July, Hazel drives out to Silver Oaks to visit her ailing mother-in-law. All she can do for her now is sit by her side for an hour and hold her hand, and sometimes she wonders what the point is of these visits. Her mother-in-law's face is impassive and silken, and occasionally driblets of spittle, thin and clear as tears, run from the corners of her mouth. It used to be such a strong, organized face with its firm mouth and steady eyes. But now she doesn't recognize anyone, with the possible exception of Hazel.

Some benefit appears to derive from these hand-holding sessions, or so the nurses tell Hazel. "She's calmer after your visits," they say. "She struggles less."

Hazel is calm too. She likes sitting here and feeling the hour unwind like thread from a spindle. She wishes it would go on and on. A week ago she had come away from Mr. Cortland's office irradiated with the conviction that her life was going to be possible after all. All she had to do was bear in mind the bargains she made. This was an obscene revelation, but Hazel was excited by it. Everything could be made accountable, added up and balanced and fairly, evenly, shared. You only had to pay attention and ask for what was yours by right. You could be clever, dealing in sly acts of surrender, but holding fast at the same time, negotiating and measuring and tying up your life in useful bundles.

But she was wrong. It wasn't true. Her pride had misled her. No one has that kind of power, no one.

She looks around the little hospital room and marvels at the accident of its contents, its bureau and tumbler and toothbrush and folded towel. The open window looks out on to a parking lot filled with rows of cars, all their shining roofs baking in the light. Next year there will be different cars, differently ordered. The shrubs and trees, weighed down with their millions of new leaves, will form a new dark backdrop.

It is an accident that she should be sitting in this room, holding the hand of an old, unblinking, unresisting woman who had once been sternly disapproving of her, thinking her countrified and clumsy. "Hazel!" she had sometimes whispered in the early days. "Your slip strap! Your salad fork!" Now she lacks even the power to wet her lips with her tongue; it is Hazel who touches the lips with a damp towel from time to time, or applies a bit of Vaseline to keep them from cracking. But she can feel the old woman's dim pulse and imagines that it forms a code of acknowledgment or faintly telegraphs certain perplexing final questions. How did all this happen? How did we get here?

Everything is an accident, Hazel would be willing to say if asked. Her whole life is an accident, and by accident she has blundered into the heart of it.

Today Is the Day

TODAY IS THE DAY THE WOMEN of our village go out along the highway planting blisterlilies. They set off without breakfast, not even coffee, gathering at the site of the old well, now paved over and turned into a tot lot and basketball court. The air at this hour is clear. You can breathe in the freshness. And you can smell the moist ground down there below the trampled weeds and baked clay, those eager black glinting minerals waiting, and the pocketed humus. A September morning. A thousand diamond points of dew.

The women carry small spades or else trowels. They talk quietly to each other, but in a murmuring way so that you can't make out the words; all you hear is a sound like cold water continuously falling, as if a faucet were left running into a large and heavy washtub.

At one time the blisterlily grew profusely on its own. By mid-May the shores of the two major lakes in the area were splashed with white, and the slopes leading up to the woods ablaze. It must have been a beautiful, compelling sight, although a single blister blossom is nothing spectacular. It springs up close to the ground like a crocus, its toothed cup of petals demurely white or faintly purple. The small, pointed, pale leaves are equally unprepossessing. By ones or twos the plant is more or less invisible. You'd step right on it if you weren't warned, crush it without knowing. It takes several million of the tiny blisterlily flowers to make an impact. And once, according to the old people of the village, there really were millions.

No one knows for sure what happened. Too much rain or not enough, that's one theory. Or something poisonous in the sunlight, radiation maybe, from the nearby power plant. Or earth tremors. Or insect pests. Or a drop in the annual mean temperature. All sorts and manner of explanations have been put forward: a vicious fungus of the sort that attacks common potatoes or a newly evolved, unkillable virus. Also mentioned is crowding by larger, more aggressive species such as the distantly related blue wort, or the towering castor plant with its prickly seed pods, or the triple-spotted tigerleaf. There is only so much root room available at the earth's surface, and the root, or bulb rather, of the blisterlily is markedly acquiescent. To the eye it may look firm and reliable, an oval of slippery pearl under a loose russety skin, like a smallish onion or a French shallot, but it is actually soft-fleshed and far too obliging for its own good. Under even minimal pressure it shrivels or blisters and loses moisture, that much is known.

All the women of the village take part in the fall planting, including, of course, scrawny old Sally Bakey. Dirty, wearing a torn pinafore, less than four feet in height, it is Sally who discovered a new preserve of virgin blisterlilies in a meadow on the other side of the shiny westward-lying lake. There, where only mice walk, the flowers still grow in profusion, and the bulbs divide year by year as they once did in these parts.

Sally lives alone in a rough cabin on a diet of rolled oats and eggs. Raw eggs, some say. She has a foul smell and shouts obscenely at passersby, especially those who betray by their manner of speech or dress that they are not of the region. But people like her smile. A troll's smile without teeth. In winter, when the snow reaches a certain height, the men of the village take its measure by saying: The snow's up to Sally Bakey's knees. Or over Sally Bakey's bum. Or clear up to Sally Bakey's eyebrows. No one knows how old Sally Bakey is, but she's old enough to remember when churches in the area were left unlocked and when people could go about knocking on any door and ask for a chair to sit down on or for a cup of strong tea.

From the railway bridge you can see the women fanned out along the highway in groups of twos or threes. Some of them work along the verge and others on the median. Right up to the horizon they go. In this part of the country, because the land is low lying and the sun reluctant, the horizon exercises an exceptionally strong influence. It presses downward like a punishing lintel. Every inch of pasture or woodland feels its weight, but roofs and chimneys and porches take the brunt of it, making the houses look squashed and stupid, thick-walled and inhospitable. It never lets up. But today the women, bending and patting their bulbs into place, then standing upright and placing their hands on their hips, taking a moment's rest, bring about a softening of the harsh horizontals. They scatter the light and, from a certain distance, the flexed silver of their bodies appears to pin the dark ground to the lowering sky, the way tablecloths and sheets are pinned to a slackly hung clothesline. There's ease in it, and merriment. Sally Bakey can be heard singing in her crone's cracked voice, a song she invents as she goes along—except for the refrain that is full of ritual cunning and defiance.

The women wear comfortable, practical clothes that are widely dissimilar in style and variously colored. Bright sports clothes. Fringed deerskin. Pants wide and narrow, reaching to the thigh, knee or ankle. Pleated skirts, leather tunics. Rayon blouses. Knitted cardigans. Aprons of terry cloth or linen. Dresses of denim, challis or finely shirred woven cotton. Age and inclination account for these differences.

Those women who are married have removed their wedding rings, and these rings are strung like beads on a length of common kitchen string that is securely knotted to form a necklace. This necklace or wreath or garland, whatever you choose to call it, has been attached to a low branch of a particular blue beech tree—not at all a common tree in the region—situated on a knoll of land north of the overpass. All day long, while the women bury the blisterlilies in the ground, this ring of gold shines in the open air, forming an almost perfect parabolic curve. Birds dive at it, puzzled. Spiders creep on its ridged surfaces and attempt to wrap it with webs. Often they succeed. The younger, unmarried girls, happening near it, glance shyly in its direction, imagining its compounded weight and how it would feel to slip such a necklace over their heads. Unthinkable; even the strongest breezes barely manage to stir it.

The midday meal is taken in the shade of a birch grove, a favored spot. Birches are clean, kindly trees, particularly at this time of year, early fall, with the leaves not quite ready to let go, but thinned down to a soft old chamoislike dryness. There's plenty of room between the trees for the women to spread their blankets, and around the edges of these blankets they sit, talking, eating, with their legs tucked up under them. Everyone brings something, sandwiches, roasted chicken, raw vegetables and flasks of ice water or hot tea. The meal ends with dried apricots, eaten out of the hand like candy. Every year it is the youngest girls who take turns passing the apricots—Sally Bakey is served first—carrying them in a very old wooden bowl that has acquired a deep nutmeggy burnish over time. Some of the women reach up and stroke the slightly irregular sides of the bowl with their fingers, exclaiming over its durability and beauty.

The planting of the blisterlily continues until late afternoon. Between the red-stemmed alder bushes and Indian paintbrush, wild carrot, toadflax, spotted dock, milkweed, Michaelmas daisies, blue chicory, and stands of rare turtlehead lie thousands of newly nested blisterlily bulbs. A few good inches of black soil have been packed on top, enough to give protection through the winter months—seven months in all, for nothing will be seen of the blisterlily until the first week of May, perhaps later if the winter is particularly severe, perhaps not at all if things go badly.

The women, dispersing at the end of the day, resettle their rings on their fingers. Since morning they have been speaking in the old secret language of which, sadly, only eight verbs and some twenty nouns remain—but these they string together inventively, weaving a stratagem of potent suggestion overlain by a wily, votive grammar of sign and silence.

Now they revert to their common tongue and set off for home. Despite their fatigue they go on foot. They feel a chill breeze, notice a graying of the air, field stubble burning somewhere not far off. All that is ordinary and extraordinary about the day converges the minute they cross their separate thresholds. Necessity and order rush together, providing a tent of calm while they go about preparing the simplest of suppers, envelopes of soup and soda crackers, or plain bread and jam.

Sally Bakey, brewing her solitary tea, has an attack of the yawns. She's tired, more tired than anyone who knows her would believe. Shadows move on the wall behind her. Her old bones complain, whimper, and her yawning shades away into an unconscious sifting of images, one burning into another, stubborn and curious. An onion trying to be a flower. A long sleep in the frozen ground. Misgivings. Dread. Unbearable pressure. Cracked earth. The first small faintly colored shoot, surprised by its upright shadow. A hard round waxy bud. Watchfulness. More than watchfulness, a strict and willing observance.

Hinterland

EVERYONE SEEMS TO HAVE STAYED PUT this year except Meg and Roy Sloan of Milwaukee, Wisconsin.

Although both Meg and Roy are patriotic in a vague and non-rhetorical way, and good mature citizens who pay their taxes and vote and hold opinions on gun legislation and abortion, they've chosen this year to ignore the exhortation of their president to stay home and see America first. The Grand Canyon can wait, Roy says in the sociable weekend voice he more and more distrusts. The Black Hills can wait. And the Everglades. And Chesapeake Bay.

And they can wait forever, he privately thinks—with their slopes and depressions and fissured rock and silence and stubborn glare. He and Meg have come this fine golden September, now turned gray, but an endurable gray, to the city of Paris, and have settled down for three weeks in a small hotel near the Place Ferdinand, determined for once to do the thing right.

For the first ten days the sun gives out a soft powdery haze. Then it starts raining, little whips of water dashing down. Beneath their hotel window the streets are stripped of their elongated shadows and stippled light; this is suddenly a differently ordered reality, foreign and purposeful, with a harsh workaday existence and citizens so bound to their routines that they scarcely notice the serious, slightly older, end-of-season tourists, like the Sloans, who are taking in the sights.

Over the years, in the seasonal rounds of business and pleasure and special anniversaries, Meg and Roy Sloan have set foot on most of the continents of the world: Asia, Australia, South America—and, of course, Europe. They have, in fact, been to Paris on two previous occasions: for a single night in 1956, early April, their honeymoon, passing through on their way to Rome; and three days in 1967, an exhausting, hedonistic, aggressive survey that embraced the Moulin Rouge and the Jeu de Paume, Montmartre and Notre Dame, the Comédie Française and Malmaison, and that terminated with the rich, suppressed shame of a dinner in the rue Royale, where they suffered a contemptuous waiter, a wobbly table, scanty servings and a yellow-eyed madame guarding the *toilette* and demanding payment of Meg—who pretended not to understand—and who muttered fiercely into her saucer of coins, *ça commence, ça commence,* meaning Meg Sloan of Milwaukee and the tidal wave of penny-pinching tourists who would follow, the affluent poor, the educationally driven, budget-bound North Americans whom Europeans so resemble but refuse to acknowledge.

And now, in the autumn of 1986, an uneasy, untrustful time in the world's history, the Sloans have returned.

"But why?" quite a number of their friends said. "Why Paris, of all places!"

Meg Sloan is a small, dark, intense woman who, though not Jewish, might easily be thought to be. In any case, it seemed that Americans were singled out by terrorists, regardless of their background: bearded soft-spoken journalists taken hostage, nuns beaten and raped, a harmless old man pushed about and then shot, innocent children propelled through the suddenly gaping side of an aircraft. Why take needless risks, the Sloans' friends said. Why go out of your way to invite disaster? Furthermore, the dollar had taken a rough punch, and you could get better nouvelle cuisine anyway right in Milwaukee, or at least Chicago, and not have to put up with people who were rude and unprincipled—remember that Greenpeace business last summer, still unresolved—besides which, three weeks devoted just to Paris seemed a lot when there was all of Europe to get a feel for.

"We're fatalists," Meg had countered, "and besides, we don't want to live out of a suitcase. Roy and I want to unpack for a change. You know, put our underwear in those big deep dresser drawers they have over there and actually hang up our clothes in one of those gorgeous armoire affairs and come back after a day of sightseeing and get into a bed we can depend on."

"What we'd really like," Roy said, "is to see how the true Parisians live."

In fact, he holds out little hope of this happening. At age fifty-five, the ability to penetrate and explore has left him, perhaps only temporarily—he hopes so. Mainly, as he sees it, he's forgotten how to pay attention, grown somehow incapacitated and lazy. At times he can't believe his own laziness. He chides himself, his sins of omission. He is a man so lazy, so remiss, he couldn't be bothered last spring to step into his own backyard for a glimpse of Halley's comet. Halley's comet won't come again, not in his lifetime—he knows this perfectly well. Unforgivable. Incomprehensible. What is the matter with him?

Both he and Meg were in need of a vacation. The long hot summer of patriotic excess at home had left him with what seemed like a bad case of flu, with aching muscles and slow settling fevers. His head felt stuffed with mineral whiteness:

too many fireworks, too many hours before a TV set regarding the costly clamor over "Lady Liberty"—the epithet drummed hard on the lining of his skull. Who are these buoyant children anyway, he asked himself, addressing the black windows of his living room, and by what power had they turned him peevish and dull and out of tune with his own instincts?

There were other problems too. The Sloans' daughter Jenny had separated from her husband, Kenneth, for reasons not yet fully explained, and returned to the family home, bringing with her from Green Bay her two small children, whose presence had unbalanced the house. Meg's nerves flared up overnight, her old insomnia came back, her eyes grew dry and jittery. Mother and daughter under one roof— the old, old story, which neither of them would have credited, and each too tactful to overstep the other, each so protective of him, Roy (father, husband), that he was continually off-balance and awaiting an explosion that he doubted would ever come.

Then the idea of a vacation presented itself, getting away, the travel agent's mystic croon—a brief respite. A trip, a holiday. Escape. And it seemed, after some initial dithering, the thing to do. September was the worst possible time of the year for Roy to get away, but arrangements could always be— and were—worked out, and he and Meg were free to go anywhere within reason; for some time now money has not really been a hindrance.

They know, though, how to travel thriftily, how to save their receipts and write off what they can as professional expenses. Meg Sloan, for the last ten years or so, has made hand-painted, one-of-a-kind greeting cards, whimsical lines and squiggles on squares of rag paper that retail for five dollars apiece, and she has come to see her trips as opportunities to scout out new ideas. Roy Sloan, who heads a technical college in downtown Milwaukee, makes solemn, uncomfortable forays to similar institutions when traveling abroad, keeping notes on curriculum and entrance requirements and capital costs. These tax write-offs serve as an enabling tactic, since both Roy and Meg grew up in frugal midwestern families and require the assurance that things are not as costly as they appear.

Certainly Paris is far from cheap. Their hotel is small, twenty rooms in all, and inconspicuous, but charges five hundred francs a night, which is one hundred dollars at the current rate. Thirty years ago the young, honeymooning Sloans stayed in this same hotel and paid the grand sum of twelve dollars. "Which included breakfast," says Meg, who, with her merciless memory for the cost of things, equivocates and subtracts and mildly despairs. Admittedly, though, there have been a number of improvements since that time: chiefly, tiny module bathrooms fitted into the corners of each room, and orange juice of an oddly dark hue served along with the croissants and coffee.

For ten days now they've sat at the same little table in the hotel breakfast room and buttered their already buttery croissants and helped themselves to apricot jam. Away from home, Meg abandons her dieting and exercise program. She grows careless and easy about her body, which, in a matter of days, takes on a sleek, milky look. She has a different fragrance about her; her hands wander more rhythmically, almost musically.

Under Roy's knife the croissant shatters, leaving rings of tender flakes on the tablecloth, and one of these she picks up with the moistened tip of her finger and transfers to her tongue. Fresh flowers with tiny blue heads lean out of a glass bottle, an ordinary glass bottle, a vinegar bottle probably.

Their waiter is young, square-jawed, from Holland. He's come to Paris to learn the business, he says, and also the French language, but to the Sloans he speaks a colloquial English, showing off. Clumsy but attentive, he brings a second jug of coffee without being asked, and more hot milk. Meg observes all this with a look of deep satisfaction; she tells Roy how rested and healthy she feels; already it seems she's forgotten she is the mother of a troubled daughter and the grandmother of two wearingly energetic children. Daylight enters the room in blocks and composes tall trembly shapes on the wallpaper behind her head. She is still a pretty woman. Roy wonders how long such prettiness lasts; his feeling is that any day now there will be an abrupt diminishment, and already he has begun to prepare himself for the tasks of pity and persuasion.

Before them, opened up on the table, is the map of Paris. They push the flowers to one side in order to make room, and Meg, with her reading glasses worn low on her nose, is pointing to the little red dot that is the Cluny Museum. Roy nods, takes a pen from his breast pocket and circles the dot. After a while they rise, sigh with contentment, and go into the street, stepping carefully around fresh dog turds, plentiful and perfectly formed, lying everywhere on the roughened oily pavement. They head for the Métro, which is just around the corner.

Arm in arm they swing along. They feel younger in this foreign city, years younger than they do at home. The first few days in Paris were hectic and wasteful, but now everything has settled into a routine, and the two of them descend into the Métro with springy nonchalance, and blithely negotiate the turnstiles. After their first day they'd decided to buy a monthly pass, a *carte orange*, that bears their signature and photograph, and this document, more than anything else, carries them over an invisible frontier and makes them part of the wave of frowning commuters who flow through the gates and take possession of the platform. The Sloans have even acquired something of the Paris look of indifference and suffering, elbows tucked close to the body, feet sturdily planted, eyes directed inward as though recalling past holidays or rehearsing those to come: Brittany, the Alps, the spicy smell of forests, distances and vistas, here and yet not here, the Gallic knack of being everywhere and nowhere, of possessing everything and nothing.

At the entrance to the museum Roy counts out the exact change, thirty-two francs, and Meg opens her handbag automatically for inspection. Today there is the additional precaution of a body search. Smiling, they hold their arms straight out. A young man, who might be a student, frisks Roy by running his hands up and down his sides and between his legs; a broad-faced woman, biting her lips, performs the same swift operation on Meg.

The Sloans have been told that the bombs currently detonated in Paris are the size of three cigarette packets, and they naturally wonder what possible good these cursory inspections can do. They've concluded that the searches are symbolic, evidence that strict security measures are being observed, even though the situation is clearly impossible. Every day for a week now a bombing has occurred in Paris; yesterday the Hotel de Ville, the day before a suburban cafeteria. Armed soldiers, looking absurdly young and pitifully barbered, stand guard on street corners, but there *is* no cure, there *are* no effective measures. The attacks are too random and insidious. The city is too large.

And yet the Sloans show no signs of alarm. They look relaxed and happy and, like everyone else entering the Cluny

Museum this morning, they comply willingly when searched, even smiling at their inquisitors, anxious to demonstrate their innocence, their gratitude for care taken, their concern about the mounting gravity of the crisis, their feeling that, all things considered, America could easily be in a similar plight.

Once inside, arriving at the first of a series of exhibition rooms, they go their separate ways. They do this wordlessly, out of long habit. On the whole they have avoided the dismal symmetry of so many married couples. They confess their differences; they are people who move at different speeds. Their senses are differently angled. Meg's response to works of art is visual or tactile, Roy's is literal. Compulsively he studies titles and dates—stooping, squinting at the tiny print, drawing on his shaky Berlitz French to translate the brief explanations. Meg, on the other hand, stands well back with one hand cupping her chin, looking intently, absorbing and stowing away in some back compartment of her brain various shapes and colors and evolving patterns. She loves texture; she loves curious hand-wrought things; it doesn't matter to her if a tapestry—and the Cluny Museum is filled with tapestries—is six hundred years old or two hundred years. She looks for emblems and symbols and whimsical objects concealed in the muted backgrounds or receding borders, a fish motif, for example, or a mermaid or a lacework construction holding fruit. Whenever some detail strikes her forcefully, she rummages in her handbag for her pen and makes a notation, usually in the form of a little sketch.

Coming together afterward and discussing what they've seen, it's as though the Sloans have attended two separate exhibitions. Today they sit at a small round table in a bistro recommended by one of their many guidebooks, eating a light lunch, a salad of potatoes, watercress and walnuts. The pleasure of travel, Roy thinks, concentrates at these small public tables, he and Meg across from each other, composed for talk as they seldom are at home.

She can be an exasperating companion, nervous in the manner of pretty women, hovering, going off on tangents, sometimes given to finding untruthful reasons for the things she does, but, for all this, he prizes their intimacies. Away from home the boundaries between them loosen. He feels he can say anything, no matter how rambling or speculative, and be understood. She listens and nods. The shine in her eyes flatters him, and he is not, as he sometimes feels at home, a marauder in her busy, bracingly cluttered life. Now, today, she lifts her hands expressively, reversing her wrists, making an airy accompaniment for herself or perhaps for Roy or for the waiter in his floor-length apron. She is describing a particular gilded Virgin she saw this morning at the Cluny Museum. "At the Cluny," she says, innocently breezy, and Roy hears a swarm of echoes: *on the Champs, at the Luxembourg.* How soon his wife is able to slide her tongue around novelty, adopting what comes her way, without hesitation.

"What Virgin?" he asks.

"In that room, you know, that little anteroom where all the coins were."

"I didn't see any coins."

"They were in the same room. At least, I think it was the same room."

"I must have missed it completely."

"It was near the end," she tells him. "You were probably getting saturated, going in circles. I certainly was."

"I suppose I could go back this afternoon." Roy says this doubtfully at first.

"I loved her," says Meg, returning to the Virgin. "I *loved* her. Not that she was beautiful, she was more odd than beautiful.

Her face, I mean. It was sort of frozen and pious, and she had
these young eyes."

"How young?"

"Very. Like a teenager's eyes. They bulged. But the main
thing was her stomach. Or her chest rather. It opened up, two
little golden doors on hinges, beautiful, and inside was this
tiny shelf. It was amazing, like a toy cupboard."

"And?"

"Inside her body, on this shelf—now this is pretty strange—
was a whole crucifixion scene, all carved with little figures,
tiny little things like dolls. I'm not describing it very well,
but—"

He waits. He can smell her perfume across the table and is
reminded of the measure of passion still stored at the heart
of his feeling for her. He has given her this particular perfume, the same bottle every birthday. The buying of it, standing at a counter in a department store in Milwaukee and
counting out bills, never fails to fill him with the skewed
pleasure of the provider. An unwholesome pleasure nowadays, he has no doubt; dishonorable, his daughter Jenny
would say, and something he should long ago have
renounced.

"That's all," Meg says. "There she was, this little golden
teenager, and inside her she was carrying a scene from the
future. Like a video or a time bomb or something. It's the one
thing I'll remember out of all that stuff we saw this morning.
Just her." She presses a hand to her chest, her neat, buttoned
suit jacket. "Opening up like that. It was—what will you
remember?"

The question takes him by surprise. She means to surprise
him, he's sure of it.

"The tapestries," he says finally.

"Which one?" She eyes him closely.

He is a little drunk; too little food with too much wine. Which one? He tries to focus, to think, then gives a helpless lopsided shrug. But Meg is poking in her bag for her address book, too preoccupied now to notice how aptly the gesture reflects his condition.

"Which one?"

"All of them," he says.

After lunch Meg leaves Roy sitting in the bistro.

Her best and oldest friend, Karen Craddock, has given her the address of a warehouse in north Paris where wonderful clothes can be had for a fraction of their retail cost. They are samples, according to Karen, worn once or twice by models in fashion shows, most of them in an American size eight, which is Meg's size—how she cherishes her smallness!—and also her daughter Jenny's.

Roy, whose feet ache, sits for an hour at the little table and makes himself drink two cups of bitter coffee. He reads the *Herald Tribune* carefully, item by item, concentrating, hoping to dispel the chalky pressure behind his eyes. Then he pays, puts on his damp raincoat and retraces his steps, back to the courtyard of the Cluny Museum.

Again he counts out money for a ticket, sixteen francs, wondering if the woman selling tickets is surprised to see him back so soon, such a zealous museum goer, so admirably greedy for an afternoon of art. She is as young as Jenny, with hair combed back roughly and a look on her face of scornful preoccupation. Stacking coins, arranging them in rows, she scarcely looks up. But the inspector, the amiable young guard who searched him earlier in the day, seems to remember him and, with a nod, waves him through.

Along with a light, early afternoon crowd, Roy enters the series of exhibition rooms. There are a great many of them, and they open logically, harmoniously, one into the next, but there are also odd turning points, raised or lowered levels and narrow staircases, a number of which are temporarily closed because of an ambitious archeological excavation going on beneath the building.

He has never had a sense of direction; it is an old family joke, how quickly he becomes lost. Within minutes today he is disoriented, twice returning to an odd, airy room holding the puzzling stone torsos of old kings and saints. He wonders if he should ask for assistance and tries to assemble a reasonable sentence. *Je cherche une vierge avec des portes sur sa poitrine.* Or is it *son poitrine?* Either way it sounds like the request of a madman.

And then, turning a corner, he finds her. She is standing on a rough stone plinth in a corner of a little room behind a glass case of coins, somewhat smaller than he imagined from Meg's description, but yes, the eyes did bulge noticeably, looking heavenward, as though dully unaware of her bright golden belly, her unimaginable destiny. The two gilded doors stand open—Roy imagines they are perpetually open, locked at a forty-five degree angle, summoning the visitor's eye. And inside, like a scene from an old play, the tiny sorrow-bent figures enact their story.

He is not alone. An elderly man and woman, each with copious white hair and each leaning upon a wooden cane, pause, peer inside, and exchange creaky looks of amusement. Close behind them glowers a lean, unpretty woman in a leather coat that she has tried to brighten with a green scarf. She shakes her head and clicks her tongue sharply, perhaps with disapproval, perhaps with wonder—Roy is unable to tell. A moment later he hears the surprise of a deep American voice uttering the words ". . . distortion of time." Someone else, another man, replies with the speed of a ping-pong player, and also the frivolity. "Yes, of course, it does have a primitive feel, but it's actually quite a sophisticated rendering."

Roy steps back so the two men can have a clear view. Both are young, a tall, bony, raincoated pair. One, carries a museum guide and regards the Virgin with hard critical eyes; the other has a priestly face and an expression of reverence. They are brothers, Roy thinks (that bony replication), or else, more probably, lovers. He longs to join in their discussion, if only to claim a bond with them, his fellow travelers. The feeling of belonging to a stalwart, foolhardy minority in an alien land gives Roy at times an unearned sense of the heroic, which he recognizes as absurd. "What do you mean by 'primitive feel'?" he would like to ask, exaggerating his own midwestern vowels, but the two men move off—they seem to glide—leaving him alone with the Virgin.

He sees that her skin beneath the gold is smoothed wood, and her general outlines are stylized and conventional. She is really an ingenious little casket for the improbable sacrifice she bears, but her upward stare now strikes Roy as being impassively self-aware; certain covert bargains made in the past must now be paid for, and this payment, luridly dramatic, is rehearsed behind the pair of peekaboo doors. The silliness of art. The crude approximations. But he is moved, nevertheless, at the way a human life drains toward one revealing scene.

The doors themselves tempt him, especially their neatly worked hinges—but to touch them, he reasons, would probably set off an alarm. The whole museum is sure to be electronically monitored; it would be madness not to, given the current situation. He wonders if Meg had been similarly tempted, and thinks how she is always stopping to shut a bureau drawer, straighten a picture, adjust a chair cushion. She is more than just nervously neat; for Meg the believable world consists of touchable objects, mainly texture and angle and curve, that tremble above and powerfully rule her place in it. Or so he thinks, never having been able, even after all these years, to uncover her separate design or the source of her will.

He looks about and sees no one, though the density of the room seems to have shifted. He senses some material displacement, and at a distance hears what he believes to be the patter of rain falling on the ancient roof, a small fretful slap-slapping against stone. Quickly he reaches out and pushes one of the little doors. The tremor in his hand conveys itself to the mechanism, and it moves obediently in a small silken arc that delights him. But as he pushes it back to its original position, he glimpses, at the periphery of his vision, a uniformed guard approaching.

The guard is wrinkled and stout, with a squashed plum for a nose. The way he tilts his stoutness at Roy gives the impression of a formal, respectful bow, but his face is crimson—with anger, Roy thinks at first—and he speaks in a loud, throaty incomprehensible French and gestures roughly toward the entrance of the room.

Roy, in turn, points to the Virgin. He smiles benignly; he wants to protest that he's done no damage, only indulged a whim. *"Elle est si belle,"* he tries, anxious to placate the reddened face and show himself properly appreciative.

"You must leave the museum," the guard announces loudly.

Roy, amazed to hear a complete English sentence coming out of this cracked old face, defends himself. "I only touched the door," he protests. Then, "I'm very sorry."

"You must leave the museum." Louder this time.

To himself, Roy says: This is ridiculous. He can hardly suppress a laugh. Here he is being scolded, reproved, being thrown out of a venerable French museum as if he were a teenage hooligan. He feels his arm firmly taken at the elbow. The old man's English apparently consists of a single phrase: "You must leave the museum."

Bewildered, Roy looks about, and then suddenly understands. *Everyone* is being asked to leave the museum. The sound that a moment ago he had taken for rain was the sound of footsteps moving across the stone floors, of people rapidly leaving the exhibition rooms and heading for the main door. To the stout old guard, who is already moving away from him, he mumbles a feeble chant—*merci, merci, merci.*

There are fifty, sixty people, maybe more, working their way to the entrance—where had they come from? Moments ago Roy had looked around and seen only a handful.

He is struck at first by how orderly the crowd is and how silently it moves along. Not one person is screaming or shouting—no one, in fact, is even talking—and how similar, too, they all seem in their breathy, melancholy, measured strides, hurrying through the calm rectangular rooms of crusted statuary and large loaf-shaped tombs; the tapestries, the porcelain, the examples of medieval glass, the paintings on wood. There is only a rattling, insectlike sound of clothing rubbing, swishing, long purposeful strides moving in waves, in a single direction.

And then something happens: for no discernible reason the gait changes. As though a signal has been given—but there has been no signal—everyone is running, and Roy too is running, squeezing through the narrow arches that divide the rooms, swerving, stumbling on his thick-soled shoes. Even the white-haired, cane-bearing couple seen earlier has somehow, by awkward shifts of weight and sideways lurching, contrived to run. A fat young woman with wild hair, a child under her arm, its head bobbling crazily, runs past Roy, and out of her frilled lips comes a wordless bleat of panic, an oink like a pig's squeal. And then the two bony American men brush past, one of them knocking against him and breathing a dutiful, constricted *pardon.*

The overhead lights blink several times. Coins jingle in Roy's pocket. As he runs toward the exit, he is thinking of nothing. Or rather, he thinks about how he is thinking of nothing. The cemented accumulation, all he has banked away inside his head, seems suddenly vaporized and lifted; everything outside the minute, *this* minute, falls away, the idle stories that pass through his brain late at night, the alternative choices he might have made, his lazy indifference and absurd fumblings. Newspapers, books, shifts of allegiance. Minor cruelties, a teacher who once said of an essay he'd written, "Where hath grammar flown?" Meg emerging from the house one winter day, fastening her coat. Inca sculpture and lost phone numbers; a brief flirtation with a very young woman, how it came to nothing; snow-banks; trees; Jenny returning early from camp with a rash on her back; Jenny bringing Kenneth home for the first time and saying with light irony, "Meet Mr. Perfect." A platter holding an immense turkey, heartless strategies, unremitting dialogue, the names of certain wild flowers, even the minor present pain of arthritis in his left thumb, a thumb broken at the age of eight, bent backward on the asphalt schoolyard by someone whose name has just this minute slipped away. It has all slipped away. Nothing, not even the smallest spindle of thought, impedes his progress as he runs through room after room toward the main door of the Cluny Museum.

He stumbles at last through the foyer and sees, dreamily, that the ticket booth has been abandoned, the insolent girl vanished. Then he is in the cobbled courtyard, and then the street beyond. There he sees a number of paneled trucks, their windows lowered, the dark squares starred with the faces of boylike soldiers, numbly staring back at him. A few soldiers stand on the pavement, clustered around the main door, and it maddens Roy to see how one of them lolls, *lolls,* against the wall. "What happened?" he asks, but already he knows. Nothing has happened, only a false alarm.

One of the young American men is vomiting quietly into a tub of begonias, and the other, he of the sacerdotal face, is standing by and murmuring, *Jesus, Jesus.* The fat girl with wild hair comes over to Roy and tells him she is from New York, Long Island. Roy explains he is from Milwaukee. The stringent circumstances make their brief exchange feel dreamlike and discordant. The white-haired couple explain they are from California. Their serious leathery faces suggest the pathos of good intentions and an unslaked hunger for human contact. They have been coming to France for twenty years, they tell Roy, and have never seen anything like this.

He walks back to the hotel, telling himself that the fresh air will do him good and, in fact, the rhythm of his shoes on the cement does bring calm—a man in a boy's shoes—as does the sight, a mere two streets away, of people selling melons and entering cafés. A well-brushed dog dances on a leash; its owner dances along behind. Every face Roy sees is clothed with the dumb shine of ignorance. He wonders, already he wonders, how he will describe this scene to Meg; he remembers nothing but the old guard tipping his capacious belly toward him and saying, "You must leave the museum." And how he ran stumbling out of the museum door into the courtyard. He is emptied out, light-headed, agonizingly alert. He feels he's been as close to the edge of his life as he's ever likely to be.

———

Meg and Roy Sloan will not always be sitting here at a little square table in La Petite Fourchette dining on marinated crab, roasted lamb cutlets with green beans, followed by a selection of cheeses, followed by sorbet cassis, followed by coffee and by two glasses of brilliantly colored cognac. The authentic world will sweep them away, attributing their brief incandescence to the lamplight or the shift of weather or the conjoined sense of having escaped what they didn't even know they dreaded.

"Of course you ran," pretty Meg Sloan says to her husband. "Anyone would run. There's nothing shameful about wanting to save your own life. I mean, there's nothing selfish about it or cowardly. If the house were on fire, you'd run out of it, wouldn't you? I know I would. I'd run like crazy."

Her shopping expedition to north Paris has failed. The warehouse, when she finally found it, had been filled with tourists much like herself, women of about her own age and size and possessed of the same financial ease and concentrated fervor. These women carried, too, the accumulated heft of discouragement; the clothes offered for sale were ugly and soiled and brought to mind instances of similar discouragement. Meg tried on one two-hundred-dollar dress that transformed her into an aged dwarf and brought tears to her eyes.

Her diminutive size, her chief vanity, seemed all at once shameful, contrived and unwholesome. She fled to a nearby post office and placed a long-distance call to her daughter in Milwaukee. The call went through quickly, much to her surprise, and caught Jenny in the throes of packing—she had patched things up with Kenneth; an understanding had been reached, a compromise of sorts, and she and the children were about to return to Green Bay. The weather in Wisconsin was glorious, frost at night, but temperatures in the daytime that qualified as Indian summer. The shrubs in the front yard had just started to turn.

Hanging up the telephone, still thrumming with her daughter's voice, its dying vibrancy, Meg had felt divided and dizzy, as though she had stepped into a room where the air was thinned and, at the same time, more tremblingly present. She was afraid she might faint or else choke and, for that reason, took a taxi back to the hotel.

"It was total extravagance," she tells Roy. "When I had my *carte orange* right in my purse. And phoning in the middle of the afternoon like that, at the most expensive time. On an impulse. I just felt—"

"It was money well spent," Roy assures her, knowing he will forever, in one way or another, be called upon for reassurance.

"We talked for ages," Meg then confesses. "I could have bought that hideous dress for the same price."

"Years from now," he tells her, "you'll look back and you'll never count the cost. You won't even remember it."

The Sloans recognize but resist the details of the future, just as Meg knows about but can't see the friable skin of her breasts beneath her white sweater, and Roy the bald, highly burnished spot on the back of his head. They will get older, of course. One of them will die first—the world will allow this to happen—and the other will live on for a time. Their robust North American belief that life consists of stages keeps them from sinking, though ahead of them, in a space the size of this small table, waits a series of intricate compromises: impotence, rusted garden furniture, disordered dreams and the remembrance of specific events, which have been worn smooth and treacherous as the stone steps of ancient buildings. A certain amount of shadowy pathos will accrue between what they remember and what they imagine, and eventually one of them, perhaps lying limply on a tautly made-up bed, will gruesomely sentimentalize this Paris night. The memory will divide and shrink like a bodily protein, and terror, with all its freshness and redemptive power, will give way, easily, easily, to the small rosy singularity of this shaded lamp, and the arc of light that cuts their faces precisely in half.

Block Out

THE WRITER MEERSHANK, vacationing in Portugal with his wife-cum-editor, Maybelle Spritz, became blocked.

The two of them spent their first morning there exploring the coastal city of Porto, which is an airy gemlike city that, as Maybelle complained, had been severely underrated—given one lousy star in the *Michelin Guide,* that was all. This was plain crazy, a single star for a dozen broad sun-splashed terraces, for countless baroque churches, for the elegant iron bridges, and the lazy smoky river lined with pungent fishing boats and dark bars. Ridiculous! She was indignant. She slapped the green guidebook hard against her long thigh. Coming to Portugal had been her idea. She was the one who had thought of flight, of leaving the Ontario winter behind, who had persuaded and cajoled and weakened her husband, Meershank, and she was determined to unearth treasures for him hour by hour. Now this insult, this chintzy rating, a gorgeous city awarded one grudging star.

"And just listen," Maybelle said to Meershank, stopping in the middle of a steep, winding cobbled street to consult the despised guide. "We're supposed to 'note the gaily colored laundry flapping overhead.' Laundry! I ask you. Never mind this incredible architecture all around us, we're asked to gape at mended tablecloths and old underpants."

Meershank looked upward. Was it the word *underpants* that caught his attention? Or Maybelle's brightly injured North American scorn, her admirable readiness to admire, and to deplore the kingly judgments of rubber tire merchants. So what does this uncultivated bunch know from anything? Back in Canada, she told Meershank, the least of these little Portuguese churches would have caused a major fussing over. A plastic dome built to protect the gold leaf and blue tiles. Tickets sold, conducted tours given, voices hushed toward a proper reverence. But here amid the riches of Portugal, tourists were asked to gaze at laundry! The condescension, the perversity! And what did the owners of the laundry have to say about it? Were they consulted about their contribution to the city's ambience? Adjured in the name of folklore to keep their colorful laundry flying? Don't you bet your sweet heart on it.

Socks, sheets, aprons, brassieres. Meershank took them in, groping for a portion of his wife's contempt. He respected cleanliness, that was the problem. He liked the thought of clothes whipped by soapy water and then bright air. Work pants, blankets—and were those diapers? Ah, diapers, yes, half a dozen in a neat row, holding hands as it were. Seeing them he felt, finally, a throat swell—wah!—of delectable sentiment.

That was the moment when his foot slipped. He felt his leg joint pull brutally at its moorings, and for a second he struggled grotesquely for balance, but to no effect. Then he was spread on the stone street, a man of some sixty-five years, lying on his back, his four limbs pointed in four different global directions.

There he rested, as grounded as any being can get, a cartoon splat: Meershank Sprawled.

A prolific and successful writer of comic novels, he immediately thrust about for droll possibilities. None appeared.

He knew only that the separate points of his pain were cleanly pinned down: back-of-head, left buttock, right elbow and a hand that was skinned and already oozing.

Around him gathered a circle of curious, amiable faces, grave but unalarmed. They drew closer. And coming into focus was his wife, Maybelle, squatting at his side. She wore long dangling earrings faced with mirrors, and white Bermuda shorts rucked back to reveal knees and thighs like waxed maple. She was crooning, or should he say keening? He loved her dearly, but had not perceived until now that she was a keening woman. Aieee! On and on; he thought the moment beautiful.

Then he saw *it*. Turning his head a quarter of an inch away from Maybelle's polished knees, he glimpsed the object that had brought him down, the agent of his disgrace. *It* was a piece of common street rubbish, a blackened, stinking, fly-encircled scrap of vegetable matter—a banana peel, no less.

Here was something he hadn't known he feared: the outrageous collision of reality and art, but art in its putrefied form. Even in his earliest novels, those puerile works he no longer bothered to list in *Who's Who* (*Babylon Babydoll, Schlepping Right Along*) he had never fallen so low as to employ a banana peel. True, in his extravagant farce *School for Sandals*, about corruption in the shoemakers' academy, he had brought the class bully, Jack Boot, down on the playing field with a slice of rotted baloney. But baloney was not bananas. There were limits. The lowest comedy has its first plateau morality.

"Do you think you can stand up?" Maybelle was saying into his ear. "Have you broken anything?"

"Just my spirit," Meershank actually said, and winced with shame.

Farther south, in the city of Lisbon, there were more churches to visit. Meershank lost count, but Maybelle made special claims for every last one. "Gorgeous," she said again and again, adding her expelled awe to the jumble of gilded relics and saints' gizzards. In shallow stone niches were dozens of sullen virgins with swords thrust into their chests. "Our Lady of Sorrows," Maybelle read from her *Michelin Guide*. Seven swords for the seven sorrows.

Our Lady?—Meershank's bone marrow liquefied. He is willing enough when required to lower his Hebraic antenna for the sake of art, but rebels at that tetchy pronoun *our*. And the designation *lady* with its suggestion of parasol and gloves. And only seven sorrows? Was that all? Such a nice finite number. She should relax, take it easy. Why this grimacing forbearance? It was embarrassing.

The bruise on his left hip had grown increasingly painful and, standing in the backs of chilly churches, one blue and golden marvel after another, he felt himself going stiff. Maybelle at last looked his way and guessed. "You're exhausted," she said. "We've earned ourselves a good lunch," and hauled him off to a large, clean, expensive restaurant where English was spoken and where they were served cold white wine and grilled sardines so tender and crisp that even the tiny tails begged to be picked up and eaten. Meershank at that instant felt he understood the point of gluttony. Eating, drinking, spreading, appreciating, he entertained a vision of an afternoon nap back at the hotel. A siesta; what could be more appropriate? He smiled across at Maybelle, who smiled back. Smooth sheets waiting to be mussed.

"Now," Maybelle said, not so easily deterred, "for the pièce de résistance."

They took a taxi to the Museum of Ancient Art, hurried past dark oily paintings of the Annunciation, of St. Anthony being tempted and retempted, portraits of sly, chinless burghers and archbishops and several more sword-struck virgins. "Almost there," Maybelle said, pointing, leading Meershank around a corner.

Ah!—there it stood! *The Adoration of St. Vincent.* A howling wall of color. Maybelle, satisfied to have found what she was after, consulted her book. "Thank God! Three stars! At last a little respect."

The six looming panels showed the saints of Portugal in all their homely wide-staring good nature. Meershank, who loved crowds, who respected healthy conviviality, felt instant affection for this mob. Besides saints there were peering, squinting beggars, knights, princes, fishermen, Queen Isabella herself, and a single Jew—all of history's gaudy gang jamming together at an impromptu hour. There was nothing here that could be deconstructed. The faces, the postures, the cheerful way they overlapped and huddled and made human space for each other suggested folks out for a picnic. And the eyes, so strong, serious and clever; the eyes were something else; in the eyes Meershank read a mission to remap the world of good and evil.

Maybelle, lost in her book, whispered something in Meershank's ear.

He croaked back. "Eh?"

"Nuno Gonsalves," she repeated, looking up.

"What's that?"—reverting to the role of curmudgeon abroad.

"The painter. That's his name. Nuno Gonsalves. Fifteenth century." Maybelle was going whispery again. "One of the treasures of Portugal."

"I see." One of the treasures. (That fragrant word.)

"Well, what do you think?" Maybelle hissed. "Pretty damn magnificent, isn't it?"

Meershank's tongue sought a sprig of irony. A pun to stick between his teeth, or a sharp little anachronism, finely sprung, needle-bright. This whispery place needed a dose of irreverence, a dollop of protein, but what?

"Yes," he said to the startled Maybelle, forsaking all verbal horseplay and looking upward. The silver of a tear glinted, and with a straight face he said, "Magnificent."

Prolific Meershank. Fecund and procreative Meershank, fructifying and endlessly flowering. The cornucopia of his imagination spills and pours its lazy plenitude, reseeding itself annually. A book a year, sometimes two. Milch-cowishly he brings them forth—this has been going on for three decades now. *The man needs a stopper for his brain.* Who said that? Who? One of his jealous contemporaries, probably, who else? What a one Meershank is to weave, forge, chisel, carve, invent, turn upside down. His fictions come off the high dive. They shoot the rapids. They burble up out of deep sleep. *Doesn't that man ever rest?* (Again the jaundiced rival, gemmed with malice.)

Of course Meershank worries about his fertility, what fool wouldn't? In his famous parodic novel, *Leapfrog Lottery,* didn't the aging protagonist, also a writer, also a family man, beg for mercy, ask to be manacled, demand a lobotomy and, when all else failed, conspire in the kidnapping and murder of his own word processor? (But true peace came only in the final chapter, when a prestigious writing award brought on a case of instant and permanent paralysis.)

Meershank has never been able to understand the devils that drive him to extravagance, since in his private life he is a man of moderation. He lives in an unpretentious three-bedroom house at Jacksons Point, Ontario. He has exactly two children, well-behaved intelligent daughters, now grown-up.

He has had two wives only, and loved them both; his first marriage of thirty-five years ended with his wife's death, and his second to his editor, Maybelle Spritz, is now in its third year. Maybelle is younger than Meershank, in her early forties, attractive and slender, but hardly in a class with Cécé Valentine. (Cécé, girl-tramp of Meershank's novel *Continuous Purring,* is considered his most Lolita-like creation, abundantly sexed, immoderately luscious, with verbiage fluttering from her lips in a blizzard of concupiscence.) No, Maybelle's wifely moderation matches the Meershank mode, as steadfast and contained as Meershank himself.

So why this writerly excess? Meershank knows immortality lies in a single quatrain, a couplet even, which is why, when he looks at the double shelves of his published books—not including paperbacks or translations—he thinks: silage, ashes. He's been ready for years to cut back, but doesn't know how. What would he do with his expendable time? He wakes in the morning with a headful of chat. It feels like a sinus infection coming on, a mosquito army. The pressure is terrible. He doesn't, has never had, the inclination to relieve the pain with alcohol or tennis. Also out of the question are gardening, long walks, birdwatching, going to the movies, going anywhere, in fact. It took Maybelle feats of timing and melodrama to get him to Portugal. She caught him off guard, between books, and held out the only sure-fire temptation she knew: the promise of material. Portugal could be mined. Gawking tourists could be made to wriggle and squeal. The awful little fates and embarrassments of dislocation could be polished up for chortles, ground down fine for guffaws and snorts, made waxy and pointed with winks and nudges. Well, yes.

But then came the humiliation of the Porto banana peel, and a week later the painting of Nuno Gonsalves, Portugal's treasure.

Meershank, moved by the astonishing work of art, asked Maybelle to show him some more of the artist's work. He snapped his fingers like a tap dancer; might as well take in the lot while he was in town.

"That's it," Maybelle said, stowing the guidebook in her woven bag.

"That's what?"

"*It*. All there is."

"You're kidding. You mean the man painted one picture and quit?"

"As far as anyone knows. That's what's so miraculous. He did it once, and he did it right."

His heart winced. Dear cruel Maybelle. She couldn't know how the words stung. Meershank would have sulked if he hadn't been so tired. His feet were tired, his head was tired. He was tired of art, tired of travel, tired of the big golden sun shining on his bare head. Enough already. One more week and he could go home.

His brain especially was in bad shape, stuffed up with sadness and red dust. Waking early in strange hotels he found himself running a cheering video through his head: his own bed back home, Maybelle in the kitchen aggressively juicing a pair of oranges, the view from their back window down the long snow-covered slope of yard, the furnace doing its sweet business day in and day out.

The high-tech quality of his reveries made him ashamed but happy, especially the flicker of his own surprising image, for there he was in his old red cardigan, still at the kitchen window, indolent, sipping cold coffee to damp down the dust, staring happily at a rectangle of sky. His desk and his word processor, it seemed, had vanished. There was nothing there but a poor old idle duffer—himself—smiling.

On their second-to-last day in Portugal, Meershank and Maybelle came across something odd. This was in the old city of Braga, in the famous cathedral. There, on the altar of one of the side chapels, they saw dozens of human parts molded in wax. "They're called *ex votos*," whispered Maybelle, quoting from the merciless guidebook. "They're sort of like concrete prayers, you might say."

Among the clutter Meershank saw wax legs, wax ears, wax hands, wax breasts, kidneys and hearts. Presumably these pale yellow bodily facsimiles had been placed at the feet of the Virgin in the hope of invoking miraculous healing. Some of them were gray with dust and fly dirt and looked as though they had lain there for years. Meershank stood well back. He found something hideous, but also innocent about their naked abandonment. He stared, then touched. The deposition, stiffened and discolored, had nothing left of original pleading, but only a candid, almost careless resignation. He found himself wanting to dive into that carelessness, to merge with it. To throw up his hands in the old classic gesture of defeat, open-palmed: so be it.

The next day, leaving Portugal, stepping with Maybelle aboard the Boeing 747 and allowing himself to be strapped in by a strapping air hostess, Meershank felt, happily, that he too had left something behind; his hands lay majestic and idle on his lap. Then the bulk of his body rose in the air, carrying with it its new lightness and sudden tight band of silence.

He loved his writer's block. Back home he found that the affliction fit him perfectly, the way a chestful of air fills a baritone's lungs. This was a silence that could be settled into. Some of life's essence stirred in it. He embraced it wholly, though for Maybelle's sake he put on a stricken face, especially in the mornings, meeting her agitated concern over the coffee pot.

"Have a second cup," Maybelle cried. "Have a third." Buoyancy was what she tried for on these mornings. Her large, handsome, bony face composed itself into vital lines, wifely empowerment. She was learning how to put on a good show of bustle. She trilled and sang. She exhorted, at first subtly, then openly. The day was ready to be packed with accomplishment; the morning hours especially squeaked their need. "More toast," she warbled. "Try this high-fiber stuff, today just may be the day." She passed butter, jam, honey, seeing in the melting calories the fuel for creation. On the way out the door, all shine and forward motion, she beamed back a smile. "A breakthrough's on the way. I feel it in my bones."

Three days a week she drove off to Toronto, where she worked for a large publishing house. All spring she'd been toiling over several manuscripts simultaneously, one of them a thousand pages long. This particular extravaganza she was trimming down to size, but it grieved her to throw words in a wastebasket when at home they were in short supply, had dried up completely, in fact; six months since she and Meershank had returned from Portugal, and not a single paragraph written. "Anything?" she would ask briskly, coming home at the end of the working day. Meershank might be reading the paper on the side veranda or brushing down the dog or clipping a hedge.

"Nothing today." His voice was cheerful. Ordinary. Life going on.

"How about trading up to a new word processor?" Maybelle suggested, a fishy shine on her face. "That monster of yours is positively antiquated."

Another day, she sprang more wildly. "Have you ever thought of a pen?" she said. "Remember pens?"

Workmen arrived one morning and installed a new sky-
light in his study. "Surprise!" Maybelle said. "An early birthday present."

Accustomed to Meershank's activity, she found its cessation
worrying. She connected it with depression, and being a
woman, particularly the woman she was, she linked his depression with herself, some failing on her part, some act omitted.

But Meershank was happy in his inactivity, he swore it. He
felt—what?—fond of himself, fonder than he had for years,
this pathetic stricken fellow caught in the human tide. It was
a relief after his long gilded hubris to be among the dispos-
sessed, newly numbed before his art, which was growing
steadily more noble as it slipped out of his reach. So this was
what it was like, this agony of drought. Hmmmmm. Well,
now he knew. He felt curiously flattered to be one with his
fellows, those sincere scribblers he had so avidly avoided and
scorned. Fraternity renewed him, the communal part of himself—here he stood, witness to the feast and famine of the creative cycle. The suffering of the throttled was his, and he felt
appropriately shriven, haunted, beset and blessed. Hadn't he
always suspected that profligacy could be cured, austerity
accomplished? A spare Beckettish brevity might yet come his
way—he could at least hope—or failing that, well, silence.
Why the hell not?

Filling time was not nearly the problem he had imagined
since hours could be spent thinking about getting started,
and further hours cursing the darkness, making false starts and
reading them aloud with rich grunts of disgust. Crumpling
sheets of paper was a satisfying activity and could be done
very, very slowly. A whole hour—generally following a lunch of
warmed-up soup—could be devoted to philosophical speculation, addressing that fleshy, many-fingered question: Does

the world really need another book? No. Yes. No. Well, it depended, didn't it? (One of the treasures of Portugal, one of the treasures of . . .)

Or he could give himself over to gossip, to speculation. The publishing world being what it was, he imagined that word had got round: ungirdled, unbraked Meershank had been brought to heel. (Serves the old boy right.) It was July. Then came August. His first bookless autumn was fast approaching. The thought was crisp, bracing. He inhaled it with a sense of awe. There were tragic proportions here if he cared to take them up, but why should he? One more word-smith muzzled, the old babbler, the old conveyor belt, scribbler, stumbler. Arghhhh!

Idleness, and an impulse for self-flagellation, led him to the reading of book reviews. Just how were his fellow *écrivains* faring? Aha!—there was old S—with yet another of his prolix empty potherings; didn't the man realize his life's work was nothing but goosedown! Had he no respect for the value of words, the craft itself, its intrinsic gold?

These pious, envious pangs were delicious to Meershank; he couldn't get enough.

"It's my fault," Maybelle grieved, "for dragging you to Portugal."

"No," he told her truthfully, it had started before Portugal, almost a year before.

He had been invited to a Toronto TV station for what was to be an in-depth interview. He arrived promptly in the late afternoon and discovered that the interview slot had been double-booked. Would he mind, Nana Beanflower asked him, if she went ahead and interviewed Slas Stanley, the figure skater, first? "Not at all," said Meershank. He knew his adopted country, he knew his place in it. Besides, what was half an hour in a lifetime?

He had come to discuss, promote, that is, his latest book, *Maple Foot Jelly,* and couldn't help noticing when his turn came that Ms. Beanflower, a fresh copy in hand, had stuck her bookmark at what looked like page ten. An old story: too busy to read, these media youngsters. "Shall we begin?" she said violently.

Her hair was brilliant media orange, and she wore violet clothing made of layers of wrinkled cotton. Her feet in their thong sandals could have been cleaner. Meershank took a keen interest in costume, believing it revealed what the north half of the brain repressed, but Ms. Beanflower, he decided, seemed unsteady in her yearnings. Still, he had not come to analyze; he had come to discuss his new book.

The plot first. They always wanted the plot; they thought it mattered. Then a little personal background, what he was working on next, his thoughts about the dark side of humor, what he was really saying underneath all his puns and jabber.

"I really *am* saying what I'm saying," Meershank said wearily, slipping thinly away from her gaze.

"Ah, come on now?" The voice coy. The twinkle turned on high.

"There *are* no hidden meanings, Ms. Beanflower." She bit her lip wickedly, leaned close to the microphone and said, "They say you're an old toughie, Meershank, but do you know what you remind me of?"

"No, what?" he said stupidly.

"A great big teddy bear, that's what."

"Ah."

In the following weeks he speculated on what might have been a fitting reply to this announcement. Thank you? Pardon? This interview is now terminated? Would you tell John Updike or Slas Stanley or Pierre Trudeau that *he* looked like a teddy bear? What exactly does a teddy bear look like? Is looking like a teddy bear something that serious and enlightened men aspire to? Is it media policy to pin labels on the teddy bear minority? Is this resemblance to a teddy bear physical or metaphysical? Is a teddy bear man lovable or grotesque? Deeply cute or profoundly shameful?

It was a mistake, he knew, to take Nana Beanflower seriously. What lapped between her ears was orange Jell-O. What motivated her was the wish to be adorable. Nevertheless, she had managed to make him doubt himself. Something intensely frivolous about his work, about himself, had encouraged her contempt, entered his body and deeply injured him. A sword stuck in his chest.

And that, he told his wife, Maybelle, skipping the details, had been the real start of his writer's block.

Maybelle Spritz knew what it was to be blocked.

As a young woman of twenty-five, starting work in a large publishing house, she had been appointed Meershank's editor. It was a fluke for someone so young to be assigned a major writer, but somebody or other in charge had had the wit to see that the Spritz warp matched the Meershank woof.

She loved him from the first day, falling upon his scrambled, pencil-whorled manuscripts, her hands flying over the stacked pages, smoothing them hot or cool, taking possession. Turning over the sheets she often laughed her big-girl laugh. Other times she circled and queried. It was said she had the Meershank canon by heart. But that was all she had.

Every year on her birthday he took her to lunch; Zuckerman's on Bathurst, boiled noodles and brisket. At Christmastime he bought her items that reflected the privacy of his affection, jokey jewelry or sternly ironic travel books, one year a beautiful seashell, another time a blue teapot shaped like a flower and covered with images of itself.

And she was always included at the Meershanks' annual Boxing Day parties. There in the crowded, scented, noisy house, whose windows and banisters were trimmed with holly, Maybelle was embraced by Meershank's adored wife, Louise, that good and gentle, blameless and bloomingly pretty woman.

These parties made Maybelle go dreamy. Always she drove out to Jacksons Point with the idea of taking a single cup of punch and slice of holiday cake, then fleeing. But year after year she was seduced, before she knew it snuggled between the cushions of a broad tufted sofa and told she was irreplaceable, priceless, one of the family, a fiction she fleetingly— that is, for an hour or so—believed.

This went on for fifteen years. She adored Meershank, not so much ardently as hopelessly, and sometimes she forgot about it for days at a time. A kind of lankiness came over her as she got older. She grew taller, it seemed, along with her name and title: Maybelle Spritz, Senior Editor. Her own office. A member of the Board. Meershank came more and more to rely on her judgment, and his twenty-ninth book, *Monkey Funk,* was dedicated to "The Spritziest Girl in Town." That made her bawl.

It never occurred to her, even in her dreams, that Meershank's wife would grow ill, would die, and that Meershank would be "free." (Maybelle Spritz is a clever woman with a blue pencil, a sorceress some say, but she lacks basic imagination.) Her life had taken a particular shape and could not be reinvented. It wasn't so terrible. She had her friends, her holidays, her work, her birthday lunches, her Boxing Day tributes. She wasn't crippled or crazy. She wasn't dead.

She was only blocked.

Maybelle brought her blocked husband smoked fish wrapped in butcher's paper. Also wonderful pears. Also gossip, sweet as candy. But the truth is, though it is very seldom admitted to, there is very little anyone can do for anyone else. Interesting excursions can be planned, people invited to dinner, noodle puddings produced, orange juice squeezed, lamps left burning, bed covers turned invitingly down. Kisses can be dropped on the tops of heads, and news brought from one person's world to another, but in the end it's a matter of waiting things out in an improvised shelter and thinking as kindly of yourself as possible.

Mimi Cornblossom (purple curls, orange garments) is the heroine show-biz star of Meershank's new book, published the third week in December, and bearing the generic title *Blockbuster;* it made this year's fall list by a split hair's breadth. A rollicking read, a hydra-headed offering, it has the same off-the-kitchen-wallishness as Meershank's pre-block books, and also a style that's teased and tenderized by all-night writing sessions, late-hour editing and a dangerous drive to the printers over narrow, icy streets. It's a broth of old injuries and pleasures, of the wounded heart and its stitched-up hole. Actual writing time? A dozen November days; for Meershank a record.

The prologue has Mimi waking one morning with a tune in her head, a tune she can't place. It's a talky, sparky tune, full-lipped and bright. She carries it with her to the Narcissus Pool, where she works as a manicurist, and all day long as she pushes back cuticles and trims and files and polishes she feels a set of lyrics beating at her temples, stabbing her through the stomach.

It's driving her crazy trying to figure out where this song comes from, its Latin sunniness and breezy flash. She hums and jerks, and breaks an emery board across the nail of an elderly client, forgets to eat lunch, jingles the coins in her uniform pocket, eyes the clock, stares out the window.

She asks everyone she sees about the song: her best friend, Virgie Allgood, her fiancé, Ken Kool, her little nephew, Lester Lou. "That's a great tune," they all say, but no one knows where it comes from.

It skips into her dreams, waxy, amber, hollow. There's a forward lean on it now, and some unexpected punctures that by morning have been repaired. She smiles in the mirror, wincing at her own hot, puzzled face. Two days ago her head was empty and now it's filled with a chorus and kickline. What is this?

She puts in a call to her favorite rock station and does a version for Big Larry. "Wild," is what he says. Then, "Solid!" Then, "Hey, you got yourself a real high spinner there."

"I do?" she says. "Really?" And feels a small brass gear of consciousness engage. She's no fool: she's got a good voice, not a great voice, but this is her tune. *Hers!*

Between the old Mimi and the new Mimi lies the thinnest of membranes. It's made out of air. It's colorless. It's not in the dictionary, not in the phone book, not in the bureau drawers or hall cupboard, but does this worry Mimi Cornblossom?

Of course not. She's already slipped like a fish into Meershank's Chapter 1, and now she's rehearsing for Chapter 2. She's got treasure to unearth and plot lines to bind. Suffering waits for her, and recompense too. Ending and mending, squaring and cubing. There she goes, there she goes! Eyes wide open, lurching blindly into the future.

Collision

TODAY THE SKY IS SOLID BLUE. It smacks the eye. A powerful tempered ceiling stretched across mountain ranges and glittering river systems: the Saône, the Rhine, the Danube, the Drina. This unimpaired blueness sharpens the edges of the tile-roofed apartment block where Martä Gjatä lives and hardens the wing tips of the little Swiss plane that carries Malcolm Brownstone to her side. What a dense, dumb, depthless blue it is, this blue; but continually widening out and softening like a magically reversed lake without a top or bottom or a trace of habitation or a thought of what its blueness is made of or what it's *for*.

But take another look. The washed clarity is deceiving, the yawning transparency is fake. What we observe belies the real nature of the earth's atmosphere, which is adrift, today as any day, with biographical debris. It's everywhere, a thick swimmy blizzard of it, more ubiquitous by far than earthly salt or sand or humming electrons. Radio waves are routinely pelted by biography's mad static, as Martä Gjatä, trying to tune in the Vienna Symphony, knows only too well. And small aircraft, such as the one carrying Malcolm Brownstone eastward across Europe, occasionally fall into its sudden atmospheric pockets. The continents and oceans are engulfed. We are, to speak figuratively, as we more and more do, as we more and more *must* do, smothering in our own narrative litter bag.

And it keeps piling up. Where else in this closed lonely system can our creaturely dust go but up there on top of the storied slag heap? The only law of biography is that everything, every particle, must be saved. The earth is alight with it, awash with it, scoured by it, made clumsy and burnished by its steady accretion. Biography is a thrifty housewife, it's an old miser. Martä Gjatä's first toddling steps are preserved, and her first word—the word *sjaltë*, which means honey—and her dead father's coldly aimed praise—"For a girl you have sharp ways about you."

These are fragments, you say, cracker crumbs, lint in your shirt pocket, dizzy atoms. They're off the map, off the clock, floating free, spring pollen. That's the worst of it: there's nothing selective about biography's raw data, no sorting machine, no briny episodes underlined in yellow pencil or provided with bristling asterisks—it's all here, the sweepings and the leavings, the most trivial personal events encoded with history. Biography—it sniffs it out, snorts it up.

Here, to give an example, is Malcolm Brownstone's birth squall from fifty-odd years ago, a triple-note *yawolll* of outrage bubbling up through the humid branches of his infant lungs, and again, *yawolll*. And the sleepless night he spent, aged twelve, in a rain-soaked tent in the Indian Hills, and also the intensity with which he reads newspapers and promptly forgets most of what he reads, and his dreamy neurotic trick of picking up a spoon and regarding his bent face in the long sad oval of its bowl.

In a future world, in a post-meltdown world, biography may get its hands on the kind of cunning conversion that couples mass and energy. We may learn, for instance, to heat our houses with it, build bigger lasers with its luminous run-off or more concentrated fictive devices.

But for the time being, every narrative scrap is equally honored and dishonored. Everything goes into the same democratic hopper, not excluding the privately performed acts of deceased spinners and weavers, or contemporary ashtray designers and manicurists, or former cubists and cabinet ministers, and young mothers pushing prams and poets who seek to disarm their critics—even these seemingly inconsequential acts enter the biographical aggregation and add to the weight of the universe.

It's crowded, *is it ever crowded!* Inside a single biographical unit, there are biographical clouds and biographical shadows, biographical pretexts and strategies and time-buying sophistries and hair-veined rootlets of frazzled memory. Long complex biographies, for example, have been registered and stored for all the ancestors, friends and acquaintances of the Japanese pop singer who right this minute is strolling in the sunshine down the Champs Élysées wearing a leopard (genuine) jacket and a pair of pale pressed jeans. There are detailed dossiers for each of the twelve girls and twenty-six boys who competed for the state whistling championship in Indianapolis in 1937. Every particular is recorded, and also every possibility and random trajectory, even those, to cite the case of Martä G. and Malcolm B., that have only a partial or wishful existence.

Written biography, that's another matter, *quite* another matter! Memoirs, journals, diaries. Works of the bio-imagination are as biodegradable as orange peels. Out they go. Psssst—they blast themselves to vapor, cleaner and blonder than the steam from a spotless kettle. Nothing sticks but the impulse to get it down. Consider Martä Gjatä's four great-grandfathers. Three of them were illiterate shepherds;

the fourth was a famous autodidact, a traveler, a minor politician, a poet of promise and, in his old age, the writer of a thick book entitled *The Story of My Life* (Lexoni Bardhë Këtë). Copies of this book can still be found in rural libraries throughout the Balkans, but not a word of the text has entered the cosmology of biography, of which the four great-grandfathers, shepherds and sage alike, have a more or less equal share.

Martä herself does not keep a diary, living as she does in a part of the world where one's private thoughts are best kept private. She is a droll, intelligent woman of wide-ranging imagination, as anyone on the streets of her city will tell you, but the one thing she cannot imagine is her encounter, just a few hours away, with the large, clean-faced, bald-headed North American named Malcolm Brownstone. The meeting, if such a slight wordless collision can be called a meeting, will originate in the lace-curtained coffee salon of the Hotel Turista. She will arrive early, a few minutes before Malcolm Brownstone, and will wear a green checked linen dress and polished leather shoes with rather higher than usual heels.

She is a citizen, indeed a Party member, of a small ellipsoid state in eastern Europe resembling in its dimensions a heaped-up apple tart viewed in profile. The top crust presses north-ward toward a sparsely populated mountainous area that still erupts from time to time with primitive vendettas whose roots go back to the time of the Turkish occupation. This is harsh terrain for the most part, with scanty soil and rough roads, but the southern corner of the geo-pie plate tilts onto a green curve of the Adriatic, and this short, favored stretch is about to be developed into a full-scale tourist facility. At present there is only a four-story concrete hostel suitable for the bus-loads of students or workers who have lately been encouraged to come here for their twenty-four-day vacation period.

But the time for expansion has arrived; even in this part of the world people are talking foreign currency; foreign currency's the key. The beaches here are broad and breezy, and despite an overrun of tufted sea grass, the potential's unlimited. A recreational consultant, Malcolm Brownstone, is being sent, today, by an international cooperative agency to advise on the initial stages of development.

A mere thirty miles from this future fantasyland is the capital city, where Martä Gjatä lives. Hers is a country often confused with toy principalities like Andorra and Monaco, but in fact is a complex ensemble of mountains and streambeds and rich deposits of iron and chromium and annual rainfall statistics going back to the year 1910. There are also some Roman ruins and a number of mosques, now turned into museums, and the busy capital city (pop. 200,000) where Martä and her mother and her mother's brother Miço live. (A fourth member of the household is old Zana, a family servant before Liberation, now lingering on as an honorary aunt and in winter sharing her bed with Uncle Miço, an *Ethnoggraphi Emerti* at the National University.) The apartment is small. The cooking facilities are rudimentary and the food somewhat monotonous, but Martä, aged forty-two, prides herself on creating a style to suit her confining circumstances. She makes a delicious *mjarzadjpër,* which is a mixture of cabbage, cheese and onions spiced with pepper. And the green checked dress she wears today is one she made herself.

She is a worker in the state film industry, which last year produced fourteen feature films and more than twenty documentaries. She is also one of the few women to have been promoted to *Direktor.* This was three years ago. Before that time she was a celebrated film actress. *The Scent of Flowers* and *Glorious Struggle* are her most beloved films and the ones that have made her famous in her country. In the first of these she played the daughter of a patriot. She wore a kerchief and an embroidered apron (borrowed from Zana, since there was no such thing as a wardrobe department in the early days) and served glasses of raki to filthy, wounded soldiers, falling passionately in love with one of them, a mere boy whose legs had been crudely amputated after battle. (In real life this young man, Dimitro Puro, had been run over by a tractor.) The film closes with a village wedding scene (Dimitro and Martä) that is exuberantly folkloric but sadly muted by the spotty black-and-white film then in use, color film having been forbidden before the cultural revolution of 1979.

The cultural revolution lasted two days and consisted of a letter written by Martä Gjatä to the Minister of Kulture pleading for a change from black-and-white film to bourgeois color. Martä delivered the request herself, placing it in the Minister's hand and giving his wide cheek a playful pat. That was the first day. The next day she had her answer, a typed directive delivered to her apartment saying: "If you think the time has come, my darling Martä, then the time has come." Both letters were immediately destroyed, though they continue to exist as part of the biographical patrimony, along with all other gestures, events and texts of this curious period. Biography works both sides of the street. Iron curtain, velvet curtain, it's all the same to biography.

In her final film, *Glorious Struggle*, Martä played the perplexed middle-aged mother—though she was herself still in her thirties—of a brilliant eighteen-year-old daughter who elects a career in Civil Engineering. The film was immensely popular, but was later criticized for its too obvious didacticism, its repetitious and ultimately tiresome plea for gender equality. Still, Martä's performance, her face passing through wider and wider rings of comprehension, raised it to the level of near-art, and there was talk for a time of international distribution. "No" came an order from higher—much higher—up. "Not yet."

A year ago the Minister of Kulture died. He and Martä had been lovers for some twenty years, but out of oversight or mutual evasion had not married. His death was caused by choking; a laurel leaf buried in a mutton stew caught in his throat. This was during a dinner at the Romanian Embassy. He was not yet fifty, still a relatively young man with dark hair rising cleanly from a blank forehead. He might have grown beautiful with time; white hair might have given him distinction, putting edges on his large, weak face and blunted features, connoting kindness or refinement. Maybe.

Martä was away at the time of his death, directing a documentary on the glass industry in the north of the country. This was not at all the kind of film she was used to working on, and the thought came to her that her lover had sent her away deliberately in order to get her out of the way. She has no proof of this, only a suspicion that confirms itself by a muttering inattention. She knows what she knows, just as her tongue apprehends the crenellations of her teeth but can't describe them. The love affair had grown desultory on both sides; occasionally she had felt herself straining to play refining fire to her lover's rather dainty brutality. "Little Martä," he often said, kissing her small breasts and giving a laugh that came out a snicker.

There is no laugh like a snicker. We want to cover our ears with shame and shut it out, but in biography the snicker lives on, a laugh trying to be a good laugh but not knowing how. Like radioactive ash or like the differentiated particles of luminescence that cling to the dark side of the globe, the chambered beginnings, middles and ends of human encounters persist, including aberrations, nervous tics and malfunctions of the spirit. A snicker cannot easily be disposed of, certainly not a habitual snicker, and thinking about her lover after his death, Martä is unable to imagine him without the stale accompaniment of snorting air. It condenses on her neck and eyes. Her remembrances taste of yellow metal, not nostalgia, and her lover's glum, puffy face continues to retreat behind a series of small puckered explosions. She did not return to the capital for his official interment and memorial ceremony, claiming quite rightly that the documentary on the glass industry must come first.

Glass has been manufactured in Martä's country only since the 1950s, before which time it was imported from Yugoslavia. The quality of domestic glass is poor. (Tumblers and wine glasses possess an ineradicable greenish tinge, and it has proven difficult to achieve quality control; household glassware is either too thick or too thin and often breaks the first time it's put into hot water.) But there has been considerable success with industrial glass, perhaps because a higher priority has been assigned, with the result that there is now a surplus of such products, and it has been decided to seek foreign markets. Hence the making of the documentary film.

Martä has always loved glass, and her biography is punctuated with references to the colors of glass, the clarity, the fluid shapes and artful irregularities, to the opaque glass grotto of her earliest memory, the time as a young child when she scratched her name, Martä Gjatä, on a frost-coated window, putting the scrapings of shirred ice on her tongue, where they deliciously melted. Around her neck, on a fine chain, she wears a pendant of seaglass, a gift from the legless actor/soldier, now a translator of textbooks, who played opposite her in *The Scent of Flowers*. A shelf in her apartment holds an antique goblet of lead crystal brought back from

Venice by the Minister of Kulture shortly before his death. When Martä flicks at it, hard, with her duster (a pair of old underpants), she is forced to balance the slack fleshiness of his face against their many tender hours of love, sometimes in the woods outside the city, sometimes very quietly on the dusty linoleum floor of a storeroom in the basement of the Palace of Kulture. She has time while dusting for her memories to bloom into flower silhouettes and glide slowly past her, a shadow parade with a cracked element of confusion. She's glad at these times that she has her work to distract her and deaden her thoughts.

The creation of the documentary presented certain structural problems, and these Martä solved by dividing the glass-making process into a series of elegant steps, and running beneath them a counter-process of poetic permutation that sent transparency flowing backward into elemental sand. She spent several weeks editing the footage, insisting on doing it herself, working even on Sunday, which was the day she had once spent walking in the woods outside the city with her lover. The work took her mind off the unfilled space ahead of her, which seemed now, with its blocky weekends and solid uncomplicated months, too large to contain her small, patient undertakings and too indifferent to provide the sort of convulsion she is secretly hoping for.

For its kind, the glass documentary is a success—thirty minutes of witty, visual exposition in which even the machinery of the glass factory seems to be smiling. It has already been dubbed into four languages, French, Italian, German and English—not one of which Martä understands, languages being her single failing—and an illustrated catalog has been prepared. Martä has brought the catalogs to the Hotel Turista today, where she will shortly be meeting a two-man trade delegation from Austria.

She is early, seated at a low, rather battered table, drinking coffee. Her cardboard satchel of film catalogs is on the floor beside her. From time to time she peers out the window through the lace curtains and sees that the blue sky is now blackened with cloud, what looks like forewarnings of rain. The Austrians apparently are still in the dining room, taking their time over lunch, and the coffee salon is empty except for Martä herself in her checked dress and, at the far end of the room, a bald-headed man bent heavily over a pile of papers. Martä glances in his direction and identifies him as a for-eigner—there's a certain opacity about him, a largeness and lope to his shoulders and arms, and a visitor's face on his face—but she has no way of knowing who he is or why he's here.

The arrival of a Recreation and Resort Consultant (Malcolm Brownstone's official title) is a portent, a sign the country is opening up and welcoming the high-tech wizardry of the West. Even more remarkable is the notion of exploitable hedonism, a new idea in this country and one which Malcolm ironically represents (a biographical fault line here, since he is known to be a hard-working man of puritan tastes, but one whose last thirty years have been beamed in the direction of pleasure).

He is comfortable with the lace curtains in the Hotel Turista, more than comfortable; he loves them and is reminded of the small frame house where he grew up, a rented house with a curved brow of shingles and two upstairs win-dows like staring eyes. The house held many of the usual mid-continental variables: bibles, hairbrushes, folded blan-kets on shelves, an enamel breadbox with the word *bread* stamped on its hinged lid, a modest, lean-bodied father with a mild passion for horseshoe pitching and a mother with a tinkling laugh and reserves of good health. There were two sisters, both of them scholarly, both of them pretty. The

sisters, and Malcolm too, made the most of their opportunities, never suspecting that their opportunities were limited.
They married, bore children, were rewarded and punished,
sought friends, took vacations, saved their money, also spent
it, and grew older, making regular compulsory deposits as
they went along to biography's vast holdings.

Out of all this planetary chaff it might be thought that a
mathematical model could be fashioned, an orderly super-
bio whose laws and forms are predictable and reduced. But
this is where anarchy enters in, or, depending on your perspective, systematic rebellion. At various times, for instance,
it has been forbidden to eat tomatoes, to poach pheasants, to
curse God, to strangle infants and to break promises. Still,
people did these things and survived and contributed their
chapters of anomaly and exception. The otherwise cases, the
potent singularities—they also survive, along with precarious
half-heard harmonies and the leaky disrepair of memory
(Malcolm Brownstone's mystic experience on a Ferris wheel
in 1947, when he observed curls of crisp gold raveling off the
sun; Martä Gjatä's love letter—to a paraplegic film actor—
which she later tore into forty-three pieces and hurled into a
weedy pond).

One of Malcolm Brownstone's first undertakings as
a young architect was the development of a "theme park" in a
region of his own country that seemed to possess no out-
standing characteristics (high unemployment figures
notwithstanding) and very little in the way of historical resonance. There was nothing, *nothing,* he could draw on other
than the longings of displaced agricultural workers to
become once again solvent and respectable. These longings
he translated into dreams, and thus Dreamland was born, a
commercial wonder, then as now. It contains a Dream City,
a Dream Palace, a Dream Mountain, a Dream-o-rama, where

Dreamobiles race along banked curves, and a Dream Stream, on which floats a Dreamboat commandeered by Dream Maids dispensing at reasonable prices such dream favors as Dreamy Candy Floss and Dreamy-Ice.

Wisely, he bought shares and immediately incorporated himself, an act of biographical distortion in which a single life sometimes gives the impression of multiple tracks. He grew rich, which did not surprise him. What surprised him was his baldness at the age of thirty-five. His biography is starred with attempts to reconcile himself to his few last scurrying hairs and the melon of scalp rising above an eave of bone. He cannot pass a mirror, even today, without a stab of confusion—who is this person? Today at the airport he was met by an official car; the driver, he noticed, had a head-ful of thick, thrusting hair. The two of them drove silently past fields of cabbages and women with scarves wrapped around their heads leading donkeys down the road, but all he could see was the driver's strongly rooted hair and his own slicked skull bouncing whitely off the rear-view mirror.

He is an earnest man, an Organization man, but with the kind of dislocated piety that the Organization finds awk-ward. His ordered, monotone missions to marginal-economy countries are undertaken with unfashionable fervor. He wants, he says aloud, to help people. His sense of vocation arrived suddenly during a trip he and his wife took to North Africa in 1976. Standing in a village souk, his eyes traveled accidentally past a wool dyer's stall to the dark room beyond, where he beheld an earthen floor and children who were of an age to be in school. He seemed to hear the words: "You are close to discovering a way to make life meaningful." A month later, in a mood of panic and high drama, he disincorporated himself—another bio blip—and joined the Organization as a dollar-a-year man.

His wife sniffled and wept. She hated to travel, to pack and unpack, to plug her hairdryer into complicated converters and risk danger. On one occasion she was startled by a large oily beetle that climbed out of a bath drain. She had frequent gastric upsets and skin rashes. Some of the countries where they were sent had unreliable water supplies and incomprehensible languages (neither she nor her husband had any aptitude for foreign languages) and systems of public morality that seemed whimsically derived from the demands of long-standing hunger.

Two years after Malcolm joined the Organization, his wife died of a stroke. Her last words before slipping into the coma that ended her life were, "You were always such a cold potato."

That's what he lives with, this icy epitaph—not even, in fact, true—and his awareness, always with him, of his scraped head. The two images overlap cruelly—potato/head—and churn him to action. Spareness, openness, bareness—these he avoids for the organized compression of public gathering places, parks and fairs, playgrounds and carnivals, pleasure domes and civic squares, the whole burning convivial world where he feels the massed volume of other lives. The truth is, though he doesn't realize it, there is not one corner of our cold, green, rocky world that isn't silted down by biography's buzzing accumulation. It's a wonder we can still breathe, a miracle we can still move about and carry on with the muffled linearity that stretches between the A of birth and the B of death. Malcolm Brownstone imagines that he is two-thirds along that mortal line, an alarming thought, but also a comforting one.

Today, in the coffee salon of the Hotel Turista, he is joined by three *functionari* from the Ministry of Interior Development. They are all of them men with short necks and copious hair— is there no end to this hair?—and dressed alike in suits so dark that the folds of cloth are without shadows. Against Malcolm's vast beige wall of tweed they seem to merge one into the other. An interpreter is necessarily present. A very young woman, still a student, she has made an attempt at fashion by pinning a crocheted collar to a plain brown sweater. This collar she touches now and then as she transforms Malcolm's preliminary recommendations into the furze and petals and throaty moss of the national language. Her biographical density is powerful, since very little as yet has been expended, and it hurts Malcolm's heart to look at her, the way she fingers her collar and twists an earring as she exchanges the sprawled flowers of her native tongue for the thudding bricks of his own English.

It puzzles him, but only a little, that official business in this part of the world should be conducted in the homey, lace-curtained public rooms of hotels rather than in offices or boardrooms. He is not at all sure that such offices and boardrooms exist. But what does it matter, he asks himself, as long as progress is made.

And in the next two hours, between three-thirty and five-thirty, two small international agreements are reached, one in each end of the coffee salon. The room darkens subtly as though in acknowledgment. Raki is ordered, and cakes are brought around.

To her Austrian visitors Martä Gjatä delivers nothing, promises nothing, but through a burly boy of an interpreter persuades them that their opportunities will be diminished if they return home without her explanatory brochures and a copy of her film, which has been given the engaging title *Jepnï Nje Lutëm* (*A Gift of Brightness*).

Malcolm Brownstone has determinedly sold his vision to his hosts, assuring them that Pleasure with a capital *P* is the springboard not only of profit but of progress, that healthy relaxed bodies roasted by the sun and bathed in a benign sea are all the more ready to stand on guard for the State. Though he won't actually visit the site until the following morning, he has already studied the pertinent maps, charts, graphs, blueprints and photographs. He mentions matching funds, contract requirements, climate variables, the components of tide, wind and hours of annual sunshine.

By chance, or perhaps by some diminution of an electric charge running from one end of the room to the other, the two meetings break up at the same moment. The Austrian duo shakes hands with Martä and heads for the *boit de nuit* in the basement of the hotel, where they will while away a few hours with green beer and illicit dancers. They kindly suggest that Martä join them, but she declines. She is expected at home, she says; she must catch her bus at the People's Square.

The three dark-suited *functionari,* through the medium of their blushing translator, bid good evening to their distinguished guest, Malcolm Brownstone. They wish him a pleasing night. They are sorry, they say, that the rain has spoiled the evening, but the countryside has been needing such a wetting. His suggestions have greatly animated them, and they look forward to traveling with him on the morrow to the coast. A car will call for him at eight-thirty, and it is hoped that this very hour is agreeable.

Badly translated languages fill Malcolm with sentiment, touching his primal sense of what a language should be, every word snugged in a net of greeting. He is charmed by inversions. He welcomes the derangement of grammar and the matching derangement of his senses. Affection surges. He would like to embrace these three chunky men, as well as the earnest translator, who is now giggling helplessly and struggling into a raincoat. Instead, he bows elegantly, like an oversized actor, and shakes hands all round. A minute later he finds himself, too suddenly, alone.

A walk is what he needs. A stroll on the Boulevard Skopjerlë, at dusk, at twilight, a look at the famous People's Square in the center of the city. Outside, the rain is pouring down, but luckily in his briefcase he has a folding umbrella, a marvel of hinged ribs and compacted nylon. He never travels without it.

At the wide front door of the hotel—marble flooring stained and splitting—he collides with Martä Gjatä. She salutes him with her droll eyes and the smallest of shrugs. *Rain* is what her look says, *rain, and me without an umbrella.* She bites her lower lip and smiles.

The smile might mean anything. Malcolm interprets it as the spasm of tension that often follows a moment of disconnection. He feels the same tension himself, and so returns the smile, but doubles the kilowatts. A real smile; no cold potato here, but a man of warmth and spontaneity; charming, helpful.

Not only does Martä not have her umbrella with her, she has no raincoat, not even a square of plastic to tie around her head. She doesn't mind about this. It's the cardboard briefcase she's worrying about; will it melt away in this deluge, and what about the rest of the brochures? They'll be ruined. She takes a tentative step forward, one high-heeled shoe advancing through the doorway and onto the flooded marble steps, then quickly retreats to the dry lobby.

Ssschwippp—the noise of an umbrella unfurling, Malcolm's made-in-Montreal umbrella; a cunning button pressed, and *voilà!* He gestures broadly at Martä and then at the umbrella. His forehead is working rhythmically, saying the unsayable in lines of brow.

In response Martä swings a dramatic arm in the direction of the open door, a perennial actress with unstartled eyes and a cheerful shrug of complicity. She points to the cardboard valise, *helpless, helpless,* and pulls a rueful face.

Time to take charge. Malcolm nods northward in the direction of the People's Square. A query, a proposition. He touches his tweed chest, a vigorous me-too sign and, with surprising delicacy for such a large person, mimes the classic gesture of invitation, a hand uncurled, beckoning, one finger leading and the others following quickly. Why not? his look says.

Why not? Martä mimes back. No coyness here, not at age forty-two, not from a woman whose biography drills straight through to struggle and achievement and recent pools of terrible loneliness. She ducks under the umbrella, and together they set off, down the broad marble steps, a turn to the right smoothly performed, and then along the wide pavement skirting the boulevard.

"You a visitor here also?" asks Malcolm, shouting above the noise of battering rain and reverting to the wooden English he uses when visiting foreign countries.

"*Ko yon skoni?*" Martä asks, waving a pretty arm, baring her teeth.

"A rainy night," Malcolm says loudly.

"*Por farë feni* (with great pleasure)," Martä replies.

They both stop suddenly and smile. The futility of language. The impossibility.

Hundreds of people fill the street, some of them running, only a few equipped with umbrellas, most of them comically drenched. Who would have thought the weather would turn so suddenly! Men, women and children. The end of the working day. Everyone seems to be carrying a bundle of some sort, vegetables or kindling or books, and these they attempt to shield from the downpour. Under Malcolm's strong black umbrella Martä and her cardboard case stay dry. She has given up on conversation; so has Malcolm.

They step with care. Portions of the boulevard have been smoothed with concrete, but in other places the old cobbles poke through, making the surface tricky, especially for Martä in her high-heeled shoes. In order to keep her balance (and because it is difficult for a short woman to walk with a tall man under an umbrella) she takes Malcolm's arm. Not a bold gesture, not at all, but a forthcoming one, also intimate. It is likely that Malcolm extended his elbow slightly by way of entreaty—half an inch would have done it, would have given permission; an old-worldly habit to walk arm in arm, emphatically neutral but with a ripple of protective tribute.

The distance between the Hotel Turista and the People's Square is a mere stroll, only about half a mile. The rain grows more intense, but instead of hurrying them along, it slows them down. First Malcolm must adjust his long steps to match Martä's and, after a minute or two of faltering, of amused back and forth glances, they find their ideal stride, a strolling, rolling gait, right and left, right and left. Malcolm brings his elbow closer to his body so that the back of Martä's tucked hand is in contact with the large damp paleness of his jacket. There it stays, there it fuses.

Ahead of them the lights of the People's Square blink unsteadily. It is the slashing of the rain that gives this look of unsteadiness. Lights seen through a whorl of weather throb rather than shine, producing a rhythmic pulse that is always trying to mend itself but never catching up. Martä and Malcolm are locked together by this rhythm, left and right, left and right, one body instead of two. If only they could walk like this forever. Malcolm has spent his whole life arriving at this moment; this is the best bit of walking he's ever going to do, and it seems to last and last, one quarter-hour unfolding into a measureless present.

Martä, dazed by a distortion of time and light, thinks how this round black umbrella gives an unasked-for refuge, how the rain becomes a world in itself, how the half-mile of rutted city street has become a furrow of love. It will never end, she thinks, knowing it is about to.

Biography, that old buzzard, is having a field day, running along behind them picking up all the bits and pieces. Biography is used to kinks and wherewithal, it expects to find people in odd pockets, it's used to surges of speechless passion that come out of nowhere and sink without a murmur. It doesn't care. It doesn't even have the decency to wait until Martä and Malcolm get to the People's Square, shake hands, go their separate ways and resume their different versions of time travel, not to collide again. This isn't one of Martä's movies, this is life. This is biography. Nothing matters except for the harvest, the gathering in, the adding up, the bringing together, the whole story, the way it happens and happens and goes on happening.

Good Manners

THE STERN, PEREMPTORY SOCIAL ARBITER, Georgia Willow, has been overseeing Canadian manners for thirty-five years. She did it in Montreal during the tricky fifties and she did it in Toronto in the unsettled sixties. In the seventies she operated underground, so to speak, from a converted Rosedale garage, tutoring the shy wives of Japanese executives and diplomats. In the eighties she came into her own; manners were rediscovered, particularly in the West, where Mrs. Willow has relocated.

Promptly at three-thirty each Tuesday and Thursday, neatly dressed in a well-pressed navy Evan-Picone slub silk suit, cream blouse and muted scarf, Georgia Willow meets her small class in the reception area of the MacDonald Hotel and ushers them into the long, airy tearoom—called, for some reason, Gophers—where a ceremonial spread has been ordered.

Food and drink almost always accompany Mrs. Willow's lectures. It is purely a matter of simulation since, wherever half a dozen people gather, there is sure to be a tray of sandwiches to trip them up. According to Mrs. Willow, food and food implements are responsible for fifty percent of social unease. The classic olive pit question. The persisting problem of forks, cocktail picks and coffee spoons. The more recent cherry-tomato dilemma. Potato skins, eat them or leave them? Saucers, the lack of. The challenge of the lobster. The table napkin quandary. Removing parsley from between the teeth. On and on.

There are also sessions devoted to hand-shaking, door-opening and rules regarding the wearing and nonwearing of gloves. And a concluding series of seminars on the all-important *langue de la politesse,* starting with the discourse of gesture, and moving on quickly to the correct phrase for the right moment, delivered with spiritual amplitude or impre-cation or possibly something in between. Appropriateness is all, says Georgia Willow.

Our *doyenne* of good manners takes these problems one by one. She demonstrates and describes and explains the accept-able alternatives. She's excellent on fine points, she respects fine points. But always it's the philosophy *behind* good man-ners that she emphasizes.

Never forget, she tells her audience, what manners are *for.* Manners are the lubricant that eases our passage through life. Manners are the means by which we deflect evil. Manners are the first-aid kit we carry out onto the battle-field. Manners are the ceremonial silver tongs with which we help ourselves to life's most alluring moments.

She says these things to a circle of puzzled faces. Some of those present take notes, others yawn; all find it difficult to deal with Mrs. Willow's more exuberant abstractions. As a sensitive person, she understands this perfectly well; she sym-pathizes and, if she were less well-mannered, would illustrate her philosophy with personal anecdotes culled from her own experience. Like everyone else, her life has been filled with success and failure, with ardor and the lack of ardor, but she is not one of those who spends her time unpicking the past, blaming and projecting and drawing ill-bred conclusions or dragging out pieces of bloodied vision or shame. She keeps her lips sealed about personal matters and advises her clients to do the same. Nevertheless, certain of her experiences refuse to dissolve. They're still on center stage, so to speak, frozen tableaux waiting behind a thickish curtain.

Only very occasionally do they press their way forward and demand to be heard. She is ten years old. It is an hour before dusk on a summer evening. The motionless violet air has the same density and permanence as a word she keeps tripping over in story books, usually on the last page, the word *forever.* She intuitively, happily, believes at this moment that she will be locked forever into the simplicity of the blurred summer night, forever throwing a rubber ball against the forever side of her house and disturbing her mother with the sound of childish chanting. It is impossible for her to know that the adult world will someday, and soon, carry her away, reject her thesis on the *Chanson de Roland* and the particular kind of dated beauty her features possess; that she will be the protagonist of an extremely unpleasant divorce case and, in the end, be forced to abandon a studio apartment on the twenty-fourth floor of an apartment building in a city two thousand miles from the site of this small wooden house; that she will feel in her sixtieth year as tired and worn down as the sagging board fence surrounding the house where she lives as a child, a fence that simultaneously protects and taunts her ten-year-old self.

On the other side of the fence is old Mr. Manfred, sharpening his lawnmower. She puts down her ball and watches him cautiously, his round back, his chin full of gray teeth, the cloud of white hair resting so lazily on top of his head, and the wayward, unquenchable dullness of his eyes. Twice in the past he has offered her peppermints, and twice, mindful of her mother's warnings, she has refused. "No, thank you," she said each time. But it had been painful for her, saying no. She had felt no answering sense of virtue, only the hope that he might offer again.

Tonight Mr. Manfred walks over to the fence and tells her he has a secret. He whispers it into her ear. This secret has a devious shape: grotesque flapping ears and a loose, drooling mouth. Mr. Manfred's words seem ghosted by the scent of the oil can he holds in his right hand. In his left hand, in the folds of his cotton work pants, he grasps a tube of pink, snouty, dampish flesh. What he whispers is formlessly narrative and involves the familiar daylight objects of underwear and fingers and the reward of peppermint candy.

But then he draws back suddenly as though stung by a wasp. The oil can rolls and rolls and rolls on the ground. He knows, and Georgia, aged ten, knows that something inadmissible has been said, something that cannot be withdrawn. Or can it? A dangerous proposition has been placed in her hand. It burns and shines. She wants to hand it back quickly, get rid of it somehow, but etiquette demands that she first translate it into something bearable.

The only other language she knows is incomprehension, and luckily she's been taught the apt phrase. "I beg your pardon?" she says to Mr. Manfred. Her face does a courteous twist, enterprising, meek, placatory and masked with power, allowing Mr. Manfred time to sink back into the lavender twilight of the uncut grass. "I'm afraid I didn't quite hear . . ."

Later, twenty-three years old, she is on a train, the Super Continental, traveling eastward. She has a window seat, and sunlight gathers around the crown of her hair. She knows how she must look, with her thin clever mouth and F. Scott Fitzgerald eyes.

"I can't resist introducing myself," a man says.

"Pardon?" She is clearly flustered. He has a beautiful face, carved cheeks, crisp gray hair curling at the forehead.

"The book," he points. "The book you're reading. It looks very interesting."

"Ah," she says.

Two days later they are in bed together, a hotel room, and she reflects on the fact that she has not finished the book, that she doesn't care if she ever does, for how can a book about love compare with what she now knows.

"I'm sorry," he says then. "I hadn't realized I was the first."

"Oh, but you're not," she cries.

This curious lie can only be accounted for by a wish to keep his love. But it turns out she has never had it, not for one minute, not love as she imagines it.

"I should have made things clear to you at once," he says. How was he to know she would mistake a random disruption for lasting attachment? He is decent enough to feel ashamed. He only wanted. He never intended. He has no business. If only she.

She seems to hear cloth ripping behind her eyes. The syntax of culpability—he's drowning in it, and trying to drown her too. She watches him closely, and the sight of his touching, disloyal mouth restores her composure. Courtesy demands that she rescue him and save herself at the same time. This isn't shrewdness talking, this is good manners, and there is nothing more economical, she believes, than the language of good manners. It costs nothing, it's portable, easy to handle, malleable, yet preformed. Two words are all that are required, and she pronounces them slippingly, like musical notes. "Forgive me," she says.

There. It's said. Was that so hard?

There is a certain thing we must all have, as Georgia Willow has learned in the course of her long life. We may be bankrupt, enfeebled, ill or depraved, but we must have our good stories, our moments of vividness. We keep our door closed, yes, and move among our scratched furniture, old photographs, calendars and keys, ticket stubs, pencil ends and lacquered trays, but in the end we'll wither away unless we have a little human attention.

But no one seems to want to give it away these days, not to Georgia Willow. It seems she is obliged to ask even for the unpunctual treats of human warmth. A certain amount of joyless groping is required, and even then it's hard to get enough. It is especially painful for someone who, after all, is a personage in her country. She has her pride, her reputation—and a scattering of small bruise-colored spots on the backs of her long thin hands. It makes you shudder to think what she must have to do, what she has to say, how she is obliged to open her mouth and say *please.*

Please is a mean word. A word in leg irons. She doesn't say it often. Her pleases and thank yous are performed in soft-focus, as they like to say in the cinema world. It has nothing to do with love, but you can imagine how it is for her, having to ask and then having to be grateful. It's too bad. Good manners had such a happy childhood, but then things got complicated. The weave of complication has brought Georgia Willow up against those she would not care to meet again, not in broad daylight, anyway, and others who have extracted far more than poor Mr. Manfred at the garden fence ever dreamed of. Good manners are not always nice, not nice at all, although Mrs. Willow has a way of banishing the hard outlines of time and place, and, of course, she would never think of naming names. Discretion is one of her tenets. She does a special Monday afternoon series on discretion, in which she enjoins others to avoid personal inquiries and pointed judgments.

"Courtesy," concludes Georgia Willow, "is like the golden coin in the princess's silk purse. Every time it's spent worthily, another appears in its place."

Almost everyone agrees with her. However much they look into her eyes and think she is uttering mere niceties, they are sworn to that ultimate courtesy, which is to believe what people want us to believe. And thus, when Mrs. Willow bids them good afternoon, they courteously rise to their feet. "Good afternoon," they smile back, shaking hands carefully, and postponing their slow, rhythmic applause and the smashing of the teacups.

Times of Sickness and Health

KAY'S MOTHER HAD IDEAS, notions of refinement. One of these notions was that young girls benefitted from the experience of ballet classes, and so all three of her daughters were enrolled—Kay's sister Joan, a second sister, Dorrie, and Kay herself, who was the youngest in the class, the youngest by far, being not quite five years old.

The lessons were held in a large mirrored room on the second floor of a commercial building. Kay remembers the long unbroken stairway, lit at the top and bottom, but dark in the middle. Their dance shoes they carried in their hands, soft-toed satiny slippers, not the hard-nosed shoes of classical ballet. The teacher was a thin, darkish woman. She wore a kind of short-skirted costume. Fancy, shiny. Another woman played the piano. One-two-three-jump was the way they started off each week.

The older girls seemed able to remember the order of the dance steps. Kay watched them hard, baffled by their ease and earnestness, trying to copy what their arms and feet did, but she was unable to shake off a sense of dazed confusion. There was dust on the mirror walls and on the hardwood floor. What was she doing here? It seemed to go on for a very long time, over and over again, one-two-three-jump.

There was mention of a recital. It filtered through to Kay, that charmed, important word. *Recital.* Like ice in a pitcher of water. The class was perfecting a dance routine called "The Wedding," and Kay's sister Joan was appointed the bride, a deserved tribute it seemed. Everyone else was to be a bridesmaid, except for Kay who was given the role of flower girl. She had no idea what this meant. She'd seen her mother cover her hands with flour when she made pie crust, smooth it on her fingers and palms, rub it into the rolling pin and on the pastry board.

A small berry basket filled with torn-up bits of newspaper was put in Kay's hands. These she was to scatter on the floor during the course of the wedding dance. This crude, stained basket with its improvised string handle and its rubbishy contents spelled out the fullness of her disgrace. Clearly she was being punished, but why? She did as she was told, shuffled and kicked and turned, always a shameful half-second behind the others, and threw paper on the floor, knowing she was doomed and powerless. Something was wrong, but she didn't know what. Who would she have asked? And what would she have said?

Kay, who is fifty, has no children of her own, but is interested in the way children think and the questions they like to ask. For example: Is a tomato a fruit or a vegetable? (Which is it?—Kay's looked it up but can't remember.) Do these querying children, she wonders, really want an answer? Or is there a kind of hopeful rejoicing at the overlapping of categories, a suggestion that the material and immaterial world spills out beyond its self-imposed classifications? What is the difference between sand and gravel? Between weeds and flowers? Between liking and loving?

It occurs to her that these children may be bluffing with

their bright, winning curiosity, being playful and sly, and masking a deeper, more abject and injurious sense of bewilderment. There is, after all, so much authentic chaos to sort out, so much seething muddle and predicament that it is a wonder children survive their early ignorance. How do they bear it? You would think they would hold their breath out of sheer rage or hurl themselves down flights of stairs. You would think they'd get sick and die.

"Do you know Philip Halliwell?" a woman asked Kay.

Kay was a young woman, barely more than a girl, standing in a public washroom applying lipstick, the ruby red putty people wore in those days.

"Slightly," she answered carefully.

"I wouldn't trust him farther than I could throw him," the woman said.

Kay slipped quickly past a row of women who were saying things women had always said. The same things their mothers and grandmothers have said, shaking the same powder across their broad or narrow noses and peering at their dabbed, genetically condemned faces or at a broken nail, probably bitten, held up and examined in the weak light. No, she did not trust Philip Halliwell. But she had fallen under his spell. That's what it felt like, being under a spell. She had, in fact, after a two-week courtship, married him. It was a secret marriage because she was still a student, working in the field of early English manuscripts. She lived in a women's residence and held a prestigious scholarship that would have been jeopardized, or so they reasoned. All this was years and years ago.

Recently, she was in the hospital for a week (tests, bone scans, which turned out negative, thank God), and Philip sent a basket of hydrangea. She hadn't seen him for six months, and so the gift surprised her. But she didn't know how to look after these particular flowers, and the nurses were too rushed off their feet to lend a hand. She took the nearly dead plant home, and on the way through the hospital corridor two people stopped her and instructed her in the care of hydrangeas. "Never let the roots go dry," one said. The other said, "Water daily, but don't allow the roots to actually stand in water."

Many people resent advice, and Kay has never been able to understand this. A man she knows, Nils Almquist, a cataloger in the museum where she works, tells her that this resistance to advice is a Teutonic failing, that people from Mediterranean countries—Greece, Italy, Spain—routinely ask the advice of their friends and relatives before making a major decision. It is a sign of courtesy to seek counsel. People whose opinion is sought are flattered, and at the same time no one is strictly bound to accept what is offered. This arrangement strikes Kay as having a good deal of human flexibility to it, and a crafty balance of consolation and hoarded-up responsibility.

"Never wear white pumps after Labor Day," her mother used to say, "or before the twenty-fourth of May." Kay believed this. It made a kind of sense, these permissive bracketing holidays and the broad field of liberty that lay between. "If you lose something," a girl named Patsy Tobin told her when she was about seven or eight, "just shut your eyes and pray to St. Anthony." Patsy Tobin's family was Roman Catholic, which was why she knew of the secret and specialized powers of St. Anthony. The advice worked. After uttering a short, breathy prayer ("Dear St. Anthony, please help me find . . ."), Kay almost always came across her lost shoe or doll or handkerchief or whatever. "When you have the growing pains in your legs," her Auntie Ruth said during one of her prolonged summer visits, "lie very still in bed, not moving a muscle, and count to one hundred." This proved excellent advice, practical to the point of magic, for not only did the pains ease as she counted, but she was almost always fast asleep before reaching a hundred.

"Happiness is capability." A woman Kay knows has written this sentence on a slip of paper and stuck it to her refrigerator door with one of those little magnets. "Oh, I know it sounds simplistic," she said, reading Kay's expression, "but it works. And it's the only thing that does work."

"There must be something you can do for him," Kay said to the doctor when her father lay dying—bedridden, bored, kept from his pinochle and poker cronies—in terrible pain. She had arranged the postponement of her comprehensive exams and come home for a few weeks.

"Aside from boiling up a deck of cards and feeding him the broth, we can't do a thing," the doctor said.

She liked this brand of non-advice. She found it ironic, indirect, cocky and kindly meant. It seemed like the sort of folksy palliative you might hear from a grunty old family practitioner. But this was a young doctor speaking. A very tall, good-looking man with exceptionally blue eyes. Kay had only just met him that morning. His name, he told her, was Philip. They shook hands, and then he helped her on with her coat. She looked tired, he said, especially her eyes.

For some reason—self-pity or injured vanity—this made her want to lean up against him and cry, but she remembers that she resisted.

Her father did not die, not then. Instead he made something of a limited recovery, getting out of bed eventually, getting himself dressed, taking short walks in the neighborhood, going as far as the corner for a newspaper or a loaf of bread.

His clothes hung loosely on him, looked clownish and poor, and Kay wondered at that time why her mother didn't do something about those miserable clothes. He had given up smoking at the start of his illness; now he gave up cards. If he came upon a group of men hunched over a game, he shook his head in a puzzled but unreproachful way as though powerless to understand why grown men would idle away valuable time.

He started to read a thick book about butterflies. Kay remembers that her mother bought this book in a second-hand store; she was always haunting such places. She loved a bargain. The book was old, its cover damaged, but the color plates were in beautiful condition. Better still, here and there, preserved in the pages close to the spine, were the dried pressed bodies of real butterflies, captured by some previous reader. They were exceedingly fragile but had kept their color and, like thin sheets of mica, glinted with metallic richness. When her father came across one of these flattened creatures, he left it where it was, untouched, as if it were a sign of good luck.

About this time Kay and Philip went to Sardinia. This was their so-called honeymoon, delayed nearly two years because of her father's condition and also because of revisions to her thesis. It was a terrible day when they left, an afternoon in late January. It was necessary to land in Toronto in order to de-ice the plane. They taxied into a hangar where the whole of the plane—the wings, body and nose—was covered with pink foam. Kay remembers it took more than an hour to restore the plane's silvery sides, and even then they rose with a shudder into a gray, torn-up looking sky. It seemed not all that improbable that they would perish. Philip ordered a bottle of champagne somewhere over Quebec, Kay's first taste of champagne, though she was twenty-five years old at the time, a tall, loping, solemn girl with a head full of roughly filed facts and opinions.

Crossing the Atlantic, Philip ignored her. He had struck up an acquaintance with a Belgian priest across the aisle, and the two of them were soon trading anecdotes—miracles and blessings of a medical and spiritual nature. Half-dozing, Kay listened to Philip describe the spontaneous recovery of one of his patients. It took a minute or two to realize it was her father's case he was recounting, the story was that full of echoes, pauses and resonance; her father with his flapping, shabby clothes became a kind of golden fabulation, a character in a rich folktale who had burst through to reality and health.

She has only a few memories of that time in Sardinia, and even the half-dozen, utterly faded, stiff-edged Polaroid snaps that remain seem to bear no relation to the two of them or what they hoped to find there: he sitting on a large rock with his hands stretched skyward; she in the doorway of a hotel; he stepping gracefully through the arch of an ancient chapel; she climbing into a little hump-backed rental car; he standing in the morning surf and wearing a pair of exotically printed swimming trunks; and another of him crouched on a hillside examining a small plant.

An odd thing happened. During the weeks in Sardinia they stayed in three different hotels, and in each of these places they were given the same room number, number five. Kay was the one who pointed this out to Philip, who might otherwise not have noticed. As a coincidence it seemed to her mildly amusing and, perhaps, even an omen of good luck, not that her instincts leaned toward omens. Philip, on the other hand, found it thrilling and also alarming. He brooded about the numbers and even quizzed the desk clerk in the third hotel about the way in which rooms were allotted.

Though their time was running out, he insisted on registering in a fourth hotel in order to test the pattern, then changed his mind at the last minute. One night he worked out the probability figures on the back of a menu, allowing each hotel fifteen rooms. The numbers were overwhelmingly against such a coincidence. He rechecked the figures. "Look at this," he demanded. Kay could see that he felt threatened and at the same time exhilarated. He discussed it with anyone who would listen including, one evening, a British couple they met in the hotel dining room. His voice grew implausibly overpitched, and the English pair exchanged sharp looks of apprehension—or so Kay thought. The next morning he woke up saying, "I'm making too much of this. I'm letting it get to me."

In Kay's memory the two of them took picnic lunches every day to lonely little beaches, but it may have been only two or three times that they did this. Probably they bought what they needed in the village shops, bread and sausage and a bottle of cheap wine. Kay remembers that one day—this was perhaps the same day Philip was cured of his obsession with the room numbers—they lay on their backs on the warm sand and she felt something brush her knee. It was a butterfly, not large, but quite brilliantly colored in shades of red and yellow and amber. She thought of her father's book and its brightly illustrated pages. Between the windows of color on the wings were tiny transparent panes edged in black. She held perfectly still, wondering what this creature made of the roundness of her knee, wondering if it perceived its own ephemeral grace. "Maybe it's a rare mutation," she said to Philip, who had fallen asleep. "Maybe it's the world's rarest butterfly."

This seemed possible. She was not just being whimsical. Almost anything she could imagine seemed possible and, for the moment, at least, she felt she knew everything she needed to know to stay alive in the world.

"The world's yours, honey, if you want it," Kay's Auntie Ruth used to say. Auntie Ruth was her mother's younger sister. She arrived every June for a visit and stayed until the first of August, sometimes longer if she judged she was not getting on her brother-in-law's nerves. For his part, he was fond of her, but found her noisy chattering tiresome, and objected in a mild, manly way to her many toiletries lined up along the toilet tank. Kay's mother defended this array of lotions and powders; Auntie Ruth suffered from eczema, also heat rash and various unidentified allergies. Besides, she got it all for free since her husband, Uncle Nat, was a pharmacist.

Uncle Nat was left at home in Brandon. He was too tied down with the drugstore, Auntie Ruth maintained, to go for a vacation. He wasn't one for travel anyway, being older than Auntie Ruth, twenty years older, and suffering from piles and also backache. She, and Kay's mother too, referred to him as The Old Poke. "I'd better drop a few lines to The Old Poke," she would say a week or so into her visit.

Auntie Ruth's visits had an effect on Kay's mother: they made her girlish. The two of them set up folding cots on the screened porch so they could talk half the night away. They made themselves twin cotton dresses with wide circular skirts and wore them downtown. Once they dipped gumdrops in lemon extract, arranged them on top of a chiffon cake and set them alight at the table. Another day they dropped in on an old friend of Kay's mother, who told them she had had an exhausting morning—she had rinsed out her shoelaces and brushed her teeth. They couldn't stop laughing at this, repeating it time and again and inventing variations. "I'm so tired, I just washed my feet and ironed a hanky." "I'm just

done in, I've blown my nose and changed my underpants."
On and on they went. Afternoons in the backyard, drinking
glasses of iced tea, they speculated on their niece Ethel's
hurry-up marriage. "You only have to put two and two
together," Kay's mother said knowingly. "You only have to
put *one* and *one* together," Auntie Ruth hooted, pitching
them into spasms of hilarity.

At the end, though, there was trouble between them. Kay's
mother lay in the hospital for four months with cancer of the
lungs, this despite the fact that she had never smoked a cigarette in her life. Her sister Ruth sent her a card every single day,
but in all those months she never once came to visit. "I can't,
honey," she said to Kay on the telephone, speaking up because
of the long distance. "Since your Uncle Nat passed on, I just
can't face hospitals, they get me down so." Kay's mother
refused at last to open the cards. She was bitter. She made her
daughters promise they would have nothing to do with Auntie
Ruth in the future, and they did promise. But, in fact, it was a
promise that none of them has kept, or ever intended to.

It grieved Kay, though, that her mother should die with
her heart hardened and set. She seemed to have forgotten all
the good times, how the two sisters, she and Auntie Ruth,
would move the sewing machine out on the porch and, in the
space of an afternoon, recover a chair or make a new set of
kitchen curtains. They made these things for almost nothing, cutting them out of remnants they scrambled for in
backstreet fabric outlets.

Kay's mother sewed beautifully, but considered herself a
novice beside her younger sister. "Anyone can do plain
sewing," she would say, "but your Auntie Ruth is a genius
with the needle." Then she went misty-eyed with recollection.
"Remember the year she came early to help with the ballet
costumes? For the recital? They were tricky as can be, those

little satin insets and the netting on the hats and at the wrists. Itchy to work with too, especially in hot weather. We worked right down to the wire. But we got them done."

"I don't remember," Kay said.

This was not true—she did remember, but saying she didn't was a way to strike out at her mother, letting her know she distrusted the touched-up trivia that formed the bulk of her remembrances and the treacly voice she used when invoking them. "I don't remember." She said it harshly, tossing it off.

"Well," her mother said, wistful, "you were very young. Just a baby. Probably too young to get anything much out of ballet lessons."

There was a coolness between them at this time because of Philip. Her mother had taken Kay aside. She had things to say to her. Handsome men, she said, can bring about problems in a marriage. They think they can go their own way. They get spoiled by flattery, by women falling about them. This leads to a lack of responsibility on their part. You can't count on them, and that's what marriage is in the long run, two people counting on each other, in good times and bad as it says in the wedding service, always having, no matter what, that one person in the world you can turn to.

The trouble was, this wasn't advice she was giving. It was prophecy. And already too late.

Kay has always believed herself fortunate in having sisters. Her sister Joan, white-haired, heavy in the hips, already several times a grandmother, lets her talk on and on. She thinks it does her good, and it does. Kay's other sister, Dorrie, is equally sympathetic, but has a different style. She prods and interrupts and brings up tricky points. "What do you mean he forgets you?" she asked once. "Do you mean just birthdays and anniversaries and so on?"

That too, but much, much more. Once he met an old friend in a restaurant and they decided to fly to Whitehorse just like that. He phoned her the next day to let her know.

"Once," Dorrie pronounced, shrugging. "A lapse." Then asked, "And other women?"

Of course there were other women, almost from the start, but that wasn't really the problem. "He forgets I exist. Who I am. He looks at me but sees the wallpaper. He's courtly in the wrong way, like a man on automatic pilot. Even in bed—"

"Yes?"

Kay hadn't meant to get into this. "Even then I feel him slipping away. His arms are around me, yes, but his head's somewhere else. We might as well be in different rooms."

Kay also has long, frequent talks with her good friend Nils Almquist. Two or three times a month they have a drink together after work, around the corner at a place called The Laughing Moose. They favor a special table near a bank of potted begonias. Nils is every bit as good-looking as Philip, but built along different lines, and Kay is about ninety-five percent sure he's gay. She can tell him almost anything. He's one of those unusual people without twitches, able to sit for long periods of time with his body still and solid. It's this, she thinks, that encourages her confidences. One night not long ago she told him about Philip's final leaving, how he slipped off without a word, as though he'd suddenly remembered he had another existence elsewhere. How had she known it was the last time? Because of a sense of lightness that stole over her. To herself she said, almost laughing, "Well, that's that." She felt like someone getting up out of a sickbed, all her bones stiff but still in working order.

Besides her sisters and Nils and other assorted friends, she belongs to a weekly conversation group. A talk circle is the official term. This group meets at Trinity Church Hall on Monday nights in a room furnished with easy chairs and soft lights.

Some years earlier, when things were going badly, she had come across a little printed notice that said: "Feeling alone and alienated? Coffee and conversation may be the answer."

She feared the usual unctuous welcoming remarks, braced herself for forced joviality and whining accord. Normally she was scornful of such endeavors, preferring to believe that liberal, educated people, nurtured from the cradle on communication skills, had no need for such organized embarrassment.

At the first meeting the discussion centered on the subject of favorite smells. One woman said mothballs. Another said coffee just after you grind the beans. A man said old ice skates when you bring them up from the basement. Kay said the smell of new cloth spread on a table, before you pin a pattern to it. The mothball woman said yes, that was hers too, only she hadn't thought to mention it. She and Kay became close friends. It's she who has "Happiness is capability" on her refrigerator door.

Ecology is a frequent topic of discussion on these Monday nights, how to live more naturally and harmoniously in the world. Also the problem of public responsibility and private yearnings, the question of tolerance and instinct, or the spiritual self versus the material world.

But when things get too serious, someone in the group will say, "Aren't we getting a bit heavy here?" and for a while they'll retreat to the primary edge and talk about such things as My Most Trying Moment or The Book That Has Meant the Most to Me or My Favorite Color and Why. Last week they talked about My Earliest Memory.

Kay described the dance recital. By some trick of inversion this memory precedes the rehearsals themselves.

The recital was held in a new, strange place, not the big mirrored room with the dusty floor. Kay was told to wait in a dark place behind heavy curtains. She was shushed by one of the bigger girls, told to stand still or she'd rip her costume, and someone else handed her a large golden basket. Not real gold, but a graceful willow basket, probably spray painted; the handle was twisted and elegant and fit smoothly over the crook of Kay's arm. A whisper welled up: "Isn't she darling!" "Yes."

Then somebody, her sister Joan probably, gave her a push forward, whispering, "One-two-three-jump," and the next minute they were filing onto a small stage beyond which was nothing but a row of blinding lights and a wall of darkness. The darkness was false, full of held breath and heated expectations, that much Kay could understand.

A number of things seemed wrong. Her dance shoes made a different wash-wash sound on the slippery floor. There was a worrying sense of crowding and falling, and dazzle from the lights. Nevertheless she kept her eyes on the others, tried to do what they did, and reached, when the time came, into her basket. But what was this? This fragrant silky handful? Whatever it was fluttered upward into the air, a rounded spray of particles that drifted soundlessly to the floor. Again and then again.

There was too much surprise in this, too much of shock and disorder. She observed the cascade of waxy pink and white flakes as they slipped from the angle of her hand, falling on the floor and on the toes of her shoes, and at last identified what they were.

The flower petals, the enchanting basket, her own exalted role, so unexpected—none of these things diminished in any way the humiliation she felt. She had been tricked, caught in a loop of incomprehension, given the hard slap of adult license. Adults were allowed to fool children, to withhold vital information, and this insult was sealed by the banked thunder of anonymous applause, as dense, unstartled and indiscriminate as the applause that comes out of a radio. Still, she curtsied and smiled, feeling sick with shame.

Sick, Kay tells the Monday night group, and when she says sick, she means sick. She means weakness, fever, dizziness, shock, shortness of breath, all the fearful symptoms, but she had curtsied and smiled nevertheless.

Consciousness narrowed down to the width of her small hand in front of her face and the little dot of false light floating over the audience that she was unable to blink away.

But she stared straight ahead and willed herself to hold steady for a few seconds longer. Already she knew she would recover.

Family Secrets

ACRES OF CORN, WHEAT FIELDS and oats led right up to the town of DeKalb, Illinois, where there was a state normal school that prepared farm girls to go out and become school teachers, one of them being my young mother. This was not long after the First World War. She was sent first to teach in a four-room school in a place called Cortland, where she stayed for two years. Why only two years? I must have asked her this at one time, or else my brother, Barclay, did. "I got sick," she said, "and had to go home for a while."

Where did she go? She went back to the forty-acre farm near Lemond where her mother and father lived, and after a year she got a job teaching on the west side of Chicago, where she soon met our father and got married and began her real life.

I've thought lately about that time of sickness; what kind of sickness is it that makes a young woman leave a job and go home to her parents for a whole year? The last time I saw Barclay I said to him, "I think Mom must have got pregnant that year she had to quit her first job."

It took him a minute to figure out what I was talking about. For a man so intelligent he has a poor memory for the details of our childhood. Once I tested him on the color of the garage doors we had at home in Maywood. "Blue," he said. "No," I shot back, "brown."

I had to remind him about Mom leaving the school in Cortland. I had to trot out the whole story, and then he leaned back and smiled his off-focus smile and said, oh yes, now he remembered.

"Well," I said, "what's your honest opinion? Do you think she got herself in trouble, as they used to say in those days?"

He shook his moony face. "I doubt it."

"A year's a long time to be sick." I made my voice curl up at the end, pointed it accusingly at the memory of our dead mother.

"Girls *didn't* then," Barclay said in a deceptively prim way he has.

"Oh no? What about Mary Morgan?"

His face squeezed into a wide smile. He remembered Mary Morgan, all right, one of the old schoolteacher friends our mother used to talk about, Mary Morgan, who was unmarried and Catholic, and who got pregnant and jumped one night off the top of a player piano in an attempt to bring about a miscarriage. For us the story of Mary Morgan's desperate leap has the sheen of legend about it, and shares space with my mother's other girlhood legends. Brave little crippled Grace, for instance, who went to DeKalb Normal in a wheelchair, and another friend, someone called Lily, who had the habit of signing her letters, "Lovingly, Lily," one word swimming coyly beneath the other (an example is preserved in my mother's "memory book," floating loose between pressed gardenias and locks of hair).

Barclay and I were having this conversation about Mom and Mary Morgan and Grace and Lily in a downtown bar that serves good roast pork sandwiches. Barclay works as a systems engineer in Houston, and normally, when he comes to Chicago, I invite him out to the house for a family dinner. I wondered if he thought it was funny that I'd suggested we meet down in the Loop like this instead, and that I hadn't even mentioned Ray and the children. Maybe he thought I was being evasive. Probably not; he has a calm, incurious nature. He'd put on weight, I saw. Even his fingers curving around the wine glass looked puffy. What do you do for love? is the question I would like to have asked him. I imagined the words leaving my mouth and entering his soft body. No, impossible. We talked instead about our mother's friend Mary Morgan, whom neither of us had ever met.

"Do you suppose it worked?" Barclay said. He meant, did she have a miscarriage, and the question surprised me. "Why, I don't know," I said with amazement.

Why didn't I know? This was an old story, after all, and I'd heard it from our mother countless times. The picture was vivid: a carved oak piano draped with some sort of fringed scarf; a woman in a flapper dress with flushed Catholic cheeks is climbing first up onto the keyboard and then onto the top of the piano itself; she crouches, then springs, and there, frozen in mid-air, she has remained. Rings of surprise surround her spread-eagled body, which is weightless in flight, but determined, righteous and stiff with terror.

"Either it worked or it didn't work," said Barclay in his committee voice. Then he said, "Maybe she died."

I said no, I didn't think so. We would have remembered that.

Neither of us could believe that our mother had told us only half the story. We agreed that we must have blocked out the ending, the moment of actual impact. "Maybe it was a nervous breakdown," Barclay said, getting back to the subject of our mother's year of illness.

This was a good possibility, and one that had also occurred to me. Our mother had been a nervous woman. Insomnia, hives, headaches, fits of harsh weeping, all the usual symptoms. "Mom's in the sadhouse again," our father would tell us from time to time. But that sad self was her later self, the self that came into being after the betrayal of her veins and the stringy deterioration of her hands. I see her as cool-skinned and calm, as a young woman in her sunny Cortland schoolroom, rather like Barclay in the matter of personality.

Barclay said, "Maybe it was one of those mysterious girlish fevers women used to get. Or, what do you call it—wasting disease?"

"No one's had wasting disease since the eighteenth century," I told him.

"How about TB?"

"Impossible. She'd have gone to the San."

"Mono?" he flung out. We tried to think if people had mono in those days, it sounds so much a disease of our own generation. But no, it's an old illness; we remembered that it was once called glandular fever.

"That's a real possibility." I drummed my fingers on the dark wet table, pleased. Barclay, what a good man he was, sensed my pleasure and poured me more wine from the bubbly-sided carafe. Glandular fever. People who had glandular fever had to go to bed and stay there, perhaps as long as a year.

"Why don't you ask Auntie Ingrid?" Barclay suggested.

"I suppose I could."

"You still write back and forth, don't you?"

"Twice a year. Christmas and her birthday. I think she'd go through the floor if I just wrote to her out of the blue and asked her about a thing like that."

"Well, if you really want to know . . ." He let his voice trail off mildly, but managed to suggest I'd been wasting his time with my speculation.

"Maybe I will," I decided. "But that's not to say I'm going to find anything out. You know how secretive our family is."

"Oh, I know that," Barclay said.

In my mother's family there were two amputations, Auntie Ingrid's finger and Uncle Harvey's leg. Even in a family with nine children this seems to me unusual.

Aunt Ingrid is my mother's twin sister; they were identical twins, the Lofgren girls from Lemond, Illinois, who looked so much alike that one of them once took a Latin test for the other without their teacher catching on. Later they liked to fool their boyfriends, my mother, Anna, going to the door when Ingrid's beau arrived and saying in her sly teasing voice, "I'm all ready if you are." They believed, as many twins do, that they were joined by a bond closer than mere sisterhood. In later years, Aunt Ingrid, married by then to Uncle Eugene and the mother of four children, would write from Napoleon, Indiana, where she had moved, and tell my mother that she had a new perm, and it would turn out to have been on the very day my mother in Maywood gave herself a Toni. Or they would find they had had colds at the same time or bought new spring coats in the same color, or tossed and turned throughout the same restless night. More often than not their letters crossed, and this more than anything else provided proof of their joined natures.

As girls they were each other's best friend. When they were seventeen they enrolled in the teacher training course at DeKalb, traveling back and forth each day on the Interurban that ran for miles past the town limits, into the rolling countryside and stopped not far from the side road where they lived. One afternoon, arriving at their stop, my mother jumped gaily off the car, followed by Ingrid. But Ingrid was wearing a ring on her finger, a cheap ring of imitation gold, and the ring caught in the mechanism of the door. My mother remembered a strip of brown skin unwinding like a peeling off an apple. There was surprisingly little blood, but considerable confusion and shouting, and someone on the street car said loudly, "The poor girl, she's going to lose that finger."

The driver of the Interurban took Aunt Ingrid straight back to the DeKalb hospital, where she did indeed lose her finger, the fourth finger on the left, that very night.

It fell to my mother to go home and tell her parents that there had been an accident. But she did *not* tell them. She could not, she later said; her mother could not have borne it. Instead, she told them that Ingrid had gone to a friend's house in DeKalb to spend the night, and then she lay awake all night with her teeth chattering, the longest night she was ever to endure. In the morning a doctor from DeKalb drove his Model T into the farmyard, knocked at the kitchen door and informed the astonished parents that their daughter's finger had been amputated.

"I was lucky it was on the left hand," Aunt Ingrid said. "It was lucky I lost it when I was young." She graduated and became a teacher; later she married Uncle Eugene and moved to Napoleon and became a prize-winning knitter. When she wore gloves, she tucked the extra finger to the inside so that nothing showed but a neat little seam. Barclay and I, as children, used to ask to see her tiny knobbed stump, which was pinker and harder than the rest of her hand. Did it hurt? we asked. Not a bit, she told us, not in the slightest. Now she's eighty years old and lives in a retirement center in southern California, and last year she wrote that she has begun to experience a twinge of arthritis in her stump, just a twinge, nothing serious, she says, but a reminder that a finger had once been there.

———

Uncle Harvey, my mother's oldest brother, lost his leg in the war in 1916. There are no firm facts about how this loss occurred, whether it was a bullet or a bomb or what, the leg was just "lost in the war," mysteriously swallowed up in the smoking distances of Europe. He came home wounded, a man with a wooden leg and two canes to help him get around. After a few weeks of hobbling about on the farm, he took the train into Chicago and got a job as a machinery operator, and he worked at that for the rest of his life, a life that was long and alcoholic and that had a quality of deep distress about it. Whether it was the wooden leg that caused his distress I don't know, but I do know that his mother, our grandmother, was never told her son had, in fact, lost his leg. He was lame, that was all she knew. She lived until the fall of 1942, this poor deluded woman, and then she succumbed to double pneumonia, still not knowing.

My husband, Ray, who comes from a more forthcoming family, has never understood how this could have happened. Was this grandmother, this short, fat-faced woman—we have only the photographs to inform us—kept in a state of innocence because of her status as Mother, the being most closely tied to the legless man? Or was she a woman with a singular sensitivity to life's darker offerings? Would she have screamed if she'd been told? Might she have fallen into a faint or slashed her wrists or sunk into years of melancholy? Or might she have shrugged—did anyone consider this?—and said, well, that's a shame, but other boys have lost their legs, and some are a lot worse off than Harvey. On one occasion the truth was almost discovered. Uncle Harvey, home for a Thanksgiving dinner, was sitting at the table lifting a turkey wing to his mouth. His mother, who was setting down a bowl of peas, put her hand on his shoulder and felt through his shirt the heavy leather strap that held the artificial leg in place. "What's this?" she said in a sharp voice.

There was a moment's awful silence. Then Uncle Harvey said, "It's for a hernia, Ma. Nothing serious."

My grandmother set down the peas and went back to the stove for the potatoes; nothing more was said. Perhaps she didn't know what a hernia was; perhaps she thought it was too delicate a subject to pursue; maybe she had her suspicions but resisted them. This, after all, was a woman who could not be told about her daughter's mutilated finger. How was she expected to bear the news of a son's lost leg? But what if suspicion gave birth to a secret, and what if the secret became part of her, like a small, benign tumor under the skin that had long since been accommodated? Turning to the stove, serving out potatoes, keeping her back turned, she may have been saying: I don't want to know, I don't want to know.

Whew, the aunts and uncles must have said afterward; whew, that was a close call. I can imagine they made adult faces at each other over the table, mock expressions of shock and guilty amusement, as though they had brushed close to something unspeakable and also foolish, something they were deeply ashamed of, but could do nothing about.

In 1925 my mother recovered from her mysterious year of illness and came to Chicago to teach school. She and Aunt Ingrid and Mary Morgan and another girl called Gladys Heinz found an apartment on the third floor of a house in Oak Park. The house was on Kenilworth Avenue, just north of Lake Street.

And the strange part of this is that the house belonged to the Hemingway family, the parents of Ernest Hemingway.

Of course, my mother had never heard of Ernest Hemingway. No one, for that matter, had really heard of him.

All she knew was that the family had a son who was living in Paris, France. He was married, and his family spoke about him with a certain coolness. My mother, in her simple way, assumed that the family disapproved of their son living abroad, or else they didn't like the girl he had married. She had no idea he was a writer.

Dr. and Mrs. Hemingway interviewed the four young women on a hot, late summer day. My mother and Aunt Ingrid and Mary Morgan and Gladys Heinz all wore hats and gloves and stockings, and they sat uneasily in the airless front room, the living room, as Mrs. Hemingway called it. The Hemingways explained that they didn't normally rent out their third floor, but that their daughter, Sonny, was in college and that college was expensive. This statement was allowed to float for a minute on the still air, and then Mrs. Hemingway explained a few household rules: the rent was payable at the beginning of each month. She herself was a light sleeper and could not tolerate noise after ten o'clock. The gas bill would be shared and so would the bill for water. Baths were to be limited to two inches in the tub, which was all she herself ever required. She said that she and her husband had considered carefully the kind of people they preferred as tenants, and they both thought that young women in the teaching profession represented all that was ideal. They regretted that their son, Ernest, had not considered a career in education. They regretted it deeply.

The third-floor apartment contained two bedrooms and a sitting room with a shuttered-off kitchen at one end. The ceiling sloped sharply in the kitchen part of the room and, standing at the sink, they had to duck their heads, especially Mary Morgan, who was taller than the others.

They took turns cooking. My mother's specialty was cheese rarebit, a soggy dish that she occasionally made for us when we were children. Aunt Ingrid made chicken à la king in toast cups. Gladys Heinz made a good nutritious meat loaf, and Mary Morgan, hopeless when it came to cooking, washed dishes night after night with her long neck bent against the ceiling.

On one occasion they were invited downstairs for Sunday dinner. There was a standing rib roast, mashed turnips, canned peas and tapioca pudding. The four of them were astonished to learn that Dr. Hemingway had done all the cooking himself. Speechless, they turned their eyes to Mrs. Hemingway, who pronounced in a deep voice, "I have never taken an interest in cooking." After dessert the Hemingways talked about their children. There had been a recent letter from Sonny, but it was some time since they had heard from their son in Paris.

"Is he an artist?" Aunt Ingrid asked.

"He's a time waster," Dr. Hemingway said in a stern, settled voice.

After a brief silence my mother, anxious to prove she was *not* a time waster, said, "Can we help wash the dishes?"

"That would be useful," Mrs. Hemingway said.

Later they told each other it was all they could do to choke back their laughter. Mrs. Hemingway's stiff autocratic phrase became their private invitation to hysteria. They inverted its icy finality and made of it the signal for hilarity. If Aunt Ingrid offered to give Gladys a manicure, for instance, as she often did, Gladys would say, "That would be useful." If Mary Morgan said she was thinking of strolling down to the public library, they would all call out after her, "That would be useful." When a man named Eugene Propper proposed to Aunt Ingrid, she swore she came close to giggling out, "Why, that would be very useful."

A year later, Ernest Hemingway published *The Sun Also Rises* and became famous, but by that time my mother and

Ingrid and Mary and Gladys had moved to an apartment on the west side.

This has always seemed to me to be a tragedy of timing. "Why did you move after only one year?" I used to badger my mother, and her answer was always the same: "That house was so cold, we couldn't stand it another winter. We complained and complained about the heat, but they never did a single thing about it."

My mother never read Hemingway; his reputation intimidated her, I think. I started early, at fourteen, reading him with eager pleasure, but also out of a compulsion to fulfill a side of a family contract that I felt had been allowed to lapse. It seemed to me I had been willed the sharp perspective of privilege. For instance, I would look up from certain passages in *Green Hills of Africa* and suddenly think: This is the voice of a man who grew up in an insufficiently heated house. The drafty stairs, the icy bedrooms, the two inches of bath water, all these things tore brokenly into the smoothness of his sentence parts, or so I thought, and I wanted to reach through the pages and warn him that he was in mortal danger of exposing himself. Didn't he realize what those soft places in the prose revealed? Couldn't he see what was so clearly apparent to the most casual observer, what his pathetic evasions revealed?

Lately, since I've had lots of time, I've reread his earlier books. A man I know, a man I thought I was in love with, teased me about being on a Hemingway trip, but it's really an inverse journey. I see these books differently now; what I thought were unconscious evasions, I now see as skillfully told lies, lies that have given me a new respect for Hemingway and the way he coped with a difficult life. I even started to think that perhaps I could cope with my own.

Then Aunt Ingrid's letter arrived, not a Christmas letter, not a birthday letter, but a letter that arrived in April in reply to my own unseasonable note. First she told me about the weather in San Diego, which is always superlative, and then about the complete lack of cooked vegetables at the Center. She expressed surprise at hearing from me and regretted that I hadn't sent news about Ray and the children. She assumed, though, that they were all fit and fine.

On the second page she explained that she had very little recollection about my mother's year of illness. She vaguely remembered a sickness of some kind, but was sure it was of shorter duration, six weeks at the most. She suggested influenza and then, as an afterthought, eyestrain. She went on to say, "I can't for the life of me see why you want to delve into all this ancient history."

The tone was rough, cross; she meant to put me in my place, and she did. I couldn't really blame her. Lies, secrets, casual misrepresentations and small failures of memory, all these things are useful in their way. History gobbles everything up willy-nilly; it doesn't care a fig for distinctions; it was all the same. My mother's illness has the same weight as a missing finger or a wooden leg or a fizzled-out love affair. Eventually, everything gets stuck between a pair of parentheses or buried in the bottom of a trunk.

I was thinking about this when the phone rang. It was my husband, Ray, suggesting we have dinner together. Why not? I said. We met at a place on Rush Street known for its good authentic Basque food, and afterward we sat talking for an hour or two.

He told me the saddest thing that had ever happened to him was seeing the movie *Easy Rider,* and then coming home and climbing into a pair of striped pajamas and going to bed. I asked him why he'd never told me this before, and he said he didn't know. I accused him of being secretive, and he smiled and said he'd probably learned it from me.

I started to tell him the saddest thing in my life was the bundle of worthless secrets I carry around in my head, but then I smiled back at him and said that I loved my secrets, that I would be lost without them, that they were the only things in the world I could call my own.

Fuel for the Fire

WHEN YOU THINK ABOUT HOLIDAYS like Thanksgiving and
Christmas and Easter, and those huge traditional dinners
with roast meat and bowls of mashed potatoes and fruit pies
laid out, you tend to imagine city families wrapping up in
their warm coats and climbing into cars and driving out to
the family farm. That's the way it was with us, but no longer.
Now, since Mom died three years ago, my dad comes into
Winnipeg for those special days. He drives the pickup, not
the Pontiac. He's used to it, he says. It hugs the road better,
and it seems there's always something or other he needs to
haul. As a matter of fact, he's here most Sundays too. It's
only forty-five miles, and he's careful to pick a time when
the highway's relatively quiet.

He's never been the world's best driver. Not that he's ever had
a real accident, but traffic makes him nervous. He gets heart
palpitations, so he says. He's okay on secondary roads, and
around McLeod, but not in the city. When Mom was still in
good health, he always tried to wheedle her into taking the
wheel when they went to Portage to shop. We used to kill ourselves laughing about that, the traffic in Portage la Prairie. But
now he sails into Winnipeg almost every week. He comes in on
the Number 1 Highway, takes a left at Silversides Boulevard,
another left at Union, and then a sharp right into our driveway.

I always give him a cup of coffee the minute he gets here. Or, if it's lunchtime, a bowl of soup. He can sink down a pan of soup just like that, cream of chicken or asparagus, if I've got it on hand. Campbell's asparagus, that's his idea of real gourmet. He doesn't mind trying new things, even lasagna or beef curry. I read an article not long ago about how old people's taste buds shrivel up with age so that they actually need more spice in their food, not less. When I told him we were having goose for New Year's Day dinner, he looked really interested. He's never had goose before. Neither have I for that matter. Neither has Dennis.

But we're all sick of turkey. We had turkey last week for Christmas, and a pork loin for Boxing Day, and I know Dad wouldn't touch lamb. So what's left? There aren't all that many edible animals when you think about it. Which is why I decided to try a goose this year, a ten-pounder. I ordered it special from DeLuca's downtown, and if Dad knew what I paid for this hunk of bird he'd have a conniption. If he asks me outright, as he's apt to do, I plan to start humming loudly or put the radio on.

It's early morning, only eight o'clock, when I get out of bed on New Year's Day. Dennis and I were out at our annual potluck last night, just four couples, the same bunch every year, and didn't get home till three-thirty—but I don't need all that much sleep. Today a dozen sirens kicked me awake. First, I forgot to take the goose out of the deep-freeze yesterday, and now I'm having to fast-thaw it in a sinkful of warm water, poking my arm way up into its icy ribcage. Its skin looks bluish gray and very prickly around the thighs, not especially appealing. Then there's the stuffing to make. I'm trying out a new mushroom and cashew recipe, and I'm also going to serve a squash soufflé with green onions and chopped parsley for color. I put chopped parsley on everything; it's got lots of iron. When Dennis and I were first married, he used to give me a hard time about my chopped parsley and said I'd probably sprinkle a handful on his dead corpse if he went first. Now he's used to it; he's actually got so he likes it.

He's still asleep, Dennis. I always get up first on holidays, there's so much to do. Besides the stuffing and the squash thing, I want to mop the kitchen floor and clean out the fireplace. I like to have things organized before the kids get too wound up and before Dennis starts thinking up projects. He'll want to take the tree down, I know that, but I want it up one more day. I'd just as soon take it down myself tomorrow when he's gone back to work and the kids are back at school.

There are going to be eight of us for dinner. Besides Dad and Dennis and the three kids and myself, I've invited Sally and Purse from next door. They're older than we are, just halfway in age between Dad's seventy-five and my thirty-four, and their two kids have grown up and moved east. Purse is a commodities dealer, oil seeds, mainly, and Sally's been selling real estate for the last eight years. She's good at it. She's already made it into the Million-Dollar Club. She had her membership key imbedded in a silver disc and wears it like a brooch on the lapel of her coat. Dad gets a kick out of her. He really likes to get her going, and she eggs him on. He can't believe the prices of houses in Winnipeg, what people will pay for jerry-built construction and hanky-sized lots. Last week, never mind the slow December market, Sally sold a house in Tuxedo for half a million dollars, and it didn't even have a full basement. The heating bills for this particular house are more than Dennis and I pay every month for our mortgage and taxes combined, but then our heating bills are pretty high too. Like everyone else around here, we switched from oil to gas a few years ago. This is a cold climate. You've got to put out a lot of your income on heat in this part of the country, but every night, from September to May, we have a fire in our fireplace, and I like to think that that takes some of the burden off the furnace.

Most of our friends who have fireplaces use them maybe three or four times a year. Cordwood's expensive, they say, but then they admit it's really the mess and bother of cleaning out the ashes. I do it fast first thing in the morning, a little whisk broom and dustpan and a metal pail for the ashes. I can clean our fireplace in three minutes flat. I've timed myself. The ashes I save to put on the garden in the springtime.

I love a fire. I'm addicted, we both are, but especially me. I get the kids to bed at night and, by the time I come downstairs, Dennis has a fair blaze going. We got into the fire habit when he was doing his graduate work in England (genetics, swine). We had a little rented house there, two rooms up, two rooms down. We didn't have a TV, we couldn't afford a baby sitter, but we had this real fireplace. Of course it wasn't a luxury there, it was how we heated the house more or less. But neither of us had grown up with a fireplace. It was something new. It was company, like a person, like our best friend. We made toast in it sometimes for a bedtime snack and, if I happened to have any orange peels left over, I'd throw them in and wait for the orange smell to fill up the room. We burned pinecones too, if we found any, and once I remember we put in one of those padded book envelopes and watched the little plastic pillows of air explode in the heat. It was only a year and a half we were there, but it seemed to stretch out much longer, sitting in front of that fireplace with the radio on low and reading library books. We hadn't counted on this, it was a surprise. It was like living in a dark crack, just the two of us keeping warm in our own dust, and Danny sleeping in his crib upstairs.

Back home we borrowed money from my folks and started looking around for a house of our own. The one thing I wanted most was a fireplace. It was at the top of the list. I pretty well knew by then that being content had to do with crackling flames and baked shins. I didn't care about a garage or a family room or whether there was four inches of insulation in the roof, as long as we had something hot and alive to sit around at night, keeping *us* alive.

Our Winnipeg fireplace is painted-over brick, off-white to match the living-room walls, with a rounded opening like one of those old-fashioned bread ovens. It draws like a dream, and it's got a damper we can open and close, which is very important in our climate. Next to it is a brass stand for the fireplace implements, and next to that is a woven brass basket holding birch logs. The birch logs are just for show; at the moment we're burning scrap lumber Dad hauled in from the farm.

He's crazy about our fireplace. He says he sees all kinds of pictures in the flames, a hundred times better than anything on TV. For a while he even tried to talk Mom into getting one installed at the farm. She wasn't too fussy about the idea, not after all those years she spent dealing with a cookstove, but she told him to go ahead if he had his mind made up. In the end he decided it was too much money. According to Sally, it costs about six thousand to install a fireplace after construction, but adds only fifteen hundred dollars to the value of a house.

In her old age my mother shrank down to nothing. Her feet ached all the time. She stopped driving the car, she stopped cooking. She got little fruity eyes and a dented chin. I hardly recognized her. She refused to go out of the house in wintertime, even to Portage. She didn't want to miss her shows, she said. She and the TV and the living-room rad were like a little unbreakable triangle. She wore a pair of wool and angora socks that came up over her knees, and a thick cardigan, and always had an afghan at hand. She hardly talked to us toward the end, she was so occupied with keeping warm and staying off her feet. It scared me seeing her like that, which is why, more or less, I signed up for the refresher course at the hospital this year with the idea of maybe going back to work part-time when Tom starts first grade.

By midmorning I have the table set in the dining ell. I'm using Mom's old damask tablecloth today, which is murder to iron but shines flat like ice under my good tulip china. But not the damask napkins, not with three kids and a goose that looks like it's got a lot of bluish fat on it. I've splurged on big thick paper napkins in a soft shade of rose, also six pale pink candles for my crystal candlesticks. Knowing Sally and Purse, we'll have pink flowers on the table too, and Lara, our nine-year-old, will want to make place cards. I'll tell her to do them on white cardboard with a pink felt-tipped pen.

Dennis is a little crabby when he gets up. He watches me pile mushroom stuffing into the goose's insides and says, "You sure that's going to be big enough to go around?"

"It's supposed to serve twelve," I tell him, and I think again how much I paid for it. The thought just washes over me for a minute, all that money, what we used to spend on food in a whole week.

"Hmmmmm," he says, in his skeptical voice, which I don't really appreciate. I ask him to carry some firewood up from the basement for tonight. Yes, yes, he says automatically, but he stands there drinking coffee and just looking at me.

Last summer my dad demolished an old shed in back of his barn. We don't know why he took it down. Dennis thinks he was just trying to keep himself busy. He doesn't actually farm anymore, but he lives in the old house and rents out the acreage. I've tried to talk him into moving to Winnipeg, and

Sally even took him to view some basement suites not far from here. For a while he seemed interested. We tried to impress on him that he could walk over here and have dinner with us at night and see a lot more of the kids as they grew up. But I think he worried about what he'd do all day in a dinky basement suite. He's a very, very sociable man. Every morning, for as long as I can remember, he's driven the half mile into McLeod for coffee and toast at the McLeod Luncheonette. He'll generally sit there for an hour, shooting the breeze. There are five or six of them, all farmers from around the area. He'd miss that. Sally finally took me aside and said she didn't think it was such a great idea, his moving to Winnipeg. She doesn't think he's ready. Maybe later on, she says, when he's less self-sufficient.

Besides being sociable, he's extremely active physically. Taking down that shed was hard work. You have to be methodical taking down a building, more so than putting one up, especially working on your own. You have to pay attention, or the whole thing can come crashing down on your head. It took him about a week, and at the end of the week he drove into Winnipeg and delivered the first of several truckloads of two-by-fours and other assorted bits of wood. "You might as well make use of this," he said. "In the fireplace."

It wasn't that big a shed as I remember, but somehow we've ended up with this basement full of ugly lumber. Dennis says it's going to last us forever. The boards are full of nails and, when I clean out the ashes in the mornings, I have to gather up the blackened nails too. Some of them get stuck in the grate, and it's a real job prying them out. But, on the other hand, there's not much point in buying firewood when we've got all this scrap wood to use up. It isn't as though we're heating the house with the fireplace, as Dad says. It's just for enjoyment. He can't believe that people actually go into supermarkets and buy Prestologs. Prestologs floor him completely, the whole idea of manufacturing something for the purpose of burning it up.

Around noon I give Dennis and the kids a pickup lunch, and while we sit talking at the kitchen table I look up and see Dad passing by the window. We never even heard him drive up. He smiles at us through the frosted glass, and I can see how we must look to him with our grilled cheese and glasses of milk and talk. The shoulders of his big plaid jacket are stippled with snow, and his eyes seem vague, as though the pupils are only parked there temporarily. "Is that goose I'm smelling?" he asks, coming in through the back way. I say yes, that I put it in the oven an hour ago. He looks happy, anticipatory.

In the afternoon, while the goose spits and crackles in the roasting pan, Dennis takes Dad to the New Year's Day Levee at the Legislative Building. This happens here every New Year's Day. In the old days it was a military affair, a strictly male-only event, but now the general public is invited, even kids. For entertainment there's an RCMP band and a troop of Scotch pipers in full regalia. You line up and shake hands with the premier of Manitoba and his wife, the lieutenant governor and *his* wife, and then you have a glass of Gimli Goose, which is a kind of pinkish wine, and some fruitcake or shortbread.

Our two older kids look as though they wouldn't mind going along, but I like the idea of Dennis and Dad being off on their own for a change. Dennis's folks live down in Nova Scotia, and they're not the sort that gets together anyway. A few times Dennis has tried taking Dad to hockey games, but it's not easy for an older man sitting so long on those hard seats. He always looks forward to the New Year's Levee. Today he's brought along his suit on a hanger and his white shirt and tie. He changes just before they set off, and on the way they drop the kids off at the rink.

The afternoon is slow and dozy, and the sun pouring in through the front window makes me feel sleepy. I settle down on the chesterfield and read an article in the paper about the right kind of clothes to wear for job interviews. I've read this same kind of article a thousand times, but I still need to read it, something makes me. Not too much jewelry. No sandals. A well-made suit in a neutral tone is still the best bet, with a muted scarf for a feminine touch. That's as far as I get before dropping off to sleep.

I can't have slept for long, maybe three-quarters of an hour, but when I wake up I sniff the air for the smell of goose and don't smell anything. I head straight for the kitchen, and sure enough the oven's barely warm. So down I go to the basement to check the fuses, but they're all in order. Then I put on my oven mitts and jiggle the element at the bottom of the oven, in case it's worked its way loose. A corner of it looks black and slightly shriveled. This happened once or twice before, a burnt-out element, but not on a holiday, and not when I was cooking an expensive goose.

My first idea is to carry the roasting pan over to Sally's and finish it off in her oven, but then I remember that she and Purse are out for the afternoon. And all the other people around here are using their ovens for *their* holiday dinners. I consider what would happen to the poor old thing if I tried cooking it very slowly on top of the stove, maybe pouring a little wine around to keep it from burning. It would probably get rubbery, or else stringy. Boiled goose doesn't sound like much of a dish. But at that moment, luckily, Dennis and Dad come through the back door.

They take off their coats and go straight to work. First Dennis takes the goose out and wraps it up with foil to try to preserve what little heat is left. Then he and Dad pull the stove away from the wall, disconnect it, and start examining the bolts that hold the element in place. Definitely burnt out, Dennis says, sounding not one bit dismayed, not an iota, just the opposite.

From the basement he carries up a set of screwdrivers and wrenches, as well as his soldering gear. Before buckling down to work, he pours Dad a tall rye and ginger ale, a heart-starter he calls it, and one for himself. He's humming away and concentrating hard as he slips his wrench around the first of the bolts.

I pull up the aluminum foil for a peek at my goose. It looks pale and glum with its dead meaty chest cooling down fast. I remember the time Dennis and I went to the British Museum to look at the mummies, how depressed I was to find just how dead you could actually get, but Dennis was all over the room, peering at everything and snapping photographs, though, strictly speaking, this wasn't allowed.

He'll have the stove working in less than an hour, he tells me. He doesn't even stop to think about what he's going to do. It's as though he's got a pocket of his brain filled with little mechanical puzzles that he can undo at will. He's going to remove the burnt-out unit and move the broiler element temporarily down to the bottom of the oven. An emergency tactic. He's whistling now. Unlike me, he appreciates the unexpected. Dad is handing him tools in a rhythmic nurse-to-surgeon manner and trying hard, I can tell, to bite his tongue and keep from giving Dennis advice. It's hard for him not being in full charge. He's a sweetheart, but pigheaded at times.

Right after Mom died—I'm talking about one month after she went—Dad cut down all the lilac bushes around their house. These lilacs were old, more like trees than bushes.

They'd always been there, protecting the house from the wind and the open stare of the road. He claimed he and Mom had often talked about chopping them down so they could get more sunshine into the house. I have my doubts about this—my mother loved those lilacs—but we let the story stand.

He cut the twisted old lilac wood into short lengths and bundled them up for our fireplace. Good for kindling, he said. And he also hauled the roots, sixteen of them, into town. First he shook off as much dirt as he could. Lilac roots are dense, damp, shrubby things, irregular in shape and amazingly large. I think he was surprised himself at the size of them.

They burned very slowly. A single lilac root takes a whole evening to burn. You have to poke it continually to keep it going, and it smolders rather than flames. Now and then it gives a turquoise color, just a flash. There's no smell of lilac at all, but from time to time the whole root takes on a sort of glow, shadowy and three-dimensional like a human face burning, eyes and mouth and wrinkled cheeks all lit up and keeping itself intact right to the point of disintegration. We still talk about it, Dad and his lilac roots. Even the children remember, or say they can.

By five o'clock the goose is back in the oven, sputtering fat and getting golden. And by seven o'clock the eight of us are seated at the table. Our faces look coral. Dennis carves, looking not quite at me, across the table. Dad carefully tastes a bit of goose, then says, as if he's looking a long way back into the past, "It reminds me a bit of pheasant, only meatier." Sally runs through her recent Tuxedo triumph, and Purse shares his nice rambling educated laugh around the table. We go counter-clockwise, telling our New Year's resolutions. Dad says he's going to think seriously about a trip to Florida, which I'll believe when I see it. Sally's signed up for calligraphy.

Purse is giving up white sugar. The kids look giggly and secretive and won't say, even when I prod them. Dennis announces his resolution to run the mini-marathon in April. He says this in a staunch, wilful, but kindly way. I'm going to master the art of crepe-making, I say, but my real resolve, the one I don't mention, is to stop managing everyone's lives for them.

After dessert the three men insist on doing dishes. Sally and I sit in the living room waiting for them. The waiting seems like a treasure we've piled up, something we owe ourselves. We settle back into soft cushions and put up our feet in front of the fireplace. But then I remember I've forgotten to lay a fire. And what with the goose crisis, Dennis has forgotten to bring up any firewood. We look at each other, at the birch logs sitting there, and say, why not?

"Hold on a sec," Dad says, coming in from the kitchen. "I'll be right back." He puts on his coat and boots, and five minutes later he's back with a large carton of bowling pins.

The bowling alley in McLeod's been shut down for years, just like the old McLeod movie theater and the old high school and just about everything else. A lot of the small central region towns are shrinking away to nothing, and McLeod suffers particularly by being just a little too close to Portage. The old buildings were boarded up ages ago, but somewhere Dad heard about the stockpile of bowling pins sitting there going to waste in the abandoned bowling alley.

A signal must have registered in his head, a dotted line stretching from the old bowling lanes direct to our fireplace. Other people might see something nostalgic or sad, but he took a look and saw fuel. Bowling pins are wood. They're burnable.

It never before occurred to me to wonder what a bowling pin might look like on the inside, but I would have guessed they were solid through and through, cut with a lathe out of chunks of tough dry hardwood. But they're not. They're glued together in two lengthwise sections, and there's a little hollow—oval shaped—in the middle.

They take a while to catch alight. You need lots of kindling, little chips of hardwood or balled-up newspaper. Then you see a flare of white light, which is the paint catching fire (the pins are painted an ivory color with a red stripe around their middles), and before you know it the entire skin is flaky ash. Then the fire finds a way into the core. The center burns brightly, deeply red, so that the sides look transparent, more like glass than wood, more like bottles than bowling pins. The red heart keeps getting brighter and brighter and then, suddenly, with a snap it cracks open. "Thar she blows," Sally says, seconds before the third pin splits itself exactly in two.

Dennis leans over and gently places two more nose to nose on the grate. He's loving this. By now we've turned out the floor lamp and all the table lamps, leaving just the lit tree and the light from the fire.

It makes me dizzy looking at those pins burning. I think, now they're going, now they're gone. I remember the last time Dennis and I were on a plane, and the pilot, crossing a time zone, asked us to adjust our time pieces. Our time pieces. What a word. We twiddled a dial, and there was an hour erased.

Purse is talking about growing up in Swan River, how he used to set pins after school, earning thirty cents an hour and how he read *True Detective Magazine* between lanes. The kids stare at his face, which happens to be a rather large, quiet, undemanding face, and I can tell they're wondering how things get so displaced and changed like this.

I look over at Dad, who's asleep in his chair. It's been a longer day than he's used to, and I'm glad he's decided to sleep over. There's pink light from the fire coloring up his forehead and cheeks. It's extravagant looking, rich, and I can't decide whether it makes him look very old or young like a boy.

Sally sits close to me. Earlier, while the men were doing the dishes and the kids were tearing around the house, I told her I was thinking of going back to work as soon as possible, not waiting till next fall after all. She listened hard. She has a lot of strong curiosity about her. "Don't rush," she said. "Work is only work."

"One more?" Dennis asks us, and balances another pin delicately on its side in the glowing ashes. It flares, catches, glows, splits open and dies. I pay attention to it. Usually I'm so preoccupied, so busy, I forget about this odd ability of time to overtake us. Then something reminds me. Cemeteries—they stop me short, do they *ever* stop me short—and old buildings and tree stumps, things like that. And the sight of burning fires, like tonight, like right now, this minute, how economical it is, how it eats up everything we give it, everything we have to offer.

Milk Bread Beer Ice

"WHAT'S THE DIFFERENCE between a gully and a gulch?" Barbara Cormin asks her husband, Peter Cormin, as they speed south on the Interstate. These are the first words to pass between them in over an hour, this laconic, idle, unhopefully offered, trivia-contoured question.

Peter Cormin, driving a cautious sixty miles an hour through a drizzle of rain, makes no reply, and Barbara, from long experience, expects none. Her question concerning the difference between gullies and gulches floats out of her mouth like a smoker's lazy exhalation and is instantly subsumed by the hum of the engine. Two minutes pass. Five minutes. Barbara's thoughts skip to different geological features, the curious wind-lashed forms she sees through the car window, and those others whose names she vaguely remembers from a compulsory geology course taken years earlier—arroyos, cirques, terminal moraines. She has no idea now what these exotic relics might look like, but imagines them to be so brutal and arresting as to be instantly recognizable should they materialize on the landscape. Please let them materialize, she prays to the grooved door of the glove compartment. Let something, *anything*, materialize.

This is their fifth day on the road. Four motels, interchangeable, with tawny, fire-retardant carpeting, are all that have intervened. This morning, Day Five, they drive through a strong brown and yellow landscape, ferociously eroded, and it cheers Barbara a little to gaze out at this scene of novelty after seventeen hundred miles of green hills and ponds and calm, staring cattle. "I really should keep a dictionary in the car," she says to Peter, another languid exhalation.

The car, with its new-car smell, seems to hold both complaint and accord this morning. And silence. Barbara sits looking out at the rain, wondering about the origin of the word *drizzle*—a likeable enough word, she thinks, when you aren't actually being drizzled upon. Probably onomatopoeic. Drizzling clouds. Drizzled syrup on pancakes. She thrashes around in her head for the French equivalent: *bruine,* she thinks, or is that the word for fog? "I hate not knowing things," she says aloud to Peter. Musing. And arranging her body for the next five minutes.

At age fifty-three she is a restless traveler, forever shifting from haunch to haunch, tugging her blue cotton skirt smooth, examining its weave, sighing and stretching and fiddling in a disapproving way with the car radio. All she gets is country music. Or shouting call-in shows, heavy with sarcasm and whining indignation. Or nasal evangelists. Yesterday she and Peter listened briefly to someone preaching about the seven *F*'s of Christian love, the first *F* being, to her amazement, the fear of God, *the feah of Gawd.* Today, because of the rain, there's nothing on the radio but ratchety static. She and Peter have brought along a box of tapes, Bach and Handel and Vivaldi, that she methodically plays and replays, always expecting diversion and always forgetting she is someone who doesn't know what to do with music. She listens but doesn't hear. What she likes are words. *Drizzle,* she repeats to herself, *bruiner.* But how to conjugate it?

In the back seat are her maps and travel guides, a bundle of slippery brochures, a book called *Place Names of Texas* and another called *Texas Wildlife*. Her reference shelf. Her sanity cupboard. She can't remember how she acquired the habit of looking up facts; out of some nursery certitude, probably, connecting virtue with an active, inquiring mind. *People must never stop learning;* once Barbara had believed fervently in this embarrassing cliché, was the first in line for night-school classes, tuned in regularly with perhaps a dozen others to solemn radio talks on existentialism, Monday nights, seven to eight. And she has, too, her weekly French conversation group, now in its fourteenth year but soon to disband.

Her brain is always heating up; inappropriately, whimsically. She rather despises herself for it, and wishes, when she goes on vacation, that she could submerge herself in scenery or fantasy as other people seemed to do, her husband, Peter, in particular, or so she suspects. She would never risk saying to him, "A penny for your thoughts," nor would he ever say such a thing to her. He believes such "openers" are ill-bred intrusions. He told her as much, soon after they were married, lying above her on the living-room floor in their first apartment with the oval braided rug beneath them pushing up its rounded cushiony ribs. "What are you thinking?" she had asked, and watched his eyes go cold.

The rain increases, little checks against the car window, and Barbara curls her legs up under her, something she seldom does—since it makes her feel like a woman trying too hard to be whimsical—and busies herself looking up Waco, Texas, in her guidebook. There it is: population figures, rainfall statistics, a naive but jaunty potted history. Why, at her age, does she feel compelled to know such things? What is all this shrewdness working itself up for? Waco, she learns, is pronounced with a long *A* sound, which is disappointing. She prefers—who wouldn't?—the comic splat of wham, pow, whacko. Waco, Texas. The city rises and collapses in the rainy distance.

Leaning forward, she changes the tape. Its absolute, neat plastic corners remind her of the nature of real things, and snapping it into place gives her more satisfaction than listening to the music. A click, a short silence, and then the violins stirring themselves like iced-tea spoons, like ferns on a breezy hillside. Side two. She stares out the window, watchful for the least variation. A water tower holds her eye for a full sixty seconds, a silver thimble on stilts. *Château d'eau,* she murmurs to herself. Tower of Water. Tower of Babel.

Almost all her conversations are with herself.

Imprisoned now for five long days in the passenger seat of a brand new Oldsmobile Cutlass, Barbara thinks of herself as a castaway. Her real life has been left behind in Toronto. She and Peter are en route to Houston to attend an estate auction of a late client of Peter's, a man who ended his life not long ago with a pistol shot. For the sake of the passage, admittedly only two weeks, she has surrendered those routines that make her feel busy and purposeful. (With another woman she runs an establishment on Queen Street called the Ungift Shop; she also reads to the blind and keeps up her French.) Given the confining nature of her life, she has surprising freedoms at her disposal.

We should have flown is the phrase she is constantly on the point of uttering. Driving had been Peter's idea; she can't now remember his reasons: Two reasons he gave, but what were they?

He has a craning look when he drives, immensely responsible. And a way of signaling when he passes, letting his thumb wing out sideways on the lever, a deft and lovely motion. She is struck by the beauty of it, also its absurdity, a little dwarfish, unconscious salute, and silent.

There is too much sorrowful sharing in marriage, Barbara thinks. When added up, it kills words. Games have to be invented; theater. Out loud she says, like an imitation of a gawking person, "I wonder what those little red flowers are." (Turning, reaching for her wildlife book.) "We don't have those in Ontario. Or do we?"

The mention of the red flowers comes after another long silence.

Then Peter says, not unkindly, not even impatiently, "A gully's deeper, I think."

"Deeper?" says Barbara in her dream voice. She is straining her eyes to read a billboard poised high on a yellow bluff. IF YOU SMOKE PLEASE TRY CARLETONS. The word *please,* it's shocking. So!—the tobacco industry has decided to get polite. Backed into a corner, attacked on all sides, they're hitting hard with wheedling courtesies, *please.* Last week Barbara watched a TV documentary on lung cancer and saw a set of succulent pink lungs turning into what looked like slices of burnt toast.

"Deeper than a gulch."

"Oh," says Barbara.

"Unless I've got it the wrong way round."

"It's slang, anyway, I think."

"What?"

"Gully. Gulch. They're not real words, are they? They sound, you know, regional. Cowboy lingo."

Peter takes a long banked curve. On and on it goes, ninety degrees or more, but finely graded. His hands on the wheel are scarcely required to move. Clean, thick hands, they might be carved out of twin bars of soap. Ivory soap, carbolic. He smiles faintly, but in a way that shuts Barbara out. On and on. Rain falls all around them—*il pleut*—on the windshield and on the twisted landforms and collecting along the roadway in ditches. "Could be," Peter says.

"Does that look brighter up ahead to you?" Barbara says wildly, anxious now to keep the conversation going. She puts away the tape, sits up straight, pats her hair, and readies herself for the little fates and accidents a conversation can provide.

Conversation?

Inside her head a quizzing eyebrow shoots up. These idle questions and observations? This dilatory response? This disobliging exchange between herself and her husband of thirty-three years, which is as random and broken as the geological rubble she dully observes from the car window, and about which Peter can scarcely trouble himself to comment? This sludge of gummed phrases? Conversation?

It could be worse, thinks Barbara, always anxious to be fair, and calling to mind real and imaginary couples sitting silent in coffee shops, whole meals consumed and paid for with not a single word exchanged. Or stunned-looking husbands and wives at home in their vacuumed living rooms, neatly dressed and conquered utterly by the background hum of furnaces and air-conditioning units. And after that, what?—a desperate slide into hippo grunts and night coughing, slack, sponge-soft lips and toothless dread—that word *mute* multiplied to the thousandth power. Death.

An opportunity to break in the new car was what Peter had said—now she remembered.

Barbara met Peter in 1955 at a silver auction in Quebec City. He was an apprentice then, learning the business. He struck her first as being very quiet. He stared and stared at an antique coffee service, either assessing its value or awestruck by its beauty—she didn't know which. Later he grew talkative. Then silent. Then eloquent. Secretive. Verbose. Introspective. Gregarious. A whole colony of choices appeared to rest in his larynx. She never knew what to expect. One minute they were on trustworthy ground, feeding each other intimacies, and the next minute they were capsized, adrift and dumb.

"Some things can't be put into words," a leaner, nervous, younger Peter Cormin once said.

"Marriage can be defined as a lifelong conversation," said an elderly, sentimental, slightly literary aunt of Barbara's, meaning to be kind.

Barbara at twenty had felt the chill press of rhetorical echo: *a religious vocation is one of continuous prayer, a human life is one unbroken thought.* Frightening. She knew better, though, than to trust what was cogently expressed. Even as a young woman she was forever tripping over abandoned proverbs. She counted on nothing, but hoped for everything.

Breaking in the new car. But did people still break in cars? She hadn't heard the term used for years. Donkey's years. Whatever that meant.

A younger, thinner, more devious Barbara put planning into her conversations. There was breakfast talk and dinner talk and lively hurried telephone chatter in between. She often cast herself in the role of ingenue, allowing her husband Peter space for commentary and suggestions. It was Barbara who put her head to one side, posed questions and prettily waited. It was part of their early shared mythology that he was sometimes arrogant to the point of unkindness, and that she was sensitive and put upon, an injured consciousness flayed by husbandly imperative. But neither of them had the ability to sustain their roles for long.

She learned certain tricks of subversions, how with one word or phrase she could bring about disorder and then reassurance. It excited her. It was like flying in a flimsy aircraft and looking at the suddenly vertical horizon, then bringing everything level once more.

"You've changed," one of her conversations began.

"Everyone changes."

"For better or worse?"

"Better, I think."

"You think?"

"I know."

"You say things differently. You intellectualize."

"Maybe that's my nature."

"It didn't used to be."

"I've changed, people do change."

"That's just what I said."

"I wish you wouldn't—"

"What?"

"Point things out. Do you always have to point things out?"

"I can't help it."

"You could stop yourself."

"That wouldn't be me."

Once they went to a restaurant to celebrate the birth of their second son. The restaurant was inexpensive, and the food only moderately good. After coffee, after glasses of recklessly ordered brandy, Peter slipped away to the telephone. A business call, he said to Barbara. He would only be a minute or two. From where she sat she could see him behind the glass door of the phone booth, his uplifted arm, his patient explanation, and his glance at his watch—then his face reshaped itself into furrows of explosive laughter.

She had been filled with a comradely envy for his momentary connection, and surprised by her lack of curiosity, how little she cared who was on the other end of the line, a client or a lover, it didn't matter. A conversation was in progress. Words were being mainlined straight into Peter's ear, and the overflow of his conversation traveled across the dull white tablecloths and reached her too, filling her emptiness, or part of it.

Between the two of them they have accumulated a minor

treasury of anecdotes beginning with "Remember when we—" and this literature of remembrance sometimes traps them into smugness. And, occasionally, when primed by a solid period of calm, they are propelled into the blue-tinged pre-history of that epoch before they met.

"When I was in Denver that time—"

"I never knew you were in Denver."

"My mother took me there once . . ."

"You never told me your mother took you to . . ."

But Barbara is tenderly protective of her beginnings. She is also, oddly, protective of Peter's. Eruptions from this particular and most cherished layer of time are precious and dangerous; retrieval betrays it, smudges it.

"There's something wrong," Barbara said to Peter some years ago, "and I don't know how to tell you."

They were standing in a public garden near their house, walking between beds of tulips.

"You don't love me," he guessed, amazing her, and himself.

"I love you, but not enough."

"What is enough?" he cried and reached out for the cotton sleeve of her dress.

A marriage counselor booked them for twelve sessions. Each session lasted two hours, twenty-four hours in all. During those twenty-four hours they released into the mild air of the marriage counselor's office millions of words. Their longest conversation. The polished floor, the walls, the perforated ceiling tile drank in the unstoppable flow. Barbara Cormin wept and shouted. Peter Cormin moaned, retreated, put his head on his arms. The histories they separately recounted were as detailed as the thick soft novels people carry with them to the beach in the summer. Every story elicited a counter-story, until the accumulated weight of blame and blemish had squeezed them dry. "What are we doing?" Peter Cormin said, moving the back of his hand across and across his mouth. Barbara thought back to the day she had stood by the sunlit tulip bed and said, "Something's wrong," and wondered now what had possessed her. A hunger for words, was that all? She asked the marriage counselor for a glass of cold water. She feared what lay ahead. A long fall into silence. An expensive drowning.

But they were surprisingly happy for quite some time after, speaking to each other kindly, with a highly specific strategy, little pieces moved on a chessboard. What had been tricky territory before was strewn with shame. Barbara was prepared now to admit that marriage was, at best, a flawed and gappy narrative. Occasionally, some confidence would wobble forward, and one of them, Barbara or Peter, might look up cunningly, ready to measure the moment and retreat or advance. They worked around the reserves of each other's inattention the way a pen-and-ink artist learns to use the reserve of white space.

"Why?" Barbara asked Peter.

"Why what?"

"Why did he do it? Shoot himself."

"No one knows for sure."

"There's always a note. Wasn't there a note?"

"Yes. But very short."

"Saying?"

"He was lonely."

"That's what he said, that he was lonely?"

"More or less."

"What exactly did he say?"

"That there was no one he could talk to."

"He had a family, didn't he? And business associates. He had you, he's known you for years. He could have picked up the phone."

"Talking isn't just words."

"What?"

Barbara sees herself as someone always waiting for the next conversation, the way a drunk is forever thinking ahead to the next drink.

But she discounts the conversation of Eros, which seems to her to be learned not from life, but from films or trashy novels whose authors have in turn learned it from other secondary and substandard sources. Where bodies collide most gloriously, language melts—who said that? Someone or other. Barbara imagines that listening at the bedroom key-holes of even the most richly articulate would be to hear only the murmurous inanities of *True Romance*. ("I adore your golden breasts," he whispered gruffly. "You give me intense pleasure," she deeply sighed.) But these conversations actually take place. She knows they do. The words are pronounced. The sighing and whispering happen. *Just the two of us, this paradise.*

"We can break in the car," Peter said to her back in Toronto, "and have a few days together, just the two of us."

Very late on Day Five they leave the Interstate and strike off on a narrow asphalt road in search of a motel. The cessation of highway noise is stunningly sudden, like swimming away in a dream from the noises of one's own body. Peter holds his head to one side, judging the car's performance, the motor's renewed, slower throb and the faint adhesive tick of the tires rolling on the hot road.

The towns they pass through are poor, but have seen better days. Sidewalks leading up to lovely old houses have crumbled along their edges, and the houses themselves have begun to deteriorate; many are for sale. Dark shaggy cottonwoods bend down their branches to meet the graceful pitch of the roofs. Everywhere in these little towns there are boarded-up railway stations, high schools, laundries, cafés, plumbing supply stores, filling stations. And almost everywhere, it seems, the commercial center has shrunk to a single, blinking, all-purpose, twenty-four-hour outlet at the end of town—pathetically, but precisely named: the Mini-Mart, the Superette, the Quik-Stop. These new buildings are of single-story slab construction in pale brick or cement block, and are minimally landscaped. One or two gas pumps sit out in front, and above them is a sign, most often homemade, saying MILK ICE BREAD BEER.

"Milk ice bread beer," murmurs the exhausted Barbara, giving the phrase a heaving tune. She is diverted by the thought of these four purposeful commodities traded to a diminished and deprived public. "The four elements."

In the very next town, up and down over a series of dark hills, they find a subtly altered version: BEER ICE BREAD MILK. "Priorities," says Peter, reading the sign aloud, making an ironic chant of it.

Farther along the road they come upon BREAD BEER MILK ICE. Later still, the rescrambled BEER MILK ICE BREAD.

Before they arrive, finally, at a motel with air conditioning, a restaurant and decent beds—no easy matter in a depressed agricultural region—they have seen many such signs and in all possible variations. Cryptic messages, they seem designed to comfort and confuse Peter and Barbara Cormin with loops of flawed recognition and to deliver them to a congenial late-evening punchiness. As the signs pop up along the highway, they take it in turn, with a rhythmic spell and counter-spell, to read the words aloud. Milk bread beer ice. Ice bread milk beer.

This marks the real death of words, thinks Barbara, these homely products reduced to husks, their true sense drained purely away. Ice beer bread milk. Rumblings in the throats, syllables strung on an old clothesline, electronic buzzing.

But, surprisingly, the short unadorned sounds, for a few minutes, with daylight fading and dying in the wide sky, take on expanded meaning. Another, lesser world is brought forward, distorted and freshly provisioned. She loves it—its weather and depth, its exact chambers, its lost circuits, its covered pleasures, its submerged pattern of communication.

Dressing Up for the Carnival

Dressing Up for the Carnival

ALL OVER TOWN PEOPLE are putting on their costumes. Tamara has flung open her closet door; just to see her standing there is to feel a squeeze of the heart. She loves her clothes. She *knows* her clothes. Her favorite moment of the day is *this* moment, standing at the closet door, still a little dizzy from her long night of tumbled sleep, biting her lip, thinking hard, moving the busy hangers along the rod, about to make up her mind.

Yes! The yellow cotton skirt with the big patch pockets and the hand detail around the hem. How fortunate to own such a skirt. And the white blouse. What a blouse! Those sleeves, that neckline with its buttoned flap, the fullness in the yoke that reminds her of the Morris dances she and her boyfriend, Bruce, saw at the Exhibition last year.

Next she adds her new straw belt; perfect. A string of yellow beads. Earrings, of course. Her bone sandals. And bare legs, why not?

She never checks the weather before she dresses; her clothes *are* the weather, as powerful in their sunniness as the strong, muzzy early morning light pouring into the narrow street by the bus stop, warming the combed crown of her hair and fueling her with imagination. She taps a sandaled foot lightly on the pavement, waiting for the number 4 bus, no longer just

Tamara, clerk-receptionist for the Youth Employment Bureau, but a woman in a yellow skirt. A passionate woman dressed in yellow. A Passionate, Vibrant Woman About to Begin Her Day. Her Life.

Roger, aged thirty, employed by the Gas Board, is coming out of a corner grocer's carrying a mango in his left hand. He went in to buy an apple and came out with *this*. At the cash register he refused a bag, preferring to carry this thing, this object, in his bare hand. The price was $1.29. He's a little surprised at how heavy it is, a tight seamless leather skin enclosing soft pulp, or so he imagines. He has never bought a mango before, never eaten one, doesn't know what a mango tastes like or how it's prepared. Cooked like a squash? Sliced and sugared like a peach? He has no intention of eating it, not now anyway, maybe never. Its weight reminds him of a first-class league ball, but larger, longer, smooth-skinned, and ripely green. Mango, mango. An elliptical purse, juice-filled, curved for the palm of the human hand, his hand.

He is a man of medium height, burly, divorced, wearing an open-necked shirt, hurrying back to work after his coffee break. But at this moment he freezes and sees himself freshly: a man carrying a mango in his left hand. Already he's accustomed to it; in fact, it's starting to feel lighter and drier, like a set of castanets that has somehow attached itself to his left arm. Any minute now he'll break out into a cha-cha-cha right here in front of the Gas Board. The shriveled fate he sometimes sees for himself can be postponed if only he puts his mind to it. Who would have thought it of him? Not his ex-wife, Lucile, not his co-workers, not his boss, not even himself.

And the Borden sisters are back from their ski week in Happy Valley. They've been back for a month now, in fact, so why are they still wearing those little plastic ski passes on the zipper tabs of their jackets? A good question. I SKIED HAPPY

MOUNTAIN these passes say. The Bordens wear them all over town, at the shopping center, in the parking lot. It's spring, the leaves are unfolding on the hedges in front of the post office, but the Borden girls, Karen and Sue, still carry on their bodies, and in their faces too, the fresh wintry cold of the slopes, the thrill of powder snow and stinging sky. (The air up there chimes with echoes, a bromide of blue.) It would be an exaggeration to say the Borden sisters swagger; it would be going too far. They move like young ponies, quivery and thoughtful, with the memory of expended effort and banked curves. They speak to each other in voices that are loud and musical, and their skin, so clear, pink, bright and healthy, traps the sunshine beneath its surface. With one hand, walking along, they stroke the feathering-out tops of hedges in front of the post office, and with the other they pull and tug on those little plasticized tags—I SKIED HAPPY MOUNTAIN. You might say it's a kind of compulsion, as though they can't help themselves.

And then there's Wanda from the bank, who has been sent on the strangest of errands. It happened in this way: Mr. Wishcourt, the bank manager where Wanda works, has just bought a new baby carriage for his wife, or rather for their new baby son, Samuel James. The baby carriage was an impulsive lunch-hour purchase, he explains to Wanda, looking shamefaced but exuberant: an English pram, high-wheeled, majestically hooded, tires like a Rolls-Royce, a beauty, but the fool thing, even when folded up, refuses to fit in the back of his Volvo. Would she object? It would take perhaps three-quarters of an hour. It's a fine day. He'll draw her a plan on a sheet of paper, put an X where his house is. He knows how she loves walking, that she gets restless in the afternoon sometimes, sitting in her little airless cage. He would appreciate it so much. And so would his wife and little Sam. Would she mind? He's never before asked her to make coffee or do personal errands. It's against his policy, treating his employees like that. But just this once?

Wanda sets off awkwardly. She is, after all, an awkward woman, who was formerly an awkward girl with big girlish teeth and clumsy shoulders. The pram's swaying body seems to steer her at first, instead of *her* steering *it*. Such a chunky rolling oblong, black and British with its wambling, bossy, outsized keel. "Excuse me," she says, and "Sorry." Without meaning to, she forces people over to the edge of the sidewalks, crowds them at the street corners, even rubs up against them with the big soft tires.

All she gets back are smiles. Or kindly little nods that say: "It's not your fault" or "How marvelous" or "What a picture!" After a bit she gets the hang of steering. This is a technical marvel she's pushing along, the way it takes the curbs, soundlessly, with scarcely any effort at all. Engineering at its most refined and comical. Her hands rest lightly on the wide white handlebar. It might be made of ivory or alabaster or something equally precious, it's so smooth and cool to the touch.

By the time Wanda reaches Pine Street, she feels herself fully in charge. Beneath the leafy poplars, she and the carriage have become a single entity. Gliding, melding, a silvery hum of wheels and a faint, pleasing adhesive resistance as the tires roll along suburban asphalt. The weight of her fingertips is enough to keep it in motion, in control, and she takes the final corners with grace. Little Sam is going to love his new rolling home, so roomy and rhythmic, like a dark boat sailing forward in tune with his infant breathing and the bump-dee-bump of his baby heart.

She stops, leans over and reaches inside. There's no one about; no one sees her, only the eyes inside her head that have rehearsed this small gesture in dreams. She straightens the blanket, pulling it smooth, pats it into place. "Shhh," she murmurs, smiling. "There, there, now."

Mr. Gilman is smiling too. His daughter-in-law, who considers him a prehistoric bore, has invited him to dinner. This happens perhaps once a month; the telephone rings early in the morning. "We'd love to have you over tonight," she says. "Just family fare, I'm afraid, leftovers."

"I'd be delighted," he always says, even though the word *leftovers* gives him, every time she says it, a little ping of injury.

At age eighty he can be observed in his obverse infancy, metaphorically sucking and tonguing the missing tooth of his life. He knows what he looks like: the mirror tells all—eyes like water sacs, crimson arcs around the ears, a chin that betrays him, the way it mooches and wobbles while he thrashes around in his head for one of those rumpled anecdotes that seem only to madden his daughter-in-law. Better to keep still and chew. "Scrumptious," he always says, hoping to win her inhospitable heart, but knowing he can't.

Today he decides to buy her flowers. Why-oh-why has he never thought of this before! Daffodils are selling for $1.99 a half dozen. A bargain. It must be spring, he thinks, looking around. Why not buy two bunches, or three? Why not indeed? Or four?

They form a blaze of yellow in his arms, a sweet propitiating little fire. He knows he should take them home immediately and put them in water for tonight, but he's reluctant to remove the green paper wrapping, which lends a certain legitimacy; these aren't flowers randomly snatched from the garden; these are florist's flowers, purchased as an offering, an oblation.

There seems nothing to do but carry them about with him all day. He takes them along to the bank, the drug-store, to his appointment with the foot specialist, his afternoon card club at the Sunset Lodge. Never has he received more courteous attention, such quick service. The eyes of strangers appear friendlier than usual. "I am no worse off than the average person," he announces to himself. He loses, gracefully, at canasta, then gets a seat on the bus, a seat by the window. The pale flowers in his arms spell evanescence, gaiety. "Hello there," a number of people call out to him. He is clearly a man who is expected somewhere, anticipated. A charming gent, elegant and dapper, propounding serious questions, bearing gifts, flowers. A man in disguise.

Ralph Eliot, seventeen years old, six feet tall, killingly handsome, and the best halfback the school team has seen in years, has carelessly left his football helmet hanging on a hook on the back of his bedroom door. An emergency of the first order; his ten-year-old sister, Mandy, is summoned to bring it to the playing field.

She runs all the way up Second Avenue; at the traffic light she strikes a pose, panting, then pounds furiously the whole length of Sargent Street, making it in four minutes flat. She carries the helmet by its tough plastic chin strap, and as she runs along, it bangs against her bare leg. She feels her breath blazing into a spray of heroic pain, and as her foot rounds on the pavement, a filament of recognition is touched. The exactitude of the gesture doubles and divides inside her head, and for the first time she comprehends *who* her brother is, that deep-voiced stranger whose bedroom is next to her own. Today, for a minute, she *is* her brother. *She* is Ralph Eliot, age seventeen, six feet tall, who later this afternoon will make a dazzling, lazy touchdown, bringing reward and honor to his name, and hers.

Susan Gourley, first-year arts student, has been assigned Beckett's *Waiting for Godot*. She carries it under her arm so that the title is plainly visible. She is a girl with a look of lusterless inattention and a reputation for drowsiness, but she's always known this to be a false assessment. She's biding her time, waiting; today she strides along, *strides,* her book flashing under her arm. She is a young woman who is reading a great classic. Vistas of possibility unfold like money.

Molly Beale's briny old body has been propelled downtown by her cheerful new pacemaker, and there she bumps into Bert Lessing, the city councilor, whose navy blue beret, complete with military insignia, rides pertly over his left ear. They converse like lovers. They bristle with wit. They chitter like birds.

Jeanette Foster is sporting a smart chignon. Who does she think she *is!* Who *does* she think she is?

A young woman, recently arrived in town and rather lonely, carries her sandwiches to work in an old violin case. This is only temporary. Tomorrow she may use an ordinary paper bag or eat in the cafeteria.

We cannot live without our illusions, thinks X, an anonymous middle-aged citizen who, sometimes, in the privacy of his own bedroom, in the embrace of happiness, waltzes about in his wife's lace-trimmed nightgown. His wife is at bingo, not expected home for an hour. He lifts the blind an inch and sees the sun setting boldly behind his pear tree, its mingled coarseness and refinement giving an air of confusion. Everywhere he looks he observes cycles of consolation and enhancement, and now it seems as though the evening itself is about to alter its dimensions, becoming more (and also less) than what it really is.

A Scarf

TWO YEARS AGO I WROTE A NOVEL, and my publisher sent
me on a three-city book tour: New York, Washington and
Baltimore. A very modest bit of promotion, you might say,
but Scribano & Lawrence scarcely knew what to do with me.
I had never written a novel before. I am a middle-aged
woman, not at all remarkable-looking and certainly not
media-smart. If I have any reputation at all it is for being an
editor and scholar, and not for producing, to everyone's
amazement, a "fresh, bright, springtime piece of fiction," or
so it was described in *Publishers Weekly*.

My Thyme Is Up baffled everyone with its sparky sales. We
had no idea who was buying it; I didn't know, and Mr.
Scribano didn't know. "Probably young working girls," he
ventured, "gnawed by loneliness and insecurity."

These words hurt my feelings slightly, but then the reviews,
good as they were, had subtly injured me too. The reviewers
seemed taken aback that my slim novel (two hundred pages
exactly) possessed any weight at all. "Oddly appealing," the
New York Times Book Review said. "Mrs. Winters' book is very
much for the moment, though certainly not for the ages,"
the *New Yorker* said. My husband, Tom, advised me to take
this as praise, his position being that all worthy novels pay
close attention to the time in which they are suspended, and

sometimes, years later, despite themselves, acquire a permanent luster. I wasn't so sure. As a long-time editor of Danielle Westerman's work, I had acquired a near-crippling degree of critical appreciation for the sincerity of her moral stance, and I understood perfectly well that there was something just a little bit *darling* about my own book.

My three daughters, Nancy, Chris and Norah, all teenagers, were happy about the book because they were mentioned by name in a *People* magazine interview. ("Mrs. Winters lives on a farm outside Lancaster, Pennsylvania, is married to a family physician, and is the mother of three handsome daughters, Nancy, Christine and Norah.") That was enough for them. Handsome. Norah, the most literary of the three—both Nancy and Chris are in the advanced science classes at General MacArthur High School—mumbled that it might have been a better book if I'd skipped the happy ending, if Alicia had decided on suicide after all, and if Roman had denied her his affection. There was, my daughters postulated, maybe too much over-the-top sweetness about the thyme seeds Alicia planted in her window box, with Alicia's mood listless but squeaking hope. And no one in her right mind would sing out (as Alicia had done) those words that reached Roman's ears—he was making filtered coffee in the kitchen— and bound him to her forever: "My thyme is up."

It won the Offenden Prize, which, though the money was nice, shackled the book to minor status. Clarence and Dorothy Offenden had established the prize back in the seventies out of a shared exasperation with the opaqueness of the contemporary novel. "The Offenden Prize recognizes literary quality and honors accessibility." These are their criteria. Dorothy and Clarence are a good-hearted couple, and rich, but a little jolly and simple in their judgments, and Dorothy in particular is fond of repeating her recipe for enduring fiction. "A beginning, a middle and an ending," she likes to say. "Is that too much to ask!"

At the award ceremony in New York she embraced Tom and the girls, and told them how I shone among my peers, those dabblers in convolution and pretension who wrote without holding the reader in the mind, who played games for their own selfish amusement, and who threw a mask of *noir* over every event, whether it was appropriate or not. "It's heaven," she sang into Tom's ear, "to find that sunniness still exists in the world." (Show me your fatwa, Mrs. Winters.)

I don't consider myself a sunny person. In fact, if I prayed, I would ask every day to be spared from the shame of dumb sunniness. Danielle Westerman has taught me that much, her life, her reflection on that life. Don't hide your dark side from yourself, she always said, it's what keeps us going forward, that pushing away from the unspeakable brilliance. She wrote, of course, amid the shadows of the Holocaust, and no one expected her to struggle free to merriment.

After the New York event, I said goodbye to the family and got on a train and traveled to Washington, staying in a Georgetown hotel that had on its top floor, reserved for me by my publisher, something called the Writer's Suite. A brass plaque on the door announced this astonishing fact. I, the writer in a beige raincoat, Mrs. Reta Winters from Lancaster, entered this doorway with small suitcase in tow and looked around, not daring to imagine what I might find. There was a salon as well as a bedroom, two full baths, a very wide bed, more sofas than I would have time to sit on in my short stay, and a coffee table consisting of a sheet of glass posed on three immense faux books lying on their sides, stacked one on the other. A large bookshelf held the tomes of the authors who had stayed in the suite. "We like to ask our guests to contribute a copy of their work," the desk clerk had told me, and I was obliged to explain that I had only a single reading copy with me, but that I would attempt to find a copy in a local store. "That would be most appreciated," she almost whistled into the sleeve of my raincoat.

The books left behind by previous authors were disappointing, inspiration manifestos or self-help manuals, with a few thrillers thrown in. I'm certainly not a snob—I read the Jackie Onassis biography, for example—but my close association with writers such as Danielle Westerman has conditioned me to hope for a degree of ambiguity or nuance, and there was none here.

In that great, wide bed I had a disturbing but not unfamiliar dream—it is the dream I always have when I am away from Lancaster, away from the family. I am standing in the kitchen at home, producing a complicated meal for guests, but there is not enough food to work with. In the fridge sits a single egg and maybe a tomato. How am I going to feed all these hungry mouths?

I'm quite aware of how this dream might be analyzed by a dream expert, that the scarcity of food stands for a scarcity of love, that no matter how I stretch that egg and tomato, there will never be enough of Reta Winters for everyone who needs her. This is how my friend Gwen, whom I am looking forward to seeing in Baltimore, would be sure to interpret the dream if I were so foolish as to tell her. Gwen is an obsessive keeper of a dream journal—as are quite a number of my friends—and she also records the dreams of others if they are offered and found worthy.

I resist the theory of insufficient love. My dream, I like to think, points only to the abrupt cessation, or interruption, of daily obligation. For twenty years I've been responsible for producing three meals a day for the several individuals I live with. I may not be conscious of this obligation, but surely

I must always, at some level, be calculating the amount of food in the house and the number of bodies to be fed: Tom and the girls, the girls' friends, my mother-in-law next door, passing acquaintances. Away from home, liberated from my responsibility for meals, my unexecuted calculations steal into my dreams and leave me blithering with this diminished store of nourishment and the fact of my unpreparedness. Such a small dream crisis, but I always wake with a sense of terror.

Since *My Thyme Is Up* is a first novel, and since mine is an unknown name, there was very little for me to do in Washington. Mr. Scribano had been afraid this would happen. The television stations weren't interested, and the radio stations avoided novels unless they had a "topic" like cancer or child abuse.

I managed to fulfill all my obligations in a mere two hours the morning after my arrival, taking a cab to a bookstore called Politics & Prose, where I signed books for three rather baffled-looking customers and then a few more stock copies that the staff was kind enough to produce. I handled the whole thing badly, was overly ebullient with the book buyers, too chatty, wanting them to love me as much as they said they loved my book, wanting them for best friends, you would think. ("Please just call me Reta, everyone does.") My impulse was to apologize for not being younger and more fetching, like Alicia in my novel, and for not having her bright ingenue voice and manner. I was ashamed of my red pantsuit, catalog-issue, and wondered if I'd remembered, waking up in the Writer's Suite, to apply deodorant.

From Politics & Prose I took a cab to a store called Pages, where there were no buying customers at all, but where the two young proprietors took me for a splendid lunch at an

Italian bistro and also insisted on giving me a free copy of my book to leave in the Writer's Suite. Then it was afternoon, a whole afternoon, and I had nothing to do until the next morning, when I was to take my train to Baltimore. Mr. Scribano had warned me I might find touring lonely.

I returned to the hotel, freshened up and placed my book on the bookshelf. But why had I returned to the hotel? What homing instinct had brought me here when I might be out visiting museums or perhaps taking a tour through the Senate chambers? There was a wide springtime afternoon to fill, and an evening too, since no one had suggested taking me to dinner.

I decided to go shopping in the Georgetown area, having spotted from the taxi a number of tiny boutiques. My daughter Norah's birthday was coming up in a week's time, and she longed to have a beautiful and serious scarf. She had never had a scarf in all her seventeen years, not unless you count the woolen mufflers she wears on the school bus, but since her senior class trip to Paris, she had been talking about the scarves that every chic Frenchwoman wears as part of her wardrobe. These scarves, so artfully draped, were silk, nothing else would do, and their colors shocked and awakened the dreariest of clothes, the wilted navy blazers that Frenchwomen wear or those cheap black cardigans they try to get away with.

I never have time to shop in Lancaster, and, in fact, there would be little available there. But today I had time, plenty of time, and so I put on my low-heeled walking shoes and started out.

Georgetown's boutiques are set amid tiny fronted houses, impeccably gentrified with shuttered bay windows and framed by minuscule gardens, enchanting to the eye. My own sprawling, untidy house outside Lancaster, if dropped into this landscape, would destroy half a dozen or more of these meticulous brick facades. The placement of flowerpots was so ardently pursued here, so caring, so solemn, and the clay pots themselves had been rubbed, I could tell, with sand-paper, to give them a country look.

These boutiques held such a minimum of stock that I wondered how they were able to compete with one another. There might be six or seven blouses on a rod, a few cashmere pullovers, a table casually strewn with shells or stones or Art Nouveau picture frames or racks of antique postcards. A squadron of very slender saleswomen presided over this spare merchandise, which they fingered in such a loving way that I suddenly wanted to buy everything in sight. The scarves—every shop had a good half-dozen—were knotted on dowels, and there was not one that was not pure silk with hand-rolled edges.

I took my time. I realized I would be able, given enough shopping time, to buy Norah the perfect scarf, not the near-perfect and certainly not the impulse purchase we usually settled for at home. She had mentioned wanting something in a bright blue with perhaps some yellow dashes. I would find that very scarf in one of these many boutiques. The thought of myself as a careful and deliberate shopper brought me a bolt of happiness. I took a deep breath and smiled genuinely at the anorexic saleswomen, who seemed to sense and respond to my new consumer eagerness. "That's not quite her," I quickly learned to say, and they nod-ded with sympathy. Most of them wore scarves themselves around their angular necks, and I admired, to myself, the intricate knotting and colors of these scarves. I admired, too, the women's forthcoming involvement in my mission. "Oh, the scarf absolutely must be suited to the person," they said, or words to that effect—as though they knew Norah personally and understood that she was a young woman of highly defined tastes and requirements that they were anxious to satisfy.

She isn't really. She is, Tom and I always think, too easily satisfied and someone who too seldom considers herself deserving. When she was a very small child, two or three, eating lunch in her high chair, she heard an airplane go overhead and looked up at me and said, "The pilot doesn't know I'm eating an egg." She seemed shocked at this perception, but willing to register the shock calmly so as not to alarm me. She would be grateful for any scarf I brought her, pleased I had taken the time, but for once I wanted, and had an opportunity to procure, a scarf that would gladden her heart.

As I moved from one boutique to the next, I began to form a very definite idea of the scarf I wanted for Norah, and began, too, to see how impossible it might be to accomplish this task. The scarf became an idea; it must be brilliant and subdued at the same time, finely made, but with a secure sense of its own shape. A wisp was not what I wanted, not for Norah. Solidity, presence, was what I wanted, but in sinuous, ephemeral form. This was what Norah at seventeen, almost eighteen, was owed. She had always been a bravely undemanding child. Once, when she was four or five, she told me how she controlled her bad dreams at night. "I just turn my head around on the pillow," she said matter-of-factly, "and that changes the channel." She performed this act instead of calling out to us or crying; she solved her own nightmares and candidly exposed her original solution—which Tom and I took some comfort in but also, I confess, some amusement. I remember, with shame now, telling this story to friends, over coffee, over dinner, my brave little soldier daughter, shaping her soldierly life.

I seldom wear scarves myself; I can't be bothered, and besides, whatever I put around my neck takes on the configuration of a Girl Scout kerchief, the knot working its way straight to the throat, and the points sticking out rather than draping gracefully downward. I was not clever with accessories, I knew that about myself, and I was most definitely not a shopper. I had never understood, in fact, what it is that drives other women to feats of shopping perfection, but now I had a suspicion. It was the desire to please someone fully, even oneself. It seemed to me that my daughter Norah's future happiness now balanced not on acceptance at Smith or the acquisition of a handsome new boyfriend, but on the simple ownership of a particular article of apparel, which only I could supply. I had no power over Smith or the boyfriend or, in fact, any real part of her happiness, but I could provide something temporary and necessary: this dream of transformation, this scrap of silk.

And there it was, relaxed over a fat silver hook in what must have been the twentieth shop I entered. The little bell rang; the updraft of potpourri rose to my nostrils, and the sight of Norah's scarf flowed into view. It was patterned from end to end with rectangles, each subtly out of alignment: blue, yellow, green, a kind of pleasing violet. And each of these shapes was outlined by a band of black, colored in roughly as though with an artist's brush. I found its shimmer dazzling and its touch icy and sensuous. Sixty dollars. Was that all? I whipped out my Visa card without a thought. My day had been well spent. I felt full of intoxicating power.

In the morning I took the train to Baltimore. I couldn't read on the train because of the jolting between one urban landscape and the next. Two men seated in front of me were talking loudly about Christianity, its sad decline, and they ran the words *Jesus Christ* together as though they were some person's first and second names—Mr. Christ, Jesus to the in-group.

In Baltimore, once again, there was little for me to do, but since I was going to see Gwen at lunch, I didn't mind. A young male radio host wearing a black T-shirt and gold chains around his neck asked me how I was going to spend the Offenden prize money. He also asked what my husband thought of the fact that I'd written a novel. (This is a question I've been asked before and for which I really must find an answer.) Then I visited the Book Plate (combination café and bookstore) and signed six books, and then, at not quite eleven in the morning, there was nothing more for me to do until it was time to meet Gwen.

Gwen and I had been in the same women's writing group back in Lancaster. In fact, she had been the informal but acknowledged leader for those of us who met weekly to share and "workshop" our writing. Poetry, memoirs, fiction; we brought photocopies of our work to these morning sessions, where over coffee and muffins—this was the age of muffins, the last days of the seventies—we kindly encouraged each other and offered tentative suggestions, such as "I think you're one draft from being finished" or "Doesn't character X enter the scene a little too late?" These critical crumbs were taken for what they were, the fumblings of amateurs. But when Gwen spoke, we listened. Once she thrilled me by saying of something I'd written, "That's a fantastic image, that thing about the whalebone. I wish I'd thought of it myself." Her short fiction had actually been published in a number of literary quarterlies, and there had even been one near-mythical sale, years earlier, to *Harper's*. When she moved to Baltimore five years ago to become writer-in-residence for a small women's college, our writers' group first fell into irregularity, and then slowly died away.

We'd kept in touch, though, the two of us. I wrote ecstatically when I happened to come across a piece of hers in *Three Spoons* that was advertised as being part of a novel-in-progress. She'd used my whalebone metaphor; I couldn't help noticing and, in fact, felt flattered. I knew about that novel of Gwen's—she'd been working on it for years—trying to bring a feminist structure to what was really a straightforward account of an early failed marriage. Gwen had made sacrifices for her young student husband, and he had betrayed her with his infidelities. In the early seventies, in the throes of love and anxious to satisfy his every demand, she had had her navel closed by a plastic surgeon because her husband complained that it smelled "off." The complaint, apparently, had been made only once, a sour, momentary whim, but out of some need to please or punish she became a woman without a navel, left with a flattish indentation in the middle of her belly, and this navel-less state, more than anything, became her symbol of regret and anger. She spoke of erasure, how her relationship to her mother—with whom she was on bad terms anyway—had been erased along with the primal mark of connection. She was looking into a navel reconstruction, she'd said in her last letter, but the cost was criminal. In the meantime, she'd retaken her unmarried name, Reidman, and had gone back to her full name, Gwendolyn.

She'd changed her style of dress too. I noticed that right away when I saw her seated at the Café Pierre. Her jeans and sweater had been traded in for what looked like large folds of unstitched, unstructured cloth, skirts and overskirts and capes and shawls; it was hard to tell precisely what they were. This cloth wrapping, in a salmon color, extended to her head, completely covering her hair, and I wondered for an awful moment if she'd been ill, undergoing chemotherapy and suffering hair loss. But no, there was a fresh, healthy, rich face. Instead of a purse she had only a lumpy plastic bag with a supermarket logo; that did worry me, especially because she put it on the table instead of setting it on the floor as I would have expected. It bounced slightly on the sticky wooden surface, and I remembered that she always carried an apple with her, a paperback or two and her small bottle of cold-sore medication.

Of course I'd written to her when *My Thyme Is Up* was accepted for publication, and she'd sent back a postcard saying, "Well done, it sounds like a hoot."

I was a little surprised that she hadn't brought a copy for me to sign, and wondered at some point, halfway through my oyster soup, if she'd even read it. The college pays her shamefully, of course, and I know she doesn't have money for new books. Why hadn't I had Mr. Scribano send her a complimentary copy?

It wasn't until we'd finished our salads and ordered our coffee that I noticed she hadn't mentioned the book at all, nor had she congratulated me on the Offenden Prize. But perhaps she didn't know. The notice in the *New York Times* had been tiny. Anyone could have missed it.

It became suddenly important that I let her know about the prize. It was as strong as the need to urinate or swallow. How could I work it into the conversation?—maybe say something about Tom and how he was thinking of putting a new roof on our barn, and that the Offenden money would come in handy. Drop it in casually. Easily done.

"Right!" she said heartily, letting me know she already knew. "Beginning, middle, end." She grinned then.

She talked about her "stuff," by which she meant her writing. She made it sound like a sack of kapok. A magazine editor had commented on how much he liked her "stuff," and how her kind of "stuff" contained the rub of authenticity. There were always little linguistic surprises in her work, but more interesting to me were the bits of the world she brought to what she wrote, observations or incongruities or some sideways conjecture. She understood their value. "He likes the fact that my stuff is off-center and steers a random course," she said of a fellow writer.

"No beginnings, middles and ends," I supplied.

"Right," she said. "Right." She regarded me fondly, as though I were a prize pupil. Her eyes looked slightly pink at the corners, but it may have been a reflection from the cloth that cut a sharp line across her forehead.

I admire her writing. She claimed she had little imagination, that she wrote out of the material of her own life, but that she was forever on the lookout for what she called "putty." By this she meant the arbitrary, the odd, the ordinary, the mucilage of daily life that cements our genuine moments of being. I've seen her do wonderful riffs on buttonholes, for instance, the way they shred over time, especially on cheap clothes. And a brilliant piece on bevelled mirrors, and another on the smell of a certain set of wooden stairs from her childhood, wax and wood and reassuring cleanliness accumulating at the side of the story but not claiming any importance for itself.

She looked sad over her coffee, older than I'd remembered—but weren't we all?—and I could tell she was disappointed in me for some reason. It occurred to me I might offer her a piece of putty by telling her about the discovery I had made the day before, that shopping was not what I'd thought, that it could become a mission, even an art if one persevered. I had had a shopping item in mind; I had been presented with an unasked-for block of time; it might be possible not only to imagine this artifact, but to realize it.

"How many boutiques did you say you went into?" she asked, and I knew I had interested her at last.

"Twenty," I said. "Or thereabouts."

"Incredible."

"But it was worth it. It wasn't when I started out, but it became more and more worth it as the afternoon went on."

"Why?" she asked slowly. I could tell she was trying to twinkle a gram of gratitude at me, but she was closer to crying.

"To see if it existed, this thing I had in mind."

"And it did."

"Yes."

To prove my point I reached into my tote bag and pulled out the pale, puffy boutique bag. I unrolled the pink tissue paper on the table and showed her the scarf.

She lifted it against her face. Tears glinted in her eyes. "It's just that it's so beautiful," she said. And then she said, "Finding it, it's almost like you made it. You invented it, created it out of your imagination."

I almost cried myself. I hadn't expected anyone to understand how I felt.

I watched her roll the scarf back into the fragile paper. She took her time, tucking in the edges with her fingertips. Then she slipped the parcel into her plastic bag, tears spilling more freely now. "Thank you, darling Reta, thank you. You don't know what you've given me today."

But I did, I did.

But what does it amount to? A scarf, half an ounce of silk, maybe less, floating free in the world. I looked at Gwen/Gwendolyn, my old friend, and then down at my hands, my wedding band, my engagement ring, a little diamond thingamajig from the sixties. I thought of my three daughters and my mother-in-law and my own dead mother with her slack charms and the need she had to relax by paint-ing china. Not one of us was going to get what we wanted. Imagine someone writing a play called *Death of a Saleswoman*. What a joke. We're so transparently in need of shoring up our little preciosities and our lisping pronouns, her, she. We ask ourselves questions, endlessly, but not nearly sternly enough. The world isn't ready for us yet; it hurts me to say that. We're too soft in our tissues, even you, Danielle Westerman, Holocaust survivor, cynic and genius. Even you, Mrs. Winters, with your new, old useless knowledge. We are too kind, too willing, too unwilling too, reaching out blindly with a grasping hand, but not knowing how to ask for what we don't even know we want.

Weather

My husband came home from work in a bad mood. There'd been a sudden downpour as he was driving in the direction of our village, and the rain, as usual, found its way into the distributor of his ancient car. Twice he'd had to stop at the side of the road, raise the hood and apply a rag to the distributor cap.

His shirt was soaked by the time he came muttering up the back steps into the house, and his hair, what remains of it, was plastered to his head, exaggerating his already petulant look. To make matters worse, he'd heard on the car radio that the National Association of Meteorologists was going on strike the following day.

I cheered him up as best I could and fed him a hot meal even though it was the height of summer, his favorite braised lamb chops with mint sauce, the mint coming fresh from our own garden, that wild strip running along the side of the garage. "Never mind about the strike," I said. "It'll only last a day or two."

How wrong I was!

We kept tuned to the radio as the hours passed, but learned little more. Heated discussions were taking place, that was all we were told. For some reason these talks were kept highly secret. Conducted behind closed doors. Hush-hush.

"They're stuck on wages, I bet," my husband said. "This world of ours is getting greedier every year."

He likes to think he is above ordinary greed and materialistic longing, and he is. The neighbors are forever trading in their lawn mowers for bigger and better models, or investing in swimming pools, which he believes are pretentious and foolish, though I myself would be happy to think about installing a small concrete pool next to the porch, a glint of turquoise water meeting my eye as I glance out the window in the early morning; even a goldfish pond would give a kind of pleasure.

He cares nothing about such luxuries. He has his job at the plant nursery, his decent-though-troublesome car, his paid-for house, his vegetable garden, and he has a glassed-in porch from which he can watch the side-yard trees as they bend in the wind, a sight that never fails to rouse his spirits. I think—indeed he confided this to me in one of our rare tender moments—that he likes to imagine the immensity of the trees' root systems, plunging downward beneath the surface of the complacent lawn, then branching sideways and adding foot by fibrous foot to a complex network of tentacles that grab at the earth's clumped particles, securely anchoring the great oaks and maples, never mind how rambunctious the wind gets, never mind the weather warnings. Roots, he said to me the evening we had this strange conversation, perform the job they're designed to do, no more, no less. They don't take time off for coffee and a smoke, and they don't bellyache about remuneration. (You need to understand that my husband is the sort of man who appreciates a high degree of application and tenacity. He wishes that his fellow human beings were just as dutiful and as focused in their day-to-day lives as he himself is.)

The first twenty-four hours of the strike stretched to forty-eight and then seventy-two. My own opinion was that the meteorologists were holding out for a better pension plan. Retirement and pensions are all everyone talks about these days, though I'm frightened of retirement myself, my husband's retirement that is. What will he do with himself, a man with his ever-present tide of irascibility? "It's probably working conditions they're quibbling about," my husband barked. His own work conditions suit him perfectly, since he is an outdoors man by nature. I sometimes sense, but then I have known him for a long time, that he can barely distinguish between where his body stops and the elements begin—though he does, as I say, hate getting soaked in the rain.

The first week of the strike affected us both. There was talk about arbitration but, as is often the case, it came to nothing. Meanwhile, without weather, we struggled against frustration and boredom. I had never before thought about deprivation on this scale, but I soon discovered that one day is exactly like the next, hour after hour of featureless, tensionless air. We were suddenly without seasonal zest, without hourly variation, without surprise and complaint, dislocated in time and space. There was nothing to press upon the skin, nothing for the body to exert itself against, nothing that satisfied. The idea of umbrellas was suddenly laughable (though we didn't laugh, at least I don't remember laughing). And there was no thought of drawing the living-room blinds against the sun.

The garden more or less disowned its responsibilities. The row of tomato plants—Mexican Ecstasy was what we were trying out this year—bore well enough, though the tomatoes themselves refused to ripen. Ripeness requires long periods of bright, warm light, as everyone knows, but for the duration of the strike we were stuck in a bland width of greyness with day after day of neither heat nor cold. "At least we don't have to worry about frost," my husband grumbled in one of his reasonable moments, but his forehead was warped with anger, and his patience further tried by yet another extension of the strike. Deadlocked, they said on the eleven o'clock news; the two sides still miles apart.

A neighbor—he owns one of those satellite dishes and is therefore able to tune in to five hundred news sources—told us the government was thinking of calling in the troops. What good would that do? I thought. "What good would that do?" my husband said loudly. He'd gone off his food by now. Nothing I put on the table seemed right, not my special potato salad, not even my New Orleans gumbo. Winter fare, summer fare, it didn't matter. The cherry vanilla ice cream we like so much withheld its flavor during this weatherless period, as did my spiced beef stew and dumplings. Our own green beans from the garden, needless to say, shriveled before we could pick them.

Like children, we were uncertain as to how to clothe ourselves in the morning. Longs or shorts? Wool or cotton? Denim or polyester? My green short-sleeved rayon dress that I'm quite fond of—and so too is my husband, if I can read his eyes—seemed inappropriate, out of place, too loaded with interseasonal deliberation. As for his own work shirts, should he put on the plaid flannel or the boxy open-weave? How were we to decide, and what did it matter anyway? This lack of mattering smarted like a deerfly's sting. I found it impossible to look directly at my husband during those early morning decisions.

Something that surprised me was how much I missed the heft of daily barometric reassurance, and this was particularly curious since all my life the humidity index has felt obscurely threatening, informing us in a firm, masculine radio voice that we were either too wet or too dry for our own good. For our health and happiness. For the continuation of the planet. No one ever indicated we might reach a perfect state of humidity/dryness balance, and perhaps there is no such thing. But to be *unsituated* in terms of moisture, without either dampness or aridity to serve as a guide, is to be nowhere. The skin of my inner thighs was suddenly in a state of ignorance, not knowing how to react. My breasts itched, but the itch could not be relieved by scratching or by the application of calamine lotion. I mentioned to my husband a rustic barometer I remembered from childhood, a mechanism consisting of a tiny wooden house with two doors. When the humidity was high and rain imminent, the right-hand door opened and a little lean boy-doll, mild-faced and costumed in Alpine dress, appeared. When it was dry, a smiling little girl swung into view, promising sunshine.

My husband, his elbows on the kitchen table, listened. His nicely trimmed beard twitched and vibrated, and I thought for a minute he was about to ask a question, raising a point that, in fact, had just occurred to me: Why should the little boy signify rain and the girl sunshine?

Did humidity and dryness possess such specific and biologically assigned qualities, each of which could be measured and interpreted?

But all he said was, "You never told me that before."

"You never asked me," I said, exasperated.

The strike was into its third week, and I found myself impatient with the dulling and rounding of each twenty-four-hour segment, marked by a pencil check on the calendar and nothing else. Our lives have always been uncertain, owing to my husband's disposition, and mine too, perhaps, but at least we'd had the alternating rhythm of light and darkness to provide continuity.

To live frictionlessly in the world is to understand the real grief of empty space. Nostalgically I recalled the fluting of air currents in the late afternoon hours, hissing against the back-yard shrubs and the fetid place where we stashed the garbage cans. And the interlace of heat and coolness on my cheeks as I carried home my sacks of groceries. I wondered if my husband remembered how, only days ago, the wind used to slide against the west side of the porch, arriving in chunks or else splinters, and how it rattled the glass in the window frames, serving up for us a nervous, silvery sort of evening music that produced, simultaneously, a sense of worry and of consolation.

I felt an urge to voice such thoughts aloud but, as usual, was uncertain in my husband's presence. To speak of propul-sive sunshine and solemn shade, and the jolts of expectation that hang between the two, would be to violate a code of inti-macy we had long since established.

What I remember most from that painful, weatherless period is the sky's mute bulk of stillness. Day after day it con-tinued in its building up—pressureless, provisional and, most heartbreaking of all, exhibiting a cloudlessness that was unrelieved. Clouds. After a month I began to think that per-haps clouds were something I had only imagined. How could anything exist as lovely and as whimsical as these masses of whipped cream that transformed themselves an hour later into bright rapturous streamers of scratched air?

I dreamed one night of a tower of cloud rising in the vivid setting sun, its fringed edges painted the deep-fried gold of apple fritters, and, at the center, shading inward with a sly, modulated subtlety, the dense pewtery purple that announces a storm either approaching or receding, it didn't matter which. By morning I was sobbing into my pillow, but my hus-band, who had risen earlier, was not there to offer comfort.

Weather

We woke and slept. My husband's job was cancelled for the duration of the strike, and so we were thrown more and more together. We tended to bump into each other around the house, getting on each other's nerves, and one day I discovered him on the porch staring out at the vacant air; he was stooped and looked older than he is, and on impulse I laced my hands around the bulk of his back, pressing the side of my face against his shirt.

Later that same day we heard the news about the settlement of the strike. It seemed the meteorologists had wanted nothing all along but the public's appreciation and gratitude, and this now had been unanimously promised and even written into their contract.

My husband and I slept in each other's arms that night, and it was shortly after midnight when we were stirred out of profound unconsciousness by a breeze loosened in the elms and carried to us through the mesh of the house's various window screens.

Then, after an hour or so, drifting in and out of wakefulness, we heard, or perhaps imagined, the ballet-slipper sound of raindrops on the garage roof. A bank of coolness and damp arrived together at first dawn and entered the valved darkness of our lungs, mine and his.

I touched his mouth with my thumb then, rubbing it back and forth. We held on to each other tightly during those minutes, feeling the essence of weather blow through us, thinking the same thoughts, and I remembered that thing that, for stretches of dull time, I tend to forget. That despite everything, the two of us have learned the trick of inhabiting parallel weather systems, of making for ourselves—and no one else—snowstorms in August, of bringing into view the air of autumn whenever we wish, the icy pain at the bottom of every breath, and then arriving at the gateway of illogical, heat-enhanced January and imagining the April wind on my face, and his too, which is no louder nor more damaging than a dozen friendly bees, so that we have curiosity enough to rise and begin another day.

Flatties: Their Various Forms and Uses

A TRADITIONAL FLATTY IS COMPOSED of flour, fat, still-water, and salt. The flour commonly used in our islands derives from *bjøerne,* a hearty local barley, almost black in color and longer in the grain than Elsewhere barley. *Bjøerne* is gathered by the young boys of the isles in middle or late summer, depending on wind and weather conditions, and winnowed on the first three days following St. Ulaf's Night, except during those years in which the full moon precedes the usual holy oblations. On these rare occasions winnowing may occur at any hour or day, provided a hollyberry candle is first lit in the barnplace opening. Ordinary tallow will suffice should hollyberry prove scarce.

In the old days, flour for flatties was ground in a stone quern. Today the intercession of wind or water is more frequently invoked, and it is said that the Island of Strell mills a goodly portion of its flour nowadays with the assistance of wavelight.

You will already be acquainted with the longitude and latitude of our archipelago, as well as its annual rainfall, and so I will confine myself here to a few domestic particulars. The islands of our homeplace are Naust, Spoy, Strell, Upper Strell, Cailee, Papa Cailee, Nack, Breen, Little Breen (where the barelegs live) and Lum, my own place of birth and lifebeing.

Flatties are consumed by the peoples of all these islands except for Naust, where inhabitants decline to eat them. They fear even to touch them. Instead, a small loafbread constitutes their chief nourishment, a mixture of crumbled meal and milk over which a prayer is uttered so that its volume doubles and trebles. The people of Naust fasten horseshoes to the hooves of their draught animals in order to protect the beastfeet from poisons that are stirred up by the action of plough and harrow.

The indigenous folk of Strell and Upper Strell are alike in their fondness for flatties that are shaped in a circle with a small depression in the middle. Their horseshoes too reflect an inclination for circularity, the two traditional points having long since merged so that there is no visible break or separation. Boys are presented with their horseshoes at the age of twelve, girls at fourteen.

The small Island of Spoy has not yet adopted the Lum-Bode. The people there rely instead on baking their flatties in a vertical passageway of shaped stone or brick that is said to carry smoke away from their dwellings. They nail their horseshoes over these passageways before a baking takes place, being careful that the prongs point skyward in a gesture of respect and also imprecation. Flatties are sometimes referred to by the oldenfolk of Spoy as *fletcake* or *platter-brød,* but these locutions are now in decline.

Though flatties abound on the Island of Cailee, it is believed there are no women among the inhabitants from whom sailors may purchase a foodhoard. These brave seamen must set sail without a supply of flatties and without the womanly benedictions that protect other island folk from disorder and caprice. Caileeans wear their horseshoes suspended from a thong of leather around their necks, and before a voyage they bend forward in a deep bow, kissing the

curve of iron in the ceremonial way, and in this manner preserve all that blesses and encourages them in their lives.

On the Isle of Papa Cailee, flatties are baked communally,
owing to the small number of inhabitants. By tradition,
Caileean men stir the flour and water together in a great pot,
after which the women gather together and add the needed
fat and salt. A single horseshoe is placed at the bottom of the
baking pan for the purpose of enhancing flavor and goodness. Before being eaten, the flatties of Papa Cailee are spread
with beehoney and folded in quarters.

The dwellers of Nack are partial to the savor of strong salt.
Their flatties, therefore, possess a unique character, and a
heat that is teasing to the tongue. Preserved fish is sometimes pressed between a pair of Nack-flatties and this *skørpe,*
as it is called, is eaten from the hand in the open air.
Nackfolk, when they are at leisure, enjoy a pursuit in which
they hurl their horseshoes in the direction of a stationary
wooden peg. Men, women and children also are known to
participate in this activity.

On the westward-lying Isle of Breen, flatties are baked but
once a year. The baking takes place in the old chapelyard, and
the first flatty to emerge from the bakeoven is broken over the
ground where the thighbone of Saint Gårtrude is buried.
There is no stone to mark this place; instead, a circle of
horseshoes serves to remind folk that they are treading near
holy-earth and cautions them to observe silence and to abide
in a state of peace with their neighbors.

Just half-a-daysail north lies Little Breen, where flatties are
cooked on a griddle instead of an oven. They are eaten three
times a day, and also at the feasts of sowing and harvesting.
Those folk who fall sick are given flatties that are first soaked
in sourmilk and sprinkled with the fine-ground meat of
acorns. When a death occurs, the people of Little Breen throw

a horseshoe into the sea so that the soul of the departed will be anchored to the earth and not lose its way.

Here on the Isle of Lum we prefer to add one or two eggs to each baking of flatties, most especially in the summertime when hens are clean-laying. A well-polished horseshoe is placed beneath the straw of each nest, and this greatly encourages the eggyield. It is the very young children who collect these eggs and carry them in baskets to the bakehouse. They never stumble, no egg is ever broken. Children born on islands differ from Elsewhere children in that they are knowing of each rock and fencepost of their homeplace, of every field-corner and doorway, every spit of sand and beach pebble. This knowledge imbues them with good health and strong trust, so that they are able to look out across the widewater and observe the wonder and diversity of our earthhome. May it ever be so.

Dying for Love

MY FIRST THOUGHT THIS MORNING is for Beth, how on
earth she'll cope now that Ted's left her for the dancer
Charlotte Brown. I ask myself, what resources does a woman
like Beth have, emotional resources? Will she get through the
first few days and nights? The nights will be terrible for her,
I'm sure of that, long and heavy.

For four years they've been together, almost five, perhaps
longer. Habits accrue in that time, especially habits of the
night, when bodies and their routines get driven into hard
rituals of washed skin, brushed teeth, programs of solemnity,
then the light switch flicked off, then, *then* the orchestrated
folding back of the almost weightless cotton blanket—for it's
spring now, late May—and the mattress buttons pushing
upward. Five years gives time to study and absorb and take
on the precise rhythms of another person's breathing pattern
and to accommodate their night postures, whether they
sprawl or thrash or curl up tight. Beth curls, but sinuously;
her backbone makes a long smiling capital C on the bedsheet,
or used to, before Ted told her he was leaving her for Charlotte.

Before bed, ever since Ted left, she drinks a cup of hot milk.
This milk holds a dose of self-destruction, since she hates the
taste and can only choke it down if it's accompanied by a slice
of toast spread with peanut butter, and this exacerbates her

weight problem, which was one of the issues between her and Ted. He has an unreasoning fear of fat, though from a certain angle his own face looks fleshy and indulged. Charlotte Brown the dancer is so thin it breaks your heart. Even off her pointes, walking diagonally across a room, she has a tripping look of someone balancing on little glass stilts; also a pair of hip bones shaved down like knives, also a high thin ribbony voice.

Beth's met Charlotte twice, once at a pre-performance party, which is also where Ted first met her, and again, recently, when the three of them, Ted, Beth and Charlotte, had a drink together in a bar called the Captain's Bridge and discussed the surprisingly long list of domestic details that now needed reordering. Ted and Charlotte are planning to be married, something Ted and Beth in their five years had never considered, at least Ted had not. On this particular evening, out of embarrassment possibly, he lifted his glass and attempted a witticism so derivative—"You only get married for the first time once"—that Beth pressed her hands to the sides of her head, causing her blouse to rip under one arm.

Ted took out a pencil and notepad. There was the lease to consider; he would pay his share through the end of June. And some stemware to split up, and two sets of oven mitts. "We won't discuss oven mitts." Beth said this nicely, with dignity. Then a desk chair, his. A brass umbrella stand, hers. A monkey fern that Ted claimed to have nursed through a bad spell after Beth neglected it. There was also, at the bottom of the list, a certain six-cup, hard-to-replace aluminum coffeepot.

Beth had planned to be relaxed and offhand for this meeting; that was the reason she was wearing an old red cotton blouse with buttons fastening on the side. She worked hard to keep the toads from leaping out of her mouth. She kept her hand away from the dish of smoked pecans and held her head bravely erect as though she were sniffing a long-stemmed rose, a trick she learned from an article in a beauty magazine. Airily preoccupied, she managed to convey the impression that she was about to rush off to meet friends in a restaurant, close friends, old friends, and that she was already late and would probably have to take a cab, but that she was perfectly prepared to bear this expense, happy, in fact, to part with her last ten dollars, so eager was she for sympathetic companionship, to be among her own kind of people. She glanced frequently at her watch, at the same time quietly maintaining her right to the six-cup coffeepot.

"I don't drink coffee," Charlotte Brown said in a dazed, injured voice.

"All right then, keep the coffeepot," Ted said, none too gently, causing Beth to grab her jacket, white linen, and rush out the door without saying goodbye or wishing the two of them happiness and good fortune in the years ahead.

Later she thought of stuffing one of Ted's stray socks in the coffeepot and mailing it to his new address. Or filling it with her birth-control pills and leaving it at his door. Or donating it to a money raiser for the victims of AIDS.

Instead she put the coffeepot on the top shelf of a cupboard, where she would hardly ever have to look at it.

I find it difficult to imagine how Beth will cope emotionally. Nevertheless, despite her insomnia, she somehow manages to get up most mornings, get herself dressed and go to work in the office of a very large swimwear factory.

A woman named Jennifer Downs who works in the same office pressed a little packet into Beth's hand one day. Sleeping pills, she whispered. Just a few. To get you through the next couple of weeks. You need your sleep, you need to keep yourself from falling apart.

Beth has a bottle of gin in her cupboard and wonders what would happen if she took all twelve pills plus the gin. She doesn't know. I don't either. Probably nothing would happen; this is what she decides anyway—nothing. But just in case she empties the gin bottle down the kitchen sink. The pills she grinds in the disposal unit.

Then she wanders into her bathroom, her hot milk in hand, and permits herself an admiring look in the ripply mirror, but nonchalantly, coolly, out of the corner of her eye. What she sees is the profile of someone who had considered joining that tiny company of women who have died for love. She salutes the side of her face with her thick pottery mug, across which is written the word SMILE.

Life is a thing to be cherished, she thinks, and this thought, slender as a handrail, gets her through one more night.

But then there's Lizzie in Somerset; my fears for Lizzie grow day by day. Her predicament is clear, and so is her fate, although I can perhaps imagine a way to assist her in the avoidance of that fate.

It is now a fortnight since Ned quit the lodgings where the two of them have sheltered these last several months. Ever since his departure Lizzie has grieved, and repeated over and over to herself their final hour together, a long damp scene in which Ned's confession of temptation and weakness had gone on and on, running out of his mouth so wastefully, and all for her account, when a single phrase would have done: he was sodden with love, and for a music hall performer named Carlotta. When he pronounced the word *love*, the little muscles around his lips strained toward a decency that surprised her.

The first shock of silence once Lizzie found herself truly alone in the room was chilling. She dealt, finally, with her necessary calculations, adding and subtracting while pacing the length of the pink wallpapered room overlooking the filthy cobbled street.

Small rented rooms such as this have the power to accumulate sharp clarities, particularly the relentless press of time passing, how it can never be turned backwards. Lizzie's small breasts, over which Neddie had sighed with disappointment, or so she fancied, were now engorged, swollen against her muslin bodice, their tips shivering with hurt. She was only eighteen, but of country stock, and knew the signs. An older sister, married and living in Oxfordshire, had spoken to her gently of female vulnerability, of the moon and its controlling power, but this was before Neddie made his appearance in the region.

He was a manufacturer's representative from Bolton. His hours were irregular. It seemed he could work when he liked, and more often he went his rounds in the early evening when, as he said, people were most easily persuaded in their buying and selling. His shirts—he possessed three—had seen better days, but his coat, which was of dark woolen stuff, and elegant, and was buttoned in the new single-breasted way, spoke of reliability. So too did his gold watch and chain and the glossy manner in which he fingered these objects. Lizzie worried about his shoes, their scraped toes and cracked uppers, wondering what, if anything, they signified.

He teased her with foolish compliments and practiced on her a perverse magic, for, by praising her simplicity, he urged her to abandon it. By exclaiming over her devotion, he hinted that her pretty ways fell somehow short of full womanly expression. Her sincerity of affection was so forthright, so cheerful, candid and unstinting, that he fell into a sulk and accused her of loving everyone else as well as she loved him. His restlessness, his tapping foot, his drumming fingers, the tiny working muscles around his mouth beseeched her to give up that token he most truly desired, and finally, in the cushiony orchard, under a sky of depthless black, she surrendered.

Now she sat in a small room counting off days. A series of pictures tripped through her head, joining the pink flowers on the wall and receding finally into a continuous blur of grief. She has told Mrs. Hanna, who keeps the lodging house, that her husband will pay the rent as soon as he returns from a brief journey to Derbyshire, a journey necessitated by a sudden illness in her mother's family. Poor creature, said Mrs. Hanna, with her munching gums, poor creature, and Lizzie has turned these words over in her mind at least a hundred times.

Late one spring night, in the tender darkness, she flung a cloak across her shoulders, swiftly pinned a hat to her head and strode toward the site of the New Bridge.

The New Bridge is a wonder. Great iron spans swing between tapering stone piles in a manner so harmonious that mountains are brought to mind, and feudal strongholds and brave deeds. The graceful railings are decorated with iron Tritons and plunging sea creatures, thrusting their green painted heads boldly forward and interlacing their scaly tails. Far below, the flooded river roars and sings.

A yellowish light now forms on the bridge railing, a spumy brightness as clear as paint, but cut over and across by shapes of heavy leaves and whip-like branches, and above them a watery aisle outlined and tinted by a three-quarters-full moon. *Now*, Lizzie whispers. And hoists herself up among the molded mermaids. Now!

But two thoughts quickly intervene. First, that she is a remarkably able swimmer. Her father, who drank, who told lies, who pocketed money he had no right to, who blasphemed, who could scarcely read, who was prideful and superstitious—this same man had taught each of his seven children, daughters as well as sons, to swim. He stood waist-high in pond water and supported their bodies with the shelf of his broad arms, encouraging them to kick for their lives and thrash and keep their heads above the treacherous surface; over and over until they had it right, until it became second nature—which is why Lizzie knows that the moment she breaks through the white foam, a phantom courage will drive her smoothly and swiftly in the direction of the river bank.

Her second thought is for her hat, which is yellow straw with a band of cut-felt violets around its crown, given her by the Oxford sister on her last birthday. She holds the hat in little regard, but senses at the same time the absurdity, the impossibility, of drowning in such a hat. Nor will she leave it on the bridge railing to be picked up by the first passerby.

Suddenly, like a wave riding well above its fellows, her sorrow collapses. She smiles, licks her lips, and turns her back on the tide of river water with its glints and crescents and riding knots of gold. Down there in the swirling currents her dear Neddie's behavior is suspended. Not only that, but she imagines possibilities of rescue. Mrs. Hanna. Her Oxford sister. Some few remaining coins in the bottom of a purse. Who can tell.

It is to my advantage that I can discard the possibilities Lizzie can't even imagine. All she understands is that both love and the lack of love can be supported. Loneliness might even be useful, she thinks—and clinging to this slender handrail of hope she readjusts her hat and strikes off down the road.

Elsewhere, much nearer home, a woman named Elizabeth is lying on her bed in the middle of the afternoon with a plastic dry cleaner's bag drawn up over her face, like a blanket in freezing weather. She is no longer young. A week ago she apprehended herself, not directly in a mirror, but by catching hold of her image, almost by chance, in the presence of its encircling flesh, and realized that this disintegrating quilted envelope would accompany her to the end, and that she had lost forever the power to stir ardor.

Nevertheless, she is surprisingly calm, breathing almost indifferently against the thin plastic covering. She inhales and exhales experimentally, playfully, observing the way the membrane puckers and clings, then withdraws at her pleasure. She has been married for twenty-five years, and is still married, to a man who no longer loves her; it's gone, it's used up, it's worn away, and there's nothing to bring it back; half her despair derives from knowing that this thing that's collapsed so suddenly in her has been dead to him for years, and she thinks how much more bearable an abrupt abandonment of love would have been.

How much more acceptable, like a cleanly applied knife, if he were to leave her for someone else, one of the secretaries in his office, for instance, some girl with a swaying, gliding pelvis, with carelessly bundled dark massy hair and bright coral mouth and fingernails—perhaps her name would be Coral as well, Coral of the swervy body and rhythmic hands who would bring about an honest spasm of betrayal and not this slow airless unassuageable absence.

She tries hard to picture the two of them together, her husband and this woman Coral, and for an instant a color photo flickers on her eyelids. But she has trouble keeping it in focus. Instead she is imagining the legions of other women who have almost died for love, how they are all fetched from the same province of illusion, the same fraying story, and how they employ the same shadeless metaphors. A tragic narrative, unbearable, except that the recurrent episodes—of ecstasy, shock, loss and lament—are similarly, cunningly, hinged to a saving capacity for digression and recovery, for the ability to be called back by clamorous objects and appointments. A woman at the end of love, after all, is not the same as a woman at the end of her tether. She has the power to create parallel stories that offer her a measure of comfort.

Already the plastic bag has loosened its hold and slipped down below her face, a bag that only yesterday enclosed a heavy gray overcoat, her husband's, and was carried home by Elizabeth herself from the dry cleaner's in a nearby shopping mall and put away in a cedar closet until next winter.

Close to the dry cleaner's establishment—her brain drifts and skitters as it refills with oxygen—is a florist's where she sometimes buys cut flowers, and next to the florist's is a delicatessen where rare honeys and olives can be found. She is a woman whose life is crowded with not-unpleasant errands and with the entrapment of fragrant, familiar and sometimes enchanting items, all of which possess a reassuring, measurable weight and volume.

Not that this is much of a handrail to hang on to—she knows that, and so do I—but it is at least continuous, solid, reliable as a narrative in its turnings and better than no handrail at all.

Ilk

By now everyone's seen the spring issue of *Ficto-Factions,* page 146, in which G.T.A., whoever he/she may be, summarizes the various papers that were presented at the recent NWUS Conference on Narrativity and Notation. Put your finger on the third paragraph of the summary, move it halfway down, and you'll see that the astute and androgynous G.T.A. refers to me by name. The bit about "the new theory of narrative put forward at NWUS and how it illustrates the atemporal paradigms of L. Porter and his ilk."

It happens that I am L. Porter—but you already know that. It's printed right here on my name tag.

I prefer to be direct in my responses, so I'll admit straight-away that an inexplicable gust of sadness passed through me when I came across G.T.A's pointed but oblique mention, and I realized too, after some reflection, that I was subtly injured to see myself accompanied by a faithful, though imaginary, pool of "ilk." By the way, that should be *her* ilk, not *his,* the L in my name standing for Lucy, after my no longer living and breathing Aunt Lucy. (Traditionally, of course, Lucy has been a female name, and one that comes embedded with complementary echoes of *lacy,* and also the lazy-daisy womb of its final *y.*) Nevertheless, my good friends, as distinct from my "ilk," have persuaded me that if I'm really serious about getting tenure I'd better sign my published articles with my initial only. In these days of affirmative action, Lucy Porter gets interviews, plenty of them, but L. Porter gets people to read her "ilkish" ideas about narrative.

So where exactly do I stand, then, on narrative enclosures? Or, to put it another way, how small can ficto-fragments get without actually disappearing? First, forget all that spongy Wentworthian whuss about narrative as movement. A narrative isn't something you pull along like a toy train, a perpetually thrusting indicative. It's this little subjunctive cottage by the side of the road. All you have to do is open the door and walk in. Sometimes you might arrive and find the door ajar. That's always nice. Other times you crawl in through a window. You look around, pick yourself a chair, sit down, relax. You're there. Chrysalis collapses into cognition. You apprehend the controlling weights and counterweights of separate acts and objects. No need to ask for another thing.

All right, most of us know this instinctively. Where Dick Wentworth (R.S. Wentworth, teacher/scholar/critic) goes wrong is in confusing narrative containment with sequentiality and its engagé/dégagé assumptions concerning directedness, the old shell game, only with new flags attached. "Look," I explain to him at the ANRAA Symposium in January—we collide while checking our coats at the opening night wine-and-cheese reception—"a fictive module doesn't need a fully rigged sailing vessel. A footstool is all it needs. Or a longing for a footstool."

And I'm not just talking minimalism here. I'm saying that fiction's clothes can be folded so small they'd fit inside a glass marble. You could arrange them on those little plastic doll hangers and hook them over the edge of Dick Wentworth's name tag. There's a bud of narrativity opening up right there behind the linked lettering, as there is beneath all uniquely arbitrary signs. There's (A) the dickness of Dick, all it says and gestures toward. And (B) the sir/surname, Wentworth, with its past-tense failure rubbing up against the trope of privilege, not to mention (C) the underground wire pulling on Jane Austen's *Persuasion*. Like it or not, Professor Wentworth's name bursts with narrative chlorophyll. His beard, his belly, they're separate stories. His pale face too. A wide, bashful, puzzled face. His wife killed herself. Someone told me that at last year's meeting.

I watch him draw his scarf slowly into the tunnel of his coat sleeve before handing it over to the coat-check person, all the way in, with the little fringed ends hanging out at the shoulder and cuff. His scarf is a cheap tan scarf and doesn't deserve this kind of care. He turns to me. His mouth open. "As Barthes says—"

"Excuse me," I say. "I'm starving. That looks like shrimp over there."

"So, how's the job search going?"

"And real champagne," I say gushingly. Ilkishly.

My Aunt Lucy, already referred to, had a short life, thirty-six years, then cancer got her, grabbed her. She lived in Bedford, New Hampshire, where she worked as a secretary-receptionist in a piano factory. She couldn't play the piano herself, not a note. She wasn't very bright. She wasn't eccentric, either. She almost never remembered to send me birthday cards or small gifts. The alignment of her teeth was only so-so. So why do I insist that her skinny, maladroit, cancer-eaten body housed an epic, a drama, a romance, a macro-fiction, a ficto-universe? Because narrativity is ovarian, not ejaculatory as so many of our contemporary teachers/scholars/critics tend to assume.

I give you my poor old relation as an example only, putting my trust in the simplifying afterlight of metaphor, which is all we have. The point is, as I try to explain to Professor Wentworth: "Narrative fullness thrives in the interstices of nanoseconds. Or nano-people, like my aunt. Though oddly enough, Professor Wentworth, I was crazy about her."

"It's Dick. Please. Don't you remember our last conversation, when we agreed—?"

"Dick, yes."

"Ovarian? You were saying—?"

"I should have said egg. Egg's a good word. A single cell—"

"A single cell—hmmm." He strokes his chin at this point, stroke, stroke.

"—holds the surfaces of the real."

"But. But, Lucy, tension absolutely cannot be created in a vacuum."

Is this a trick? Starting a sentence with a double *but*? I call that aggressive. Or else aggression's reverse side, which is helplessness. "Look, Professor Wentworth, Dick. There's plenty of high-octane tension flowing between the simple states of being and non-being—"

"Which points," he says, "to the other side of this discourse."

"Every discourse is born of a micro-discourse," say I, wanting to press his sad effusions into something ardent and orderly. Something useful.

"Uh-huh."

There is only one shrimp left on the plate. It lies curled on its side, paler than a shrimp should be, and misshapen. I feel a yearning to know its story.

Also, I can't help noticing that its ridged shrimpy curl matches almost exactly the configurative paisley splotches on Professor Wentworth's tie. I stare at that tie, something makes me. The mixed blues and reds strike me as boyishly courageous, but it is the knot that brings a puddle of tears to my throat. Or rather, it is the way he, Dick Wentworth, keeps touching that knot as he speaks, applying pressure with his thumb, pushing against the spread stiffness of buttoned oxford cloth and into the erect column of the neck itself. A good enough neck, soapy, a forty-year-old neck, or thereabouts. I remember that his wife hanged herself. From a water pipe. In the basement of their house. In Ithaca, New York.

"I'm afraid I don't quite see—" he begins, his thumb rising once again, preparing to push.

His whole life seems gathered in that little silky harbor. Mine too, for some reason. Probably the champagne fizzing up into my nose.

Did I make up that part about the water pipe? Me and my ilk and I, we're given to such exiguous notation. Doublings. Triangulations. Narrativistically speaking, our brush strokes outreach our grasp.

"You've probably heard," says Dick Wentworth, "that we, ahem, have an opening in the department for next year. It's, hmmmm, in composition and rhetoric, but reassignment is always an option," he continues, "once tenure is confirmed," he goes on, "and you might, if you will excuse me for saying so," he concludes, "be ready for—"

I did say, didn't I, that my Aunt Lucy was thirty-six when she withered away? Exactly the age I will be in four years and three ilkly months.

Cross that last bit out. There's no room for self-pity in the satellite-bounced fictions of today. Ellipsis, though crownless, is queen. I remind Dick Wentworth of this insight.

"I'm afraid I didn't quite catch what you said. This noise, all these people, that execrable music."

"I said I'd give it some thought."

"What?"

"The position. The post. The post/position."

"Oh."

He was away attending another conference when it happened. The combined SWUS/NWUS biannual, the year he gave his paper on "Stasis and Static in Early Twentieth Century Cowboy Imbroglios." Brilliant. Shedding light on. Now it seems he can't forgive himself for signing up for the post-conference mini-session on the couplet.

"Really? The couplet?"

"The line, actually."

She'd been dead, apparently, for just twenty-four hours when he got home. The police, even in off-the-map places like Ithaca, are good at figuring out things like the amount of water left in the body cells after the heart stops. It decreases at a known rate. Experts have considered this, done graphs and so on.

"The line, you said?"

"Well, perhaps I should have said the word."

Of course she left a note. On the kitchen table, probably. Or pinned to her bathrobe. It doesn't matter where. What matters is what the note said. Only one word, rumor has it. Scratched in pen or pencil or chalk, scratched into the laminated tabletop, into the wood paneling of the basement rec room, with a nail, with a nail file, with a piece of glass, scratched on her wrists—it doesn't matter.

"Salary?"

"Small."

"How small? Do you mean, hmmmm, ridiculously small?"

"Annual increments, though. And benefits."

"Benefits!"

What matters, at least to L. Porter and her ilk, is the exact word she left behind. Its orthography, its referents. The word is the central modality, after all. The narrational heart.

There are infinite possibilities. A dictionary of possibilities. You'd think that little scratched word would come scuttling toward me on jointed legs, wouldn't you, eager to make itself registered. It might have been something accusing (betrayal). Or confessional (regret). Or descriptive (depression), or existential (lost, loose, lust)? or dialogic (a simple goodbye). No, all too predictable. Reactive rather than initiative.

My guess is that she left some kind of disassociative verbal unit: leaf, water, root, fire, fish.

"Love."

"What did you say?" To narrativize is to step back from spontaneous expression, even as one consolidates the available, accessible, amenable material of the world.

"Love," he says again, looking down, sideways, then up at the ceiling fan, ready to withdraw his narratival disjuncture and press forward to other, wider topics.

"Pardon?"

"We'd love to have you aboard."

The spine of the final shrimp is parked between his front teeth now. Sitting there rather sweetly, in fact, though it makes it difficult to catch his next words. "My ilk is your ilk" is what I think I heard.

Stop!

THE QUEEN HAS DROPPED OUT OF SIGHT. At the busiest time of the court season too, what with the Admiral's Ball coming up, and the People's Picnic. No one knows where she's disappeared to. Has she gone to the seaside? Unthinkable. A person who is sensitive to salt water, to sand, to beach grass and striped canvas, does not traipse off to the seaside. Well, where, then? It used to be that she would spend a few days in the mountains in late summer. She loved the coolness, she said, the grandeur. But now her sinuses react to balsam and pine. And to the inclines of greenness and shadow.

No, she is a stay-at-home queen. A dull queen. Not exactly beloved, but a queen who is nevertheless missed when she is absent. People are starting to talk, to wonder. They understand that the pollen count is high, and so it is not unreasonable that she remain enclosed in her tower. But why have the windows been bricked in? Can it be that she has developed an intolerance to sunlight too? Poor soul, and just at the turning of the year, with the air so fine and pale.

Music, of course, has been anathema for years. Bugles, trumpets and drums were confiscated in the first triannulus of her reign, and stringed instruments—violins, cellos—inevitably followed. It was heartbreaking to see, especially the moment when the Queen's own harp was smashed by hammers and the pieces buried deep in the palace garden.

Simple nourishment has always been for her a form of torture. Fruits and vegetables, meat and milk bring on duodenal spasms, but, worse, she is unable to bear the shape of a spoon in her mouth. The finest clothing rubs and chafes. The perfume of flowers causes her to faint, and even oxygen catches in her windpipe so that she coughs and chokes and calls for the court physician.

Ah, the physician! What grave responsibility that man bears. It was he, after all, who first recognized the danger of ragweed and banished it from the realm. Then roses. Then common grass and creeping vines. It was he who declared the Queen to be allergic to her courtiers, to her own children, to the King himself.

But at least life went forward. Acts of proclamation. The Admiral's Ball, already mentioned. And the Spring Rites on the royal parade grounds, where the Queen could be glimpsed by one and all, waving her handkerchief, bravely blessing her subjects with the emblem of her disability. People are fed by that kind of example. Yes, they are. People find courage in stubborn endurance.

But recently the Queen has disappeared, and matters have suddenly worsened. There has been an official announcement that clocks and calendars are to be destroyed. It is forbidden now to utter the names of the days and months, to speak of yesterday or tomorrow or next week. Naturally there will be no Spring Rites this year, for the progression of seasons has been declared unlawful. Meteorologists have been dismissed from their positions and weather disallowed. The cause of Her Majesty's affliction has been identified. It has been verified absolutely. It seems the measured substance that pushes the world this way and that, the invented sequentiality that hovers between the simple raising and lowering of a teacup, can no longer be tolerated by the Queen.

At last the people understand why the palace windows have been closed up. The temporal movement of the sun and stars must be blocked from her view. Rhythmic pulsations of light threaten her existence, suggesting as they do the unstoppable equation that attaches to mass and energy. She lives in the dark now, blindfolded, in fact. Her ears too have been covered over for fear she will hear the cries of birds, a cock at dawn, a swallow or an owl hooting its signature on the night sky. She no longer speaks or thinks, since the positioning of noun and verb, of premise and conclusion, demands a progression that invites that toxic essence, that mystery.

But they have overlooked her heart, her poor beating queenly heart. Like a mindless machine it continues to add and subtract. A whimsical toy, it beeps and sighs, singing and songing along the jointed channels of her blood. Counting, counting. Now diminishing. Now swelling. Insisting on its literal dance. Tick-tock, tick-tock. Filling up with deadly arithmetic.

Mirrors

WHEN HE THINKS ABOUT THE PEOPLE he's known in his life, a good many of them seem to have cultivated some curious strand of asceticism, contrived some gesture of renunciation. They give up sugar. Or meat. Or newspapers. Or neckties. They sell their second car or disconnect the television. They might make a point of staying at home on Sunday evenings or abjuring chemical sprays. Something, anyway, that signals dissent and cuts across the beating heart of their circumstances, reminding them of their other, leaner selves. Their better selves.

He and his wife have claimed their small territory of sacrifice too. For years they've become "known" among their friends for the particular deprivation they've assigned themselves: for the fact that there are no mirrors in their summer house. None at all. None are allowed.

The need to observe ourselves is sewn into us, everyone knows this, but he and his wife have turned their backs on this need, said no to it, at least for the duration of the summer months. Otherwise, they are not very different from other couples nearing the end of middle age—he being sixty, she fifty-eight, their children grown up and married and living hundreds of miles away.

In September they will have been married thirty-five years, and they're already planning a week in New York to celebrate this milestone, five nights at the Algonquin (for sentimental reasons) and a few off-Broadway shows, already booked. They stay away from the big musicals as a rule, preferring, for want of a better word, *serious* drama. Nothing experimental, no drugged angst or scalding discourse, but plays that coolly examine the psychological positioning of men and women in our century. This torn, perplexing century. Men and women who resemble themselves.

They would be disinclined to discuss between them how they've arrived at these harmonious choices in the matter of playgoing, how they are both a little proud, in fact, of their taste for serious drama, proud in the biblical *pride* sense. Just as they're a little proud of their mirrorless summer house on the shores of Big Circle Lake.

Their political views tend to fall in the middle of the spectrum. Financially, you might describe them as medium well off, certainly not wealthy. He has retired, one week ago as a matter of fact, from his own management consulting firm, and she is, has always been, a housewife and active community volunteer. These days she wears a large stylish head of stiffened hair, and he, with no visible regret, is going neatly bald at the forehead and crown.

Walking away from their cottage on Big Circle Lake, you would have a hard time describing its contents or atmosphere: faded colors and pleasing shapes that beg you to stay, to make yourself comfortable. These inviting surfaces slip from remembrance the minute you turn your back. But you would very probably bear in mind their single act of forfeiture: there are no mirrors.

Check the medicine cabinet in the little fir-paneled bathroom: nothing. Check the back of the broom cupboard door in the kitchen or the spot above the dresser in their large sky-lighted bedroom or the wall over the log-burning fireplace in what they choose to call "the lounge." Even if you were to abuse the rules of privacy and look into her (the wife's) big canvas handbag you would find nothing compromising. You would likely come across a compact of face powder, Elizabeth Arden, but the little round mirror lining most women's compacts has been removed. You can just make out the curved crust of glue that once held a mirror in place.

Check even the saucepans hanging over the kitchen stove. Their bottoms are discolored copper, scratched aluminum. No chance for a reflective glimpse there. The stove itself is dull textured, ancient.

This mirrorlessness of theirs is deliberate, that much is clear.

From June to August they choose to forget who they are, or at least what they look like, electing an annual season of non-reflectiveness in the same way other people put away their clocks for the summer or their computers or door keys or microwave ovens.

"But how can you possibly shave?" people ask the husband, knowing he is meticulous about such things.

He moves a hand to his chin. At sixty, still slender, he remains a handsome man. "By feel," he says. He demonstrates, moving the forefinger of his left hand half an inch ahead of the path of an imaginary razor. "Just try it. Shut your eyes and you'll see you can manage a decent shave without the slightest difficulty. Maybe not a perfect shave, but good enough for out at the lake."

His wife, who never was slender, who has fretted for the better part of her life about her lack of slenderness—raged and grieved, gained and lost—has now at fifty-eight given up the battle. She looks forward to her mirrorless summers, she says. She likes to tell her friends—and she and her husband are a fortunate couple with a large circle of friends—that she can climb into her swimsuit and walk through the length of the cottage—the three original rooms, the new south-facing wing—without having to look even once at the double and triple pinches of flesh that have accumulated in those corners where her shoulders and breasts flow together. "Oh, I suppose I could look down and *see* what I'm like," she says, rolling her eyes, "but I'm not obliged to take in the whole panorama every single day."

She does her hair in the morning in much the same way her husband shaves: by feel, brushing it out, patting it into shape, fixing it with pins. She's been putting on earrings for forty years, and certainly doesn't require a mirror for that. As for lipstick, she makes do with a quick crayoning back and forth across her mouth, a haphazard double slash of color. Afterward she returns the lipstick smartly to its case, then runs a practiced finger around her upper and lower lips, which she stretches wide so that the shaping of pale raspberry fits perfectly the face she knows by heart.

He's watched her perform this small act a thousand times, so often that his own mouth sometimes wants to stretch in response.

They were newly married and still childless when they bought the cottage, paying far too much, then discovering almost immediately the foundations were half-rotted, and carpenter ants—or something—lived in the pine rafters. Mice had made a meal of the electric wires; ants thronged the mildewed cupboards. Officially the place had been sold to them furnished, but the previous owners had taken the best of what there was, leaving only a sagging couch, a table that sat unevenly on the torn linoleum, two battered chairs, a bed with a damp mattress and an oak dresser with a stuck drawer. The dresser was the old-fashioned kind with its own mirror frame attached, two curving prongs rising gracefully like a pair of arms, but the mirror it had once embraced was missing.

You would think the larceny of the original owners would have embittered the two of them. Or that the smell of mold and rot and accumulated dirt would have filled them with discouragement, but it didn't. They set to work. For three weeks they worked from morning to dusk.

First he repaired the old pump so they might at least have water. He was not in those years adept with his hands, and the task took several days. During that period he washed himself in the lake, not taking the time for a swim, but stopping only to splash his face and body with cold water. She noticed there was a three-cornered smudge of dirt high on his forehead that he missed. It remained there for several days, making him appear to her boyish and vulnerable. She didn't have the heart to mention it to him. In fact, she felt a small ping of sorrow when she looked up at him one evening and found it washed away. Even though she was not in those days an impulsive woman, she had stretched herself forward and kissed the place where the smudge had been.

Curiously, he remembers her spontaneous kiss, remembers she had washed her hair in the lake a few minutes earlier, and had wrapped a towel around her head like a turban. She was not a vain woman. In fact, she had always mourned too much the failures of her body, and so he knew she had no idea of how seductive she looked at that moment with the added inch of toweling and her face bared like a smooth shell.

At night they fell exhausted into the old bed and slept as though weights were attached to their arms and legs. Their completed tasks, mending and painting, airing and polishing, brought them a brimming level of satisfaction that would have been foolish to try to explain to anyone else. They stepped carefully across their washed floorboards, opened and shut their windows and seemed to be listening at night to the underhum of the sloping, leaking roof. That first summer they scarcely saw a soul. The northern shore of Big Circle Lake was a wilderness in those days. There were no visitors, few interruptions. Two or three times they went to town for groceries. Once they attended a local auction and bought a pine bed, a small table and a few other oddments. Both of them remember they looked carefully for a mirror, but none was to their liking. It was then they decided to do without.

Each day they spent at the cottage became a plotted line, the same coffee mugs (hers, his), the comically inadequate paring knife and the comments that accrued around it. Familiar dust, a pet spider swaying over their bed, the sky lifting and falling and spreading out like a mesh of silver on the lake. Meals. Sleep. A surprising amount of silence.

They thought they'd known each other before they married. He'd reported dutifully, as young men were encouraged to do in those days, his youthful experiences and pleasures, and she, blocked with doubt, had listed off hers. The truth had been darkened out. Now it erupted, came to the surface. He felt a longing to turn to her and say: "This is what I've dreamed of all my life, being this tired, this used up, and having someone like you, exactly like you, waking up at my side."

At the end of that first married summer they celebrated with dinner at a restaurant at the far end of the lake, the sort of jerry-built knotty-pine family establishment that opens in May for the summer visitors and closes on Labor Day. The waitresses were students hired for the season, young girls wearing fresh white peasant blouses and gathered skirts and thonged sandals on their feet. These girls, holding their trays sideways, maneuvered through the warren of tiny rooms.

They brought chilled tomato juice, set a basket of bread on the table, put mixed salad out in wooden bowls, then swung back into the kitchen for plates of chicken and vegetables. Their rhythmic ease, burnished to perfection now that summer was near its end, was infectious, and the food, which was really no better than such food can be, became a meal each of them would remember with pleasure.

He ate hungrily. She cut more slowly into her roast chicken, then looked up, straight into what she at first thought was a window. In fact, it was a mirror that had been mounted on the wall, put there no doubt to make the cramped space seem larger. She saw a woman prettier than she remembered, a graceful woman, deeply tanned, her eyes lively, the shoulders moving sensually under her cotton blouse. A moment ago she had felt a pinprick of envy for the lithe careless bodies of the young waitresses. Now she was confronted by this stranger. She opened her mouth as if to say: Who on earth?

She'd heard of people who moved to foreign countries and forgot their own language, the simplest words lost: door, tree, sky. But to forget your own face? She smiled; her face smiled back; the delay of recognition felt like treasure. She put down her knife and fork and lifted her wrists forward in a salute.

Her husband turned then and looked into the mirror. He too seemed surprised. "Hello," he said fondly. "Hello, us."

Their children were six and eight the year they put the addition on the cottage. Workmen came every morning, and the sound of their power tools shattered the accustomed summer-time peace. She found herself living all day for the moment they would be gone, the sudden late-afternoon stillness and the delicious green smell of cut lumber rising around them. The children drifted through the half-completed partitions like ghosts, claiming their own territory.

For two nights, while the new roof was being put on, they slept with their beds facing straight up to the stars.

That was the year her daughter came running into the kitchen in a new swimsuit, asking where the mirror was. Her tone was excited but baffled, and she put her hands over her mouth as though she knew she had blundered somehow just presenting this question.

"We don't have a mirror at the cottage," her mother explained.

"Oh," the child replied. Just "Oh."

At that moment the mother remembered something she had almost forgotten. In the old days, when a woman bought a new purse, or a pocketbook as they were called then, it came packed hard with gray tissue paper. And in the midst of all the paper wadding there was always a little unframed rectangle of mirror. These were crude, roughly made mirrors, and she wasn't sure that people actually used them. They were like charms, good-luck charms. Or like compasses; you could look in them and take your bearings. Locate yourself in the world.

We use the expression "look *into* a mirror," as though it were an open medium, like water—which the first mirrors undoubtedly were. Think of Narcissus. He started it all. And yet it is women who are usually associated with mirrors: mermaids rising up from the salty waves with a comb and a mirror in hand; Cleopatra on her barge. Women and vanity go hand in hand.

In his late forties he fell in love with another woman. Was she younger than his wife? Yes, of course she was younger. She was more beautiful too, though with a kind of beauty that had to be checked and affirmed continually. Eventually it wore him out.

He felt he had only narrowly escaped. He had broken free, and by a mixture of stealth and good fortune had kept his wife from knowing. Arriving that summer at the house on Big Circle Lake, he turned the key rather creakily in the door. His wife danced through ahead of him and did a sort of triple turn on the kitchen floor, a dip-shuffle-dip, her arms extended, her fingers clicking imaginary castanets. She always felt lighter at the lake, her body looser. This lightness, this proof of innocence, doubled his guilt. A wave of darkness had rolled in between what he used to be and what he'd become, and he longed to put his head down on the smooth pine surface of the kitchen table and confess everything.

Already his wife was unpacking a box of groceries, humming as she put things away. Oblivious.

There was one comfort, he told himself: for two months there would be no mirrors to look into. His shame had made him unrecognizable anyway.

He spent the summer building a cedar deck, which he knew was the sort of thing other men have done in such circumstances.

She had always found it curious that mirrors, which seemed magical in their properties, in their ability to multiply images and augment light, were composed of only two primary materials: a plane of glass pressed up against a plane of silver. Wasn't there something more required? Was this really all there was to it?

The simplicity of glass. The preciousness of silver. Only these two elements were needed for the miracle of reflection to take place. When a mirror was broken, the glass could be replaced. When a mirror grew old, it had only to be resilvered. There was no end to a mirror. It could go on and on. It could go on forever.

Perhaps her life was not as complicated as she thought. Her concerns, her nightmares, her regrets, her suspicions—perhaps everything would eventually be repaired, healed, obliterated. Probably her husband was right: she made too much of things.

"You remind me of someone," she said the first time they met. He knew she meant that he reminded her of herself. Some twinned current flowed between them. This was years and years ago.

But her words came back to him recently when his children and their families were visiting at Big Circle Lake.

The marriages of his son and daughter are still young, still careful, often on the edge of hurt feelings or quarrels, though he feels fairly certain they will work their way eventually toward a more even footing, whatever that means.

He's heard it said all his life that the young pity the old, that this pity is a fact of human nature. But he can't help observing how both his grown children regard him with envy. They almost sigh it out—"You've got everything."

Well, it's so. His mortgage is paid. There's this beautiful place for the summer. Time to travel now. Old friends. A long marriage. A bank of traditions. He imagines his son and daughter must amuse their separate friends with accounts of their parents' voluntary forswearing of mirrors, and that in these accounts he and his wife are depicted as harmless eccentrics who have perhaps stumbled on some useful verity that has served to steady them in their lives.

He longs sometimes to tell them that what they see is not the whole of it. Living without mirrors is cumbersome and inconvenient, if the truth were known, and, moreover, he has developed a distaste in recent years for acts of abnegation, finding something theatrical and childish about cultivated denial, something stubbornly willful and self-cherishing.

He would also like to tell them that other people's lives are seldom as settled as they appear. That every hour contains at least a moment of bewilderment or worse. That a whim randomly adopted grows forlorn with time, and that people who have lived together for thirty-five years still apprehend each other as strangers.

Though only last night—or was it the night before—he woke suddenly at three in the morning and found his wife had turned on her light and was reading. He lay quiet, watching her for what seemed like several minutes: a woman no longer young, intent on her book, lifting a hand every moment or two to turn over a page, her profile washed out by the high-intensity lamp, her shoulders and body blunted by shadow. Who was this person?

And then she had turned and glanced his way. Their eyes held, caught on the thread of a shared joke: the two of them at this moment had become each other, at home behind the screen of each other's face. It was several seconds before he was able to look away.

The Harp

THE HARP WAS FALLING through the air, only I didn't know it was a harp. It was only this blocky chunk of matter, vaguely triangular, this *thing*, silhouetted against the city sky, held there for a split second like a stencil's hard-edged blank, more of an absence than a real object of heft and substance. It threw off a single glint of gold as it spun downward, I remembered that afterward.

Everyone stopped and stared, which is surprising in a city this size, and especially at that hour, the end of the workday, and people hurrying home or stopping to do a little last-minute Christmas shopping. Yesterday's fall of snow was fast turning to urban slush. I remember thinking how oddly comforting the cold slush felt against the side of my face and along the exposed part of my leg, a sort of anaesthetic or sensory diversion. My own father, when seized by shoulder cramps last spring, had favoured ice packs over a hot-water bottle, and this was one more thing he and my mother quarreled about. That long list made up their life together. Leisure, food, work, housing, the sentient pleasures, the hour of bedtime, tea versus hot chocolate, heat versus cold; they agree on nothing.

Someone near me let out a shriek, there were scuffling sounds as I went down hard on the pavement, and then a sudden closed silence as people in their overcoats crowded around me. I blinked and saw a man stoop and put his gloved hand on my bare leg. My pantyhose; what had happened to my pantyhose?—a brand new pair put on earlier in the day. "You're going to be fine," he said, and someone else pronounced the word "harp," that puzzling little word leaping out of a strand of other, less audible words.

It seems—yes, it was true—I had been struck on my left leg by the wood post of a large concert harp falling from an overhead window, and this smashed instrument lay next to me now in the soft grey slush, two inert bodies side by side. It and me. Fallen sisters. A streetlight shone overhead. I flung out a hand and, with more reflex than intention, struck violently against the harp's strings, and was rewarded by a musical growl, very low in tone and with the merest suggestion of vibrato. The crowd around me applauded. What could they have been thinking? That I, wounded on the street, ambushed, had decided to perform an impromptu concert? "There, there," one of them said, "the ambulance is coming."

Explanations followed, although there are no explanations that quite cover this kind of random accident. There had been a Christmas party on the second floor of the Blair Building, a gathering of accountants and their spouses standing about drinking spiced wine and eating little hot rolled-up tidbits of bacon and cheese, and one of the more bibulous guests had stumbled against the harpist—it was said by someone that he had been flirting openly with her—and knocked the instrument against the window, which immediately shattered.

"What a good thing you were hit by the harp and not the glass," people said. "How fortunate you were to be struck on the leg and not the head," others offered. I cried for two days, drenching my hospital sheets with my tears, weeping from the shock and the pain and the stupidity of people's remarks, and also because I had not been invited to the accountants' party, never mind that I am not an accountant myself or acquainted with one.

Was there any justice in the world? Think about it. Why should I have been shivering along on a dark slush-strewn street when I might have been standing aloft in that warm, crowded, scented room, reaching for one more pastry puff, one more glass of fragrant wine, and taking in, as though it were my right, the soft background tinkling of harp music; my name printed on the invitation list, part of the ongoing celebration of the season.

X-rays were taken, of course, and it was determined that a chip of bone had broken away from my left shin. Nothing could be done about this detached piece of tissue, I was going to have to live my life without it, just as I have learned to accommodate other subtractions. The bruising would disappear in a week or so. Painkillers were prescribed. A counselor arrived to help me deal with trauma, and the chaplain enjoined me to give thanks for having been spared even greater injury. The newspapers requested interviews, but these I resisted.

I phoned my mother in Calgary. ("You always were clumsy," she said.) And my father in Montana. (Did I mention that my parents have decided to separate after all these years?) He, with his hearing impairment, came away from our conversation believing I had been struck not by a harp but by a heart. "That doesn't sound too serious to me," he said in his fatherly way. "A heart is a relatively soft and buoyant organ." And then he said, "You'll get over it in no time."

The harpist visited me in the hospital. Her body was tense. Her face was red. She kept her coat on, buttoned up, during the whole of the visit. The harp was being examined by experts. It might be repairable or it might not, but in any case the expense was going to be exorbitant—and here was she, without insurance, and for the time being without any means of earning a living. It seemed only reasonable, she said, that I contribute to her costs.

Only my dreams are benign. In these nightly visitations the harp is not plummeting but floating. The December air presses on its gilded strings tenderly, with the greatest tact, and I am transformed, unrehearsed, into the guest of honor, awarded the unexpected buoyancy of flight itself, as I reach out to catch the whole of my life in my arms.

Our Men and Women

OUR EARTHQUAKE MAN IS UP EARLY. He greets the soft dawn with a speculative lift of his orange-juice glass. "Hello, little earth," he hums quietly. Then, "So! You're still here."

He puts in a pre-breakfast call to the E-Quake Center. "Nothing much," he hears. "Just a few overnight rumbles."

Overnight what? Really?

He resents having missed these terrestrial waves, but his resentment is so faint, so almost non-existent, he swallows it down, along with his vitamin C. He should be grateful. So he's missed a tremble or two! What does it matter?—the earth is always heaving, growling, whereas last night he'd slept seven uninterrupted hours with his arms and legs wrapped around the body of his dear Patricia, his blond Patricia, graceful, lithe Patricia, fifteen years his junior, blessed replacement for Marguerite—perpetrator of sulks, rages, the hurling of hairbrushes and dinner plates. Thirty-five years he and Marguerite were together. Their four grown children are almost embarrassingly buoyant about this second marriage of his. At the time of the wedding, last Thanksgiving, two days after a 3.5 Richter-scale reading, the kids chipped in together to buy their old dad and his new wife an antique sleigh bed. Actually a reproduction model, produced in a North Carolina factory. Sleek, beautiful. Closer in its configuration to a cradle than a sleigh.

Now, in the early morning, Patricia is grilling slices of seven-grain bread over the backyard barbecue. She has a thing about toasters, just as he has a thing about the instability of the earth. You'd think he'd be used to it after all this time, but his night dreams are of molten lava, and the crunch and grind of tectonic plates. As a graduate student he believed his subtle calibrations could predict disaster; now he knows better. Those years with Marguerite taught him that making projections is like doing push-ups in water. The world spewed and shifted. There was nothing to lean against. You had to pull yourself back from it, suck in your gut, and hold still.

His solemn, smiling Patricia is flipping over the toast now with a long silvery fork. Sunlight decorates her whisked-back hair and the rounded cotton shoulder of her T-shirt. What a picture! She stands balanced with her bare feet slightly apart on the patio stones, defying—it would seem—the twitching earth with its sly, capricious crust. "Ready?" she calls out to him, skewering the slices of toast on her fork and tossing them straight at his head.

But no. It's only an optical illusion. The toast is still there, attached to the fork's prongs. It's a hug she's thrown in his direction. Her two skinny arms have risen exuberantly, grabbed a broad cube of air and pushed it forcefully toward him.

It came at him, a tidal wave moving along a predestined line. This is what his nightmares have promised: disorder, violence.

A man of reflexes, his first thought was to duck, to cover his face and protect himself. Then he remembered who he was, where he was—a man standing in a sunlit garden a few yards away from a woman he loved. He can't quite, yet, believe this. "Tsunami," he pronounced speculatively.

"Me too," she whispered. "Hey, me too."

―――

Our Rainfall woman is also up early. She parts her dotted-Swiss curtains and inspects the sky. Good, fine, okay; check. A smack of blue, like an empty billboard, fills in the spaces behind her flowering shrubs and cedar fence; she finds this reassuring, also disappointing. Her whole day will be like this, a rocking back and forth between what she wants and what she doesn't. "I am master of all I can stand," her father, the great explainer, used to say. She can't remember if he meant this thought to be comforting or if he was being his usual arrogant, elliptical self.

At eleven o'clock she conducts her seminar on drought. At four-thirty she's scheduled to lecture on flood. Lunch will be a sandwich and a pot of tea in the staff room. They expect her to be there. Today someone asks her about the World Series, who she's betting on. "Hmmmm," she says, blinking, looking upward, moving her mug of tea swiftly to her lips. Then, "Hard to say, hard to say."

Her night dreams, her daydreams too, are about drowning, but in recent months she's been enrolled in an evening workshop at the Y that teaches new techniques guaranteed to control nocturnal disturbances. It works like this: in the midst of sleep, the conscious mind is invited to step forward and engage briefly with the dream image, so that a threatening wave of water closing over the dreamer's head (for example) is transformed into a shower of daisies. Or soap flakes. Or goose feathers. An alternative strategy is to bid the conscious mind to reach for the remote control (so to speak) and switch channels. Even her father's flat elderly argumentative voice can be shut off. Right off, snap, click. Or transmuted into a trill of birdsong. Or the dappled pattern of light and shadow.

She lives, by choice, in a part of the country where rain is moderate. There's never too much or too little. Except—well, except during exceptional circumstances, which could occur next week or next month, anytime, in fact. Planetary systems are enormously complicated; they tend to interact erratically. She understands this, having written any number of articles on the very subject of climate variability, on the theory of chaos. Meteorologists, deservedly humbled in recent years, confess that they are working *toward* eighty-five percent accuracy, and that this thrust applies only to twenty-four-hour predictions. Long-term forecasting, the darling of her graduate school days, has been abandoned.

There's no way people can protect themselves against surprise. Her father, for instance, was one minute alive and the next minute dead. The space in between was so tightly packed that there wasn't room to squeeze in one word.

Our Fire fellow is relatively young, but already he's been granted tenure. Also five thousand square feet of laboratory space, plus three research assistants, plus an unlimited travel allowance. Anything he wants he gets, and he wants a lot. He's gassed up on his own brilliance. And with shame too. No one should need what he needs, and need it ten times a day, a hundred times a day.

He's a man of finely gauged increments, of flashpoints, of fevers and starbursts, of a rich unsparing cynicism. Up at five-thirty, a four-mile run, a quick flick through the latest journals, half a dozen serious articles gulped down, then coffee, scalding, out of a machine. This part of the day is a torment to him, his night dreams still not shaken off. (Has it been made clear that he lives by choice in a motel unit, and refuses even the consolation of weekly rates?)

By seven he's in his office, checking through his e-mail, firing off letters that become quarrels or sharp inquiries. Everywhere he sees slackers, defilers and stumblers. His anger blazes just thinking of them. He knows he should exercise patience, but fear of anonymity, or something equally encumbering, has edged the sense of risk out of his life.

Small talk, small courtesies—he hasn't time. His exigent nature demands instant responses and deplores time-wasting functions. Like what? Like that wine-and-cheese reception for old What's-His-Name and his new wife! Like staff-room niceties. Blather about the World Series. And that lachrymose young Rainfall woman who keeps asking him how he's "getting along."

Well, he's getting along. And along and along. He's going up, up. Up like a firecracker.

Right now he's doing fifty double-time push-ups on the beige carpet of his office in preparation for one of his popular lectures on reality. His premise, briefly, is that we can only touch reality through the sensations of the single moment, that infinitesimal spark of time that is, even now as we consider it, dying. We must—to use his metaphor—place our hand directly in the flame.

He pursues his point, romping straight over the usual curved hills of faith, throwing forth a stupefying mixture of historical lore and its gossamer logic, presenting arguments that are bejeweled with crafty irrelevance, covering the blackboard with many-branched equations that establish and illuminate his careful, random proofs. On and on he goes, burning dangerously bright, and ever brighter.

Notes are taken. No one interrupts, no one poses questions, they wouldn't dare. Afterward the lecture hall empties quickly, leaving him alone on the podium, steaming with his own heat, panting, rejoicing.

But grief steals into his nightly dreams, which commence with a vision of drenching rain, rain that goes on and on and shows no sign of ever ending, falling into the rooms of his remembered boyhood, his mother, his father—there they are, smiling, so full of parental pride—and a brother, especially a brother, who is older, stronger, more given to acts of shrugging surrender, more self-possessed, more eagerly and more offhandedly anointed. The family's clothes and bodies are soaked through with rain, as are the green hedges, the familiar woods and fields, the roadway, the glistening roofs and chimneys, inclines and valleys, the whole world, in fact. Except for him, standing there with his hands cupped, waiting. For him there has not been, so far, a single drop.

She's something else, our Plague and Pestilence woman. She's just (today) won the staff-room World Series pool—a lucky guess, she admits, the first four games out of seven. No one else risked such a perfect sky-blue sweep.

"You were an accident," her mother told her when she was a young girl, just ten or eleven years old. "I never meant to have a kid, it just happened. There I was, pregnant."

Unforgivable words. But instantly forgiven. Because her mother's voice, as she made this confession, was roughened with wonder. An accident, she said, but her intonation, her slowly shaking woman's head, declared it to be the best accident imaginable. The most fortunate event in the history of the world, no less.

Our Plague and Pestilence woman married young, out of love, a man who was selfish, moody, cruel, childish. But one day, several years into the marriage, he woke up and thought, "I can't go on like this. I have to change. I have to become a different kind of person."

They are thankful, both of them, that their children have been spared the ravages of smallpox, typhoid, diphtheria, scarlet fever, poliomyelitis. Other diseases, worse diseases, hover about them, but the parents remain hopeful. Their histories, their natural inclinations, buoy them up. She dreams nightly of leaf mold, wheat rot, toads falling from the sky, multiplying bacteria, poisoned blood, incomprehensible delusions, but wakes up early each day with a clean sharp longing for simple tasks and agreeable weather.

It was our Plague and Pestilence woman who, one year ago, introduced her assistant, Patricia, to the recently widowed Earthquake man, and this matchmaking success has inspired another social occasion—which occurred just last night, as a matter of fact. A platter of chicken, shrimp, saffron and rice was prepared. A table was set in a shaded garden. The two guests—our Rainfall woman, our Fire person—were reluctant at first to come. They had to be persuaded, entreated. Once there, they were put, more or less, at their ease. Made to feel they deserved the fragrant dish before them. Invited to accept whatever it was that poured through their senses. Encouraged to see that the image they glimpsed in the steady candlelight matched almost, but not quite, the shapeless void of their private nightly dreams.

Our P and P woman, observant as she is, doesn't yet know how any of this will turn out. It's far too soon to tell.

We can't help being proud of our men and women. They work hard to understand the topography of the real. It's a heartbreaking struggle, yet somehow they carry on—predicting, measuring, analyzing, recording, looking over their shoulders at the presence of their accumulated labor, cocking an ear to the sounds of their alarm clocks going off and calling them to temperature-controlled rooms and the dings and dongs of their word processors, the shrill bells of approval or disapproval, the creaks of their bodies as the years pile up, and the never-ending quarrel with their smothered, creaturely, solitary selves. Limitations—always they're crowded up against limitations. Sometimes our men and women give way to old nightmares or denial or the delusion that living in the world is effortless and full of ease. Like everyone else, they're spooked by old injuries, and that swift plummeting fall toward what they believe must be the future. Nevertheless, they continue to launch their various theories, theories so fragile, speculative and foolish, so unanchored by proofs and possibilities, and so distorted by their own yearnings, that their professional reputations are put at risk, their whole lives, you might say. Occasionally, not often, they are called upon to commit an act of extraordinary courage.

Which is why we stand by our men and women. In the end they may do nothing. In the meantime, they do what they can.

Keys

BIFF MONKHOUSE, THE MAN WHO BROUGHT bebop to
Europe, collapsed and died last week in the lobby of the
George V Hotel in Paris. His was a life full of success and fail-
ure, full of love and the absence of love. The famous "teddy
boy" attire he affected was a kind of self-advertisement saying:
I am outside of time and nationality, beyond gender and class.

No wallet or passport was found on his person.

No coins, snapshots, receipts, letters or lists were found on
his person.

No spectacles, prescriptions, pills, phone numbers, credit
cards were found on his person.

No rings, wristwatches, chains, tattoos or distinguishing
scars were found on his person.

No alcohol, caffeine, heroin, crack or HIV-positive cells
were found in his bloodstream.

No odor attached to his body.

His hair had been recently cut. His nails were pared, his
shoes only lightly scuffed. His right hand was closed in a
tight fist.

An ambulance attendant pried open Biff Monkhouse's
fist half an hour after the collapse and found there, warm
and somewhat oily, a plain steel key ring holding nine keys of
various shapes and sizes.

Dr. Marianne Moriarty of Agassiz University read the Biff Monkhouse news item (Reuters) and found it not at all surprising. She's evolved her own complex theory about keys, why people cling to them, what they represent. Every time you turn a key in a lock you make a new beginning—that's one of her beliefs. Keys are useful, portable and highly metaphorical, suggesting as they do the two postures we most often find ourselves in—for either we are locked in . . . or locked out. In her 1987 doctoral thesis she reported the startling fact that North Americans carry, on average, 5.3 keys. (Those who are prudent have copies hidden away, occasionally in places they no longer remember.) She herself carries twelve keys—condo, office, mailbox, garage, jewelry box and the like, also a hotel key (Hawaii) she can't bear to send back. Using an approved statistical sample, she's worked out the correlation between the number of keys carried and the educational or economic or age level of the key carrier. Her mother, Elsie, for instance, a sixty-six-year-old housewife in the small town of Grindley, Saskatchewan, carries only three keys—back door, front door, safe-deposit box, period—while Marianne's lover, Malcolm Loring, professor emeritus of the Sociology Department, a married man with a private income, carries sixteen keys, one of which unlocks the door of a boathouse that burned down two years ago.

Arson was suspected, but never proven. Sixteen-year-old Christopher MacFarlane, skinny, ponytailed, bad skin, a gaping, shredded hole in the left knee of his blue jeans and a single unattached, unidentified key in his back pocket, happened to be in the vicinity at the time of the fire. He was questioned, but later released after a somewhat rougher-than-usual body search. The young police sergeant eyed him closely and said, "We'd like you to tell us, sonny, exactly what this key is you've got in your pocket." "I don't know," the boy replied.

He had found the little key in the grass behind the marina. He'd been lying there flat on his belly, running the palm of his hand back and forth across the dry, colorless, shaven blades, feeling the unbreathable heat and thinking about sex—the fundamental circularity of sexual awakening, first longing, then intention and discharge, then satisfaction and finally quiescence. What was the use of it, he wondered, this wasteful closed rhythm that presented itself again and again like an old fable that wheezes out its endless repetition. It wore away at him. He kept hoping to drive it away, but a kind of anxiety was forever regrowing around his heart, and he felt he would never be free.

And then he saw something burning in the grass near his head, a coin or a bottle cap. But no—when he reached out, he found it was a key. It lay lightly in his hand, small and almost weightless, rounded at its head and punched with a ridged hole. The other end—the business end, as some people call it—was dull-toothed, cheaply made, stamped out rather than cut; possibly it was a bicycle key or the key to a locker. Or else—and he pushed himself up on one elbow, peering at it closely, turning it over in his hand—or else it was the key to money or mystery or fame or passion. He slid the little key into his back pocket, where it remained for several weeks, long enough for its silhouette to leave an imprint on the faded denim material, a thready raised patch of white shading off into blue.

The key was later discovered in the dryer of the Harbor Heights Laundromat by one of its regular clients, Cheryl Spence, thirty-four, who lives on the fourteenth floor of a high-rise across the street. It was a Saturday morning. She dumped in her blouses, her full cotton skirts and sundresses, her socks and underwear, her pillowcase and duvet cover. She turns all these items inside out when she launders them, giving them a hard shake as her mother had done, as her grandmother once did, and then she examines the pockets for stray tissues and paper clips. Buttons are buttoned and zippers zipped. She checks the temperature setting, measures the detergent in the little Styrofoam cup provided by the management.

Oh, how orderly and careful I am, she says to herself, how *good!* In her change purse there are plenty of quarters to feed the machines, little silvery stacks of them lying on their sides, rubbing solidly together. If other people doing their laundry on a Saturday morning run short of change, Cheryl can always help them out. Whenever this happens, she reflects on what a kind, generous and altruistic person she is, and what a pity there aren't more good-hearted people in the world like herself. She thinks this, but doesn't say it. As a very young child, not more than six or seven years of age, she understood that she was scheduled to have a double existence—an open life in which her actions were plainly visible, and a hidden life where thought and intention squatted darkly. This powerful separation seems wholly natural to her, not a thing to rage against or even to question. The real world, of course, is in her own head, which she sometimes thinks of as a shut room provisioned with declaration and clarity, everything else being a form of theater.

The little key she found at the Harbor Heights Laundromat was bent from being tossed about in the dryer's drum. Some of its particularity had been rubbed away by heat and friction. She straightened it as best she could between her fingers, dropped it into her purse and carried it home. Who knows when she might be confronted by a lock she can't open?

For several months it sat, or rather lay, in a kitchen drawer, in a cracked teacup to be precise, along with a single hairpin, a handful of thumbtacks, a stub of a candle, half an eraser, a blackened French coin, a book of matches from the Infomatic Center, a rubber band or two and a few paper clips. Odds and ends. Flotsam and jetsam.

In the evenings, tired out from a day at the accounts office, she likes to read long romantic novels and listen to music on her CD player. One night—it was in the middle of January, in the middle of an ice storm—she sat reading a book called *The Sands of Desire* and listening to a concert of soft rock when she felt herself seized by an impulse to purify her life. The way her thighs broadened out as she sat in her chair, the printed words slipping out of focus, the notes of music—their excess and persistence crowded up against her, depriving her for a frightening moment of oxygen. She opened a window and let the icy air come into her apartment, but it was not enough. She grasped a small corduroy cushion and hurled it out the window, observing with satisfaction the way it spun around in the dark air as it descended, a soft little satellite of foam and fabric. Next she threw into the driving phosphorescence a compact disc she had bought on sale only one week earlier, a medley of country ballads, wailing, weak and jerky with tears. In a kitchen cupboard she found a family-sized package of Cheese Twists, then a brown-edged head of lettuce in the refrigerator—out they went, one after the other, sailing off the tips of her fingers. And finally, in a gesture that was a kind of suicide or ritual cleansing, she didn't know which, she emptied out the cracked china cup with its miserable, broken, mismatched contents, its unsorted detritus of economy and mystery. It seemed to her she could hear the separate items rattling down through the frozen tree branches and landing like a shower of meteorites on the rooftops of the cars parked below—the paper clips, the thumbtacks, the little bent key. Ping. Tut. Tsk, Tick. Gone.

This same Cheryl Spence has visited the Pioneer Museum at Steinbach and the Reptile Museum on Highway 70 and the Wax Museum in Minneapolis, but she has never even heard of the Museum of Keys in the city of Buffalo, that dark old American city of cracked alleys and beef-colored bricks. A rough place, a tough place—but underlying its rough toughness, buried there like a seam of limestone, is the hoarded and invested money of a dozen or so millionaires no one's ever heard of, men made rich on meat, screws, plastics, textiles, optics, leather and the like. One of them, a manufacturer of table silver, established the Museum of Keys some years ago as a showcase for his own extensive key collection.

His interest in keys began at the age of sixty, at a time when he was recovering from a serious heart attack. It was Christmas morning. He was seated in an armchair, a blanket over his knees, ashamed of that soft-fringed covering, ashamed of his cold feet in their slippers and the weak light that drifted in from the east-facing window. His wife presented him with an antique porcelain music box shaped like a shepherdess. Always before she had given him practical, manly objects such as fountain pens or fishing gear. What was he to make of a figurine with flounced china skirts, revolving slowly and playing the same merry waltz tune again and again and again? He sensed some covert meaning in his wife's offering—for there she stood, inches away from him, so rounded, pale-fleshed and mildly luminous, so timid in her posture and so fragile (with a head that tipped sideways and one hand clasping the pleats of her skirt), though her gaze at the moment of gift-giving was oddly sharpened and sly; she held her breath in her throat as though it were something breakable like ice or glass or part of the solitude she sometimes drew around herself.

He loved her, and had never thought of her as a shrewd or demanding woman, yet here she was, waiting to be thanked, that much was clear, to be awarded an explosion of gratitude he had no way of formulating. He was not schooled in such expressions. Tact or shyness had kept him ignorant.

Her name was Anna. He knew, intimately, after thirty years of marriage, the floury cellular creases of her neck and elbows, her breasts, hips and round, shining ankles; he knew too, or rather sensed, that real intimacy was essentially painful—to those locked in its embrace as much as those shut out. In his confusion, his embarrassment, he seized on the exquisitely fashioned silver key, which at least possessed familiar weight and form.

How beautifully it fit his hand. How concentrated was its purpose. He had only to insert it in the shepherdess's glazed petticoats, that slender place at the back of her waist that has no name, and the mechanism was engaged. A twist or two released a ruffling of bells in triple meter. In the moment before the music began—and this was the part he grew to love best—there could be heard a brief sliding hum of gears shifting into place, anxious to perform, wonderfully obedient to the key's delicate persuasion.

The second key he acquired belonged to the lost oak door, or so he imagines it, of a demolished Breton chapel. It is thirteen inches long, made of black iron, rough in texture but beautifully balanced. "Notice the beautiful balance," he says when showing it off, always employing the same exclamatory phrase and allowing the key to seesaw across the back of his wrist. Some of his other keys—before long there were hundreds—are made of rare alloys; many are highly decorated and set with semiprecious stones, pieces of jade or turquoise. One of the most curious is fifteen hundred years old, Chinese, and another, dating from the days of the Roman Empire, is made so it can be worn on the finger like a little ring. There are keys from the Middle Ages with elaborate, ingenious warding devices and there is also a small, flat, unprepossessing key—entirely unornamented—which is said to be the prototype of the Yale (or pin tumbler) key invented in Middletown, Connecticut, in the year 1848.

The Museum of Keys is located in the southwest corner of the city, admission free, closed on Mondays, and offering school tours every Tuesday. A portrait of Anna ____, the founder's wife, 1903–1972, hangs on the wall behind the literature display. Ten thousand visitors come through the doors each year, and often they leave the museum jingling their own keys in their pockets or regarding them with new respect, perhaps thinking how strange it is that keys, the most private and secret parts of ourselves, are nevertheless placed under doormats or flowerpots for visiting friends, or hung on a nail at the back of the garage for the gas-meter man, or mailed around the world in padded envelopes, acknowledging in this bitter, guarded century our lapses of attention.

A seven-year-old boy taken along with his class to the museum in Buffalo stares into a display case. His gaze settles on a long, oddly shaped wooden key (Babylonian), and his hand flies instantly to the key he wears around his neck, the key that will let him into his house on North Lilac Avenue after school, one hour before his mother returns from her job at the bottling plant. When first tying the key in place, she had delivered certain warnings: the key must not be lost, lent or even shown to others, but must be kept buried under his sweater all day long, accompanying him everywhere, protecting him from danger.

He doesn't need protection, not that he could ever explain this to his mother; he knows how to jump and hustle and keep himself watchful. The key leads him home and into a warm hallway, the light switch waiting, a note on the refrigerator, the television set sending him a wide, waxy smile of welcome. There is no danger, none at all; his mother has been misled, her notion of the world somehow damaged. Still, he loves this key (so icy against his skin when he slips it on, but warming quickly to body temperature) and has to restrain himself, whenever he feels restless, from reaching inside his clothes and fingering its edges.

He is a solemn child whose thoughts are full of perforations (how it would feel to bite into a red crayon or put his tongue to the rain-soaked bushes behind the schoolyard fence), or else opening onto a lively boil of fantasy that tends to be dotted with bravery and tribute. And yet, for all his imaginative powers, he cannot—at his age—begin to picture the unscrolling of a future in which he will one day possess a key ring (in the shape of the Eiffel Tower) that will hold a pair of streamlined rubber-tipped car keys, as well as a rainbow of pale tinted others—house, office, club, cottage—and a time when he will have a curly-headed wife with her own set of keys (on a thong of red leather stamped with her initials) and a fourteen-year-old daughter whose miniature brass key will open a diary in which she will write out her secret thoughts, beneath which lie a secondary drift of thought too tentative, too sacred, too rare to trust to the inexactitude of print and to the guardianship of a mere key.

Absence

SHE WOKE UP EARLY, drank a cup of strong, unsugared coffee, then sat down at her word processor. She knew more or less what she wanted to do, and that was to create a story that possessed a granddaughter, a Boston fern, a golden apple and a small blue cradle. But after she had typed half a dozen words, she found that one of the letters of the keyboard was broken, and, to make matters worse, a vowel, the very letter that attaches to the hungry self.

Of course she had no money and no house-handy mate to prod the key free. Many a woman would have shrugged good-naturedly, conceded defeat, and left the small stones of thought unclothed, but not our woman; our woman rolled up her sleeves, to use that thready old metaphor, and began afresh. She would work *around* the faulty letter. She would be resourceful, look for other ways and make an artefact out of absence. She would, to put the matter bluntly, make do.

She started—slowly, ponderously—to tap out words. "Several thousand years ago there—"

But where her hands had once danced, they now trudged. She stopped and scratched her head, her busy, normally useful head, that had begun, suddenly, to thrum and echo; where could she go from here? she asked herself sharply. Because the flabby but dependable gerund had dropped through language's trapdoor, gone. Whole parcels of grammar, for that matter, seemed all at once out of reach, and so were those bulky doorstop words that connect and announce and allow a sentence to pause for a moment and take on fresh loads of oxygen. Vocabulary, her well-loved garden, as broad and taken-for-granted as an acre of goldenrod, had shrunk to a square yard, and she was, as never before, forced to choose her words, much as her adored great-aunt, seated at a tea table, had selected sugar lumps by means of a carefully executed set of tongs.

She was tempted, of course, to seek out synonyms, and who could blame her? But words, she knew, held formal levels of sense and shades of deference that were untransferable one to the other, though thousands of deluded souls hunch each day over crossword puzzles and try. The glue of resonance makes austere demands. Memory barks, and context, that absolute old cow, glowers and chews up what's less than acceptable.

The woman grew, as the day wore on, more and more frustrated. Always the word she sought, the only word, teased and taunted from the top row of the broken keyboard, a word that spun around the center of a slender, one-legged vowel, erect but humble, whose dot of amazement had never before mattered.

Furthermore, to have to pause and pry an obscure phrase from the dusty pages of her old thesaurus threw her off balance and altered the melody of her prose. Between stutters and starts, the sheen was somehow lost; the small watery pleasures of accent and stress were roughened up as though translated from some coarse sub-Balkan folk tale and rammed through the nozzle of a too-clever-by-half, space-larky computer.

Her head-bone ached; her arm-bones froze; she wanted only to make, as she had done before, sentences that melted at the center and branched at the ends, that threatened to grow unruly and run away, but that clause for clause adhered to one another as though stuck down by Velcro tabs.

She suffered too over the *sounds* that evaded her and was forced to settle for those other, less seemly vowels whose open mouths and unsubtle throats yawned and groaned and showed altogether too much teeth. She preferred small, slanted, breakable tones that scarcely made themselves known unless you pressed an ear closely to the curled end of the tongue or the spout of a kettle. The thump of heartbeat was what she wanted, but also the small urgent jumps lodged between the beats. (She was thankful, though, for the sly *y* that now and then leapt forward and pulled a sentence taut as a cord.)

"Several thousand years ago a woman sat down at a table and began to—"

Hours passed, but the work went badly. She thought to herself: to make a pot of bean soup would produce more pleasure. To vacuum the hall rug would be of more use.

Both sense and grace eluded her, but hardest to bear was the fact that the broken key seemed to demand of her a parallel surrender, a correspondence of economy subtracted from the alphabet of her very self. But how? A story had to come from somewhere. Some hand must move the pen along or press the keys and steer, somehow, the granddaughter toward the Boston fern or place the golden apple at the foot of the blue cradle. "A woman sat down at a table and—"

She felt her arm fall heavy on the table, and she wondered, oddly, whether or not the table objected. And was the lamp, clamped there to the table's edge, exhausted after so long a day? Were the floorboards reasonably cheerful, or the door numb with lack of movement, and was the broken letter on her keyboard appeased at last by her cast-off self?

Because now her thoughts flowed through every object and every corner of the room, and a moment later she *became* the walls and also the clean roof overhead and the powerful black sky. Why, she wondered aloud, had she stayed so long enclosed by the tough, lonely pronoun of her body when the whole world beckoned?

But the words she actually set down came from the dark eye of her eye, the stubborn self that refused at the last moment to let go. "A woman sat down—"

Everyone knew who the woman was. Even when she put a red hat on her head or changed her name or turned the clock back a thousand years or resorted to wobbly fables about granddaughters and Boston ferns, everyone knew the woman had been there from the start, seated at a table, object and subject sternly fused. No one, not even the very young, pretends that the person who brought forth words was any other than the arabesque of the unfolded self. There was no escape and scarcely any sorrow.

"A woman sat down and wrote," she wrote.

Windows

IN THE DAYS WHEN THE WINDOW TAX was first introduced M.J. used to say to me, "Stop complaining. Accept. Render unto Caesar. Et cetera."

I remember feeling at the time of the legislation that the two of us would continue to live moderately well as long as we had electricity to illuminate our days and nights, and failing that, kerosene or candles. But I knew that our work would suffer in the long run.

"Furthermore," M.J. continued, "the choice is ours. We can block off as many or as few windows as we choose."

This was true enough; the government, fearing rebellion, I suppose, has left the options open. Theoretically, citizens are free to choose their own level of taxation, shutting off, if they like, just one or two windows or perhaps half to two-thirds of their overall glazed area. In our own case, we immediately decided to brick up the large pane at the back of the house that overlooks the ravine. A picture window is how my parents would have described this wide, costly expanse of glass; M.J. prefers the trademark term "panorama vista," but at the same time squints ironically when it's mentioned. We loved the view, both of us, and felt our work was nourished by it, those immense swaying poplars and the sunlight breaking across the top of their twinkling leaves, but once we sat down and calculated the tax dollars per square inch of window, we decided we would have to make the sacrifice.

Next we closed off our bedroom windows. Who needs light in a bedroom, we reasoned, or the bathroom either, for that matter? We liked to think at the time that our choices represented a deliberate push towards optical derangement, and that this was something that might add a certain . . . *je ne sais quoi* . . . to a relationship that has never been easy.

Before the advent of the Window Tax, light had streamed into our modest-but-somehow-roomy house, and both M.J. and I rejoiced in the fact, particularly since we earn our living as artists—I work in oils; M.J.'s medium is also oils, but thinly, thinly applied so that the look is closer to tempera. Light— natural light—was crucial to us. Just think what natural light allows one to see: the thousand varying shades of a late fall morning when the sky is brittle with a blue and gold hardness, or the folded, collapsed, watery tints of a February afternoon. Still, artificial light was better than no light at all. We did go to the trouble of applying to the government for a professional dispensation, a matter of filling out half a dozen forms, but naturally we were turned down.

We were, it could be argued, partly prepared for our deprivation, since both of us had long since adjusted our work cycle to the seasonal rhythms, putting in longer hours in the summer and cutting back our painting time in the dark ends of winter days, quitting as early as three-thirty or four, brewing up a pot of green tea, and turning to other pursuits, occasionally pursuits of an amatory disposition; M.J.'s sensibility rises astonishingly in the midst of coziness and flickering shadow. Our most intimate moments, and our most intense, tend to fall into that crack of the day when the sun has been cut down to a bent sliver of itself and even that about to disappear on the horizon.

It is a fact that my work has always suffered at the approach of winter. The gradual threatened diminishment of the after-noon sun encourages a false exuberance. Slap down the thick blades of color while it is still possible. Hurry. Be bold (my brain shouts and prods), and out of boldness, while the clock drains away each thrifty second of possibility, will come that accident we call art.

It seldom does. What I imagine to be a useful recklessness is only bad painting executed with insufficient light.

M.J.'s highly representational work prospers even less well than mine during the late autumn days, not that the two of us have ever spoken of this. You will understand that two painters living together under one roof can be an invitation to discord, and its lesser cousin, irritation. Ideally, artists would be better off selecting mates who are civil engineers or chiro-practors or those who manufacture buttons or cutlery. It's relatively easy to respect disparate work, but how do we salute, purely, the creative successes of those we live with, those we stand beside while brushing our teeth? How to rule out envy, or worse, disdain, and to resist those little sideways words or faked encouragement, delivered with the kind of candor that is really presumption? And so when I say, rather disingenuously, that M.J.'s work prospers less well, is overly representational, employs too much purple and lavender, and so on, you will have to take my pronouncement with a certain skepticism. And then reflect on the problems of artistic achievement and its measurement, and the knowledge that systems of temperament are immensely complicated. The salt and wound of M.J.'s vulnerability, for instance, is stalked by an old tenderness, but also by the fear of being overtaken.

It seems that most artists are frightened by any notion of subtraction, and, of course, the rationing of light falls into the category of serious deprivation. Without paint, artists can create images with their own blood or excrement if necessary, not that the two of us have ever been driven to such measures, but there is no real substitute for natural light. As the accustomed afternoon rays grow thinner, the work becomes more desperate, careless and ineffectual. We often discussed this over our tea mugs during our mid-winter days when the year seemed at its weakest point, how scarcity can stifle production or else, as in my case, clear a taunting space to encourage it. It seemed to both of us monumentally unfair.

But then, with the new tax measures, the house was dark all day. Like everyone else we had come to see the cutting back of natural light as a civic protest against a manipulative tax, *conscience de nos jours,* you might call it, and like all but the very rich we had filled in every one of our windows—with brick or stone or sheets of ugly plywood. *Obscura maxima* was the code phrase on our politicized tongues, and we spoke it proudly—and on our bumper stickers too—at least in the beginning. (Of course, we left the window in our studio as long as we were able, and only boarded it up when we were made to feel we had failed in our civic responsibility.)

In another country, at a different latitude, we might have packed up our easels and paints and sandwiches and worked *en plein air,* since no government, however avid for revenues, is able to control access to outdoor light. But "nature's studio," as the great Linnaeus called it, is seldom available in our northern climate. Our winters are long and bitter, and our summers filled with sultry air and plagues of mosquitoes. We are dependent, therefore, on a contrived indoor space, our *atelier,* as I sometimes like to call it, into which we coax as much light as possible—or at least we did before the enactment of the Window Tax.

The tax, when it was first introduced, had a beguiling logic, and even the appearance of fairness. We know, every last one of us, how widespread the evils of tax evasion are, how even the most morally attentive—and I would put M.J. and myself in that category—inflate their travel receipts or conceal small transactions that have brought them profit. More than once I've exchanged little dashed-off paintings, still lifes mostly, for such necessities as fuel oil and roof repairs, leaving behind not a trace for my accountant's eye.

The genius of the new tax was its simplicity. Some forms of wealth can be hidden in safe-deposit boxes or in dresser drawers, but the dwellings we inhabit announce, loudly and publicly, our financial standing—their size, their aesthetic proportions, the materials with which they are fashioned. And what could be more visible from the exterior than the number and size of one's windows? What feature can be more easily calculated?

A formula was worked out: so many tax dollars per square inch of window. A populist victory.

The results might have been foreseen. Overnight, with windows an index to wealth, and thus a liability, the new form of tax evasion became, as you can imagine, a retreat to medieval darkness. One by one, and then hundreds by hundreds, our wondrous apertures to the world were walled in with wood or cardboard or solid masonry. As seen from the outside, the hurriedly filled-in windows gave our houses the blank, stunned look of abandonment. Inside was trapped the darkness of a primitive world; we might just as well have been living in caves or burrows.

The plotted austerities of our own domestic life, so appealing at first, soon faded. A life in the dark is close to motionless; hour by hour the outlines of our bodies are lost—there is no armature of style, no gesture, no signifying softness of the mouth. What follows is a curious amnesia of the self. I had thought that words spoken in the dark might bring back the old force of language, words becoming deeds, becoming defined moments, but I found instead that the voice in the dark puts on a dignified yet hollow sideshow, so that we ended up speaking to ourselves and not to each other.

Of course, there was always the alternative of artificial light, which was in fact our only recourse. But a life performed under the burnt yellow-whiteness of electric illumination condemns us to perceptual distortion. There is that vicious snapping on and off of current, and the unvarying intensity, always predictable, yet always startling. The glare of a simple light bulb—think of it, that unhandsome utilitarian contrivance of glass and wire—insists on a sort of extracted/extruded truth, which those of us involved in long love affairs are wary of. Our postures and equivocations are harshly exposed, and the face we show the world subtly discolored. Is there any love that doesn't in the end insist on naming itself, showing itself to other less fortunate people, oh, look at me! at us!

When two people live and work under the same roof, the solitary nature of consciousness is frayed with a million threads of incalculability, and one of those threads is a deci-sion to avoid emotional dissonance and preserve for one's self certain areas of privacy. M.J. and I, in the months follow-ing the Window Tax, settled for an unspoken equipoise: I kept my self-doubts to myself and, in turn, was spared the usual strong doses of disrespect about my *attitude*.

No longer did we discuss our work or show our projects to each other, though we occupied as always the same studio. We kept to our separate corners. I worked mainly during the day and M.J. at night, for with the loss of daylight it scarcely mat-tered to us anymore which was which. As for our *vie intime*, well, that had declined radically after just a few days spent under the parching electric lights. While M.J. slept, I worked steadily but with a constant ache of discouragement, attempting with my range of aromatic oils to recreate on canvas the warmth and shine of inflowing light, that which I'd known all my life but now could scarcely remember. This was a flat, dull width of time, though I have always recognized that long chapters of life go on without strong passion.

It occurred to me one day that my use of canvas might be at fault. Stretched canvas, with its stiff industrial surface, possesses a withholding element and in the best of circumstances is reluctant at first to "open" its weave to what is offered. I knew that it had once been customary to paint on wood surfaces, hearty walnut planks or maple—this was an old and honorable tradition, and one that I thought worth trying.

At that moment my eyes fell on the slab of plywood we had nailed over the studio window, and the thought came to me that I might overpaint its cheap fir grain with a diverting image: one of my tossed-off still lifes, perhaps, a collection of lemons on a blue plate or a pitcher of pure water, something anyway that was more consoling than the life around me and less inviting of the late afternoon fits and starts brought on by the overhead lights.

The rectangularity of the wood seemed to demand a frame of some kind, and this I carefully painted in, exchanging the rather harsh orginess of fir for a subtly grained and beveled oak, a generous four inches in width, working my way around the two sides, the top and bottom, and then, finally, painting in a quartet of fine mitred corners. An easy trick, you might think, transforming one type of wood into another, but the task took me the rest of the day—and half of the next.

When I paint, I am composed, I am most truly myself, but I wish I could tell you how much happiness this particular craftsmanlike task gave me, exchanging wood for simple wood, coaxing ripples from dead surfaces. My usual paintings are compositionally complex and employ a rich color field. I am known for my use of the curved line. It's even been said that my management of the curve has brought to contemporary painting "an engagement for the eye and a seduction for the intellect." And yet, the strict linearity of my new "oak" frame brought a satisfaction my rondure illusions have never given.

At first I didn't know that what I was framing was, in fact, a window; the knowledge came upon me slowly as I found my brush dividing the framed space into a series of smaller rectangles, bringing about a look that was oddly architectural. Again I reached for a golden oakiness of color; again I kept my lines disciplined and sharp, but narrower now, more delicate and refined.

Mullions. The word leapt into my head. A relic of an older world from a wiser consciousness. These nonstructural bars dividing the lights or panes of the window proved relatively easy to master, being simple wood strips, slightly grooved on their edges, glinting with their barely revealed woody highlights. Each one of them pleased me, the verticals, the horizontals, and most especially their shy intersections.

That phrase *most especially*. Did you notice? M.J. has no patience with such locutions.

Harder to paint on the surface of ordinary plywood was the image of glass, and so I was forced to experiment. Window glass, as you will have observed, is a curious half-silvered substance, a steaming liquid that has been frozen into a solid plane. Glass possesses different colors at different hours of the day. Sometimes it pretends it's a mirror. Other times it gathers checks and streaks and bubbles of brilliance and elegant flexes of mood. Its transparency winks back at you, yet it withholds, in certain weathers, what is on the other side, revealing only a flash of wet garden grass, a shadow of a close-standing hedge or perhaps a human figure moving across its width—the mail carrier or a neighbor or even M.J. out for a late afternoon stroll. Glass is green like water or blue like the sky or a rectangle of beaten gold when the setting sun strikes it or else a midnight black broken by starlight or the cold courteous reflection of the moon.

Glassiness evaded me. My brush halted; it swung in the air like a metronome. What I produced were gray cloudy squares with a cardboardlike density, a kindergarten version of what a window might be.

It may have been that I was tired. Or that I was visited by that old fear of failure or by the sense of lowered consequence that arrives out of nowhere, especially when I hear M.J. tiptoeing around in the kitchen, brewing yet another pot of tea. I decided to leave it until morning.

As always I rose early and went straight to the studio and snapped on the electric lights. My "window" was waiting, but I saw immediately that it was altered. The shadows of my oak moldings had acquired a startling *trompe l'oeil* vividness, their depth and shadow augmented and their woodiness enlivened by amber flecks and streaks. I had been pleased to arrive the day before at a primitive suggestiveness—window as architectural detail, window as gesturing towards windowness, just falling short of verisimilitude, but this was now a window so cunningly made that it could almost have been opened on its casement hinges. Hinges that had not existed yesterday. The glass panes too had been tampered with. I looked closely and recognized a slick oil shine superimposed on a lake of rainy mauve.

All day I worked on the glass. It went slowly, so slowly that often an hour would pass with only one or two touches of my brush on the surface. My paint was mixed and layered, rubbed out, then reapplied. By evening I had managed to articulate, or so I thought, the spark and glance and surprise of glass without, of course, stretching towards the achievement of light or air.

I woke the next morning with a sense of excitement. Even before entering the studio I could feel a soft-shoe dance in the region of my chest, and I reflected that it had been some years since my feelings had run so dangerously out of control. My "window" shone, its oak frame burning with an almost antique burnish, and the troublesome panes giving off their glassy gifts. How is it possible to make light dance on a flat surface, and how does anyone bring transparency to what is rigid and unyielding? I sighed, then readied myself for a day of work.

It was at least a week before the task was done. By coincidence we were both there when it reached completion, standing side by side in one of our rare moments of tenderness, each of us with brush in hand. One of us reached forward to apply a final brush stroke, though we weren't able to remember afterward which it was. The moment was beautiful, but also blurred. We recall a sudden augmentation of brilliance, as though we witnessed the phenomenon with a single pair of eyes, our "window" bursting its substance, freed in such a way that light flowed directly through it.

Not real light, of course, but the idea of light—infinitely more alluring than light itself. Illusion, accident, meticulous attention all played a part in the construction of a window that had become more than a window, better than a window, the window that would rest in the folds of the mind as all that was ideal and desirable in the opening, beckoning, sensuous world.

Reportage

NOW THAT A ROMAN ARENA has been discovered in south-eastern Manitoba, the economy of this micro-region has been transformed. Those legendary wheat farms with their proud old family titles have gone willfully, happily bankrupt, gone "bust" as they say in the area, and the same blond, flat-lying fields that once yielded forty bushels per acre have been turned over to tourism.

Typical is the old Orchard place off Highway 12. Last Wednesday I visited Mr. Orchard in the sunny ranch-style house he shares with his two cocker bitches, Beauty and Trude, one of them half-blind, the other hard of hearing. The fir floors of the Orchard place shine with lemon wax. There are flowers in pottery vases, and the walls are covered by the collage works of his former wife, Mavis, who is said to be partly responsible for the discovery and excavation of the Roman ruins. I asked Mr. Orchard for a brief history.

"Quite early on," he mused, pouring out cups of strong Indian tea, "I became aware of a large shallow depression in the west quarter of our family farm. The depression, circular in shape like a saucer and some three-hundred feet across, was not so much visible to the eye as experienced by the body. Whenever I rode tractor in this area—I am speaking now of my boyhood—I anticipated, and registered, this very slight dip in the earth's surface, and then the gradual rise and recovery of level ground. We referred to this geological anomaly as Billy's Basin for reasons that I cannot now recall, although I did have an Uncle Bill on my mother's side who farmed in the area in the years before the Great War, a beard-and-twinkle sort of fellow and something of a scholar, according to family legend, who was fond of sitting up late and reading by lamplight—books, newspapers, mail-order catalogs, anything the man could get his hands on. I have no doubt but that he was familiar with the great Greek and Roman civilizations, but certainly he never dreamed that the remnants of antiquity were so widely spread as to lie buried beneath our own fertile fields here in Manitoba and that his great-grandnephew—myself, that is—would one day derive his living not from wheat but from guiding tours and selling postcards. Whether Uncle Bill would have scorned or blessed this turn of events I have no way of knowing, but I like to think he was not a man to turn his back on fortune."

At that point one of Mr. Orchard's dogs, Beauty, rubbed voluptuously against his trousers leg. "You will agree with me," he said, "that once a thing is discovered, there's no way on earth to undiscover it."

Mavis Orchard (née Gulching), who has been amicably separated from Mr. Orchard for the last six months, was able to fill me in on the circumstances of the actual discovery. She is an attractive, neatly dressed woman of about sixty with thick, somewhat wayward iron-grey hair and a pleasant soft-spoken manner. Smilingly, she welcomed me to her spacious mobile home outside Sandy Banks and, despite the hour, insisted on making fresh coffee and offering a plateful of homemade cinnamon-spiral rolls. Her collage work was everywhere in evidence, and centered more and more, she told me, on the metaphysics of time, Kiros and Chronos, and the disjunctive nature of space/matter. She is a woman with a decidedly philosophic turn of mind, but whose speech is braced by an unflinching attachment to the quotidian.

"When we think of the fruits of the earth," she led off, "we tend to think of cash crops or mineral deposits. We think"—and she held up her meticulously manicured hands and ticked off a list—"of wheat. Of oil. Of phosphates. Natural gas. Even gold. Gold does occur. But the last thing we think of finding is a major historical monument of classical proportions."

At this she shrugged hyperbolically in a way that indicated her sense of the marvelous. "Arrowheads, of course, have been found in this area from early times. Also a small but unique wooden sundial displayed now in the Morden Local History Museum, where you can also see a fine old English axe belonging to the first settler in this region, a Mr. DeBroches. But"—and she tugged at her off-white woolen cardigan, resetting it around her rather amply formed shoulders—"when the drills went into our west quarter section looking for oil and came up hard against three supine Ionic columns, we knew we were on to something of import and significance, and that there could be no turning back. This earth of ours rolls and rolls through its mysterious vapors. Who would want to stop it? Not I."

Angela and Herbert Penner, whose back porch offers the best position from which to photograph the ruined arena, spoke openly to me about the changes that have overtaken their lives.

Herbert: There are problems, of course, adjusting to a new economic base.

Angela: I wish they wouldn't throw things on the ground, gum wrappers, plastic wrap from their sandwiches and so on. Last summer our family cat, Frankie, swallowed a soft drink tab and had to be taken to the vet, which set us back fifty dollars if you can believe it. But most people who come here are just people.

Herbert: (proudly) We've had visitors from all fifty states, all ten Canadian provinces plus the territories, Western Europe, Japan and mainland China.

Angela: Would you like to see the guest book? One gentleman wrote recently: "Standing at the entrance to this site, one experiences a sort of humility."

Herbert: (piqued) A lady from California wrote: "Not nearly as impressive as Nîmes."

Angela: That's in France. Theirs seats twenty thousand.

Herbert: Not the point really, though, is it?

Angela: We've managed to keep our charges reasonable. Our color film we sell at almost cost.

Herbert: (interrupting) Coffee and sandwiches is where we make our bit of change, I'd say. Refreshments. Think about that word. Re-fresh-ments.

Angela: And next year we're edging into B and B.

Herbert: Meaning bed and breakfast.

Angela: All in all we feel we've been blessed.

Herbert: (concludingly) Oh, richly, richly blessed.

Dr. Elizabeth Jane Harkness at the Interpretative Center replied somewhat caustically when asked about the markings on the stones and columns, "The motifs we find here are perhaps closer to the cup-and-ring carvings of prehistory than to the elaborate texts found on most traditional Roman structures," she admitted, patting her handsome auburn hair in place, "but we find it offensive and indeed Eurocentric to have *our* markings referred to as 'doodles.' It is one of the great romances of consciousness to think that language is the only form of containment and continuity, but who nowadays really subscribes? Who? Our simple markings here, which I personally find charming and even poignant, are as emblematically powerful in their way as anything the Old World has to offer."

Jay DeBroches, former grain-elevator manager and great-grandson of the first settler in the area, took me along to the Sandy Banks beer hall, now renamed the Forum, and said very quietly, with innate dignity, "Speaking off record for a moment, there was a certain amount of skepticism at first, and although I don't like to say so, most of it came from south of the border. It was like a we-had-a-Roman-ruin-and-they-didn't sort of thing. One guy claimed it was an elaborate hoax. A Disneyesque snow job. Like we'd done it with mirrors. Well, they sent their big boys up here for a look-see, and one glance at this gorgeous multitiered, almost perfect circle was enough to convince them of what was what. Now we've got some kind of international trustee setup, and that keeps them happy, though rumor has it they're scouring Minnesota and North Dakota with lasergraphs looking for one of their own, but so far no luck. I guess in my heart of hearts I hope ours is the only one. I've got the parking concession, so I'm here every morning early, and it still makes me shiver—even my fingers shiver, every little joint—when I see the dew winking off these immense old shelfy stones and giving a sense of the monolithic enterprise of that race that came before us."

The Stanners family has thus far concentrated on T-shirts, felt pennants and key rings, what Mrs. Stanners refers to as "your takeaway trade." But she has visions of outdoor concerts, even opera. "And this place is a natural for Disney-on-Ice," she says, escorting me to her veranda and offering a wicker armchair.

San (Salvador) Petty, chief zoning officer, unrolls a set of maps and flattens them on a table. I help him weigh down the edges with desktop oddments, a stapler, an onyx pen holder, a framed photograph of the arena itself during the early stages of excavation. "Here," Mr. Petty explains, pointing with the eraser end of a pencil, "is where the new highway will come. The north and south arms join here, and as you can see we've made allowance for state-of-the-art picnic facilities. We have a budget for landscaping, we have a budget for future planning and contingency costs and the development of human resources. None of this just happened, we made it happen."

"Speaking personally," said retired Latin teacher Ruby Webbers, "I believe it is our youth who will ultimately suffer. The planting and harvesting of grain were honorable activities in our community and gave our boys and girls a sense of buoyancy and direction. They felt bonded to the land, not indebted to it. I don't know, I just don't know. Sometimes I walk over here to the site on moist, airy evenings, just taking in the spectacle of these ancient quarried stones, how their edges sharpen under the floodlights and how they spread themselves out in wider and wider circles. Suddenly my throat feels full of bees. I want to cry. Why not? Why are you looking at me like that? I grant you it's beautiful, but do beautiful monuments ever think of the lives they smash? Oh, I feel my whole body start to tremble. It shouldn't be here. It has nothing to do with us. It scares me. You're not listening to me, are you? At times it seems to be getting even bigger and more solid and more *there*. It preens, it leers. If I could snap my fingers and make it disappear, that's what I'd do. Just snap, snap, and say, 'Vanish, you ridiculous old phantom—shoo!'"

Edith-Esther

EDITH-ESTHER'S BIOGRAPHER started phoning her a year ago, wanting to know her thoughts about God.

Generally he manages to catch her early in the morning, just as she's rubbing her creased eyes open and setting aside her night dreams, reaching sideways for her bathrobe, coughing her habitual morning cough.

She's noticed how he can be aggressive in his questioning or else placatory, depending on how the biography is going or what he judges her mood to be. "It's most interesting," he said one day, purring into the mouthpiece, "that you seem not to have addressed or referenced a single particularized deity in any of your novels."

"Really?" she said, belting her robe against the morning chill. "Can that be true?"

"Not unless you count the paragraph in *Lest We Be Known,* Chapter Four, page twelve of the first edition, when George Hellman says something or other about how God has damned the entire Hellman dynasty."

"Oh, hmmmm, yes." She is holding the phone tucked under her chin, which is more painful than one might think, while she struggles to find the on switch for her new Swiss coffee machine. "I think I did say something like that."

"But my sense, Edith-Esther, is that you intend this particular aside to be more metaphorical than specific."

"I believe you must be right," she said. She is eighty years old, and more and more finds that the novels she's written, their textures, their buzzing, inhabited worlds, blend into the width of a long grassy field. Or rather, the various novels can be reduced to a single brevity. Love doubted. Love lost, love renounced. Bleak, she often thinks to herself of her own work. Or, when she wants to treat herself kindly, austere.

"It would be useful," her biographer said, "if you could state, one way or another, on which side of the belief debate you sit."

"Debate?"

There! She'd found the switch. In a few minutes there would be four inches of coffee in the glass pot, dark and flavorful, a Brazilian blend, her daily ration. With coffee she would be set for the morning, held alert and upright. "Now, which debate would you be referring to?"

They both recognized that she was being disingenuous. Stalling.

"The classic debate, Edith-Esther. Does He or does He not exist?"

"I'm surprised at you," she said. "You of all people even raising the question, and in that form."

"What can I say? A biographer is obliged to raise all questions. The total weave of personality must include—"

"I don't believe," she told him plainly, "in God."

Did she imagine him sighing? Yes. There was a silence, at any rate, just spacious enough to enclose a sigh. "What's wanted, Edith-Esther, is some slight spiritual breeze blowing through the life material, the merest hint of the unseen world."

This was too much for Edith-Esther, who had spent her life in flight from those who believe the body merely a sack for the soul. "I would have thought," she said, "that a man like you might appreciate that we live in secular times, and that the next century will be even more—"

"I wasn't speaking of a whole theological system. Good heavens, no. Your readers would never"—here he produced one of his small, appeasing, updraft chuckles—"expect any such thing. I think they'd be happy with just, you know, some small tossed coin at the fountain of faith. Some offhand salute to a Creator or Supreme Being. Or even the mention of an occasion when you reflected, however briefly, on the nature of the Life Force."

Life Force? The term, so old-fashioned and Shavian, brought her a smile. She looked down, and abruptly stopped smiling. Her left arm displayed a veiny ridge of fine purple. Was it there yesterday?

She poured a stream of coffee into a thin white mug and sipped cautiously, seeing even without the aid of a mirror how her upper lip puckered grotesquely at the ceramic edge, trembling and sucking like a baby's greedy mouth. She was at an age when eating and drinking should be done in private. "I may have reflected on such matters," she said, "but I was not at any time rewarded with proof."

"I see." Disappointment raised his voice to a croak. "Well, perhaps I might say that in the biography, quote those very words you've just uttered."

"No, absolutely not. That would give a false impression. That I'm some sort of desperately seeking pilgrim."

Edith-Esther can imagine her biographer at this moment, 112 green miles away, past four loops of major highway, across a concrete bridge, eighteen stories into the air, sitting at his blocky desk and holding a Bic straight up on its point, trying to think of another angle from which he might approach the subject of Edith-Esther's non-existent religious impulse.

She understood how careful you had to be with biographers; death by biography—it was a registered disease. Thousands have suffered from it, butchery by entrapment in the isolated moment. The selected moment with its carbon lining. Biographers were forever catching you out and reminding you of what you once said. *But back in 1974 you stated categorically that . . .*

He was, if only he knew, just one inch more tactful and patient than she actually demanded. It was exasperating, but also amusing, the way he tiptoed, advanced and withdrew, then advanced again. She supposed this show of courtesy masked his very real powers of extraction and was what made him who he was—one of the world's most successful and respected biographers, at least in the literary arena. Robert Sillerman, Roche Clement, Amanda Bishop—he'd done them all. His portrait of the prickly Wilfred Holmsley was considered a model of a private life turned inside out, yet each of its revelations seemed perfectly stitched in place so that nothing really surprised or shocked, not even the disclosure of Holmsley's plagiarism in his late sixties, that dramatic accident scene, lifted almost word for word from a newspaper report. (Inadvertent, the judge ruled when the case came to trial, a question of Mr. Holmsley copying an arresting text into his notebook and forgetting the quote marks. Also pertinent was the question of just how many ways it was possible to describe a simple decapitation.)

"Well, then," Edith-Esther's biographer continued, "do you believe in anything at all?"

She considered. "I suppose you must mean astrology or tea leaves or something of that sort."

"I mean," he said, "just anything. *Anything.*"

"For some reason I have the sense you're trying to bully me into belief, and I'm not sure that's fair. Or useful."

"Not at all, Edith-Esther, not at all. No biographer worth his or her professional salt manipulates the material. Or the subject. Don't even entertain the thought. Pulling cords of memory is what I'm really trying to do. Helping you to put a finger on some moment, partly obscured perhaps, that would be perfectly understandable, when you might have, you know, transcended this world for an instant and then buried it in the text, which is something writers are wont to do, and—"

"Do you remember when you and I signed our initial agreement two years ago this March?"

"Of course. A wonderful occasion."

"Which we celebrated, you'll recall, with dinner at Mr. Chan's."

"The most delicate shrimp dumplings I've ever had the pleasure of tasting. Little clouds, saffron-scented. We actually asked the waiter to refill the serving dish, didn't we?"

"And do you remember the moment when the fortune cookies arrived?"

"How could I forget? Oh! Oh! Mine said, 'Persevere and you will arrive at truth.'"

"You will also recollect that I refused to open my fortune cookie."

"Because—"

"I knew I was disappointing you, but I am less willing than some to be drawn into the realm of the spurious and super-stitious. You will remember that I was not what is known as a good sport that evening."

"Come, now, Edith-Esther, no one really believes in fortune cookies."

"You did, at least on that particular occasion. You decreed it was an omen. By perseverance you are going to arrive at the truth of my life. I believe you called it my 'kernel of authenticity.'"

"Oh, yes. That!"

"I admit I was troubled by the phrase. Thinking to myself, what if there were no kernel, what then?"

"I never meant to put forward something you'd find disturbing—"

"I must have lost my rationality, at least for a moment. The fact is, I slipped my fortune cookie into my handbag and brought it home. Just before going to bed I opened it up."

"Bless you, dear Edith-Esther. And what did it say?"

"It informed me that romance was about to enter my life."

"Ah."

"Now do you see why I reject all projections from beyond?"

"But your opening of the fortune cookie suggests, in a sense, your willingness to test your faith."

"Absolutely not," she said, draining her cup. "It suggests the opposite. A test of my disbelief."

One day Edith-Esther's biographer phoned earlier than usual. He was excited. He'd found something. "I've been rereading *Wherefore Bound*," he said.

Wherefore Bound. She tried to remember which one that was. Part of an early trilogy. The second volume? Or else the first. The air in front of her eyes filled for a moment with a meadow landscape, classic birds, wild grasses, a blur of shredded cloud. "Oh, yes," she said.

"Remember Paul Sinclair? He's the defrocked priest, the one who renounces his faith and—"

"Of course I remember."

"Your strongest work, in the opinion of the more astute critics—that tiny, ever-diminishing troupe. What I mean is, the character of Paul Sinclair is densely and beguilingly ambiguous."

"I wouldn't say ambiguous, not at all, in fact." She raised her cup to her mouth. Her coffee machine was broken. It was under guarantee, but so far she has been unable to find the required certificate. Meanwhile, she was making do with Nescafé, which she found bitter. "I'd say Paul Sinclair is very firm in his position."

"The fact is, Edith-Esther, he repeats and repeats his disconnection with the Godhead."

"Wouldn't you say that shows—"

"He repeats himself so often that one begins to doubt his doubt. Don't you see? Protesting too much? It seems very clear to me. Faith's absence pressed to the wall and brought to question. And then he leads the hundred children on their march and later overcomes—"

"He never admits anything."

"I was caught too by the symbolism of his lover's name. Magdelena. Now, there's a name with spiritual resonance, oh, my, yes, and—"

"I've always liked that name. I met someone a long time ago in Mexico named Magdelena, who became—"

"And there's the place where you're talking about Magdelena's lips and you say—surely you remember—you say, 'her lips form a wound in her flesh.'"

"I can't believe I said anything as silly as that."

"Wounds, Edith-Esther. The wounds of Christ? Surely that rings a ding-dong."

"I must have been trying to describe the *color* of her lips, their redness, something like that. Perhaps they were chapped. Perhaps she was suffering from cold sores. I myself used to be troubled by—"

"You've always undervalued your own work, Edith-Esther.

Rejected any sense of subtext, even when it's staring you in the face."

"I've never—"

"Why is it you're always refusing comfort? Why?"

"I don't know." She really didn't. Though perhaps she couldn't help thinking, it was because she'd refused to offer her readers the least crumb of comfort.

"Never mind, forgive me. It's part of your charm, Edith-Esther. It's all right. It's you."

"My kernel of authenticity?"

"What a memory you have. You're teasing me, I know, feeding me back my own nonsense. *Une taquine.* Even over the telephone wire, I can hear you teasing. But yes, it's true. You're exactly who you are."

"Whoever that may be."

"Hello?"

"Good morning, Edith-Esther. It's me."

"So early."

"I've been up all night rereading *Sacred Alliance.*"

"Well"—she gave a laugh, rather a wobbly one—"I'm afraid you can't describe *that* one as a critical success."

"Because it was misunderstood. I mean that with all my heart. I misunderstood it myself, initially. That word *Sacred* in the title, it completely escaped me until last night, but now I see exactly the flag you were waving."

"Flag? Waving? Oh, my. The title, I'm quite sure, was meant to be ironic. I'm certain that was my intention. It's so long ago, though, and I just this minute woke up. I can't seem to find my glasses. I know they're here somewhere. Perhaps I should phone you back when I'm feeling more focused—"

"You remember when Gloria first meets Robin, page fifty-one, and admits the fact of her virginity to him, it all comes out in a burst, not surprisingly, but what she's really saying is that she's made a choice, a sacred choice, a declaration about where she ultimately intends to place her devotion—"

"I can't imagine what I did with those glasses. I left them on the bedside table last night—"

"—and so, when Gloria and Robin go off to Vienna together and after that most unsatisfactory consummation, et cetera, and when he goes out to arrange for a rental car, and she locks herself in the hotel room—remember?—and writes him a note—"

"They're broken. One of the lenses. The left one. Smashed. I simply can't understand it—"

"—and the key word in that note is in the last line, the word *intact*. She writes that she wants to keep their one glorious night together *intact*, but what she's really saying is—"

"Oh, God!"

"Edith-Esther?"

She seemed to be stumbling across a width of unleveled ground, still wet with the morning's dew. "I'll have to phone you back, I can't seem to—"

"—that she will choose celibacy, that her calling lies in the realm of the spiritual, and that she—Are you there, Edith-Esther? Hello? Hello?"

"Just a quick call. Hope I didn't wake you."

"I was just lying here dozing. Feeling guilty. Thinking about getting up."

"I had to know. Have you seen the book?"

"Which book?"

"*The* book. Your biography. *A Spiritual Odyssey?*"

"Oh."

"Surely it arrived. Surely you've had a chance to look at it."

"I've been a little under the weather. Just twinges. And my glasses are broken again."

"You're not seriously ill, surely."

"Too many birthdays. As they say."

"Not you, Edith-Esther. Not someone with your spirit."

"My spirit? My what?"

"The cover. What do you think of the cover?"

"Very arresting. It turned out well. But the title—when did you decide to change the title?"

"Last-minute kind of thing. The publisher and I agreed it captured the direction your life has taken."

"You took out that part in the second chapter about my first communion."

"No, it's there. I just gave it a slightly different interpretation."

"I dropped the host on the church floor and stepped on it."

"You may remember it that way, but in fact—"

"It's just ordinary bread, I remember saying to myself. Store bread. White bread. I wanted to see if there'd be any lightning bolts."

"You were very young. And probably excited. You dropped it by accident, and were so embarrassed you tried to cover it— the host, that is—with your foot."

"There were no lightning bolts. I was sure there wouldn't be. There was nothing, only a hard, accusing look from the priest."

"He understood your embarrassment."

"His name was Father Albert. You left out his name."

"He could still be living."

"He'd have to be a hundred and ten."

"There might be a lawsuit, though. From the Church."

"Because he liked little girls? Liked to tickle them under the arms and between the legs?"

"The implications, that's all."

"You should have asked me—"

"It isn't what people want to hear, Edith-Esther. They've heard too much of that particular story in recent years. You'd be charged with a psychological cliché, I'm afraid."

"Clichés are almost always true—have you noticed that?"

"I don't want to see you represented as one of those insipid victims—"

"I saw early on that my particular kind was considered dangerous and needed to be locked up—in the house, in the convent. Did you know women were excluded from the Latin discourse?"

"Other times, other rhymes."

"I haven't been well."

"You sound extremely weak, Edith-Esther. Your voice. Have you seen a doctor?"

"Do you think I should?"

"I can't possibly know. But I can tell you one thing. The book is getting a positive response."

"Really?"

"More than positive. The fact is, people are finding it uplifting."

"Up-what?"

"I know you detest the word. And the concept. But some of us haven't your strength. We need encouragement along the way."

"I never meant to be uplifting. The last thing I wanted was to—"

"Of course not. But your example, Edith-Esther. All you've been through. The way you've translated your spiritual struggle into enlightenment."

"My glasses are broken."

"I'm praying that it hits the bestseller lists by next week."

"You're praying? Is that what you said?"

"Edith-Esther, are you there?"

No, she is no longer there. She's walking down the long green hummocky field, which may not be a field at all but a garden in a state of ruin. Whatever it is, it slopes toward a mere trickle of a river, and this is disappointing, the reluctant flow of water over small white stones, and also the surprising unevenness of the terrain. Ugly, ugly, seen up close. She feels, or else hears, one of her ankles snap. Chitinous. Oh, God. Barbed weeds and rough sedges, they scratch her bare legs and thighs. Luckily she has the sense to squeeze her eyes shut and to make tight fists of her hands. Every muscle in her body tenses against a possible invasion of bees or whatever else might come.

Some years ago Edith-Esther's pencil jar was stolen from her kitchen by an avid literary groupie. An image of this plain glass jar returns to her at the very moment she stumbles and falls. Probably, before its pencil-jar incarnation, it had held her favorite redcurrant jelly. Its glassy neck was comfortably wide, the more freely to receive her sharpened pencils and a fat pink eraser with old rubbed edges. There was a serious pair of scissors too, black-handled, and what else? She was forgetting something. Oh, yes. A decorative letter opener given to her by a friend—Magdelena?—with the Latin words RARA AVIS stamped on the handle.

A rare bird.

She feels herself grasping the handle now and testing the blade against her arm. It is surprisingly sharp, so sharp she decides to hack at the savage purple grass rising up around her, clearing a path for herself, making her way forward.

New Music

SHE WAS TWENTY-ONE when he first saw her, seated rather primly next to him on the Piccadilly Line, heading toward South Kensington. It was midafternoon. Like every other young woman in London, she was dressed from head to toe in a shadowless black, and on her lap sat a leather satchel.

It was the sort of satchel a girl might inherit from her adoring barrister father, and this was the truth of the matter (he found out later), except that the father was a piano teacher, not a barrister, and his adoration was often shaded by exasperation—which one can understand.

After a moment of staring straight ahead, she snapped open her satchel, withdrawing several sheets of paper covered with musical notations. (*He* was on his way to Imperial College for a lecture on reinforced concrete; *she* was about to attend an advanced class in Baroque music.) He had never before seen anyone "read" music in quite this way, silently, as though it were a newspaper, her eyes running back and forth, left to right, top of the page to the bottom, then flipping to the next. The notes looked cramped and fussy and insistent, but she took in every one, blinking only when she shifted to a new page. He imagined that her head was filled with a swirl of musical lint, that she was actually "hearing" a tiny concert inside that casually combed head of hers. And *his* head?—it was crammed with different stuff: equations, observations, a set of graphs, the various gradients of sands and gravels, his upcoming examinations and the fact that his trousers pocket had a hole in it, leaking a shower of coins on to the floor as he stood up.

"I think this is yours," she said, handing him a dropped penny.

"Whose music is that?" he managed. "The music you're looking at?"

"Tallis. Thomas Tallis."

"Oh."

She took pity on him as they stepped together onto the platform. "Sixteenth-century. English."

"Is he"—inane question—"is he good?"

"Good?"

"His music. Is it, you know, wonderful? Is he a genius, would you say?"

She stopped and considered. They were in the street now. The sunshine was sharply aslant. "He was the most gifted composer of his time," she recited, "until the advent of William Byrd."

"You mean this Byrd person came along and he was better than Thomas What's-his-name?"

"Oh"—she looked affronted—"I don't think *better* is quite the word. William Byrd was more inventive than Thomas Tallis, that's all. More original, in my opinion, anyway."

"Then why"—this seemed something he had to know, even though his reasoning was sure to strike her as simplistic and stupid—"why are you carrying around Thomas Tallis's music instead of the other chap's—the one who was better?"

She stared at him. Then she smiled and shrugged. "Do you always insist on the very best?"

"I don't know," he said, not being someone who'd experienced much in the way of choices. He was conscious of his hideous ignorance and inability to express himself. "It just seems like a waste of time. You know, taking second-best when you could have the best."

"Like reading, hmmm, Marlowe when you could have Shakespeare?"

He nodded, or at least attempted to nod.

"It's *because* I believe Tallis is second-best that I prefer him," she told him then. Her chin went up. Her voice was firm. "I don't expect you to understand."

"I do, I do," he exclaimed in his awful voice. And it was true, he did.

He loved her. Right from that instant, the way she opened up her mouth and said *because Tallis is second-best.*

Imagine a woman getting out of bed one hour earlier than the rest of the household. What will she do with that hour?

Make breakfast scones for her husband and three school-age children? Not this woman, not scones, banish the thought. Will she press her suit skirt? clean out her handbag? ready her attaché case for a day at work? No, this woman works at home—at a computer set up in what was once, in another era, in another incarnation, a sewing room. It's a room with discolored wallpaper, irises climbing on a sort of trellis, which doesn't make sense for a non-climbing, earth-bound flower. Against one wall is her writing table, which is really a cheap plywood door laid flat on trestles. She has been offered, several times, a proper desk, but she actually prefers this makeshift affair—which wobbles slightly each time she puts her elbow on the table and stares into the screen.

That's where she is now. At this hour! Her old and not-very-clean mauve dressing gown is pulled tight against the chill. It is not a particularly flattering color, but she doesn't know this, and besides, she's as faithful to old clothes as she is to inferior wallpaper. It's as though she can't bear to hurt their feelings. She's tapping away, without so much as a cup of coffee to cheer her on. It's still dark outside, not black, exactly, but a brew of streaked gray. You'd think she'd put up a curtain or at least a blind to soften that staring gray rectangle, but no. Nor has she thought to turn on the radio for a little musical companionship, she of all people. She's tapping, tapping at her keyboard, her two index fingers taking turns, and for the moment that's all she appears to need.

Is she writing a letter to her mother in Yorkshire? A Letter to the Editor complaining about access ramps for the handicapped? A suicide note full of blame and forgiveness and deliberate little shafts of self-pity? No. Today she's writing the concluding page (page 612) of a book, a book she's been working on for four years now, the comprehensive biography of Renaissance composer Thomas Tallis, ca. 1505–1585. The penultimate paragraph is already on the screen, then the concluding paragraph itself, and now, as a scarf of soft light flows in through the window and lands on her shoulders, she taps in the last sentence, and then the final word—which is the burnished, heightened, blurted-out word *triumph*. The full sentence reads: "Nevertheless, Tallis's contribution to English music can be described as a triumph."

Nevertheless? What's all this *nevertheless* about, you're probably asking?

Squinting into the screen, she taps in "The End," but immediately deletes it. My guess is that she's decided writing "The End" is too self-conscious a gesture. Did her husband write "The End" when he finished his monograph *Distribution of Gravel Resources in Southwest England?* Yes, certainly, but then he's not as fearful of self-indulgence as she.

She's spent four years on this book. I've already said that, haven't I?—but to be fair, the first eight months were passed listening to Tallis's music itself. The Mass for Four Voices, *Spem in alium, Lamentations of Jeremiah,* nine motets and so on. She lay on our canted, worn sofa—the kids at school, the husband at the office—and listened with notepad and pencil on her sweatered chest, waiting for the magnetic atoms of musical matter to come together, one and one and one, and give shape to the man who created them. There's so little known about him, and what is known is made blurry with *might have, could have, possibly was*—all the maddening italics of a rigorously undocumented life. The only real resource is the music, which, curiously, has come down to our century intact, or so I'm told, and that is why this woman spent eight months absorbing each separate, self-contained, cellular note.

Occasionally she fell asleep during those long sofa days. I'm no expert, but I've been told that Tallis is not particularly interested in counterpoint as such, and that the straightforward way he develops his musical ideas produces a sense of serenity that can be an invitation to doze. She admits this, but insists he can be experimental when he wants to be and even mildly extravagant. (*In nomine,* she gives as an example.)

Tallis's ghost lives in our house, his flat, hummy, holy tones and the rise and fall of Latin phrasing; it's permeated the carpets and plaster; it clings to the family hair and clothing and gets into the food. And for several months now an inky photocopy of his portrait has been stuck on the fridge, a little wraith of a man with a small pointed beard and abundant shoulder-length hair brushed back from his forehead. He is vain about his hair, one can tell.

It's not easy to calculate overall height from a head-and-shoulder image, but clearly he's got the alarmed, doubting eyes of a short man. (I am not a particularly tall chap myself, and so I instantly recognize and connect with a short man's uneasy gaze.) The children are forever asking their mother how Tom Tallis is getting along, meaning is she going to finish her book soon. They miss her rhubarb crumble, they miss the feel of ironed clothes and clean sheets and socks sorted into pairs. Her husband—he's in the sand and gravel business—he misses waking up beside her in the morning. By the time the alarm goes at half-past seven, the bed is cold, and she's already been working for an hour or more at her second-hand word processor. "There's cornflakes," she calls out when she hears footsteps in the kitchen, not for a moment lifting her eyes from the screen. "There's plenty of bread for toast." Well, sometimes there is and sometimes there isn't.

But because this is the final morning in the writing of her book, with the book's closing word *triumph* winking at her from the screen, she rises and stretches and makes her way to the kitchen, a sleepy, mauve-toned phantom. There she finds them—two sons, daughter and spouse, gathered about the toaster. She stares as though we are strangers who have entered her house sometime during the last four years and are now engaged in a mystical rite around this small smudged appliance. We're not exactly unwelcome, her look tells us, but the nature of our presence has yet to be explained.

Two months later Thomas Tallis is still on the fridge door. No one in the family has quite the courage to take him down, but the manuscript, all 612 pages, has been mailed to the publisher. This is a reasonably distinguished publishing house—though certainly not the best—and the editor is delighted to have the Tallis book on his fall list. He would much rather the author had written about William Byrd, of course, that goes without saying. There would have been *great* interest in a book about William Byrd, whereas there is only *considerable* interest in Thomas Tallis. Tallis, if the truth be known, must always be identified along with his famous student, who, according to tradition, overshadowed him. Part of Tallis's essence, in fact, is that he is stuck in an inevitable frame of reference. He also ran. Ran a good race, but . . .

Imagine what a woman does who has suddenly, after four long years, completed an arduous task. She cleans her house, for one thing, not perfectly, but competently. She remains in bed an hour longer in the morning, and for this her husband is ecstatically grateful. They wake together, his lips trace the pearled curve of her spinal column. He is a man who stumbles about all day dealing with the exigencies of gravel production, gravel deliveries, gravel prices per cubic yard, but thinking every other minute of his wife's soft limbs, her bodily clefts and swellings.

For her clever daughter she buys tickets to the ballet, and they return from the performance drunk with pleasure, and enact mock, foolish pirouettes on the hall carpet, bumping into the walls and giggling like a pair of teenagers.

For her younger son, a boy of exceptional beauty, she spends a whole day sorting through the debris of his bedroom. She does this tactfully, tidily, thoroughly, and the child is conscious of an immense sense of relief. All those buried socks, books, pencil ends, wads of paper, coins, dust—he was unable to deal with it, but now all is order and ease.

Her middle child is neither clever nor exceptional in appearance, but she loves him best; she can't help it; he touches a spot of tenderness in her that only music has been able to reach. She kisses the top of his head while he eats his cereal. She straightens the collar of his coat before he leaves for school. She has gone back to listening to Tallis in the afternoons, a remarkable recording by the Tallis Scholars, and as she listens, something like a kite string reaches down and pulls at her thoughts, which are not quite ready to be thoughts. It might be that she's putting her own heart beside itself, making comparisons. What does it mean to be better or best?

One of the new, young music gurus, writing in the weekend papers, believes Tallis is actually a better composer than Byrd. What had been considered simple in his work is now thought of as subtle. What struck earlier critics as primitive is really a form of understated sophistication. Perhaps these judgments boil down to mere fashion. Or perhaps the recent Tallis biography has upped his reputation.

Imagine a girl just twenty-one years old—I'm aware that I probably should say "young woman," but there is so much girlishness in her face and in the way she sets off from home each morning, running a quarter of a mile to the Tube station, swinging her leather satchel at her side. She is probably in love, or at least drawn to the possibility of love. Undoubtedly she thinks about the new clenched knot of ardor in her chest, thinks of it all day long, coming and going to her classes, while seated at the piano and also at the harpsichord, which she has recently taken up. Her head may be swarming with Latin, with choral efforts, with the rising and falling and patterning of sound, but her body presses against this new, rapturous apparition.

Then one day, late in May, she meets a young man. They collide on the Tube, not the most romantic of venues. This man is awkward, he has holes in his pockets, he is ungainly in his appearance. He is really rather ordinary, as a matter of fact, immersed as he is in the drainage capability of compacted gravel, and so lacking in perception that he will never understand why she agreed to have a coffee with him instead of attending her class. He's a lad, that's all, just another face, though he flatters himself that she sees something in him. Why, otherwise, does she go to the cinema with him on that first afternoon, and then out for fish and chips, and later, only a week later, does she end up in his flat, in his bed?

Why does she marry him, him of all people? Why do they buy a house in a semi-respectable area of London, produce three quite nice children, take holidays in Scotland or else in Yorkshire, where her mother lives? And why—another question altogether—when her book on Tallis is launched at a large cocktail buffet, and her publisher suggests that she write about William Byrd, does she shake her head "no"?

Let someone else do Byrd, her look said on that occasion.

But now, one year later, she's rethinking the matter. Yes, Byrd. Why not?

The system of temperament in the family shifts once again, and so does the onward allotment of time. As before, this woman rises early each day, but this time to put together her notes on William Byrd, the divine William Byrd, who seems suddenly in danger of being eclipsed by his renowned teacher and mentor.

She allows the house to fill up with dust and clutter. When her husband drops a kiss on the back of her neck, she shakes her hair impatiently. Her word processor sends out blinding windows of authority. She's busy, she's preoccupied, she's committing an act of redemption. A choir of ten thousand voices sings inside her head. No wonder she's been looking at her husband lately with an odd, assessing, measuring clarity.

New Music

More and more he tries to stay out of her way, and more and more he refers to himself in the third person. He's an ordinary man, no one to make a fuss over. He insists on that. Nevertheless, he finds himself opening his ears to the new music that's overtaken the house.

Soup du Jour

EVERYONE IS COMING OUT these days for the pleasures of ordinary existence. Sunsets. Dandelions. Fencing in the backyard and staying home. "The quotidian is where it's at," Herb Rhinelander wrote last week in his nationwide syndicated column. "People are getting their highs on the level roller coaster of everydayness, dipping their daily bread in the soup of common delight and simple sensation."

A ten-year-old child is sent to the corner store to buy a bunch of celery, and this small isolated event with its sounds, smells and visual texture yields enough footage for a feature film. A woman bending over her embroidery pauses to admire the hitherto unremarked beauty of her thimble, its cozy steel blue utility, its dimpled perfection. A walker stumbles over a fallen log and apprehends with piercing suddenness the crumbling racy aroma of rotted wood, how the smell of history rises from such natural decay, entropy's persistent perfume, more potent than the strongest hallucinogen and free for the taking. Nowadays people ill in their beds draw courage from the shapeliness of their bedposts, the plangent software of cut flowers, Hallmark cards, or knitted covers for their boiled eggs, and such eggs! Such yellowness of yolk! Such complementary wrap and gloss of white.

Soup du Jour

Everywhere adolescent girls stare into ditches where rainwater collects and mirrors the colors of passion; their young men study the labels of soup cans, finding therein a settled, unbreakable belief in their own self-sufficiency. The ordinary has become extraordinary. All at once—it seems to have happened in the last hour, the last ten minutes—there is no stone, shrub, chair or door that does not offer arrows of implicit meaning or promises of epiphany.

Only think of Ronald Graham-Sutcliffe in his Dorset garden among his damasks and gallicas. Modern roses do not interest Mr. Graham-Sutcliffe. They remind him of powder puffs, and of periods of his life that now strike him as being unnecessarily complicated. He still feels a stern duty to weigh the suffering in every hour, but this duty is closely followed by the wish to obliterate it. He pulls on his Wellingtons in the morning, every morning now that he's retired, and does a quick stiff-legged patrol among his fertile borders. He locks his hands behind his body, the better to keep his balance as he moves forward with his old man's dangerous toppling assurance. Times have changed; he no longer counts the numbers of new buds or judges the quality of color. He's gone beyond all that. Now, standing at the middle tide of old age, it's quite enough to take in a single flower's slow, filmic unfolding. One rose, he sees, stands for all roses, one petal drifting to the soft ground matches the inevitable erosion of his own essential unimportance. This is natural harmony, this is the greatest possible happiness, he says to himself, then draws back as though the thought has come from someone more vulgar than himself.

He savors too his morning tea with its twirl of white milk. And his bedtime whisky; now that he's allowed only one a day, he's learned to divide the measure into an infinite number of sips, each sip marking off a minute on his tongue and a tingle of heat in his folded gut. At the end of the day, hot soapy bathwater laps against the thinness of ectomorphic legs, surely not his legs, these jointed shanks with their gleam of Staffordshire pearl, though he acknowledges distant cousinage. Afloat on the surface are his pinkish testicles, clustered like the roe of a largish lake fish, yes, his, definitely his, undeniably his, but nothing to make a fuss over. Not anymore. He is a man for whom ambition has been more vital than achievement, fleshly volume more imperative than mastery. He sees this clearly, and has no further expectations, none that count in the real world. His army years, his time in the colonial service, his difficulty with women (one in particular), his throat full of unconfessed longings—all have come to rest in a large white porcelain tub and a warm towel waiting, folded beautifully, over a chromium rail.

Mrs. Graham-Sutcliffe, Molly to her friends, is seated on a small green sofa in a Dorset sitting room, a book open on her lap. Lamplight throws a spume of whiteness around her which is more flattering than she can possibly know. She is memorizing French verbs in an attempt to give meaning to her life. Naturally she favors those regular, self-engrossed verbs—*manger, penser, refléchir, dormir*—that attach to the small unalarming segments of her daily existence. She loves her daily existence, which includes, although she hasn't thought to acknowledge it, the pale arc of lamplight and the hooting of owls reaching her through the open window. Entering the various doorways of present, imperfect, future anterior and subjunctive, she perceives and cherishes the overlapping of one moment with the next, the old unstoppable, unfoolable nature of time itself.

Exuberant and healthy, except for the usual grindings and twinges, she has a hearty respect for those paragraphs in a full life that need reworking. As a young child she was attacked by a madwoman on a London omnibus. The woman, who was later arrested and sent to an asylum, pulled a package of lamb chops from a leather bag and hurled them with all her strength at young Molly's straw boater. Something about the child, the yellowness of her hair, the eager wet shine of her eyes, had excited the woman's rage. Molly's hat was knocked askew. She was struck on the left cheek and ear, and the precise shape and weight of the blow have been stamped on her memory.

For a year or two she woke from sleep trembling and pressing her hands up against her face and emitting little muffled yelps of terror. In another epoch, in another sort of family, she might have been sent to an analyst in an attempt to erase the wound. Instead she learned to nurse the incident along, to touch it up with a blush of comedy. She has by now related the story to hundreds of friends and acquaintances, smoothing out its strangeness in the telling, assigning herself a cameo role of amused passivity. The story ripples with light. There is something, after all, more intrinsically droll about a packet of lamb chops than, say, a brick. Lamb chops ascend more readily to myth, as witness the greaseproof paper that has long since slipped away and the butcher's twine. Bone, flesh and gristle, and a border of hard yellow fat, are caught in midflight aboard a rather charming period conveyance, and there the image rests, shivering amid the most minor of vibrations and eliciting throttled laughter from Molly Graham-Sutcliffe's many good-natured friends.

In the same gregarious, self-mocking manner, she has transformed other, similarly seismic nightmares into the currency of the mundane and mild—her dozens of inconvenient household moves over the years, an agonizing childbirth that yielded a stillborn lump with a cord around its neck, the spreading, capricious arthritis in her elbows and knees, and

Mr. Graham-Sutcliffe's occasional indiscretions, one in particular. There is a verb, she's found, to match every unpardonable act, and every last verb can be broken down until it becomes as faultless and ordinary and innocently inquisitive as that little sleepy English infinitive *to be*.

And now, with Mr. Graham-Sutcliffe still in his bathwater and his wife, Molly, on her green sofa, nodding a little over her French grammar and feeling a slight chill from the open window, it seems as good a time as any to leave Dorset behind, thousands of miles behind, and move on to the other side of the world.

But there is a chill too in the city of Montreal, where, with the five-hour time difference, it is late afternoon on a breezy spring day. A woman by the name of Heather Hotchkiss, age forty, is standing in the kitchen of a suburban bungalow, stirring a pot of homemade soup. She is the owner/manager of a laundromat in nearby Les Ormes de Bois and finds after the long working day, Mondays in particular, that there is nothing so soothing, so cheering, as the chopping, stirring, seasoning and tasting that are part of the art of soup making. In her right hand she grasps a wooden spoon. Its handle, worn smooth by many washings, provides a frisson of added pleasure, as does the rising steam with its uplifting fragrance of onion, carrot, garlic and cabbage. She stirs and sniffs like the practical-minded ordinary woman she feels herself to be. The diced potato and celery will be added only during the last half hour of cooking in order to preserve their more fragile flavor and texture.

This much she learned from her mother, who undoubtedly learned it from her mother and so forth ad infinitum. The mysteries of soup making are ancient. You would have to go back a thousand years, perhaps further, to discover its intricacies and logic, whereas you would have to go back only ten or twelve years to uncover the portion of Heather Hotchkiss's life that she dissolves so expediently, so unconsciously, in her steaming, wholesome vegetable brews.

Ten years ago people in the movies still smoked and laughed deep within their throats. The world was extravagant and feckless. Nevertheless, churches, at least in the larger English market towns, were locked up for the first time against vandals. Heads were shaved or dyed blue. Lovers gave each other flashy gifts such as diamond cufflinks or microwave ovens, bought on the never-never. Ten years ago the pleasures of everyday existence were known only to a handful. Everyone else, Heather Hotchkiss included, wanted more.

More of everything, more risk, more moments of excited intimacy, more pain, more heightened eroticism, more self-destruction, more high-kicking desire, more altered states of consciousness, more sensual fulfillment, more forgiveness, more capitulation, more lingering surrender, more rapturous loss of breath, more unhealed grief, more hours pressed into the service of ecstasy, more air, more weather, more surfaces to touch, more damage, more glimpses of heaven. Ten or twelve years ago Heather Hotchkiss, in love with Ronald Graham-Sutcliffe, a married man old enough to be her father, would have hooted at the simple delight of soup-making, but this is where time has delivered her, across an ocean, to the suburb of a large North American city where she is the proprietor of a well-run business with a reasonable profit margin, in good health but with graying hair, bent over a stainless-steel cauldron of bubbling soup. She also knits, swims at the Y, reads books on gardening, practices meditation, and takes her son, Simon, for weekend walks on Mount Royal.

Simon, aged ten, is in love this spring with the cracks of sidewalks, their furrowed darkness and decay and their puzzling microcosmic promise. The earth opens, the earth closes; the scars are straight, uniform and accessible—or are they? Sometimes he sees the spreading stain of a burgeoning ant colony, sometimes surprise tufts of coarse grass or weeds. He never steps on a crack, never. Over the winter his legs have grown to such an extent that he can dodge the tricky cracks while pretending indifference, looking skyward, whistling, humming, daydreaming, and, more than anything else, counting. He is a ritual counter. There are ten provinces in his country. There are 34 children in his class at school, 107 iron spikes in the schoolyard fence and 322 squares of pavement between his house and the corner store, where his mother often sends him on errands. He is firmly under the spell of these sidewalk sections, these islands, compelled to count them again and again, ever watchful for variation or trickery. Sometimes, not often, he is inattentive and finds himself one or two numbers out. Then he feels a temporary diminishment of his powers and an attack of gooseflesh on his neck and arms. He knows his life depends on the memorizing of the immediate, proximate world.

But today he concentrates so hard on the task of counting squares that he arrives in front of the grocery forgetting what has brought him here. His mother sent him, true. She gave him a five-dollar bill. A single item is required, but what? He is ready to die with the shame of it. He cannot return home empty-handed, and he cannot enter the store and engage the pity of Mr. Singh, the owner, who would immediately telephone his mother and ask what it is she requires.

He freezes, hugs the points of his elbows, thinking hard, bringing the whole of his ten years into play. Today is Monday. The day when his mother is most inclined toward soup-making. He pictures the two bowls of soup, one for her, one for him, side by side on the smooth pine table.

He sees clearly the red woven placemats and the gleaming spoons with their running banners of light, and then the various colored vegetables floating in a peppery broth.

He takes a breath, pokes a stick between the squares of concrete, and begins the process of elimination. Not carrots, not onions, not potatoes. As he strikes these items from the familiar list, he experiences the same ponderable satisfaction he finds in naming such other absences as father or brother or uncle, always imagining these gaps to be filled with a leather-fresh air of possibility, just around the corner, just five minutes out of reach.

At that moment the word *celery* arrives, fully shaped, extracted cleanly from the black crack in the pavement, the final crack (as luck would have it) before the three smooth cement steps that lead up to the sill of the corner store. The boy's gratitude is thunderous. He almost stumbles under the punishment of it, thinking how he will remember it all his life, even when he is old and forgetful and has given up his obsession with counting. He says it out loud, *celery,* transforming the word into a brilliantly colored balloon that swims and rises and overcomes the tiny confines of the ordinary everyday world to which, until this moment, he has been condemned.

Invention

My grandmother, as everyone knows, was the inventor of the steering-wheel muff.

It was born of love. She was a woman who adored her young husband, she doted on him, and her invention was a tribute to that love. Never a driver herself, she worried about the way my grandfather's gloved hands slipped on the steering wheel in the winter—ours is a country with a long and bitter winter season, icy roads, danger at every turn. When Grandfather was forced to remove his gloves in order to secure a firmer grip on the wheel, his knuckles quickly turned white with cold. She was pained by the sight of that whiteness, and moved to do what she could.

It took her a single afternoon to crochet her first model, her prototype, you might say. It proved less than satisfactory, however, since it offered little purchase on the smooth surface of their Buick's steering wheel. What to do? She looked around and discovered another kind of wool with improved adhesive properties, wool that was imported from a region on the coast of west Ireland where the sheep graze on certain regional sedges and beach grass, there being an absence of ordinary turf. She also experimented with an elastic edging, then lined the "glove," as she called it in the early days, with a strip of gathered chamois.

My grandfather, a lover of gadgets, was delighted. He called it his steering wheel "chapeau," and demonstrated its usefulness to his colleagues. Soon my grandmother was busy making her little hand-wrought coverings for their many friends. She tried flannel, corduroy, fur, velvet, suede, burlap, all with greater or lesser success, and gave away her various models as hospitality gifts or stocking stuffers. One of these friends wrote her a thank-you note saying: "My steering wheel is now snug in its beautiful winter muff," and the official term—*muff*—was born, just weeks before she hired four helpers, women recruited from the Alice House for Unwed Mothers, and set up a workshop in the attic of her home on Russell Road.

Money began to trickle in, then became rivers of money, especially when she introduced her famous faux-leopard muff, which became the signature for all that was chic, young, adventurous and daring.

People were surprised at how she threw herself into the muff enterprise. A small factory was built north of the city, which she launched by breaking a ginger ale bottle across the workers' gate, and this moment was immortalized in a Pathé newsreel. (You can, if you look carefully, make out the blurred image of my grandfather, smiling proudly from the sidelines.) Other factories were put into operation, Cincinnati, Manchester, Hong Kong. To this day production has never quite managed to keep up with demand, which is more than you can say about other products. The market had been waiting, it seemed, for just such a utilitarian accessory. She in her housedress and apron, she who had been timid about speaking into her own telephone, was interviewed more than once on the radio about the benefits of the muff, which not only warmed a cold surface but brought coolness—in Arizona, New Mexico, California—to the problem of a *hot* steering wheel. Who would have thought it—that an object this simple could bring consumer satisfaction to so many.

Except to my grandfather, of course, whose spirits withered as the wheel-muff empire grew.

In his later years he went back to the cold, rigid bone of an undressed steering wheel. A serious driver, he maintained, cherished the direct touch of the hand on the steering apparatus, the control, the feeling of resonating with the working engine, of being part of the mechanism itself and not separated from it by a piece of superfluous "fluff." Almost every day he could be seen driving erratically up and down Russell Road, grasping his naked steering wheel in his hard old hands, his flesh sealed against comfort. This went on for years, not that my grandmother paid the least attention. By that time they were living apart.

Invention is a curious gift, and may well be overcredited. Invention is not so much about creation as "finding out"; the word's Latin origin says it clearly, *invenire,* meaning to come upon. My grandmother would have defined it, initially anyway, as making do, improving, stumbling across—but then success made her dizzy, then arrogant, and then she became "an inventor."

Just think of how many times that woman went to court to protect her patents! Think of how sternly she dealt with the Cincinnati strike. Where did she find the strength to confront public attention? And all the while her temperament grew discolored, so that she forgot utterly that long-ago moment when she was a young woman, passionately, tenderly in love with her handsome new husband, glancing across the width of the car at his gloved hands slipping on the wheel and thinking: what can I do to show my ardor?

It was quite otherwise for Fulham-Cooper, my famed precursor through my mother's side of the family, a late sixteenth-century grammarian whose blood I am happy to claim. Fulham-Cooper did not, of course, start out as a grammarian, but was, as his name announces, a cooper, one who earned his living by making and repairing barrels in a sleepy corner of rural England. He was greatly gifted in his trade, however, and had a head for business. *And* he was literate, something of an anomaly in that era. In time he was able to employ two or three assistants, later as many as twenty. A regional map of the period shows that his village eventually bore his name: Fulhamton. It might be thought that such a man would direct his inventive energy toward improving the traditional barrel or cask, but instead my ancestor invented the hyphen.

As you know, much medieval writing came down to us enjambed on the page, one word running smack into the next. Those monks sweating over their manuscripts and devoted to the preservation of sacred texts, gave only minimal thought to how difficult they made the act of reading. What good fortune, then, that Simon the Wise (no relation, I'm sorry to say) invented the word-space. He was widely celebrated for this device, and justly so, in my opinion, though a space, like a zero, may seem at first a negative triumph, mere air masquerading as substance.

Well, we know differently today. Emptiness has weight; absence gestures at meaning. A doorway is privileged over an actual door in its usefulness and even its beauty—to give a homely example. A caesura locks a poem into a grid of understanding; a silence distinguishes speech from speech and thought from thought.

After the discovery of the word-space came that spirited novelty the period or full stop, a collaborative invention by a pair of unmarried Jutland sisters, both skilled embroiderers, in need of a stitch (they used a French knot) to conclude or accent a line of scripture running along the length of a linen altar cloth, a treasure that is now preserved at the Victoria and Albert Museum, its precious threads disintegrating between sheets of glass, but available to public view if one applies to the curator in writing.

The cryptic comma was, I like to think, devised by one Brother Alphonse, a very distant cousin on my paternal grandfather's side, who was also known for his fine woodcuts and his habit of near-continuous prayer. One day, as he was lost in meditation, the nib of his pen slipped downward and sideways, and instead of depositing a fine, precise dot on his sheet of precious parchment, he left a curled worm of ambiguity, which he recognized at once as a sacred pause, a resting place during which time he might breathe out his thanks to God for the richness of his blessings, and prepare his next imprecation. *Let me be free in my thoughts, let me be clean in my acts, let me never lose connection with the holy bonds between me and Thee, and the everlasting earth, amen, amen, amen, ad infinitum . . .*

My own ancestor's invention of the hyphen derives directly from his barrel-making skills. Consider the barrel, which is nothing more, after all, than a circle of bent staves held together by an iron hoop. The simple hoop connects what is otherwise unconnectable, since the barrel-maker's wooden strips long to spring apart.

A hyphen takes on the same function. A diacritical mark of great simplicity, it joins what is similar and also what is disjunctive. Two words may be read as one, a case of compounding meaning and doubling force, but this horizontal bar, requiring only a sweet, single stroke of the pen, divides as well as marries. How clever of my kinsman to know that successful inventions are both functional and elegant. Aesthetically, the hyphen is superior to the slash, you will agree, and it makes a set of parentheses look like crude homemade fencing.

Fulham-Cooper, later Sir Fulham-Cooper, may have been a genius, or he may simply have "fallen upon" his useful contribution. I am proud to come from a long line of inventors, but I recognize, at the same time, that invention is random and accidental. For instance: someone discovered one idle afternoon that a loop of plastic tubing will defy gravity if gyrated rapidly around the human body. Someone else, in another slot of time, noticed that a mixture of potassium nitrate, charcoal and sulphur will create a new substance that is highly explosive. Some unsung hero invented the somersault, not to mention the cartwheel. Other people—through carelessness or luck or distraction or necessity—invented keys, chairs, wheels, thermometers and the theory of evolution.

As I say, the spirit of invention seems rooted in my own family history. The proof is there. I have tracked this genetic facility carefully, and friends of mine have even been kind enough to suggest that I might qualify as a professional genealogist, especially since I have managed, finally, to document my family tree all the way back to Titus the Shepherd— one of my Greek-speaking forebears. His invention, though he himself was a lazy young man, and naturally was thought by his parents to be a wastrel, altered the entire nature of human consciousness.

It happened late on a summer afternoon. Titus, a shepherd like his father and grandfather, was bored. The sheep were stupid with heat that day, slow in their movements, and abjectly obedient. None strayed. Instead they huddled miserably in the shade of a small fig tree, unmoving. There was no breeze, no cloud overhead, nothing to break through the emptiness in Titus's head.

He waved his staff in the direction of another shepherd on another hill, a greeting of sorts, anything to interrupt his ennui, but met with no response. It would be hours yet before he might return home, eat his mother's soup of onions and fennel, and endure his father's bitter complaints, and another hour or two before he would be able to take refuge in his bed.

All day long he yearned for his bed. There he at once fell asleep and dreamed, and his dreams made him happy.

When he was a very small boy he asked his father what this thing was that happened at night. How did the night stories enter the house and find their way behind his eyes with their colors and shapes and drama? Such richness. "These are dreams," he was told. "Everyone is given dreams."

Sometimes his dreams frightened him. He was chased by a bear and eaten. His mother fell ill. He was naked, shamed. He felt a terrible hunger, a thirst. But even these visions of tragedy brought their gifts, their excitement. They carried movement, possibility, a raising of the blood. Furthermore, their shadow would soon shift sideways, he knew this, and make space for the good dreams he had come to depend upon; even their decaying presence offered the promise of the next night and the next dream story. The world could be made and unmade in this way. It could go on forever.

The most skilled genealogist—and I am only an amateur, as I have said—cannot give an account of another's dreams. Titus has left no records himself, but it is established that he was healthy and able. And one can easily guess what a young man's dreams might consist of. Feats of courage, no doubt. Saving one of his father's lambs, for instance, and earning extravagant public tribute. And surely he would dream of women, young women, old women, their clean skins and secret clefts. Their songs and offerings and quick, dark-eyed glances. And the heaving of a sudden rhythmic rapture that quickly emptied itself and began again, again, and again, played out in the darkness, a story unfolded and made brilliant.

But for now there are no dreams to distract and amuse. The sun, he notices, is still almost straight overhead. The sheep make their soft, useless noises of appetite and suffering in their hotly lit circle. It will be hours before Titus will be in his cool bed, dreaming. The thought is unbearable, unbearable.

To offer himself a measure of solace, and to pass the time, he begins to dream about dreaming. It is as though he has opened a small, previously unknown door in his head. He does not dare shut his eyes, of course, for his father's small flock is his responsibility; he doesn't dare let even one sheep out of sight. He breathes in and out, and at that moment feels a dividing of consciousness. He exists in two places at once, stubbornly rooted to this dull hillside, solitary, dimly aware, but at the same time he feels himself carried into a story of splendor and bravery. There is music, vibrancy. His spine stretches. The grip on consciousness is firm, yet a woman is walking towards him, a beautiful woman with a thin band of gold around her left wrist. She is reaching out her slender arms. What can she be saying? He can scarcely believe what he hears: she is chanting his name. Titus. I've found you.

A distortion of time occurs, though he isn't sure whether it is elongated or shortened. A dozen strands and subplots creep into the dream story. Opportunities for bold deeds multiply, and he hears himself named on a roll of honor: Brave Titus, Noble Titus. Circling the crowded scenes of action are softer lights, alternative arrangements, where a vague beauty presses and offers ease. Its glaze covers the hillside, even the flanks of the standing sheep and the pathetic little fig tree bent against the air.

For a moment it seems the vision is about to collapse, but he manages to draw it back to life. Onward. A new, freshly furnished story rumbles into view with its defining line of phosphorescence. And next . . . and then . . . and finally . . .

The rest of Titus's day passes in what seems a moment. In no time he is ducking through the doorway of his parents' house, where the smell of soup greets him. He can't wait to tell them what he has discovered. He makes them sit down and listen carefully. He can dream in the daytime as well as at night, he says. He can dream with his eyes wide open, never for a minute losing his concentration on the silly sheep.

"A daydream," his father says, full of wonder. "I must try this out for myself."

"You have chanced upon something of great value," his mother says, and she touches his shoulder with respect, understanding at once that this new form of consciousness will bring creativity and salvation and grace where before nothing but dullness had been.

No wonder I feel fortunate to be a humble leaf on my family tree. This tree thrives, its energy flows into the world making its offerings and inventions. The fact that I myself lack inventive fervor is not a cause for sadness, you must believe me; I know perfectly well that if the spirit of invention were too widely distributed, the world would implode.

Some of us are needed who merely keep the historical record. We count, we describe, we make our small forays into the archives. We keep track of our findings.

We interpret, we analyze, we speculate. And sometimes we risk our small emendations. Perhaps this too is part of invention.

Death of an Artist

THE OLD MAN IS DEAD.

At least, he appears to be dead, lying there, *nested* there in oaky repose, relaxed under a demi-coverlet, the coffin lid tufted and ribboned and stuck with flowers. People shuffle by and stare down at him, remarking how like himself he looks. His last disguise.

In fact, his face is fleshier, angrier, than it appeared on the screen, knobbed and prehistoric with its thug's nose, long, bony, white-tipped ears, thickish lips and a tongue that now and then deceived him on the tube, wagging and twitching while he thrust about for one of those Anglo-Gallic witticisms of his, Oscar Wilde with a dash of maple syrup, always playing the role, the wimpled satyr. Now you see him, now you don't.

No one knew him, really knew him. The history of his choleric, odd, furiously unproductive and thoroughly unsatisfying life is most clearly set out in his diaries, eight plump volumes, but difficult to decipher because of the red crayon he affected, and the cheap lined schoolboy paper. These "undiaries," as he himself once called them, are best read in reverse, that is, you should begin with the final entry and work your way backward.

Never mind the smiting, toxic scrawl. Begin. Observe him, then, at age eighty-eight, the infant's tongue lolling and speaking his need. His weepy red script holds the glare of old regrets and fresh insights. "This has been the most remarkable day of my life," he writes after making his desperate and theatrical journey, actually hoisting himself onto a train one June morning and going back to that country crossroads where he was born.

As a pilgrimage it was heroic, he with his tick-tocky heart and plugged lungs, playing the hoary sage, the native son. He required two canes, if you remember, to move himself along, wheezing and wiping the tears from his eyes. That was a side of him that perhaps only Emily knew: his sentimentality, his foundering in the folds of memory, those long sighs and leaky snuffles, just barely audible in his broadcasts.

The two canes, of course, were part of his getup, his self-relishment. In his left hand he grasped the aluminum rod, spare and modern, government-issue; in his right, the burnished sycamore wand owned by his putative grandfather, former choir member and townsman. Between these two symbolic props he balanced himself, blinking at the camera, a tottery old paradox, eliciting sympathy while projecting scorn, disdainful of the particular but committed to the whole. Wink, blink. "Well, yes," he barked into the microphone. The sun shone down. His beard was handsomely stiff and speckled. It was said that before his public appearances he shampooed it with the yolk of an egg, and that he considered it a mark of virility, though probably only Emily was entirely privy to this remark.

His seventies were his best decade, when, as he himself said, he was most nearly himself. The pension helped, also the milder climate. Often he strolled in the park of an afternoon, for the sheer pleasure of its symmetrical flowerbeds and settled statuary. During the whole of this era his only shred of posture was a Victorian parasol, printed with poppies, bought

for ninepence in a north London market. "Forgive this artifice," he said to a reporter who asked why he carried it. "But
one must protect one's self from one's self." The same
reporter inquired as to his political views (and he admitted to
a rather filthy vision of the future). And about his costive use
of semicolons; and his opinions on his fellow "artistes"; and
why he now referred to himself as "one." A photographer
captured him forever, standing by a singing fountain, his
parasol raised, fending off not sun but rain, and uttering one
of those off-the-cuffers that we now know to have been laboriously prepared and memorized and repeated. "One is ultimately faithful to one's infidelities," he twice uttered.

So much for his seventies, his sun-strewn seventies, when
even Emily appeared to be taken in by his little affinities
with nature, his ornithological potherings, his urban
botanizing. "*Les mauvaises herbes,*" he sniffed, returning
home from his afternoon strolls and tucking away the parasol for another day.

In his sixties he was in his full strength, or, to quote from
his "anti-journal," at the zenith of his weakness. He roared
and whimpered, bellowed and bled. It was said he perfected
the grunt. Made it his. He bought a ruff to wear around his
neck and a pair of tights for his not-yet-completely-withered
shanks. Emily has left a suitable account of this period, in
which she submits her theory of possible drug dependency,
Valium to be precise. Just to see him before the medicine
cabinet was to feel an unstitching of certainty. Chemical
tranquility brought an instant alias, transported him effortlessly into his other selves. When he drooped and sighed, he
did so with authenticity and vigor. She worried, though,
about his predilection for Turkish toweling (the term *terry
cloth* was anathema to him) and speculated with her usual
perspicacity that a thwarted sexuality was at the core. He

received during this decade several mysterious phone calls, generally late in the morning, and worked tirelessly on his telephone mannerisms, cupping the receiver in a malevolent fashion and glancing upward at the ceiling tiles as though the ultimate tabulation of those acoustical squares might bring about the onslaught of popular acceptance—something he both courted and feared. He was, Emily says, an afternoon aristocrat and a twilight prole. Suppers he took in silence, like a monk.

His fifties were another matter. Some biographers suggest that it was during this period that his masquerade became the most elaborate and self-defoliating. He once, for instance, borrowed (stole) a child's wagon, filled it with bedding plants, and went door to door through the western suburbs, offering his wares, gratis, to anyone kind enough to accept. No one did; doors were slammed; he wrote about this experience later in his "neo-diaries" (vol. 6), calling it a national disgrace and a symptom of global paranoia. It was not a happy time. More than once he threatened retirement—"one wearies, one wearies"—but something hammy in his thundering brushed close to truth. In short, he made the mistake of becoming picturesque, forgetting that subterfuge requires more than consistency.

In his mid-forties he fell in love. Emily, of course, a case of feminine predicament and masculine opportunity or perhaps the reverse. May and December, one of those doomed unions, but one that was also blessed. "Entirely glandular," he blustered to his public, "and also deeply spiritual." They were snapped in a discount store by the paparazzi, she pushing a cart with her look of benighted luster and he playing the fool with a clutch of credit cards. At the checkout the girls winked, but at the bank there was trouble. He was forced into a radical reassessment during which his persona received a touch-up job, almost a replating. "I am at heart an average person," he sincerely announced at a small ad hoc press conference in the vicinity of his neighborhood.

In his thirties—his chimera period, he called it—he was a sought-after dinner guest, and it was his habit, during this epoch, to carry a set of car keys in his hand. They gave him a sweet jingle, a certain cachet, becoming a trademark or, if you like, a kind of statement to the world. These keys, he seemed to say, spell evanescence. Transience. Fleeting grace.

An apocryphal story from the same period has him traveling about town carrying a mandolin, the origins of which are unknown but much disputed. On buses and streetcars, generally sitting toward the front, he rested this instrument across his knees in a lateral position, and frequently tapped its varnished frame with his fingers, creating a rhythmic effect.

And, of course, there is his toque, acquired in his twenties, that remarkable chapeau of knitted wool with its famed double tassel, worn throughout his life, tilted over his left or right ear. Often, once or twice a day, he lifted his hand and touched it lightly in a kind of ironic salute to the unhatted universe. "Hey, do you sleep in that thing?" a cheeky radio reporter once asked him, stopping him in the middle of his midday walk.

Throughout his teenage years he visited, not surprisingly, country churches and sat beneath any number of trees. "Were you starting to get self-aware during this period?" is a question often posed, and the probable answer is: Perhaps. Certainly he was assembling the philosophy of non-merciless adaptation we find today limned in his "crypto-diaries." His around-the-house costume in those teen years consisted of a rough cotton robe (forerunner of his Turkish toweling period?) and a pair of comfortable slippers said to have been presented to him by his mother on his thirteenth birthday. A coming-of-age gesture, perhaps. Ceremony has always figured importantly in his rubric, and a pair of slippers at such an auspicious age cannot have been without meaning.

No serious person pays attention to his childhood, he is said to have said, though evidence points to the contrary. A small set of building blocks, for instance, cannot be discounted. And a spinning top. *Spinning!* A silver cup with his name misspelled at the lip. And, of course, the red crayon, without which his name would be only a name and his life less than a life.

"I am utterly alone," he wrote (in red) across the top of the final page.

There has been no mention of an inquiry.

The Next Best Kiss

TODD AND SANDY HAD BEEN FRIENDS for just a few weeks, and Sandy knew they were about to say goodbye to each other.

This thing between them was an episode taking place on a small screen. A mini-flick, as Todd would say, a scenario, a sketch. A million words had flown by, but nothing had been promised or declared, and Sandy could sense the way she and Todd were using each other up minute by minute, one talky voice drinking the other dry.

Both of them loved to talk—or, more accurately, they felt compelled to talk. A hyperverbal compulsion was what they shared, way up there on the glottal thermometer, and that was putting it kindly. This talkiness might have been genetic, or it might have been what was expected of them. They were both professors, he on the West Coast, she on the East; she was in history, he was in sociology/film studies/cultural exegesis. ("Professor of et cetera"—that was one of Todd's little jokes on himself, almost his only joke.)

Friends introduced them to each other at the reception that launched the 1998 Darlington Conference, in Detroit, devoted to the subject of *fin de siècle* crisis. Todd gave a paper titled "End of the Self," about the instability of the self, the self as the sum of incalculable misunderstandings, and the selfishness of even claiming a self. Todd confided to Sandy that the text for his talk might eventually find its way into the *New York Review of Books,* although the editors were asking for substantial changes, which Todd was questioning—and quite rightly, he said.

Sandy presented an afternoon seminar, "Diatribe and Discourse in the Twenty-first Century," prophetic in its pronouncements, spacy, brilliant (she hoped), loaded with allusive arrows (Lacan in particular) and followed by a vigorous Q-and-A session, with Todd, seated out there in the audience, contributing a number of thoughtful comments and reservations.

"He's an asshole," Sandy's colleague Chloe said afterward.

"No," Sandy countered, "not an asshole. Just an ass. One of those silly, old-fashioned asses." She said this with a fond smile, all the muscles in her face and body relaxed for once. "Like our fathers were. Or our uncles. Total asses."

"He talks in clauses, Sandy. You're not supposed to *talk* in clauses. And especially not with semicolons intervening. I can hear those semicolons coming at me. Little squash balls hitting the wall."

Sandy was still smiling; she couldn't help herself. "There's no law against semicolons."

Since their first meeting Sandy's jaws and Todd's jaws had not stopped moving. They had a verbal ping-pong game going, a monsoon, unstoppable. Sexually, they seemed to belong to the same nation—the strenuous, the informed, the adventurous, the currently unattached. On the other hand, anyone could see that they were far from being matched linguistically. Todd's ruminations tended to be speculative, Sandy's narrative.

For example: "We've probably said farewell to the world of sermons and to the clenched piety of holy pilgrimages," Todd said in his lecture, question marks hovering over his words

like a jangle of surprised coat hangers. "We may soon be sur-
rendering our sacred objects and perhaps the practice of
prayer—even the notion of prayer."

"You seem to be hedging your bets a bit," Sandy told him
after the presentation, not wanting to smother him in blanket approval—it was too soon for that. "The use of 'probably'
and 'perhaps' and 'may be' and so on."

She had learned that women are obliged to interrupt their
own discourse for the discourse of others, using standard
probes and thrusts and "sincere" attempts at interrogation—
the same strategies their mothers once used.

"It's ironic, but the *probable* now holds more force than the
certain," Todd told her mysteriously, cradling her in his arms
that first night, stretching his neck and kissing the tender
place where her hairline met the back of her neck. "Because
it more and more appears to be self-evident that nothing is
really conclusive."

"You could be right," Sandy said. She was having trouble
with her breathing and wasn't sure whether the cause was
emotional or physical. Todd had a large, solid body. She
appreciated its weight (she had been a long time between
men and their bodily heft), but at the same time she felt vulnerable being pinned down like this.

"Everything's smaller now," Todd continued, minutely
shifting his body. "Our idea of love is smaller. Our friend-
ships are smaller."

"Yes," she said. "Emphatically. Why, back in the nineteenth
century love was big stuff. As big as those balloons people
used to ride around the world in. Now it's more like the kind
of grit that gets left behind in your jeans pocket."

"Yeah, sort of," Todd said.

He listened politely enough to her account of childbirth,
the moment eleven years earlier when Jenny burst from her

womb, as wet and compacted as a supermarket chicken with her folded limbs and tight whorls of dark hair, but Sandy, who liked to make a terse drama of her birth event, could tell that Todd's thoughts were elsewhere.

His eyes were squeezed shut, and he had gone suddenly critical in a pedagogical way that was quickly becoming familiar; his arms were around her, but in her imagination he was standing a few feet away, holding a clipboard in his hand and a microphone to his lips, analyzing her narrative structure and syntax.

"Womb?" he murmured. "Now, that's a somewhat romantic, nineteenth-century word to bring into a modern clinical procedure."

"It's not clinical at all," Sandy was about to say, but Todd started telling her about his automobile accident in Mexico— Baja California, to be exact—as though there were some connection between birth and highway injury.

Perhaps there was; the cooler half of her brain bleeped this possibility. Human tissue. Tearing and bleeding. Sudden intervention. She had noticed that people who have been in car crashes always get around to these stories fast. They love their accidents. Road disasters are like five-star movies in their lives, the only time they've been allowed to be major actors. "They had to pry open the door to get me out," Todd was saying. "The ambulance attendant kept saying it was a miracle I was still breathing." His voice went rough and shy with remembrance.

"It must have been terrible."

"Worse than terrible."

"How much worse?" She hoped she didn't sound as though she were mocking him.

"What?"

"I mean, how do we measure these things?"

"Do you always have to measure everything?"

A good question—or was it? "I suppose," she said slowly, easing his elbow off her upper arm, which was beginning to tingle, "that we do try to estimate the weight of experience in our lives."

"As if we can." He said this with a little snort that she found unaccountably piglike. He said it with disappointment.

"How else can we stand back and see where we are?" she said. "Or *who* we are?"

"Who we are." He echoed this observation lazily, without any fight in his voice or even a pull of breath. "You know that the 'who' of that particular question is something that absolutely cannot be isolated. Our identity shifts from one moment to the next, so that we are always in a state of becoming or diminishing."

Sandy set the "we" aside for the moment. As a historian, she believed obstinately in the roundness and accessibility of events. Every date had a doorway, if you could only locate it. Every recorded birth and death had its corporeal and metaphorical dust, composed or else scattered, the little lost frights and ecstasies of fragile existence. And there was something else that lived on top of her thoughts: the notion that everyone had a mother, and from that mother, from that tight little purse with its fleshy space and opening lips, came the desire for expanded air and space.

She felt the need to say so, even if it meant risking a non sequitur. "Each of us has had a mother," she murmured into Todd's neck.

"Yes," he said, but clearly without taking in the weight of her thought. "True enough."

"And yours?" she said, prodding.

"My what?"

"Your mother. You haven't mentioned your mother. Not so far, anyway. Is she, you know, living?"

"Living, breathing. Housewife. San Diego. Arthritis in her fingers. Goes to Bible study. Cooks turkeys."

"Mine too. Amazing. All that same stuff. Only it's Danville, Ontario, not San Diego." She didn't tell Todd that she had put as much distance between herself and her mother as possible, or that she broke into a sweat when she heard her mother's voice on the telephone.

"My mother worries about beetles getting into her breadbox," Todd went on jovially.

"Really?"

"It's only happened once, in 1946, I think, before I was born, but it's given her a reason to stay alive."

"Has she read your book on seismic stasis?"

"Ha!"

"How reductive," Chloe said to Sandy, hearing about this conversation the next day. "Believing his mother's only worry is beetles in her bread. Her big worry is probably *him*. What a jerk she has for a son. Men who dismiss their mothers that easily can't be trusted."

"He said it rather sweetly, I thought."

"And I don't blame her one bit for not reading his book. Why the hell should she?"

"My mother read *my* book. She said I used too many big, show-off words."

"Really?"

"'Who do you think you are?'—that's what she said."

"If I were you, I'd wind this Todd thing up, and fast!"

"It's easy for you to say," Sandy told her. "You have Bernard. I haven't had anyone for a long time."

"Does he make you happy?"

"Happy?"

"Now, Sandy, that's a simple, straightforward question. Yes

or no. Does he make your happiness gland wiggle and beg for more?"

"No. But."

It was summertime; Todd and Sandy were both free. He followed her back to Halifax and moved into the apartment she shared with her daughter. Just temporary, a few days. There was a heat wave. Then a cool wave. They spent a lot of time in bed—at least when Jenny was off at day camp. The rest of the day fell into a rhythm—reading the paper, cooking, shopping—that was comfortable, and that persuaded Sandy she was almost, in a summer kind of way, happy with her life.

At the same time, she had to admit that those twin demons, happiness and sadness, had lost their relevance. Happiness was a crock; no one, except maybe Chloe, really had it for more than a minute at a time. And sadness had shrunk, become miniaturized and narrowly defined, a syndrome, a pathology—whereas once, in another time, in a more exuberant century, in a more innocent age, there existed great gusts of oxygen inside the sadness of ordinary people, carpenters, tradesmen, housewives and the like. Sadness was dignified; it was referred to as melancholy; it was described as autumnal in tone and tinged with woodsmoke. Nobody got blamed for the old sadness. It was a real affliction, like color blindness or flat feet.

Matthew Hooke, for instance, could not be described as a happy man, and yet he was thought of as a valuable person in his society.

"Who actually is Matthew Hooke?" Todd had the courtesy to ask after a week or so.

"English botanist, 1809 to 1883."

"Yeah, right. The guy you wrote the book about."

"Uh-huh."

"Do you actually connect to this person? I mean, can he say to you anything that is actually meaningful? He's eighteenth-century—"

"Nineteenth-century." She had noticed that Todd was careless about dates.

"—and probably superstitious as hell and missing half his teeth. And here you are, this very twentieth-century woman who's lying in bed at three o'clock in the afternoon in a modern high-rise apartment in the middle of Halifax, and you haven't got any clothes on, just your skin against these sheets, and the traffic going by, and you turn your thoughts to this Hooke person—"

"Matthew Hooke."

"Right. Matthew."

"You sound jealous."

"What!"

"Jealous that I can be thinking of this mildly depressed but nevertheless intelligent and accomplished nineteenth-century gentleman at the same time you've got your hand between my legs."

"Well?"

"Well what?"

"Well, who's it going to be, then? Him or me?" He tried to express this thought as a joke, but he was not, as Sandy had noticed, good at jokes.

"So." She attempted a playful tone. "Do I have to make a choice?"

"What, exactly, was so great about this man, anyway? What's he done to get a biography written about him?"

"It's not a biography. It's more of a contextual monograph. A background inquiry into what made him who he was—"

"Whatever that was."

"I'm just a tiny bit surprised you don't know his work. Don't take this the wrong way, but, I mean, this was a man who paralleled Darwin, and whose ideas—"

"Look, I don't happen to be in that particular field. Who can know everything?"

"He did."

"He did what?"

"He was one of those late, late, late medieval polymaths who extended right into the nineteenth century. He knew science, literature, classical languages, philosophy, architecture, music. And botany—well, that goes without saying."

"The epistemological world was smaller then."

"You are jealous, aren't you?"

"It isn't as though he was Bach or Malthus or Kant or one of the great giants of human thought."

"He was an autodidact. A rustic from the wilds of Somerset. Never went to school."

"Oh, I get it. That's his excuse for being minor. He had hay coming out of his ears."

"Think of him as a synthesizer. That's how I describe him, anyway, in the book. Someone who skipped the heavy theoretical work and just talked about how plants looked, how they presented themselves. How they could change shape with a little encouragement."

"You don't need to be a genius to describe the various parts of a wood lily."

"Only a genius would think it's necessary to do so."

"What's that noise?"

"Oh God, it must be Jenny letting herself in the door."

"Jenny already?"

"Yes," Sandy said carefully, heavily. "Day camp is over for today. As it has been every day at this time. Children are put on the bus and brought home by their counselors around about the middle of the afternoon. This happens all over the Western world."

"That's it, then, I suppose, for today."

She looked at him sternly, her schoolmarm look, and then let her face soften, pumping a theatrical puff of air into her cheeks. "There's always tomorrow."

Todd made a delicious macaroni-and-cheese supper for Sandy and Jenny, miles beyond the Kraft Dinner they sometimes shared on busy days. Rat trap cheese, tender pasta elbows, real grated onion, salt and pepper, all this baked slowly in cream until crisp. Ordinarily Sandy didn't keep cream in the house. This cream was left over from the veal recipe she'd cooked for Todd on the weekend.

"Can we eat in front of the TV?" Jenny asked.

"No."

"Why not?" The beginning of a whine.

"Because we should use the time to talk. You haven't told us what you did at day camp."

"We did a folk dance—I told you already. What Irish people do."

"That sounds very interesting," Todd said. "Some of those dances go back hundreds of years."

"Yes," Sandy said. "That's true."

"Courting dances," Todd said. "Or, more primitive still, dances that celebrate signs of fertility—the beginning of menses, for instance."

"So we did this folk dancing and then we did woodwork and then we had lunch and then we did birds and wildflowers and environment and then we waited for the bus to come."

"Well, maybe a little TV won't hurt. But only for half an hour."

"I know we agreed not to plunge into each other's history," Sandy said later to Todd, "and we've been pretty good about observing that pledge. But did you and your ex ever have children?"

"No," Todd said. "We thought about it a lot and we talked about it a lot. But it didn't happen."

"That's what I thought," Sandy said.

More and more, Sandy's men friends tended to be talky types, but perhaps they always had been. Her ex-husband, Jenny's father, Stephen, was a case in point: a man of bursting garrulousness, a physicist now employed at a research institute in Kansas City—thundering at his staff, no doubt, and filling the sedate laboratories with his galloping cadence. He was descended from a line of Missouri farmers who expressed themselves not sparingly, as country people are assumed to do, but colorfully, rapturously, endlessly, about crops, weather and sports, and who exchanged the effervescent kind of quips that spin off from a more laconic tradition or else lean on common male assumptions: salesman jokes, penis jokes, beer jokes, jokes about city slickers or women's lib.

On the other hand, Stephen hadn't believed that every single issue under the sun warranted prolonged debate. The promotion of argument for its own sake sprang from a buried need for drama, according to Stephen. Talk should be a diversion, a pleasure, a pursuit, not something that spilled out of confession or declaration, so that the self was placed on trial. For instance, he, Stephen, did not plan to be in the labor room coaching Sandy when their baby was born. He wasn't at all frightened of the phenomenon, or repelled by it. He simply wasn't interested, period. Yes, he loved her and yes, yes, he would love the baby when it emerged, but he was not up to what he termed "the medical side of things."

His reluctance had seemed a big thing to Sandy at the time, a major betrayal that came to represent a number of other, smaller failings. Later she wondered why she had made such a big deal of it. Shouldn't she have appreciated the honesty of his response? "He's got a tongue on him," her mother had said, "but he won't ever bring you real trouble."

Later Sandy and her little Jenny lived for two years with a man named Christopher Swift, who sold computer stock. His was the kind of calling that demanded a quick phrase, a smooth delivery, a word-tumbling manner that forestalled interruption. The trouble was, he couldn't shut it off. He hovered over Sandy in the evenings, showered her with words on weekends, entertaining her, persuading her, pressing against her common sense, talking her into ridiculous ventures—a time-share in Hawaii, a hiking trip to Thailand, where Jenny nearly died of diarrhea and then dehydration.

There were others. Some lasted a matter of days. Mike Something-or-other and his philosophical divagations. He was a man who could turn a glimpse of an ordinary tree or shrub into an instant thesis on the insularity of the soul or hermeneutics of regeneration. Toby Shawn (six months) was given to meditations about his grandfather's incivility, his mother's spite, his brother's fecklessness—a circle of incrimination that widened endlessly and came to include, to no one's surprise, Sandy and eight-year-old Jenny. There was no refuge.

On lonely nights Sandy would head for the neighborhood video store, where she rented old movies, particularly those from the forties, a time when her parents were children growing up. She would make a pot of tea, hunker down on a pile of cushions and sit up half the night, eyes stuck to the screen, eager for the fiction of how men were once believed to behave.

She was particularly drawn to that American icon known as the strong, silent type, and a hopeful part of herself prompted her to believe that such men actually existed off the screen. Didn't Hollywood effusions, for all their carelessness, persist in the refining and sharpening of our vision of ourselves? That period creature the silent male did not babble or condemn or theorize or hold forth. He might open his mouth from time to time and speak when required, a dense, manly rumble in his throat introducing a terse, tender monologue of withheld energy, but he was not at any point bent crooked with the weight of his opinions. Instead, his bone marrow quietly tapped into the world around him, the suppressed words subtly infantilizing his sexual bulk, so that you wanted to hug him like a baby and at the same time bed him down for a night of breathless, wordless, stunned satisfaction.

That was how it was in the old days, if you chose to believe it.

Sandy got a postcard from Chloe and Bernard, who were in Maine, stating, in Chloe's private cryptography, "Hope you're well out of the claws of Mr. Clause."

Everyone was surprised that Todd hung around right up until early September, when classes began at San Diego State, and that the usually impatient Sandy was not altogether exasperated by his presence. He fit in, more or less. He took Jenny to a dinosaur movie and out for pizza afterwards. His theory about the slippery self, its detachment from any fixed point of proof, had its own virtues, and even its comforts—at least for Sandy. Why should we be tethered to our inherited packet of DNA and to the tyranny of our mothers' and fathers' good intentions—what they might have done, what they could have said, if only they had been smarter, kinder, more feeling, less selfish? Does anyone apprehend human vibrations when they are filtered through choked time waves and genetic matter? How much can we know we know?

She had work to do at the end of the summer, lectures to prepare, her office to set in order. While she was out of the apartment, Todd busied himself reading about Matthew Hooke. He did this on the sly at first, working his way straight through Sandy's shelf of Hooke literature and then, finally, reading her book, *Matthew Hooke: Silent Visionary*. He restrained himself, he later told Sandy, from making his usual marginal notations.

"What kind of notations would you have made?" She was surprised at how nervous she suddenly felt.

But all he said was, "Just the usual queries. Like 'Is this statement supported?' Or 'More information needed here.'"

She decided not to take this as a criticism. She decided to imitate the even-handed, non-judgmental woman she aspired to be. "Well, you've probably noticed that there isn't a lot of hard information about Hooke's life."

"Yes, I did notice."

"The only thing to do was to fill in around the edges with the historical background."

"Right."

She looked at him. "Eccentrics don't often leave complete records. They don't think they need to be forever explaining themselves."

In fact, his botanical journals aside, almost nothing was known of Matthew Hooke, nineteenth-century botanist, other than that he seldom spoke.

"Good day," he is believed to have said when presented to the Royal Court and honored for his accomplishments in cross-breeding peas and, some years later, broad beans. He delivered his minimalist greeting, according to Sandy's text, not in the innocent manner of a rustic but in the full knowledge that his accomplishments released him from heavier forms of tribute or obeisance. He never married, never had children. He appeared to have lived without the consolation of sex—he who dabbled so happily, so tirelessly, with the tender male and female parts of plants.

Others who inhabited the same southwesterly English village as Matthew Hooke, a place called Little West Nutley, or sometimes simply West Nutley, knew him as a man of silence. Was he perhaps even simple, they might have wondered—a man so stretched by intensity and so out of joint with other human creatures that he misread the demands of common intercourse? The comments of his neighbors regarding his taciturnity were, of course, apocryphal, as was almost everything about poor Hooke's life: how he discovered his bent for natural science, how he overturned contemporary ideas of hybridization, how the tug of his thought moved ever toward the useful and practical, without losing for a minute the undertow of biological miracle.

"The kissing part took me by surprise," Todd told Sandy.

"Of course, we don't know quite how to read that aspect of his life," Sandy said. "I mean, we don't really know how weird or non-weird that kind of behavior was."

"I'd say it was very, very weird," Todd said.

The kissing part was revealed in a single sentence inscribed by an unnamed West Nutley vicar who had undertaken to write a sort of village history. "Good Mister Hooke speaks to no one excepting his pea blossoms," the vicar wrote, "but does love to kiss the ladies whenever an occasion is given."

"The guy was a pervert," Todd told Sandy. "A rapist *manqué.*"

"I don't see it that way," Sandy said crossly.

"Leaping out of the bushes at ladies! Come on, now. Admit it."

"There's nothing in the text about leaping out of the bushes."

Sandy felt sure that Hooke's advances, if that's what they were, amounted to an innocent hunger for women's flesh—quick, dry kisses, aimed at the cheek or perhaps even the lips, shyly stolen, timid yet assertive, silent pressings, silken, a curious mouth seeking forbidden tenderness, requiring that fleet conjunction for its own sake and not for where such a kiss might lead or even what it might declare. A Hooke kiss would be enclosed by its own small muscular effort and release, and by the impossibility of an explanation outside the momentary refreshment that it offered. Its savor would break through the common parochial strictures like a new form of cloud and be permitted, even smiled over. Touch me, touch me, let me touch you in this simple, explicit way—that's all it would say. (Sandy had read somewhere that earthworms kiss, their frontal parts briefly waving, nodding at each other. Mosquitoes too, and houseflies, if the evidence could be believed. They caught each other in midair—a fraction of a second only, but a connection nevertheless.)

"You and your friend Chloe would have him up for sexual abuse if he wandered around Halifax stealing kisses."

"Maybe not. Maybe I'd like one of those stolen kisses myself. Maybe I'd feel honored to be a recipient. Or maybe I'd think it was just, you know, sort of hilarious, but at the same time okay."

"So you believe that Matthew Hooke's personality was outside the margins. Psychologically speaking, I mean."

"Maybe. But not because he kissed ladies." She gave the word a cockney spin: *lie-dees.*

"What about his not talking?"

"I think I can understand that."

"Really! You! So you don't think he was even a little bit weird?"

"Well." She wanted to be fair. "There is that business about living with his mother."

"What business?"

"No particular business—just that he lived with her."

"Why shouldn't he live with her?"

"A grown man living with his mother. It's just—"

Sandy felt the conversation running out of control. She didn't know what it meant or who was defending whom, but she'd been here before often enough to understand how the most intricate arrangements can be dismantled by a single uttered phrase. Something hovered in the still air between Todd and her, a cloud of unbreathed thought, no bigger in size than a cantaloupe, or a human fist.

Then he said, "I live with my mother."

"Oh." Another skipped beat. "You didn't mention . . . I didn't realize."

"And I'll probably go on living with my mother."

"Oh."

"I didn't know it would matter to you. Or maybe I did know, and that's why I didn't bother to mention it."

"It doesn't mean a thing, not at all, really. You've completely misunderstood me, Todd. I have nothing against men who live with their mothers."

"Tell me about it." He said this as though his mouth were full of bitter coins.

This discussion took place on their last night together. For hours afterward they lay silent on Sandy's bed, neither one of them really sleeping, and in the morning they rose to an even deeper silence, a silence she found painful but also dignified and somehow admirable. They moved politely around the apartment, two civilized adults, one of them preparing for an early flight, closing his suitcase, checking his ticket, attaching his e-mail address to the fridge with one of Sandy's rubberized fridge magnets. She made him toast and coffee, and then drove him, in silence, to the airport. The idea of an embrace seemed obscene. Shaking hands would have been ludicrous. All he said in parting was "Be sure to say goodbye to Jenny."

And give my love to your mother.

This is what Sandy told Chloe when they were having lunch a week later. "That's what I almost said to him—*Give my love to your mother.* The words were just about to hop off my tongue."

"What stopped you?"

"I don't know. I was afraid I might laugh. Or else cry. I mean, I'm a woman who doesn't know where her next kiss is coming from."

Eros

ANN WENT TO A PARTY ONE NIGHT where the dinner conversation drifted toward the subject of sexuality. How does the sexual self get sparked into life? And when do we suspect its shared presence?

The man sitting next to Ann at the table spoke authoritatively on the subject. The sexual act, he said, requires a verbal gloss these days. Other creatures—lesser creatures, he meant—act out their sexuality instinctively, but human beings have evolved to the point where they must second-guess all natural feelings. A case of cultural over-refinement. It can happen that people, so busy learning mathematics or looking after their hair, simply don't "get it" on their own, and then they need a sort of interpretive guide like those types who take you on tours around hydraulic dams or conduct wildflower walks. "These days explication is required," he said, "in order to sanction the commands of the blood."

Ann disagreed with this man and said so. His name was Alex, and she'd been told he was a well-respected maker of medieval instruments with a studio in a converted warehouse not far from where she lives. She suspected he had been invited for her sake—it happened all the time, the well-intentioned matchmaking of her coupled friends. And so here they were, a single man, a divorced woman, the two of them seated next to each other at the long, festive dinner table. Ann thought Alex's phrase "commands of the blood" was silly and old-fashioned, like certain kinds of poetry she remembered from school.

"Which is why," Alex continued, "we have had to develop the awful institution of the birds-and-bees talk between parents and children. Otherwise, new generations could miss the whole thing, the mechanics, as it were, of what is required."

"That seems impossible," someone across the table said. "People don't grow to adulthood without knowing they're sexual animals."

Alex was adamant. He leaned his long arm forward so that the hairs on the back of his gesticulating hand were whitened by the twin circles of candlelight. "Individual children feel sexual urges, of course, but they don't necessarily know that other people do."

"You only have to turn on the TV—"

"And in prime time too!"

"—the new play at the Playhouse, I mean, talk about graphic—"

"Couldn't be more explicit."

"When I asked my mother about sex, she just wrung her hands and said, 'Don't you already know?'"

"More people than we think are locked in a circle of innocence," Alex said, nodding in a way that Ann thought was pretentious. "They resist. They block."

"All they have to do is read the newspaper."

"—spells out the whole whammy."

"—it doesn't quite, you know."

"Desire," said the woman whose dinner party it was. She stared deeply into her glass of red wine and said it again. "Desire."

The subject turned to Victorian brides who went to their marriage beds uninformed, how shocking that must have been, how perverse they must have found their husbands' expectations. *Now, my precious love, there is something I'm going to have to poke between your legs, but I promise to be gentle . . .*

"Maybe it did happen occasionally," Ann said, "but only someone terribly stupid could arrive at marriage age without adding up the perfectly obvious evidence all around them."

"You mean," someone said, "observing farm animals and the like?"

"Well, yes. And common everyday romance, which has always been out in the open. Kissing, touching. Erotic glances. You have to know something's going on, that men and women have more happening between them than polite conversation and domestic convenience."

"Some people aren't particularly observant," Alex said, which suggested to Ann that he might be one of those people. "And some people aren't good at connecting the dots even when they see them."

A woman called Nancy Doyen mentioned a story she'd read in a newspaper. An Alabama couple had been married for a period of three years, at which time they visited a doctor, wondering why they had not been blessed with a baby. The doctor asked a few tactful questions, and soon established the fact that the couple had not had sexual relations. They had believed that sharing a bed—sleeping together—was all that was required.

"My point exactly!" Alex cried out. His voice was excited.

Ann gave him a long sideways look. He was the only man at the table who was not wearing a jacket and tie. Instead, he wore a soft-looking woolen sweater in a deep shade of blue. Indigo, she supposed it would be called. The knit was particularly small and smooth for a man's sweater, and Ann reached forward and placed her hand lightly on the ribbing that formed the sweater's cuff. She had the idea that she must somehow restrain this person from making a fool of himself. He was looking into the candlelight with a Zenlike concentration, and Ann knew how, after a certain amount of wine, Zen talk leads straight to embarrassment.

He continued, though, her hand still resting on his wrist, to talk about the complicated notion of human sexuality, its secret nature and hidden surprises, its unlikelihood, in fact. As he talked he covered Ann's hand with his own, and then with one slow, almost absent-minded gesture he swept her hand into the shadows of his lap. She could feel the rough linen of the table napkin, then the abrupt soft corduroy of his trousers. She flexed her fingers, an involuntary movement, and a moment later found her hand resting against human flesh, the testicles laughably loose in their envelope of fine skin, and a penis, flaccid and small, curled up like a blind animal. Meat and two veg was how she and her girlfriends once described this part of the male body.

At first she thought she might laugh, and then she decided she might faint. She had never fainted in all her life, but this could be the moment. No one would blame her, especially those who knew about her recent surgery and chemo treatments.

Couldn't the others at the table hear the gasp gathering in her throat? She made a motion to pull her hand away from Alex's lap, but he pressed his fingers more firmly on hers. The thought came to her that these were the same fingers that constructed intricate lutes and lyres and handled small, probably beautiful tools. Her consciousness seemed to divide and to divide again, and then soften. She moved her fingers slightly, playfully, seeing what experiments she might invent.

Even so small a movement had the effect of sucking the air out of the room, though no one seemed to notice.

"Desire," the hostess said once again. She probed her salad greens gently, then put down her fork and peered around the table of guests, a long visual arc of inquiry, of solicitude. Her wineglass was empty. Her look was loving and also proprietorial. She appeared pleased with every single one of them.

When Ann was four years old she was taken to stay for a few days with a married cousin who lived in the country. She has no idea how the arrangement came about. What could it have meant—a gesture of hospitality extended to a very young child? She does remember that she considered the visit a thrilling adventure.

Her cousin Sandra was a young woman, barely twenty, with a musical laugh and curls all over her head. She lived in a small brown house on an acre of land with her young husband, Gerald, and a tiny baby, Merry-Ann. There was about these arrangements the sense of a doll family afloat in a toy landscape, and this should have constituted a paradise for little Ann, whose own parents seemed immensely old and somber and without movement in their lives.

She was allowed to push Merry-Ann in her carriage, first covering her with a crocheted blanket and tucking in the edges. She was permitted to stand on a kitchen chair and mash potatoes with Cousin Sandra's wooden masher. When Sandra and Gerald kissed, as they often did, Ann had the feeling of being inside the pages of a beautiful pop-up book with defined edges and dimensions and sudden, swallowed surprises and jokes.

Nevertheless, within a few days, three or four at the most, she grew anxious and miserable. She complained to her cousin of an earache, but the cousin identified the malady for what it was: severe homesickness. Her small suitcase was packed, and she was driven home.

She remembers that she was carried through the doorway of her own house—in whose arms she can never quite recall— and that she found the neutral, neglected rooms extraordinarily altered. In fact, only a few items had been changed. A leaf had been taken out of the breakfast table, and this smaller squarish table was now positioned at an angle under the window. Instead of the usual tan placemats there was a brightly flowered cloth, one Ann had never seen, and this too was placed at an angle. The scene was as jaunty and brave as a Rinso ad. Bright sunlight struck the edges of the plates and cups so that she had the sense of looking into a bowl of brilliant confetti, there were so many particles of color dancing before her eyes.

This transformation had occurred in the short time she'd been away. It seemed impossible.

And even more impossible was the idea that her parents had been here all along. They had not been frozen in time or whisked out of sight. They had been alive, busily transforming the unalterable everyday surfaces, and here was the evidence. In her absence they had prevailed. They possessed, it seemed clear, an existence of their own.

And there was something else that folded and filled the air. Something disturbing, vivid. It had no taste or noise to it, but it bulked in the space between her aproned mother and her father with his loosened necktie and rolled-up sleeves. "It" was a charged force, not that she could have described it as such, from which she herself was excluded, and it connected as through an underground passage with Cousin Sandra and Gerald kissing by the kitchen window, their mouths so teasing against each other, and yet so purposeful.

But that was all right. She liked it that way, and even if she didn't, she understood that this was the way things were and had, in fact, always been.

Yes, there was a thickening in the air, the spiked ether of unanswered questions.

But this was nothing new. Huge patches of mystery existed everywhere. How, for instance, to explain the halo around the head of baby Jesus? How did the voices get into the radio? That time when two neighborhood dogs got stuck together: how could such an unlikely thing happen?

Ann, age seven, was caught at school holding a note that was being passed from desk to desk. The teacher, Miss Sellers, snatched it away and quickly scanned its contents. "I'm surprised at you, Ann," she said. "I'm very, very disappointed."

The note said: "Nelly, put your belly up to mine and wiggle your behind."

Ann was asked to stay in from recess until she had copied ten lines on a piece of paper: "I will not pass notes again." Later, deeply shamed and making her way out to the playground, she saw Miss Sellers in the stairwell. She was showing the note to two other teachers, and they were laughing their heads off.

Aunt Alma and Uncle Ross came to visit every summer, and this visit was greatly anticipated, especially by Ann's mother. Aunt Alma was her favorite sister and the most beautiful. She wore daringly cut cotton dresses she made herself and was lively in her manner, spilling gossip and laughter. She knew how to "go at a tear," ripping through household tasks, the beds, the dishes, so that she and Ann's mother could head off for a day of shopping or out to lunch at a place called the Spinning Wheel. Sometimes, when Aunt Alma thought Ann was out of earshot, she told slightly off-color jokes—but with a sense of wonderment in her voice, as though she herself with her elegant posture and thick coiled hair stood just outside the oxygen of these jokes, slightly bewildered rather than amused by the small, rough ironies of human bodies and the language that attended them.

Uncle Ross was tall, thin and solemn. He spent the vacation days seated in a porch chair and going through a stack of *Reader's Digest*s he'd brought along. There was no time to read during the working year, he explained; he was kept so busy at the insurance company.

One evening at the dinner table Uncle Ross paused before taking his place next to Aunt Alma. It happened to be a particularly hot day, and Aunt Alma was wearing a backless sundress. He bent and kissed the back of her neck, a slow and courtly kiss, unhurried, serious and private—never mind that the whole family was present and about to dig into their roast beef hash.

This kissed part of Aunt Alma's neck was called the nape, which was something Ann didn't know at the time.

Ann, who must have been nine or ten years old, watched the kiss from across the table, and it seemed to her the kiss fell on her neck too, on that same shivery spot. She felt her whole body stiffen into a kind of pleasurable yawn that went on and on. So this was it. Now she knew.

Ann at fourteen spent hours at her desk practicing an elegant backhand, which she believed would move her life forward. Her daily life was fuzzy, composed of what felt like carpet lint and dust, when what she wanted was clarity, poignancy. She memorized a love sonnet by Edna St. Vincent Millay, and she and her friend Lorna recited it in low moony tones, making fun of the words and of their own elocutionary efforts. She

stared at the khaki pants of the boys in her class and wondered what was there, packed into the crotch and how it felt.
Some boys she didn't know stopped her on her way home
from school and poked a tree branch between her legs, which
frightened her and puzzled her too, so that she broke away
and ran all the way to her house. She cried at the movies; in
fact, she liked only those movies that made her cry; her tears
were beautiful to her, so clear, fast-flowing and willing, yet so
detached from the consciousness that she could watch them
and mock them and snort at how foolish they were and how
they betrayed her. At a New Year's Eve party a boy kissed her;
it was part of a game, something he was obliged to do by the
game's rules, but nevertheless she relived the moment at
least once each day as though it were a piece of high drama,
the softness of his lips and the giggling, eager embarrassment he'd shown. All these unsorted events accumulated in
the same pocket of her brain, breathing with their own warm
set of lungs. She read *Lady Chatterley's Lover,* and what
shocked her most was that she found the book under a chair
in her mother's bedroom.

Her mother knew; that was the terrible part. Her father
knew too, he would have to know if her mother knew.
Everyone knew this awful secret which was everywhere suggested but which for Ann lay, still, a quarter-inch out of
reach. Even Bob Hope on the radio knew; you could tell by
the way he talked about blondes and brunettes and redheads.
Oh, he knew.

"Don't ever let a boy touch your knee," Ann's mother told
her. "It happened to me once when I was your age, but I knew
that one thing could lead to another."

"A climax is like a sneeze," one of Ann's girlfriends said.
"And you know how much everyone loves to sneeze."

"Boys love it if you put your finger in their ear. Not too hard, though. Just a tickle."

"The Tantric secrets," said an article Ann read in *Esquire* magazine, "can be easily mastered in a three-day course given on the shores of the beautiful Finger Lakes."

"I hope he never touched you," Ann's father said about a neighbor. "You'd tell us, wouldn't you, if he touched you?"

High up on her inner thigh. That's where Ann touched herself. Making a little circle with her thumb.

"Sex and death. They live in the same breath, can't you feel that?" This from an English professor who detained Ann after class one day in order to discuss her essay on Byron.

"Be a nun and you get none," said an actress in a play Ann attended. The woman pronounced it loudly from center stage, full of sly winks and meaningful shrugs.

"The body is a temple. Keep that temple sanctified for the man you are going to spend your life with. On the other hand, it's usually better if the man has had a little prior experience."

Molly Bloom. Yes, she said, yes, she said, yes. Something like that.

Ann married Benjamin. She had both her breasts in those days, and Benjamin adored those breasts. "You'd think they'd squeak when the nipple goes up," he said with wonder. He toyed with them, sucked them, gnawed gently at the tender breast skin, saying, "Grrrrr." The brown color of the twin aureoles astonished him, though. He had expected pink, like in a painting. Ann wondered if the brownness frightened him slightly.

They had a wedding night, the kind of wedding night no one gets anymore. Before that night there had been long, luscious sessions of kissing, accompanied by a carefully programmed fumbling with each other's bodies: nothing below

the waist, nothing under the clothes allowed, but nevertheless it was rapturous, those wet deep kisses and shy touches
on her sweatered breasts.

Now here, suddenly, was Ann in a white silk nightgown
with a lace yoke. Then the nightgown came quickly off,
which seemed a shame considering its cost. Now his whole
body was against hers; head to toe their warm young skin
was in contact. This was the best part. The rest of the business hurt, and left a sticky, bloody puddle on the bedsheet,
which worried Ann, how the hotel staff probably had to deal
with such messes all the time.

She and Benjamin had read the marriage manual their
minister had given them, and in the chapter titled "Afterward," the author had described a feeling of vague melancholy which often visits couples after a session of satisfying
sex. There was a reason for this, something chemical, the hor-
mones plunging to the baseline flatness of everyday life, a
necessary return to the reality that sustains us.

And, yes, Ann remembered that wedding night plunge.
Her whole body trembled with the sadness of it, and
Benjamin, mistaking the trembling for orgasm, was proud,
and then exhilarated, and then almost immediately ready to
go again. Grrrrr, he said against her chest wall.

Things got better, of course. Then they got worse. Then they
dramatically dwindled. There were violent quarrels in the
early years that made Ann think of cloth tearing behind her
eyes, and reconciliations so tender that even today her throat
fills with tears when she recalls them. Sex was either a healing
or an exercise in blame. Once she made the mistake of telling
Benjamin that she found something faintly hilarious about
sex, about how a man's penis suddenly blew up and wanted to
stick itself in a woman's vagina; it was so ungainly, such a

curious and clumsy human mechanism. He had taken this confidence badly. He liked to think of sex as a beautiful form of communion, he said, but Ann knows that he would not find her beautiful at this moment, with her battleground of a chest, that slicing breast scar and the curious new cords of hard tissue that join her shoulder and arm. Alex, sitting next to her at a dinner table with her thumb and forefinger on his penis, will not find it beautiful either, never mind the cheerful advice from the cancer booklets about the return of the libido and new forms of touching and holding.

Benjamin's shame, his promises, his failures, his ardor, his indecision—these formed the swampy terrain which Ann learned more or less to navigate, understanding that any minute the ground was likely to give way, but feeling at the same time stronger, and more certain about what she wanted. "I want you out," she finally said, after one particularly bitter betrayal, and then, a week later, changed her mind.

They went to Paris to patch things up.

Their hotel was located on a quiet street in the Marais and faced onto a private park where Parisians walked their dogs in the early mornings. Most of the other buildings in the neighborhood were built of a dull basement-colored stone, but the hotel where Ann and Benjamin stayed was, rather curiously, constructed of a soft, rosy, un-Parisian brick. Like many hotels, it wound its way around a rectangular air shaft so that each room looked directly into the windows of the other rooms. There was a small garden at the bottom and a few lines of laundry, still in the still air.

The hotel was classified as a luxury accommodation, but it seemed during the week they were there to be undergoing a form of entropy. The air-conditioning failed. The fax connection to the outside world failed. The extraordinarily heavy curtain on Ann and Benjamin's window fell to the floor, brass rod and all, and it took the two of them to carry it out to the corridor.

On the last day, after a breakfast of coffee and croissants, the elevator broke down. ("We do apologize, madame, but it is only five flights; just think of the guests on the top floors.") She and Benjamin climbed the stairs and entered their room. The faint and not unpleasant smell of cigar smoke greeted them, smoke that must have drifted across the air shaft from another room.

Benjamin lay on the bed, his eyes closed, and Ann settled in a chair by the open window, spreading her newspaper in front of her. She loved to read *Le Monde* when she came to France; its linguistic turns seemed a sort of crossword puzzle, and each time she managed to translate a sentence she congratulated herself.

Church bells rang out from a distance, reminding her that it was a Sunday morning. Traffic sounds rose from the street. A dog was barking, probably from the park across the street. Then she heard something else: a woman's strong orgasmic cry coming from one of the open windows of the hotel.

The innocence of it was what moved her first, the stunning lack of restraint. The music of the woman's moan was immediately recognizable to Ann, this half-singing, half-weeping, wordless release that seemed to block out all of Paris, all of the hexagon of France with its borders and seacoast and muted overhead sky.

Benjamin's eyes were suddenly open. He was smiling at her, and she was smiling back. Then they were out of their clothes—this happened in an instant—and into each other's arms. His skin felt exactly right to her that day, its silver flecks and familiar imperfections. As they moved together on the hard French bed, the rhythm of their bodies took them over, in tune for once, and it seemed to Ann that the red bricks of their hotel were melting into a pool of sensuality. She had never understood that curious, overweighted word *desire,* she had scoffed at that word, but this must be it, this force that funneled through the open air, traveling through the porous masonry and entering her veins.

Everything, it seemed, could be forgiven and mended now. She imagined that each room on the air shaft was similarly transformed, that men and women were coming together ecstatically as she and Benjamin were doing and that the combined sounds they made formed an erotic random choir, whose luminous, unmoored music was spreading skyward over the city. This was all they ever needed for such perfect happiness, this exquisite permission, a stranger's morning cry.

Of course it didn't last, how could it?

But she hangs on to the moment in these difficult days, even at this dinner table with her hand still in the lap of a man named Alex, whom she hardly knows or even likes. She is part of the blissful, awakened world, at least for a moment. What comes in the next hour or the next year scarcely matters.

Dressing Down

YOU MIGHT SAY THAT MY GRANDFATHER carried the idea of "dressing down" to new heights.

He was, of course, a social activist of national reputation and, as well, the first serious nudist in southern Ontario, the founder of Club Soleil, which is still in existence, still thriving, on the shores of Lake Simcoe, just north of Toronto. You'll recognize his name at once if you're up on your twentieth-century history.

His biography came out too late—he had been dead for some years by then—for him to comment on or defend his own beliefs as a naturist, not that he would have done so, not that he would have entertained for two minutes the rude intervention of a press interview. *But how do you carry your wallet, sir? What do you do, sir, about, um, the male body's sudden embarrassments?*

Please, he would have said to the journalists from the *Toronto Star* or the *Globe* or the *Telegram* or whatever, please! The exposure of the skin to the sun and air is a private matter, and your interest in the project, gentlemen, ladies, is—forgive me—entirely prurient.

These same questions, I confess, also occurred to me as a young boy. How had my grandfather become a nudist in the first place, and what did it mean to him to shuck off his clothes, all his clothes, for one month of the year? Was it so he could feel the gaze of a hot July afternoon spreading across the square lean acreage of his chest, and, in softer shadows, onto those other less-talked-about areas? And, another question, how did he reconcile his nudist yearnings with his Wesleyan calling, with his eleven-months-a-year job as YMCA director for Eastern Canada?

If you drive the highway to Lake Simcoe today, you'll be struck by the variety of signs greeting you left and right between the groves of pine and birch: one by one they gesture toward green-leafed darkness, offering winding trails, gravel roads, pointing the way to countless small hidden lakes, beaches and stretches of inspirational shore. "Awake-Again Bible Conference." "Bide-a-Wee Housekeeping Cottages, Reasonable Rates." "The Merit Institute. Absolutely Private." "Fish 'n' Fun with Mike and Hank." "STOP AND SAY HELLO—TED AND TINA." "ADX Yoga and More." And, finally, "Club Soleil."

Club Soleil has never, not since its founding in 1926, had more than the most discreet of highway signs, hand-painted, black on white, a single board nailed to the trunk of a long-lived elm, with a roughly fashioned arrow-tip pointing east toward a trail, one that discouraged (yet allowed) wheeled traffic.

Campers at Club Soleil slept in tents in the early years. Meals, vegetarian, were taken beneath the shade of an immense canvas structure known as The Meeting Place. Why vegetarian? Why Carrot Soufflé on Monday, Parsnip Purée on Tuesday, Swiss Chard Pie on Wednesday, and so on and so on? My grandfather was a meat eater for the rest of the year, but in July he lived on leaves, roots, seeds, the only nourishment going at Club Soleil.

The prohibition against the eating of flesh might seem to some visitors a contradiction when human flesh was everywhere displayed on the Club Soleil lawns and on the narrow strip of beach running around a promontory called The Point. The living hams and haunches of middle-aged men made their way between mixed flower and vegetable beds, another of my grandfather's innovations. And so did the necks, shoulders, throats and bellies of their wives. White-jellied breast flesh jiggled in the Ontario sunlight, tested it, defied it. Buttocks. Thighs. Calves. Fragile ankle bones belonging to city lawyers, physicians, charity organizers, household matriarchs. Patrician feet stepped carefully across the beach pebbles and drummed up and down on the grass where a volleyball court had been set up for the young people.

My grandmother had difficulty with all this. It was only after she and my grandfather were married that he told her how he had been taken by friends soon after finishing university to a naturist beach on the Atlantic coast of France. He had greeted the new experience as a door swinging wide open in his existence. Some men are brought to life by the sexual spasm; my grandfather tasted ecstasy for the first time as he lowered his trousers on the slope of a French sand-dune, then, more cautiously, dropping his underwear as well, then stepping free. Dry heat and sunlight penetrated his dark manly parts, which since birth had been confined. A hundred other bathers looked on, or rather, they *didn't* look on, that was the wonder of it, that they never so much as glanced in his direction.

He had not expected in his life to feel a breeze pass over his nether regions—this is the untethering miracle he tried to explain to my grandmother, and later to her son, my father. The pleasure was intense and yet subtle. It resonated across the width of his skin, the entire human envelope electrified— here was paradise. And it was in accord with nature's design, as he saw it. It was true; he was able to see nothing perverse about his reaction. How could it be so when he became at that pants-dropping moment larger, stronger, nobler, a man charged with a new range of moral duty? The Protestant God of shame had nodded in response, nodded and smiled and drifted away, and my grandfather, so unexpectedly twitched into life, announced himself an instant convert. He walked straight into the sea, then, where the cold salt water flowed around every mound and recess of his body and completed the arc of liberation.

But how was he to bring the same set of circumstances and appreciations to rigid Ontario? And how, a year later, to explain his passion to his young bride, my gently brought-up grandmother?

He was a man, however, who took for granted his right to make his dreams come true. Ever methodical in his dealings, he sent away to the International Naturism Institute in Switzerland for information, then began to look for a piece of well-sheltered lake property, which he was able to purchase with part of his inheritance. Next, he carefully sounded out a few of his more worldly friends. Might they be interested? Had they discovered for themselves the health-giving benefits of naturism, psychological as well as physical, the mind and body unfettered and fused? Did they know of others who might be interested in the venture? Discretion would rule the day, of course. Privacy, sanctuary, a quiet bond between comrades, an agreement to give one's self up to the pleasures that God Himself had provided.

Yes, my grandmother said, but this is not the sort of thing that remains secret, no matter how circumspect one is.

She was right. Word got around. It was inevitable. But her husband's passion for health and sun, his annual indulgence, only enhanced his dignity. It seemed he could do no wrong in those days. The imagined presence of this young, muscular, unclothed body, released to nature, to prelapsarian abandonment, and its contrast to the suited, shirted, necktied manliness he presented to the world as he went about lecturing on social justice or presiding over his YMCA duties—this misalignment only gave him a beguiling, eccentric edge, arousing even in the straitlaced a shrugging admiration and making of him an exceptional being, free-minded, liberal, a man of virility, who also happened to be clever and compelling—especially to women. He became, in the puritanical society he inhabited, rather famous.

My grandmother's disinclination for nudity would not have surprised those who knew her well. Her interest was in covering up, not stripping down. The same week she married my grandfather she'd had curtains and heavy draperies made for the windows of the house they bought on Macklin Avenue. By the following summer slipcovers dressed the wicker porch furniture. Scarves in broderie anglaise adorned every bureau. Pillows in my grandparents' house were fitted with undercovers as well as over-covers, and she herself sewed a sort of skirt in flowered chintz that was tied prettily with bias tape around the wringer washing machine when it was not in use. Lace doilies sat on the arms and back of every chair. Woolen throws were flung across the various sofas. Rugs lay scattered everywhere upon the thick carpets. Fullness, plumpness, doubleness. Hers was a house where one could imagine the possibility of suffocation.

Her own clothing, needless to say, comprised layers of underclothes, foundation garments, garters and stockings, brassieres, camisoles, slips, blouses, cardigans, lined skirts, aprons, and even good aprons worn over the everyday aprons. Her mind drifted toward texture, fabric, protection and warmth, as though she could never burrow deeply enough into the folds of herself.

Which was why she had so much difficulty taking part in the annual July rites at Lake Simcoe. Naturism was not her nature. Nudity was the cross she bore.

At first she tried to make bargains with her husband. "I'll go," she told him, "but don't expect me to go around with *my* clothes off."

He reasoned with her gently, reminding her that nudity was an activity that, once established, did not allow abstentions. Nudity implied community. The effort to throw off cultural ignorance was so difficult, he explained, that reinforcement was ever needed. A single clothed person creates a rebuke to the unclothed. One person walking across the Club Soleil lawn in a summer dress and sandals and underpants is enough to unsettle others in the matter of the choice they had taken.

But going without clothes was unhygienic, she argued.

No, he said, not at all. (He had read his material from the International Naturism Institute closely.) Woven cloth harbors mites, molds, dust, germs. Whereas nothing is easier to keep clean than human skin, which is, in fact, self-cleaning.

Infection, my grandmother pointed out. From others.

Not a chance, he argued. Not when every camper is issued a clean towel at the beginning of the day, and this towel is used on the various benches and hammocks at Club Soleil, and even carried into the dining hall and spread on the chair before the diner sits down.

"It's different for women," she protested, gesturing awkwardly, miserably. "Women have special problems."

My grandfather explained that when women campers were "having their time," they had only to wear a short pleated skirt, rather like a tennis skirt. No one thought a thing of it, six days, seven days, nature's timetable. There was, of course, no reason to cover the breasts or shoulders.

"I can't imagine Mrs. Archie Hammond going around naked, not with her sags and bags." My grandmother said this with uncharacteristic bitterness.

"Kate and Archie have both signed up."

"Naked? Those two?"

"Of course, naked. Though naked, my love, is not really a word that naturists use."

"Yes, you've told me. A hundred times. But naked is naked."

"Semantics." (My grandfather, it must be remembered, lived in the day when to snort out the word *semantics* was enough to win any quarrel.)

"You do know what people will say, don't you?"

"Of course I know. They'll say that visitors to Camp Soleil are licentious. That we are seekers of sexual pleasure, and that the removal of the artificial barrier of clothing will only inflame our lust. But these people will be wrong."

"I'm not so sure of that," she said. "I know Archie Hammond. I've seen how he looks at women, even with their clothes on."

"Our bodies are God's gifts. There are those who believe that our bodies are holy temples."

"Then why," she asked cannily, "don't you ever see pictures of Jesus without *his* clothes on? He's always got that big brown robe wrapped around him. Even on the cross he had a little piece of cloth—"

"This discussion is going nowhere."

Indeed this discussion would have gone nowhere. It would have vanished into historical silence, except that my grandfather confided its essence to his adult son—my own father—years later, where it was received, as such parental offerings are, with huge embarrassment and rejection. How could such a private argument have taken place between one's own mother and father? Why this mention of the unmentionables between them, infidelities, monthlies—was it really necessary?

"Don't you see," my grandmother, not yet thirty years old, said to her husband, "how humiliating this is for me? A grown-up woman. Playing Adam and Eve at the beach."

He was touched by the Adam and Eve reference. It brought a smile to his lips, threw him off course. This was not what she intended.

"Do it for me," he pleaded. He had a slow, rich, persuasive way of speaking. "Please just try it for me."

"Would you love me less if I refused?"

"No," he replied. But he had let slip a small pause before he spoke, and this was registered on my grandmother's consciousness.

"It's wrong, you know it's wrong. It fans those instincts of ours that belong to, well . . ."

"To what? Say it."

"To barnyard animals."

"Ah!"

"I can't help it. That's what I think."

"We are animals, my precious love."

"You know what I mean."

"Why don't we make a bargain, then?"

She was suspicious of bargains. She came from a wealthy Ontario family (cheese, walnuts, whisky) where bad bargains had been made between brother and sister, father and son. "What kind of bargain?" she asked.

"You're crying."

"I have to know. I need to know."

"I propose that during the month of July we abstain."

"Abstain?"

"From sexual intercourse."

"But"—she must have paused at this point, hating this term *sexual intercourse,* and yet shocked that her husband would relinquish so easily their greatest personal pleasure—"why?"

"To prove to you, conclusively, that going unclothed among those we trust has nothing to do with the desires of the flesh."

"I see."

My grandmother was a passionate woman, but probably shy about the verbal expression of passion—and not sure how to show her shocked disappointment in the proposed accommodation. "I don't know what to think," she said, tears lining her lashes, knowing she had somehow been trapped in her own objections.

And so she was now faced with a dilemma. Her husband had countered each of her arguments about Club Soleil, and had even offered the ultimate sacrifice, an abstention from intimate relations during the unclothed month of July. She was cornered. She must respond, somehow, and, of course, she was at an age when people believe they will become more and not less than they are.

"All right," she said to the proposed bargain. "All right."

Did she say it crossly or tenderly? With a sense of defeat or victory? The particular tone of the story has not come down to me.

And so the long succession of summers began, the humiliation of July first, when my grandmother's favorite flowered dresses came off, her girdle, her hose, her underpants. There is a certain sharp irony to be felt when cast in a role one can't quite occupy, and for my grandmother a jolt of anger must surely have accompanied her acquiescence, the beginning of a longer anger. She found a way to walk on the beach with reasonable dignity, but never with ease, and she learned to stand nodding and chatting with Kate Hammond and the other women, blocking out the sight of their bared, softening flesh, discussing the weather, the children, the latest movies and books. She never, apparently, became accustomed to her exposed body with its pale protrusions, its slopes and meadows and damp cavities. Her fair face lightly perspired in the fresh breeze. Always she carried herself with an air of dolefulness, her eyes wary, her hands crossed stiffly over the region of her pubis. Stiff with love and suffering and absence.

This went on for years. My grandparents and the other original members grew older. Some of them retired and moved to Florida, but a new and younger set of naturists joined the ranks. Archie Hammond died of a heart attack, though Kate Hammond remained a loyal summer camper, moving from a tent into one of the newer cabins. The tennis courts were upgraded. A vegetarian chef was brought from Banff.

Then, suddenly, one summer my grandmother refused to take part. The cause of her refusal was me, her ten-year-old grandson, who was to be taken to Club Soleil for the first time. It was one thing, she felt, to take off her clothes in front of her husband and friends; she had hardened herself to the shame of it. But she would not become a naked grandmother, she would not allow herself to surrender to this ultimate indignity. This was asking too much.

She remained in Toronto that summer, and the rupture between herself and my grandfather was never completely mended.

It might be wondered why I was not introduced to Club Soleil until I was ten years old. I loved my grandparents, and had often wondered where they disappeared to each summer.

I sensed some reticence, distaste even, on my father's part when it came to discussing the matter. *Soleil* was a French word, he explained carefully, meaning sunshine. Our own vacations—my mother, father and I, their only child—were taken at Muskoka Lodge, where the wearing of clothes was unquestioned, and indeed may have been part of the reason for going there. It was a fashionable place in those days, and a full wardrobe of "resort apparel" was *de rigueur*. I remember that my mother possessed a pale peach dress with a little "bolero" that floated behind her as she stood leaning on the porch rail during the evening cocktail hour. My father, of course, ended each day by exchanging his golf clothes for a white dinner jacket.

Then one year they decided to go to Europe instead, and someone suggested that I should stay behind and join my grandparents at Club Soleil. The idea of perpetual *soleil* was appealing, especially since our own Muskoka Lodge summers were often cloudy or rain-soaked.

At this point the real nature of the enterprise was explained to me, and I remember my father's words as he struggled to fill me in. "It is a place," he said, "where people go about in their birthday suits."

I knew what birthday suits meant. It was one of the jokes of the schoolyard. Birthday suits meant buck-naked, stark-naked. Starkers.

"You mean with nothing on?" I was deeply shocked, though I later wondered if part of my shock was rehearsed and just slightly augmented for effect.

My father coughed slightly. "It's believed, you see, to be good for the health. Vitamin D, the sunshine vitamin."

"Not even their swimsuits?" This came out in a theatrical squeal. It seemed important to reach a full understanding at once, to get it over with.

"I know it's difficult to imagine." He patted me on the shoulder then, a rare gesture from a man who lacked any real sense of physical warmth.

Oddly, the thought of my grandmother's naked body lay well within my powers of imagination. I had inspected the plump nylon-encased feet and legs of my mother, so rosy, sleek and unscented, and I'd also seen the statues in the park and at the art gallery, the smooth marble parts of women, unblemished and still and lacking human orifices. What shocked me far more was thinking of my unclothed grand-father, a man who had always seemed to me *more* clothed than other men. His dark business suits were thicker of fab-ric and more closely woven. And there were his tight collars, black hose, serious oxfords and the silk scarf he tucked in the neck of his woolen overcoat so that not an inch of flesh, except for his hands and face, was available for scrutiny. But this was my winter grandfather, the only one I had ever seen. Could he possibly have, tucked between his trousered legs, what my father had, what I had?

Yes, it turned out that he did, but instead of hiding these parts behind a bath towel as I was taught to do at home, he strolled the grounds of Club Soleil, an elegant man at home in his own aging, pickled-in-brine skin, a revered ascetic and—it was clear—lord of his own domain, majestic in his entitlement, patting the heads of children and stopping to chat with Kate Hammond at the edge of the archery range. "You must not be afraid," he said to me kindly on the day of my arrival, "to follow the rituals we observe in our summer community."

To be encouraged in such sanctified naughtiness was beyond any dream a ten-year-old boy might have. I learned. I learned fast, but at the same time I understood that the world was subtly spoiled. People with their limbs and creases and folds were more alike than I thought. Skin tones, hairy patches; that was all they had. Take off your clothes and you were left with your dull suit of invisibility.

What I witnessed led me into a distress I couldn't account for or explain, but which involved a feverish disowning of my own naked body and a frantic plummeting into willed blindness. I was launched into the long business of shame, accumulating the mingled secrets of disgust and longing that eventually formed a kind of rattling carapace that restricted natural movement and ease.

"I'm only sorry," my grandfather said often that summer, "that your grandmother is not here to see how brown and strong you've grown."

When my grandfather died, he was buried in a plain pine coffin, just as the instructions in his will outlined.

And his tall and by now greatly withered body was laid out on the bare floor of the coffin without a stitch to conceal his nakedness and not even a blanket or sheet for comfort's sake. This was not his request, but my grandmother's, grimly decreed when the family gathered to discuss the "arrangements." She insisted it would have been what he wanted, and since the coffin was to be closed, what difference did it make. She also insisted that Mrs. Kate Hammond be barred from the funeral.

"It is impossible to bar anyone from a public funeral," my father insisted.

"Then she is not to be invited to stay for coffee afterward," my grandmother said. "She will probably come anyway, but she is not to be explicitly invited." She said this sternly, punitively it seemed to her family, in an attempt to outflank her dead husband, but by then all of us had learned to shrink from the anger that deformed her last years.

Her own death, pneumonia, occurred a mere eighteen months after my grandfather's. She too had specified in her will a plain pine box, with the additional written request that her body be put to rest unclothed and that the coffin be left open at the funeral.

It was as though she had hungered for this lewd indiscretion, as though some large smoldering ugliness had offered itself to her in her last days and she had been unable to resist. That's what I thought at the time.

Now I think of that final gesture differently. (Needless to say, the family did *not* honor her final request; the pine coffin, yes, and yes to the naked body, but the lid was firmly closed.) It seems to me now that an offering was made on her part, heartbreaking in its impropriety and wish for amends. This desire, perhaps, had acquired a grotesque life of its own, with a vividness that could find no form of expression in the scannable universe. "The unclothed body," she might have said, pouring into that vessel of a word a metaphorical cleansing, "is all we're allowed to take away with us."

The rest must have fallen away in the same moment she wrote down the words of her will: the draperies, the coverings, the fringe and feathers, the wrappings, the linings, the stuffings and stitching. Goodbye, she must have said to what couldn't be helped. Goodbye to the circular life of shame and its infinite regress.

She must have thought she could get everything back by a single act of acquiescence. In the next world, just a breath away, the two of them would greet each other rapturously. Their revealed limbs would flash among the bright vegetation, at home in the green-clothed world, and embracing each other without restraint.

She would have forgotten that nature's substance is gnarled and knotted in its grain, so that no absolutely

straight thing can come of it. They should have understood that all along, those two. It might have become one
of their perishable secrets, part of the bliss they would one
day gladly surrender.

Various Miracles was first published in 1985; *The Orange Fish* was first published in 1989; and *Dressing Up for the Carnival* was first published in 2000. The following stories were first published in these publications. In an event of an omission or error, please notify the publisher.

"Various Miracles" in *Canadian Forum/Anthology of Prairie Women Writers*; "Mrs. Turner Cutting the Grass" in *Arts Manitoba*; "Accidents" in *The Malahat Review*; "Purple Blooms" in *Quarry*; "Flitting Behavior" in *CBC Anthology*; "Fragility" in *Saturday Night*; "The Metaphor Is Dead—Pass It On" in *Prairie Fire*; "Love so Fleeting, Love so Fine" in *The Malahat Review*; "Dolls, Dolls, Dolls, Dolls" in *Aurora/CBC Anthology*; "Invitations" in *Fiddlehead*; "Home" in *Fiddlehead*; "The Journal" in *Fiddlehead*; "Salt" in *The Antigonish Review*; "The Orange Fish" in *A Room of One's Own*; "Chemistry" in *The Canadian Forum*; "Today Is the Day" in *West Coast Review* under the title "Close Observation"; "Hinterland" in *Prairie Fire*; "Block Out" in *Prairie Fire*; "Good Manners" in *West Coast Review*; "Times of Sickness and Health" in *A Room of One's Own*; "Family Secrets" in *Prism International*; "Fuel for the Fire" in *Border Crossings*; "Milk Bread Beer Ice" in *Saturday Night*; "Dressing Up for the Carnival" in *The Malahat Review*; "A Scarf" in *National Post*; "Weather" in *Story*; "Flatties: Their Various Forms and Uses" in a chapbook for the International Festival of Authors; "Dying for Love" in *West Coast Review*; "Ilk" in *Prairie Fire*; "Stop!" in *Drop Out*; "Mirrors" in *Story*; "The Harp" in *Story*; "Our Men and Women" in *North Dakota Quarterly*; "Keys" in *Border Crossings*; "Absence" in *Event*; "Reportage" in *Prairie Fire*; "Soup du Jour" in *West Coast Review*; "Invention" appeared on CBC Radio's Festival of Fiction in 1999; "Death of an Artist" in *Event*; "The Next Best Kiss" in *Atlantic Monthly*; "Eros" in *Desire in Seven Voices*; "Dressing Down" in *Saturday Night*.

CAROL SHIELDS's novels, plays, stories and non-fiction have won many awards. Her novel *The Stone Diaries* won the Governor General's Literary Award in Canada, the Pulitzer Prize and the National Book Critics Circle Award in the United States, and the Prix de Lire in France. *Larry's Party* won the Orange Prize for Fiction and was a finalist for the Giller Prize. In 2000 the government of France appointed Carol Shields a Chevalier de l'Ordre des Arts et des Lettres. Her anthologies of women's writing (co-edited with Marjorie Anderson), *Dropped Threads* and *Dropped Threads 2*, were both national bestsellers. She won the 2002 Charles Taylor Prize for Literary Non-Fiction for her biography, *Jane Austen*. Her novel *Unless*, published in 2002, was a finalist for the Man Booker Prize, the Giller Prize and the Governor General's Literary Award. Carol Shields was the Canadian Booksellers Association's Author of the Year in 2003.